# THE OVERNIGHT

by Ramsey Campbell
from Tom Doherty Associates

*Alone with the Horrors*
*Ancient Images*
*Cold Print*
*The Count of Eleven*
*Dark Companions*
*The Darkest Part of the Woods*
*The Doll Who Ate His Mother*
*The Face That Must Die*
*Fine Frights* (editor)
*Gathering the Bones*
*The Hungry Moon*
*Incarnate*
*The Influence*
*The Last Voice They Hear*
*The Long Lost*
*Midnight Sun*
*The Nameless*
*Nazareth Hill*
*Obsession*
*The Overnight*
*The One Safe Place*
*Pact of the Fathers*
*The Parasite*
*Scared Stiff*
*Silent Children*
*Waking Nightmares*

# THE OVERNIGHT
# RAMSEY CAMPBELL

TOR™

A TOM DOHERTY ASSOCIATES BOOK

NEW YORK

THE OVERNIGHT

Copyright © 2005 by Ramsey Campbell

A Tor Book
Published by Tom Doherty Associates, LLC
175 Fifth Avenue
New York, NY 10010

www.tor.com

Tor® is a registered trademark of Tom Doherty Associates, LLC.

ISBN 0-765-31299-9

EAN 978-0765-31299-0

First Edition: March 2005

Printed in the United States of America

0   9   8   7   6   5   4   3   2   1

for Tam and Sam,
with love and vegetables

# ACKNOWLEDGMENTS

In March 2000 I went to work full-time at the Cheshire Oaks branch of Borders. Most of my friends were shocked that I needed to take a job other than writing, though Poppy Z. Brite sent several enthusiastic emails. My wife, Jenny, was supportive as always. In the months I worked at the shop I made quite a few friends and conceived this book out of my experience. What more could I ask? Let me thank all my colleagues for helping make my time there so enjoyable: Mary, Mark, Ritchie, Janet, Emma, Derek, Paul, Lisa, Melanie M, Mel R, Mel of the café, Craig, Will, Annabell, Angie, Richard, Sarah H, Sarah W, Judy, Lindsay, Fiona, Barry, Laura, Colin, Vera, Millie, Joy, John and Dave. None of them resembles any character in this book, but the lift is a different matter. My editor, Melissa Singer, was once again a fount of useful suggestions.

# THE OVERNIGHT

# WOODY

**What time is this supposed to be? He seems hardly to have slept but**
already there's the travel alarm. No, it's the cordless phone that comes
with the house and is forever wandering off. The muffled shrilling
makes him feel jet-lagged all over again, though it's months since he
moved to England. He sprawls out from under the quilt that's meant
to protect him from the northern English weather, only to find he's
left the phone downstairs. A robe would be welcome, but the tag is
twisted around the hook on the door and the phone may not wait.
Maybe it's Gina thinking it's daytime this side of the ocean. Maybe
she's decided to give his bookstore a chance after all.

He slaps the switch for the barely shaded light and tramps fast
out of the room and down the stairs that aren't quite as wide as a
telephone booth. Banisters slick with chilly paint the colour of old
teeth creak a warning not to lean on them too hard. The globe over
the stairs spends most of its energy just being yellow. He wouldn't
have thought, until he walked on it barefoot, that a carpet could be
so cold, but it can't compete with the linoleum in the kitchen. The

phone isn't in there either. At least renting a house so small nobody except Brits would want to own it means there aren't many places for a phone to hide.

It's in the front room, by the chair facing the television that has so few channels it doesn't even need a *TV Guide*. The stale chocolate curtains are drawn, and he switches on the pink-shaded light on the way to the chair. The phone isn't by it, it's down the side, and what else is he dredging up? A candy wrapper decorated with hair and fluff, a greenish coin so old he doubts it's legal. He turns on the phone with his other hand. "Woody Blake."

"Is that Mr Blake?"

Did he dream he just told the man that? "You got me, sure enough."

"Mr Blake the manager of Texts?"

By now Woody has shaken the sticky paper off his fingers into the dented wastebasket embellished with the same florid paper as the walls. He risks perching his unprotected rear on the edge of the prickly armchair. "That's what I am."

"It's Ronnie on patrol at Fenny Meadows Retail Park. We've got an alarm at your shop."

Woody's on his feet. "What kind?"

"Could be false. We need someone to check."

"I'm on my way."

He's already past the shadows a flight of plaster ducks left on the stairway wall. Half a minute in the bathroom takes some of the pressure off, and then he's back into clothes that have borrowed a chill from the building. He adds the overcoat that was heavy enough for the Minnesota winter and slams the lumbering front door behind him as he steps onto the sidewalk, which is all of six feet wide. Two strides take him to the car he rented, an orange Honda, though it would be white except for the streetlights that make everything look steeped in pumpkin juice from last week's Halloween. The street—what the Brits call a terrace, houses squeezed together like a red brick concertina with their front windows bulging out—is silent except for him and his orange-tinted breath. The car marks its space with an ochreous cloud before turning one hundred and eighty degrees, past the Flibberty Gibbet pub that apparently used to be called the Hangman and the premises where half the local men seem to spend their days betting on horses. Half a mile of terraces and traffic signals showing him red lights on nobody's behalf takes him out beyond the houses and the sidewalks, past lush verges where dandelions are flowering late in the year and streetlamps colour evergreens autumnal. Two miles of highway bring him to the motorway, the freeway between Liverpool and Manchester. He's hardly topped the speed limit when he has to brake for the exit to the retail park.

He's sure the bookstore has the best position of any business in the half-mile oval. As soon as he drives onto the exit ramp he sees the giant elongated letters spelling TEXTS along the two-storey concrete wall. Fog surrounds the store with a whitish aura. He drives around the outside of the development, past several uncompleted buildings, and through the entrance between the Stack o' Steak diner and the Frugo supermarket. Trios of saplings planted in strips of grass decorate the blacktop of the parking area. They net Woody's car with shadows cast by floodlights standing guard over the stores—the Stay in Touch mobile phone showroom, Baby Bunting next to Teenstuff, TVid with its window full of televisions, the Happy Holidays travel agency sharing an alley with his bookstore. An incessant chirping like the cry of a huge maddened nightbird fills his ears as he parks across three spaces in front of the entrance to Texts.

A heavyweight in uniform with a clipboard under his arm plods to meet him. "Mr Blake?" he shouts in a voice as flat as his crew cut and an accent as broad as his earnest humourless face.

"And you have to be Ronnie. Not too long, was I?"

It takes a consultation of his fat black wristwatch and a good scratch of the scalp to let the guard say "Nearly seventeen minutes."

He's shouting louder than ever, which together with the squalling of the alarm feels capable of crowding all the intelligence out of Woody's head. "Let me just . . ." Woody yells, gesturing at Texts, and types on the keypad between the handles of the glass doors. Two twelve one eleven admits him to the mat that says READ ON! between the security pillars. He taps another code on the alarm panel, which is showing a red light for the sales floor, and then there's an aching silence except for a tiny shrill buzz he would blame on a mosquito if he were still working in the New Orleans branch. He hasn't identified the source when Ronnie says "You'll need to sign my board."

"Happy to when I've checked the store. Will you help?"

The guard is clearly daunted by the sight of half a million books, beginning with the table heaped with Tempting Texts beyond the mat. Woody switches on all the lights in the ceiling tiles and turns left past the counter with the cash registers and the Information terminal. "You could take the other side," he suggests.

"If anyone's up to no good I'll fix them."

Ronnie sounds eager to manhandle someone. He sets off fast into and out of Travel and History, where Woody noticed through the right-hand window that the shelf-end promotions are due for renewal—he'll remind Agnes, Anyes as she calls herself, that customers deserve to see something new every time they visit Texts. He's quickly through Jill's Fiction and Literature aisles in front of the left window. There's no hiding place by the side wall full of video cassettes and DVDs and compact discs, and the shelves in the middle of the floor are no taller than his shoulders. Wilf's section is so tidy you might think nobody had time for Beliefs any more, religions or the occult either, but every book has its reader—that's another Texts motto that is international now. Meanwhile, Ronnie's head is dodging back and forth in Jake's Genre Fiction aisles. "Nothing," he says as Woody catches his eye, "just books."

Woody can't help taking this personally. Nobody should be so unenthusiastic when Texts has a world of books to offer—it bothers him more than the possibility of an intruder. "What kind do you read?" he calls.

Ronnie is in Erotica before he admits "Funny stuff."

"Humour's on the side wall."

Though Woody was playing safe, Ronnie looks as if he's struggling to the conclusion that it was a joke at his expense, and so Woody turns his attention to the back wall, the children's section. Some of the alcoves look as if monkeys had been let loose on the shelves. That isn't how they should be left at the end of the day; he'll need to have a word with Madeleine. Nobody is lurking behind the chairs in any of the alcoves—it would take a dwarf to do that—but a book is sprawled on its face on the carpet in Tiny Texts. It's a first reading book with a single-syllable word opposite a picture on each of the pairs of board pages. Surely Madeleine wouldn't have left it there; perhaps its fall triggered the alarm. Woody checks that it hasn't been damaged and returns it to its shelf. He has found nothing else unshelved by the time he meets Ronnie beside Tempting Texts.

The guard is poking out his lips at them. Some best-seller appears to have captured his fancy. Woody is about to encourage him when Ronnie slams the clipboard on top of the pile of *Ringo by Jingo*. "That's for you, you little pisser."

However much he hates the Beatles or just the drummer, there's never an excuse for damaging a book—and then Woody sees what the assault accomplished. A mosquito is twitching its last on the famous nose. Ronnie scrapes the insect off with a thumbnail he wipes on his trousers, leaving a snotty trail under Starr's left nostril. "It's all this global warming," Ronnie mutters. "Weather doesn't know where it is any more."

Woody cleans the cover with his handkerchief until there's no trace of the incident. He's watching the guard pore over inking a letter on the clipboard sheet when the overhead speakers burst into song. "Goshwow, gee and whee, keen-o-peachy . . ." It's the first track on the compact disc that head office provides to liven up the staff when they're fitting out and stocking a new branch. Woody has to admit it's one of the few things that make him ashamed to be American, and why has it started up? Perhaps a similar glitch in the power supply tripped the alarm. As he turns off the player be-hind the counter, Ronnie frowns at it. "I liked that," he complains.

Woody ignores the implicit request while the guard labours over writing and at last passes him the clipboard and a ballpoint fractured by his grasp. FALS ALARM TEXT'S BOOKSHOP 00.28–00.49, says the whole of the inscription, followed by an inkspot. "Thanks for looking after my store," Woody says as he tries to incorporate the inkspot in the first of his vowels, though this lends it a resemblance to the less blind of a pair of eyes.

"That's my job."

He sounds as if he thinks Woody said too much. Maybe he thinks the manager oughtn't to be so proprietorial. Woody is tempted to reveal this is the first branch he's managed after working his way up through New Orleans and Minneapolis, but if that didn't mean enough to Gina, why should it to the guard? It was bad enough that she took a dislike to Fenny Meadows, far worse that she couldn't say why. Impressions are no use if you can't or won't put them into words. No doubt Mississippi is where she ought to stay—this wouldn't be her kind of weather. "Okay, I guess we're through for the night," says Woody, realising too late that Ronnie is nothing of the kind.

Ronnie drags his shadows past the stores and unoccupied prop-erties towards the guards' hut next to Frugo as Woody resets the alarm. The floodlights sting his eyes until he climbs into the Honda, but he'll save feeling tired for when his head returns to the pillow. As he speeds onto the slip road, graffiti on the concrete pillars un-der the motorway meet the headlamp beams, short crude words in primitive letters as giant as the mind behind them is small, he sus-pects. That's one breed of customer Texts can manage without, and Woody hopes Ronnie and his colleagues will keep them clear until the store has its own guard. Otherwise he's sure his staff are up to any challenge, including the Christmas season, however much more experience they would have brought to it if the store had opened in September. He couldn't have brought that about; the builders overran their schedule. Now he can do everything that's required, though, and he needn't expect less of the staff. It doesn't matter where he lives until he's happy with the store. Maybe that's really why Gina decided against working there: she didn't like sharing his narrow bed, though it didn't stay cold for long. The possibility brings a wry smile to his lips as he drives onto the motorway and the fog sinks into the glow of the retail park.

# JILL

**Fifteen minutes take Jill's Nova out of Bury, where delivery vans** have turned the narrow main street into an obstacle course, and onto the motorway past Manchester. A faster quarter of an hour brings her to Fenny Meadows Retail Park. Mist precedes her across the tarmac and trails across the wet green fields towards the distant Pennines, a darker jagged frieze cut out of the grey horizon. She parks behind Texts, whose final plastic letter towers like a giant worm over the car. She touches the photograph of her daughter that's perched above the windscreen mirror. "We can do this, Bryony," she declares.

The blank concrete alley between Texts and the Happy Holidays travel agency leads straight to the books she's responsible for, or at least to the sight of them through the display window. Fiction and Literature didn't sound too daunting, since Jake has Genre Fiction, but trying to invent shelf-end promotions kept her awake last night. Her seps are going septic, she can't help thinking now, and she still has to concoct a way to promote Brodie Oates, the bookshop's first

visiting author. Her doubts must have escaped onto her face, because Wilf looks uncertain how to greet her across the counter.
"Don't worry, Wilf," she says and wonders if he too has a reason as
she makes for the staffroom.

The door to the featureless concrete stairway lets her in once she
shows the plaque on the wall her staff badge. Beyond the toilets
confronting each other across the passage at the top, the staffroom
door isn't so particular about whom it admits. Though Jill is five
minutes early, the rest of her shift is seated at the laminated table in
the pale green windowless room. Jill takes her card from the Out
rack and slides it along the slit beneath the clock and drops it in the
In. Connie gives her a big pink-lipped smile bright enough for a
toothpaste ad as Jill sits down. "Ouch," Connie says and twitches
her small snub nose at the squeal of the chair on the linoleum. "No
rush, Jill. You aren't really late."

Angus makes to hand Jill a copy of today's Woody's Wheedles
sheet but snatches his hand back when Connie is faster. For a moment the August tan that's fading from his elongated face turns even
blotchier. The weekend figures are the best yet for the branch, and
now Woody wants to see the weekday sales increase. "Anybody
with ideas, just pin them on the board," says Connie as she deals
everyone printouts of the shift rota. "Gavin, that's a monster yawn,
you're shelving. Ross, could you put security tags inside anything
over twenty pounds? That's price, not weight, but it could be both.
Anyes, you can be informative at Information. Jill, you're a till till
eleven."

As Jill hurries downstairs she's hoping she'll have time to remind
herself of the various routines the till demands, but Agnes is looking
for help with a queue. Jill types her staff identification number at Till
2 and rubs her clammy hands together. "Who's next, please?"

A thin but pregnant girl in a floor-length raincoat wants to buy
six romances with her Visa card. The codes on the books scan, the
till accepts the card, and Jill remembers to lay each book on the pad
that neutralises any security tag a manager may have hidden

randomly in them. From the heap under the till she peels off a plastic Texts bag that squeaks against her nails and loads it with the books, not forgetting to smile and say "Enjoy them" as she hands the package to the customer. "Who's next, please?" brings her a large man in a small hat of the same prickly tweed as his suit. He presents Jill with his armful of a single book on fighter aircraft and then a cheque, which she has to feed into the till so that it prints the details of the transaction on the back. The till hums to itself while she pleads silently that it won't shred the cheque. At last the till sticks out its tongue, and she only has to compare signatures— they're not quite the same, but surely close enough—before she writes the guarantee card number under the print from the till. The largest bag only just accommodates the book, and she has hardly finished struggling with them when a young mother, who keeps hoisting a toddler with her left arm, dumps a handful of books on the counter, along with a Texts gift voucher for half their price and a Switch card. She delivers a running commentary on Jill's actions as the till buzzes to itself like an insect all the more dangerous for being half-awake—"Now look, the register's had its breakfast and the assistant has to give it Patricia's piece of paper that we call a voucher. Now see, the assistant has to type all mummy's big long number from her card"—and it hardly helps that she has to explain more than once that she isn't calling Jill a sister. "Enjoy your books and come back to see us soon," Jill says at last and takes the chance to tickle Patricia under the chin; at least, she tries, but the toddler draws back. "Thank you," the young woman says briskly and carries both her items out of the shop.

As Jill treats herself to a quiet but expressive sigh, Agnes sidles along the counter from the Information terminal. "Sorry I left you to serve all those people," she slightly more than whispers, stowing her black tresses behind an ear to reveal a thin pale bony cheek mottled by embarrassment. "The computer didn't seem to want to help me find a book."

"Don't worry, Anyes, we're all still learning," Jill says and is resting a look of encouragement on her when the ceiling speaks. "Jill call four, please. Jill call four."

She feels as if Connie has caught her loafing. At least she doesn't have to use the public address system to reply. She doesn't like listening to herself on the speakers, which show up her Mancunian accent as though the voice she hears in her head is a posh costume she can't quite affect, or perhaps one with holes she doesn't notice. When they're connected Connie says "Would you mind taking your lunch now? Wilf wants to shoot out at twelve and Ross does at one."

It's only eleven, and Jill is working until six. At least she'll be able to finish Brodie Oates' novel sooner, and surely then she'll have ideas. She hurries to clock off and open it while the microwave rotates her carton of last night's vegetable chili with a series of muffled metallic creaks. The cover of the book is blank except for the author's name and *Dressing Up, Dressing Down* lettered in various fabrics: no photograph, just "This is the author's first publication" on the back flap. She hasn't finished the opening paragraph of the final chapter when she glances around to discover who's peering at it over her shoulder, but of course the cold breath on the nape of her neck belongs to the air-conditioning, which also fumbled at a corner of the page. She feeds herself straight from the carton with a fork while she reads. How much of a joke is the ending supposed to be, and on whom? When the man alone in a room removes all his costumes he turns out to have been every character: the Victorian detective whose quarry, the jewel thief, proved to be himself in drag; the sergeant in the First World War who was revealed as his daughter; the mysterious Berlin nightclub singer, her child and a hermaphrodite; the sixties private eye who couldn't decide what sex he was and who discovered these were all his relatives by taking psychedelics and communing with his genes halfway through the book, which then started rewinding itself . . . Jill forks up the best mouthful, which she has saved until last, but it's a lump of foil disguised by sauce. She spits it into a sheet of kitchen roll and drops that in the pedal bin, then returns to staring at the book.

The meaning has drained out of the title by the time a mouth behind her licks its huge lips. Whoever was about to page must have decided against it, because the speaker falls silent. Surely the title has to suggest a promotion—the initials, even. "May sound like a DUDD, but it's not," or, if she's to be more honest, "Is this a DUDD? Judge for yourselves" . . . "Did B. O. write a DUDD? Buy it and find out" . . . A moment's thought exposes how bad any of these ideas would look, but now the syllable seems to be stuck in her head: not even a proper word, just a lump of less than language. It thumps in her skull like a drum or the start of a headache. Dudd, dudd, dudd, dudd . . . She's glad to have it interrupted by the sight of Wilf, except that he stands in the doorway as if he's waiting to be told what to do and assumes she knows. A beaky frown multiplies itself above his patient greyish eyes and long blunt nose before he rubs his broad not unattractively bony face. "So," he says, "er . . ."

"What can I do for you, Wilf?"

"Do you think I could slip away about now?"

Jill has to glance at her watch to convince herself what he means. How has she managed to spend an entire hour upstairs? She hasn't even had a coffee, which might have helped rouse her brain. "Sorry, of course, you head off," she gasps as she springs to her feet and makes for the stairs so fast she almost forgets to clock on. At least that means her mind is on the job, she tells herself. At least she's giving all of herself to the shop that she can. Surely that's as much as anyone could ask.

# MADELEINE

**"Look at all these books. How many books does Dan think there** are? Are there lots of books?"

"Lost."

"Not lost, Dan, lots. Dan isn't lost, is he? And these books aren't. Most of these books are on their shelves. These here are shelves. Shelves are where the shop keeps books. Does Dan have shelves at home?"

Shouldn't the boy's father know? He must think talking primers aren't supposed to. He's with his son in Tiny Texts and talking louder than the music even Mad knows is Handel on the speakers. She's in the next bay, Toddlers' Texts, where some of the books are indeed strays thin enough to be waifs and a Teenage Text is sprawling on top of a shelf of simplified fairy tales. Sometimes she thinks the only T to describe her section is Trouble. "Shells," Dan shouts and giggles just as loud.

"Shelves, Dan. Shall we find Dan a book now? Which book would Dan like?"

"These ones," Dan says, trotting out of the bay in a straightish line. "Nice."

Mad has to suppress a snorty laugh, because he's bound for Erotica. Ross catches her eye across the Psychology section but seems unsure whether to expect to share a grin, although they agreed to stay friends. When she responds with a wink he looks away quickly without finishing his grin. He's making for the little boy, who has pulled *Sensual Discipline* off a low shelf, until the father arrives and snatches the book. "Not nice," he says, slapping erotic portfolios on the top shelf with it, and stares at Ross followed by Mad. "Not nice at all."

She could fancy he has sensed some trace of their relationship, but they've nothing to regret. They aren't going to let any awkwardness develop at work. She's forgetting the solid silky feel of Ross inside her, and the shower gel his penis tasted of; she has already forgotten how his tanned square blond-topped face looked at no distance at all. She gives him a smile she doesn't mean to be too secret and returns to loading her trolley, which she hopes she's not off more than usual, with misplaced books. Dan's father chooses a book with small words in aloud and marches his son off in step with Handel, and Mad wheels the trolley into Tiny Texts, where she lets out an oh that's close to an ow. Half a dozen shelves are in a worse state than she found when she started tidying.

Ross parts his lips as he ventures over, and she remembers the trace of a flavour of minty toothpaste. "Sorry," he murmurs as he observes the disorder. "I didn't see him doing it. I wouldn't let a kid of mine do that."

"You never mentioned you had any."

"I've not. You know me, I'm cautious." A memory seems to discolour his tan while he adds "I meant if I had."

"I did know that, Ross." If they were still together he would have realised she was teasing, but now she wonders how much they need to be wary of saying. "I'd best get on," she says. "I've still got books to bring down."

She hopes hearing Dan's father hasn't turned her monosyllabic. Once Ross retreats to his territory she tidies the shelves yet again before clattering the books on the trolley into order and filing them where they ought to go. She's at full speed now, which is the way she likes to feel. When she badges herself into the concrete lobby where the shop takes deliveries, however, the lift stops her dead.

Is it the slowest object in the building? She has to jab the button twice to summon a descending rumble beyond the metal doors. They twitch as a muffled female voice that reminds Mad of a secretary says "Lift opening." Two trolleys have been going for a ride in the cage as grey as fog, but there's room for her and hers. She thumbs the Up button to be told "Lift closing."

"Go on then, there's a good lift."

She could imagine that it waits for her to finish speaking before it shivers its doors and drags them shut. As it shudders upwards the trolleys nudge one another with a sound like someone very young fumbling with a drum. "Lift opening," the voice says as the cage settles at the top of the shaft. The doors fidget, unless they appear to because Mad is staring hard at them. Frustration sends her through the gap the instant it parts wide enough; frustration makes her almost stamp as she and the trolley reach her stock racks. When she began her shift they held no more than an hour's worth of books, but now they're stuffed.

Stamping won't clear them, nor staring either. New books come with the job every day. She sets about loading the trolley so fast she doesn't understand why she's overcome by a shiver. Perhaps the air-conditioning is playing tricks—no, somebody behind her is. She twists around to find Woody watching her from the doorway to the staffroom at the far end of the aisle of metal shelves. The door must have let in a draught as quiet as he was. He fingers the squared-off tail of his flattened turfy hair as if it conceals a switch that raises his equally black eyebrows and the corners of his mouth. "Falling behind?" he calls.

"Only if my underwear's not tight enough." Whoever she might say that to, he certainly isn't among them. "Not for long," she tells him.

He pads past the Returns and Damaged racks and nods at her shelves without taking his gaze off them. He looks more patient than reproachful, but there's a hint of pinkishness about his long cheeks, and an extra furrow in his wide forehead. "The public can't buy what they don't see. Nothing should be up here longer than twenty-four hours."

"Just these have." Mad gropes for the books that today's delivery pushed into hiding. She keeps her back to him as he says "If you find you need help, talk to your shift manager."

She wouldn't need it if someone had tidied her section in her absence last night. She'd rather not tell tales about workmates—she can deal with the culprit herself. Woody leaves her to unload her shelves, but she's certain she senses him watching her. She has to laugh at herself, if a little nervously, when she turns and finds she's alone in the stockroom. She steps her pace up, though the books make so much noise on the trolley she wouldn't hear anyone behind her. At last she's able to trundle the books to the lift, where she pokes the Down button and dodges out. She can imagine feeling trapped by sluggishness if she rode the lift down.

She retrieves her trolley and hauls the door to the sales floor wide, then speeds her books through before thirty seconds can be up and trigger an alarm. By the time the metal elbow tugs the door shut she's in the Teenage bay, where armfuls of books have to be shifted to make room for newcomers. She hasn't quite stopped feeling watched, though Ross isn't watching; he's at a till, while Lorraine is behind the Information terminal. Woody can watch her on the screen in his office if he wants to, in which case he sees her shelve rather less than half her trolley load before six o'clock brings her dinner break.

She leaves the trolley by the delivery doors—trolleys are never to be left unattended on the sales floor in case children play with them and hurt themselves or someone else and Texts is sued, as happened in Cape Cod—and jogs upstairs. She fills her yellow Texts mug from the ivory percolator and sits down with her Frugo dinner. Soya prawn salad sounded tasty, but there's an underlying grittiness that reminds her of picnic food dropped on the ground. She can only persevere with eating out of the plastic carton while she borrows questions from books for her first children's quiz. When Jill clocks off at the end of her shift Mad asks her if the questions are too hard. "Bryony could answer most of those," Jill says with some pride.

"You should bring her. She might win."

"It's meant to be her father's day with her." Jill's large face is always a little too earnest for thirty, and now the wrinkles at the corners of her eyes don't look as if they have been left by smiles. She passes a hand over her decidedly red hair that's tamed by a cut just short of severe. "I'll see what she wants to do," she says.

Mad mentions that she and Ross are just friends now, and more of Jill's shift overhear. Gavin unleashes a yawn that hefts his heavy eyelids and stretches his long cheeks past his sharp raw nose towards his pointed stubbly chin, Agnes looks uncertain whether to be sad or brave or both on Mad's behalf. Everyone pretends not to be thinking about Ross as he sprints upstairs. Lorraine is close behind him, and breaks the uncomfortable silence. "Can I sling your books off the trolley downstairs, Madeleine?"

She sounds about to break into a chortle. Mad often thinks that, like Lorraine's laugh that goes with the horses she rides and her accent with ambitions to dissociate itself from anywhere near Manchester, her tone seems forced because her glossy pink lips are smaller than her face needs them to be. Lorraine raises her left eyebrow like the top of a question mark composed of golden fur, and Mad stands up to feed the last of her salad and its carton to the pedal bin. "I'm using it, Lorraine. I'll get back to it now."

"You've not had all your break yet, have you? You don't want to show the rest of us up."

"I don't, but I need to catch up on my shelving."

"Tell management to give you more time on it, then."

Mad washes her mug over the sink heaped with them and plates and utensils. She wipes the mug on a Texts towel and stands it in the cupboard above the sink, and turns to find Lorraine still gazing at her. "I wouldn't need so much time," Mad says, "if somebody had tidied it last night and a few other nights when I wasn't here as well."

Lorraine tilts her gaze up as though she's praying silently or observing her eyebrows, a gesture that provokes Mad to demand "Who was supposed to last night? Was it you, Lorraine?"

The subject of the question widens her eyes but otherwise leaves them how they are until Gavin says "I think it was, Lorraine, was it?"

"It may have been," she says, then glares at him. "Remind us all what it's got to do with you, Gavin."

His yawn may be his answer. It's Ross who comments "Weren't you saying staff should stick together, Lorraine?"

"Gracious me," Lorraine says and follows her blank gaze out of the door. "If the boys are going to gang up I think the ladies had better leave them to it."

Nobody wants to appear to be trailing after her, but Mad makes for the route through the stockroom. She's limbering up to be the swiftest she's ever been as she wheels the trolley onto the sales floor and into the Teenage alcove, only to halt as if she's been caught by the neck. Half a dozen books, no, more have been turned with their spines to the backs of the lowest shelves since she went for her break.

Did someone think it would be fun to give her more work? She stalks along the alcoves in search of the villain, but there's nobody. As she retraces her steps more slowly, daring any more books to be out of place, Ray ambles over from Information. His generously jowly pinkish face has adopted the paternal expression it wears whenever he heads a shift meeting. "Lost something?" he enquires.

"My mind if I have to put up with much more of this."

He runs his hand over his reddish neck-length hair, rendering it even more variously curly. "Of what's that when it's playing for the league, Mad?"

She knows football is second only to his family but doesn't see the relevance just now. "Look what someone did while I was upstairs."

He tramps after her into Teenage and peers where she's pointing. Once he has finished sucking his mouth small and wry he says "Well, I didn't see anyone. Did you, Lorraine? You were over here before."

Lorraine is wandering up and down the aisles. She puts on no speed at all to detour into Mad's section. After a pause for raising her eyebrows without widening her eyes she says "There was nobody."

"Don't leave yourself out," says Mad.

"I wouldn't touch your books," Lorraine says as though she feels superior to them or Mad or both.

"Like you didn't last night, you mean."

"Ladies," Ray murmurs. "Can we do our best to get on? We don't want anybody thinking us Mancunians can't sing the same tune."

No doubt he has football chants in mind. Lorraine's fleeting frown shows how she resents being associated with the game and with Manchester, which would amuse Mad more if she didn't have to ask "So why were you in my section?"

"I was looking for a trolley, as you know. Have you finished with it yet?"

"Try putting your head inside the lift."

"Is that all settled, then?" Ray hopes. "I expect you must have overlooked those books before, Mad. It'll only take a moment to fix, won't it?"

They take quite a few, not least because they turn out to be from the opposite shelf. Before she has finished the transfer Mad's fingers start to feel grubby, though she can't see why. Lorraine has strolled away to the lift, but Ray moves the last misplaced book. "You carry on shelving till you've absolutely done," he says. "I'm sure that's what the boss will want."

She would appreciate the proposition more if it didn't make her feel convicted of letting her shelving accumulate. She shuffles the contents of the trolley into order and dumps books in front of the shelves they belong to, then she returns the trolley to the lobby and sets herself a challenge: before the shop shuts, all her books will be where they should be. There are so few customers tonight that soon everyone else is shelving too—Ray, Lorraine, stocky ginger-bearded Greg—and she no longer feels singled out, not least because Woody has gone home. In less than ninety minutes she sends a trolley up and rescues it from the lift, and shortly it's back in there, almost more than full of the last of her books.

Mad is dancing from foot to foot to keep off the chill of the de-livery lobby when she hears a series of thumps beyond the metal doors. She can't help thinking of an ape determined to batter its way out of its cage, which is why the words of the lift sound like a warning. She wishes she weren't alone in the lobby—at least, she does until the lift labours open. She must have overloaded the trol-ley. Half a dozen books are on the floor.

She wedges the doors of the lift with the trolley and grabs the fallen books. Someone has recently tracked mud into the lift. By the time she makes her escape her hands need wiping on her handker-chief, which she also uses to clean a splotch off the cover of a school story, a mark that resembles a magnified fingerprint with wrinkles instead of whorls. None of the books is damaged, at any rate. The lift boasts of closing as she rushes the trolley onto the sales floor and starts arranging the contents at once.

She heaps books on the moss-green carpet and finds spaces for them on the shelves, and that's Mad for over an hour. If she thought about it she might be surprised how satisfying the task is, but its proximity to mindlessness is part of the appeal—an odd quality when it concerns books. All that's important is to live up to her own challenge, and she has only a handful of volumes to shelve when Ray picks up a phone to broadcast his voice. "Texts will be closing in ten minutes. Please take any purchases to the counter."

Two girls grab three romances each, and a pair of wilfully bald men leave the books they were leafing through in armchairs. Connie has hardly called five minutes when Mad shelves her last book with a sigh of triumph. She's ready to help search the shop while Ray stands guard at the exit. She feels absurd for checking her section twice, darting into each alcove as though she expects to catch somebody disarranging the bottom shelves. Of course nobody is hunched in a corner or crawling on the floor. She's the last to call "Clear," and feels sillier still.

Ray types the code to lock the doors as Connie uses a phone to say "Tidying time" as if she's announcing a treat. She loads a trolley with the jingling trays out of the till drawers to ferry them up to the office, and Ray wanders over to Mad. "Anything to be done still?" he wonders.

"Only the rest of the shop," she's proud to assure him.

That's scattered with vagrant books. The bald men in the armchairs had collections of cartoons about a talking penis; no doubt their grunts must have been of laughter. Three horror films about giant insects have emerged from their plastic chrysalids and crawled unnoticed into Science, and it takes Mad some time to locate their cases. Once the obvious wanderers have been escorted home the mass of books has to be tidied, and Mad wishes she didn't keep feeling compelled to glance towards her own. She doesn't know how often she has given in to the urge when Lorraine says "Aren't we supposed to have done by now?"

"By gum, she's right, you know," says Ray. "Eleven's struck."

As Mad consults her little thin gold watch her parents bought for her twenty-first last year, Greg says "No harm in a few extra minutes if they're what the shop needs."

"Tell you what, Gregory," Lorraine says, "you can give it mine too."

Ray brandishes his badge at the plaque by the door up to the staffroom. Everyone is through before thirty seconds elapse, even Greg. Ray is standing aside to let Mad and Lorraine clock off first when Connie calls from the office "Sorry I forgot to call time. The computer doesn't seem to want me to put in the figures."

Perhaps Ray resents the implication that sending the staff home was her job. "I expect we can fix it together," he tells her, and precedes everyone else down to the exit. "Drive safely," he advises as he lets them out, because Fenny Meadows has built a wall of fog less than two hundred yards from the shop.

The deserted tarmac painted with bony oblongs glistens like mud. The outer surface of the display windows is turning grey as ice. The air is laden with the thick milky glare of the floodlights. The farther away the lights are, the fatter and more blurred they grow; outside Stack o' Steak and Frugo they could be moons invisibly tethered to the pavement, the kind of fuzzy moon that always looks capable to Mad of hatching out a horde of spiders. She hurries shivering after Lorraine around the building to the staff car park.

Her little green Mazda is blanched by the spotlight above the giant X of TEXTS. Shadows make the five cars appear to be standing on or next to wet patches that have seeped up through the tarmac. Lorraine leaps into her Shogun before Mad has even unlocked her door. Greg stays his Austin and taps his horn as though he's giving his colleagues permission to leave. Mad lets her engine pant for a few seconds so that it won't stall. A blotch of light slithers across the wall and appears to vanish into the concrete—it must belong to Lorraine's retreating headlamps.

As Mad drives past the front of Texts she glimpses a blurred shape wandering among the shelves—Ray, presumably. No doubt he's checking they're tidy for a while. She can't help wondering until she stops herself how long hers will remain that way. She drives up out of the fog that lies in the retail park and sees clear tail-lights flying like sparks along the motorway. She oughtn't to feel as if she's dredging herself and her mind out of the murk. Now it's home to St Helens and her first little flat on her own, and her bed her parents bought her to take to university, and if she's lucky nine glorious hours of not having to think about work.

# NIGEL

**How late is it now? Twelve minutes later than last time Nigel looked:** close enough to five o'clock that he should turn off the alarm in case it wakens Laura. Reaching for the clock feels like plunging his bare arm into water that has had all night to gather ice. As soon as he has found the switch with a fingernail he shelters in the tropics of the quilt, but he mustn't risk going back to sleep. He inches across the warm mattress and settles a light but lingering kiss on Laura's shoulder blade, which is as naked as the rest of her. He's easing himself away when she mumbles a sleepy protest that isn't exactly "Night" or "No" either and reaches back to take hold of his stub.

Her hand feels like all the soft heat of the bed turned into flesh. At once he's much less stubby and yearning to kiss her awake as slowly as he can bear. What with his shifts at Texts and hers at the hospital, where he sometimes thinks she's too ready to accommodate colleagues with young children, he and Laura have had few occasions recently when neither of them is too tired. But she needs her sleep, and if he succumbs now he'll end up late. He can't have the staff on his shift waiting to be let into the shop. He prises Laura's fingers gently off himself and lifts them up to kiss them before he slips from under the quilt and pads out of the room.

Even the carpet is cold as snow. No wonder his stub tries to hide like a snail. He rushes downstairs as fast as he quietly can and through the mahogany kitchen to rouse the central heating. By the time he has used the toilet and shower beyond the kitchen and donned the clothes he took downstairs last night, the chill has been driven out of the building. He tiptoes upstairs to leave a morning kiss on Laura's forehead. "Dry carely," she mumbles. "See you night." Once she's asleep again he lets himself mousily out of the house.

A milk float is humming its fitful crescendo through the village as he hooks the gates at the end of the drive open and unlocks the double garage. While West Derby has been a Liverpool suburb for most of a century, it's quiet enough to be a village still. He backs his Primera out past Laura's Micra and closes the garage and the gates. Three minutes within the speed limit bring Nigel to the dual carriageway of Queen's Drive, and he's at the motorway in less than ten.

For most of half an hour his smoky cones are the only headlights. Signs like promises of blue sky—St Helens, Newton-le-Willows, Warrington—swell up and then expose their spotlit backsides in the mirror. The sign for Fenny Meadows seems paler than its relatives; in the distance it looks white with mould. It recovers its colour as the fog drains down the slip road, to stand more of its ground in the retail park.

Fog flaps around the spotlight above an X like an illiterate giant's signature on the rear wall of the bookshop. As he leaves the car a patch of moisture wells up beneath it and subsides, but it's a befogged shadow. He hurries along the alley the colour of fog and past the window, into which an assortment of books have escaped from the vacant aisles. Typing most of Woody's surname on the keypad releases the glass doors, and his first two letters reduced to numbers quell the alarm.

As soon as Nigel is locked in he begins to shiver. The heating won't have been on long, and some fog may have crept in while the doors were open: he can't be sure if the children's alcoves across the shop are faintly blurred. He hesitates by the counter but can find no excuse to stay there. It's absurd of him to behave like this when every day that Laura is in Accident and Emergency she deals with human damage most people wouldn't want even to imagine. Perhaps it's best that he and Laura have no children if this is the kind of example he would set them—a father afraid of the dark. A surge of anger sends him to clap his badge to the plaque by the door up to the staffroom.

The walls of the passage are blanker than fog, but he has never been claustrophobic. He switches on the light as the door hauls itself shut, then he sprints up the bare concrete stairs. Beyond the door past the toilets and the name-tagged staff lockers is a light that he's especially anxious should be working. It is, and for a troubled moment he thinks he isn't alone in the building, but of course Wilf neglected to clock off—he'll need to give Ray a shift error slip. Nigel slides his own card along the groove and drops it in the In rack above Wilf's, and then he confronts the staffroom.

What could make anyone nervous? Not the walls the colour of pale moss, the straight chairs standing at attention round the table except for one resting its forehead against the edge, the cork wallboard with several Woody's Wheedles sheets pinned to it, the sink full of unwashed plates and mugs and cutlery that must be collaborating on a faint moist stale smell . . . But this isn't the room where Nigel spends much of his time and feels least at ease. He strides to throw open the door to the office.

The light in there is reliable too. Three computers attended by swivel chairs and wire trays bristling with papers keep one another company on a bench that sprouts from three sides of the room. A pair of magnetic butterflies have settled on Connie's monitor, Ray's sports a Manchester United badge, and Nigel thinks yet again that he ought to find an emblem to decorate his: it might make him feel more at home. Why should he need to force that? He must have been in windowless places before, but he has never been afraid of the dark—afraid that the lights will fail, trapping him in blackness as profound as the depths of the earth. There wouldn't even be a glow from Woody's office beyond the benchless wall. All this is non-sense, and here's his chance to prove it to himself while nobody's about. Good God, he's supposed to be a manager. He steps into the office and shuts the door behind him, then he slaps the light switch with a vigour that sends him into the instant enveloping dark.

He can't have taken many inadvertent paces when he stumbles to a halt. He meant to take them, he tells himself. He meant to sur-round himself with more of the darkness, to prove that no amount of it was the slightest threat to him, however much it feels as if he has been dragged underground. It has done its worst, which is noth-ing at all, and there's the doorbell ringing at the front of the shop. The muffled distant sound could be signalling his victory or, if he's honest about it, his release. He turns towards the staffroom, but he might as well have no eyes. There's no hint of the outline of the door.

Has the light beyond it fused, or is he wrong to think he's facing it? He can't see it anywhere around him, but he mustn't panic; he only has to advance until he encounters a wall. He takes a hesitant step and stretches out his hands. They've hardly moved when the left one touches the spongy forehead of whatever's crouched in front of him.

Nigel lets out a gasping cry that leaves him no breath. As he staggers backwards he hears the object scuttle into the dark. It thumps the bench, rattling the computers, by which time he has re-alised what it was: a chair on wheels. Of course the noise that slith-ers softly along a wall is nothing but an echo. He's farther from the door than he could have believed, but at least he's able to locate it now, by the sound of the faraway doorbell somebody's leaning on. He blunders in that direction and almost collides with the door, ex-cept for detecting the faintest hint of illumination around it. He gropes for the doorknob, which feels grubby and not too dry, no doubt from his sweaty hand. He flings the door wide and runs, not flees, downstairs.

As Nigel crosses the sales floor Gavin takes his finger off the bell-push. He continues to jig on the spot outside the glass doors while beside him Angus stops rubbing his hands together, apparently in case this looks like impatience. Both of their faces are wreathed in breath. Nigel has scarcely unlocked the doors when Gavin skips onto the READ ON! mat. "You look lively," Nigel says.

"Buzzin', all righty, that's me." Gavin jerks his eyebrows high as if to underline a quip Nigel doesn't understand, or in an attempt to hoist his heavy lids, or a tic that stretches the skin tighter on his pointed face. "How about you, Anyus?" he says, spinning around. "Sleep all night?"

Angus falters between the security pillars in front of the muddy slogan and rubs a handful of his long mottled face so hard he might be trying to erase the last of this year's tan. "He's pronouncing me like Anyes," he explains as if he's not sure how amused he's entitled to be.

"We did know that, Anyus."

Behind them a Passat driven by Jake's boyfriend cruises to a halt, and Jake gives him a quick kiss before climbing out. "I'll cope with the mob while you all clock on," Nigel says and glances at the rota on the counter. "You're tilling for the first hour, Angus. Jake and Gavin, you're shelving."

Of course there's no mob. Nobody has ever needed to unlock the doors to anyone but staff. Newspapers and magazines might bring customers earlier, but Frugo stocks those and commands the entrance to the retail park. Nigel collects yesterday's customer order forms from the shelf beneath the Information terminal, then occupies himself by lining up books in Animals to the regulation half-inch from the edge of the shelf. Once Angus reappears, Nigel heads for the route to the stockroom.

The lift is demonstrating how well it can pronounce two of its three words. As Nigel climbs the stairs a muffled clatter of books on trolleys sinks past him. The Returns and Damaged racks need to be cleared, but first the customers' orders have to be sent. He sends himself across the staffroom, where the faint irritatingly vague smell is dissipating, and switches on the office light. He's about to sit at his computer when he notices Woody's door is ajar.

That's hardly remarkable. Woody tends to leave it open when he's in his office. As Nigel pushes it wider, the baseball pennant above the desk flexes itself wormlike in the dimness and sags flat on the wall. Two of the quadrants of the security monitor up in the far corner display movements too: Gavin's on his knees in Music, and a figure is squatting in Toddlers' Texts. At least they have a customer, then, though the figure's head and indeed its whole greyish shape are too blurred for Nigel to distinguish any details. He closes the door and goes to work at the computer.

He emails most of the orders to the American warehouse or the British equivalent in Plymouth, though the publishers of a poetry collection are so diminutive he has to search for the address and send a direct request. He's close to finishing his task when Gavin's voice appears above him. "Nigel call twelve, please. Nigel buzz a dozen."

He grabs the phone to head off any further jesting. "Yes, Gavin."

"There's a customer wanting to know if you've got his order."

"Can you give me the details?"

"It's about round here."

"And his name is . . ."

"Sole. What's your first name?" A pause sounds smothered by a hand. "It's Robert," says Gavin, and not quite evenly "Mr R. Sole."

Is this a prank? When Nigel glances at Woody's monitor he sees a man in front of Gavin at the counter. His grey hair could be a tail his fur collar is dangling. Nigel opens the computer list of customers who've ordered books. Riddle, Samson, Sprigg, but not a solitary Sole or anything it could have been mistaken for. "Could you just confirm the name?" Nigel at once feels unwary for asking.

"He's wondering about your name." Another pause interferes with Nigel's breath before Gavin reports "It's like I said."

"I'm coming down," Nigel says to forestall any repetition of it, and heads fast for the stairs.

He's nearly at the Information terminal when the customer swings round with a swirl of his ponytail and a smell of old astrakhan. His lower lip helps the upper rise into a smile as he fingers the thumb-hole in his chin and then extends a hand as pudgy as his wrinkled piebald face. "Bob Sole."

"Pleasure. Nigel," Nigel offers, and hastily "I'll see to Mr Sole, Gavin. Would you happen to know when you ordered the book, Mr Sole?"

"The day you opened. I was nearly the first through the door."

"Glad you keep coming back."

"It's about time there was a bit of intelligence round here."

Nigel isn't sure if this refers to Texts or the customer, and restrains himself to asking "Would you know the author?"

"I've got his name if that's what you're after. Bottomley's the feller. Don't ask me the book."

Nigel types the surname in the Search box of the online catalogue. Soon a multiplication of the name rises up, bringing titles with it: *In the Dells of Delamere*, *Stories of a Stockport Stockbroker*, *Manchester Murders and Mayhem*, *Poems on the Peaks*, *Commons and Canals of Cheshire* . . . "Could that be it?" Nigel suggests, pivoting the screen towards the customer.

"You'd wonder what'd drive that out of your thick skull, wouldn't you?" Mr Sole enquires, presumably about himself. "Can you give it another go?"

"I will the moment I'm back at my desk. I'm sorry your order slipped through the system somehow."

"I'm not blaming any of your crew."

All the same, once he has dictated an address in Lately Common and Nigel has printed out the slip, Mr Sole scrutinises his copy before folding it pocket-sized. He's the only customer now—indeed, Nigel didn't notice when Toddlers turned deserted; there wasn't anybody there when he came downstairs. He shows the wall his badge and hurries back to his computer.

It's displaying a screensaver that he hasn't seen before. Presumably the image of several figures performing a dance or some other repetitive business hasn't fully loaded: it's too greyish and muddily blurred. He touches a key to get rid of the spectacle and search for Mancunian Press. He emails an order for Bottomley's book and glances at the security monitor in case Mr Sole is waiting to be told his order is in order, but the public is represented only by two bald men in armchairs. Each is staring at the nearest shelf as though the spines of books are quite enough to read, until one raises his face like an aquatic creature mouthing the surface of a pond.

It's time for Nigel's secret indulgence. He wonders sometimes whether everybody has one so silly they would be mortified if it were ever discovered. His is acting like a vandal towards already damaged or imperfect books; perhaps he needs the break from playing manager. Racks stir with a furtive jangle as he hurries through the stockroom to find a trolley, onto which he lobs half a dozen faulty video cassettes and more than twice as many books. He wheels them to his section of the office bench and sets about examining his take.

He isn't going to assume that any of the staff are responsible for the problems with the cassettes: no two of the original purchases bear the same staff identification number. He initials the Reason for Return slips, which say "blurred picture" or "blurred tape" or just "blurred", and lays the tapes to rest in a carton addressed to the Plymouth warehouse. The books have more reason to leave the shop— entire sections of text are repeated, or the skewed print is sliding helplessly off the page—and he's cracking spines with gusto before he slings each offender into the carton when the next book proves to be *Commons and Canals of Cheshire*. He's about to be delighted on Mr Sole's behalf, but then he sees that the entire middle section of the slim volume, including several pages where he's just able to distinguish the name of Fenny Meadows, is so blotchily printed it looks waterlogged. He drops the book in the carton and opens the most expensive item, a hundred pounds' worth of paintings by Lowry. Where's the exchange slip? He leafs through the heavy pages, past cityscapes so drab they might be composed of mud, swarming with insect figures, but they're all. Nothing is wrong with the catalogue except the jacket Nigel tore and the pages he wrenched loose from the binding when he threw the book on the trolley. He's damaged one of the most expensive books in the shop.

It shouldn't have been on the Returns racks, but that doesn't absolve him of failing to check. He grabs a slip and describes the catalogue as damaged on delivery. It could almost be true; certainly the cover feels grubby. He's lowering the book into the carton with belated care when Woody darts into the staffroom.

Is he due yet? Nigel's start of guilt sends the book half out of its jacket, which tears as he lunges to save it. As he fumbles both of them into the carton, Woody advances to watch. "Say, that's some damage," he remarks.

Does he mean the price, or wouldn't an American? "That's how it came," Nigel manages not to stammer.

"Are we seeing much of that?"

Whatever face Nigel is showing feels treacherously warm. "This is the first," he makes it reply.

"How about once we've taken delivery?"

"Just about the same, I'd say."

"As long as everyone is careful. We can't sell books we don't have." Woody passes a hand over his turfy hair as though he's feeling for overnight growth or perhaps for his next thought. "How long does the fog stay like this around here?"

"It does seem to be hanging around in the mornings."

"Seems like it's keeping customers away. We may have to think about our hours." He takes a step away from Nigel and halts to demand "Who went in my office?"

"I thought I could keep an eye on security while you weren't here and I was."

"I do take a break once in a while, you've got me there." Before Nigel can decide whether to explain he wasn't criticising, Woody says "No, you were right" and shuts himself in his room.

Nigel seals the carton with tape and heaves it onto the trolley. He sends it down in the lift and dumps it in the lobby to be collected, then hurries upstairs to tabulate the latest stock reports. The windowless rooms no longer bother him now that someone else is there. Nevertheless as he sits down Woody's muffled voice rather takes him aback. Woody must have heard him return and is calling to him. Since Nigel doesn't know what's behind the words, he isn't sure how to reply. He utters a sound that may not be audible, or perhaps it seems insufficiently agreeable. "We'll need to be here longer," Woody said, but now there's silence.

# AGNES

**"Agnes please call nine. Sorry, I mean Anyes. Anyes please call nine."**

Agnes would suspect some people of getting her name wrong on purpose, but not Jill. She sticks the last corner of her *Warm Up With Winter Breaks* notice to the end of her European Travel shelves before hurrying to the phone next to Humour. Perhaps a stray child has been playing with it; the receiver feels grubby. Agnes holds it between a finger and thumb and says "Hi, Jill."

"Sorry again. I forgot how to page for a moment. There's so much to remember, isn't there?"

"I expect we won't even think about it soon. Why did you want me?"

"Your father's on line one."

"Thanks, Jill," Agnes says and thumbs the Line One button. "Hello?"

"Annie. She's there, June. You're in one piece then, Annie."

"Such as it is. A bit pale and wrinkled but still intact."

"You always look fine to us. You ought to think of yourself more, all the same. Find someone to go away with for a couple of weeks if you won't on your own, or failing that, a few sessions on a sunbed."

"Yes, dad," Agnes says rather than revive the disagreement. Her parents took her around half the world when she was little, but now they're too frail to travel, and she would only worry if she left them alone together for any length of time. Making herself look as though she has been away appeals to her even less—it would be like suggesting slyly that she wants to go. "Anyway," she says, "you remember we aren't supposed to get personal calls at work."

"I thought it was calls from friends that are prohibited. I didn't realise it applied to family as well."

"I hope we'll always be both, but is it something urgent?"

"There was a crash on the motorway near you just now on the news. How are the conditions there?"

Agnes turns from crouching secretively over the phone and glances down her aisles towards the window. Fog that has blotted out the supermarket swells the brake lights of a mammoth lorry as it lumbers out of the retail park. "It's a bit murky," she admits.

"I can't hear you, Annie. You know our ears aren't what they were."

"I said there's a bit of fog, dad. I'll take extra care on the way home. I know that's what you want."

"I wouldn't have thought it was much."

She hears the hurt just under the thin skin of his voice—the loneliness he and her mother will never admit to feeling as their old friends grow too old to visit them, those friends who aren't older than alive. "Of course it isn't," she assures him. "You and mummy look after each other till I'm home."

"We can for longer than that, Annie."

This could be the start of another of their family disagreements that take hours to reach no conclusion, because they're all so anxious not to injure one another that they have to pick their way through every detail. She's desperate to terminate the conversation without giving him an excuse to feel slighted, because she can hear Woody's voice nearby. She peers at the computer terminal next to the phone and types in the search box the first words that come to her: Fenny Meadows. "Well, you don't need to," she's saying meanwhile. "You know I'll always come home."

"Poor girl, except you aren't one any longer, unless we've kept you that way."

"I'll always be yours." Agnes feels as if she's struggling to drag herself free of a slough of emotion that has grown stagnant. "I really must do some work," she says. "Kiss mummy for me."

"We might get up to more than that," he says, which he ought to know makes her uncomfortable. At least it shows there's some life in her parents, and she's able to replace the receiver. The computer screen has turned blank, and here comes a reflection to see why. When she spins around guiltily, however, nobody is approaching. She didn't see a blurred figure rising through the greyness after all. In a moment Woody does arrive, but from her right. "Problem, ah, Anyes?"

"It's gone."

"Try switching it off and on again."

She pokes the button on the block of the computer, and darkness wells into the screen. As she waits for a few seconds, Woody says "What were you trying to find?"

"Just the, the history of this area."

She presses the button a second time and feels his scrutiny gathering on her. She's telling herself that it can't be apparent she was talking to her father when Woody says "It's for whoever called just now, right?"

"Right. That's to say that's right, I mean, yes."

"I don't see where you took their number to call them back."

"They've, oh, they said they were going out. They'll ring in a bit, they said."

"Always get a number." At last he transfers his gaze to the

screen, which has turned blue while the computer checks for errors. "When you're through here, can you give Madeleine a hand with the quiz?" he says, and frowns towards the counter. "Keep an eye out for lines, what you Brits call queues."

There are more than a dozen customers at large in the shop, but she suspects most of them are parents of the children who are gathering around Mad in Teenage Texts—children of too many ages to compete with one another at anything but noise. As the computer produces its icons Agnes is afraid Woody will stay to watch her fake a search. She has typed Fenny Meadows in the box before he heads for the door by the lift. Once she's sure he isn't coming back she ends the search, which hasn't found a single title, and hurries into Teenage. "What would you like me to do, Mad?"

Mad raises her small wide-eyed oval face and, having shaken back her shoulder-length blonde tresses, taps her plump pink lips with a fingertip as if to release an idea. "Do you think you could take about half of them up the other end for a quiz?"

"I'll have the little ones, shall I?"

"If you're feeling mummyish. I'll try and keep order while you bring some chairs down."

Agnes badges herself through the door up to the staffroom. Ross is on his break, and Lorraine is sitting next to him, so close she's almost on his chair. She turns as if her face is being lifted by her rising golden eyebrows, while Ross seems to hope Agnes will be content with the back of his head. "It's only Agnes," Lorraine reassures him. "Anyes, I know we're meant to say."

"Please don't if it's too much trouble."

"There are worse things round here. Are you coming for your break?"

"No, I'm here for Mad."

Ross twists to face Agnes. "You mean she sent you up?"

"That's what she did."

"Sometimes I think she's sending us all up," Lorraine says in her almost chortling voice.

Ross won't be distracted from his theme. "If that's what she calls still being friends—"

"She sent me to get some chairs for the quiz."

"You might have said that."

"I just did. We only need one in here at the moment, don't we? There's only supposed to be one of us having our break at once."

"About time a few of us queried that," says Lorraine with very little of a chortle. "I don't know about anyone else, but I don't like being up here by myself."

"So I'll take that one if I may, Lorraine."

Lorraine rests her fingertips on Ross's shoulder while she stands up. "There's your little chair, Agnes. I'll see you later, Ross."

He looks uncomfortable until the stockroom door closes behind her, and then he jumps to his feet. "Here, I'll take some," he says and stacks five chairs as Agnes picks up four. He bumps his way into the stockroom, where Lorraine is planting books on a trolley, more loudly when she sees him and Agnes. "Shall I come down with you?" he asks Agnes.

"You finish your break. Thanks, Ross," she adds over the voice of the lift.

As the doors close he saunters over to Lorraine. "Want a hand as well?" he says so coyly it makes Agnes suck her teeth. Their conversation dwindles and grows blurred as the windowless cage lumbers downwards. Before it settles at the bottom of the shaft she can't hear them. It tells her that it's opening in a voice that seems slower than last time she heard it—perhaps the tape or whatever it uses to speak is developing a fault. The doors quiver like slabs of grey mud as a preamble to heaving themselves apart, and she blocks them with the chairs. She dodges out and drags the chairs after her and hobbles them onto the sales floor, to be greeted with a cry from Mad. "Here's the chair lady."

About as many of the children cheer as mutter "Big deal" or one more word. "We'll pretend we didn't hear that, shall we," Mad says without looking directly at anyone, "and let's make sure we don't again. Anyes, I think you'd better take the little ones before their ears can get any grubbier."

Agnes isn't certain only older children said the word, but she lifts six chairs off the stack to move them to the farthest alcove. A little girl jumps up from sitting cross-legged on the floor and lays her book on top of a shelf. "Shall I help carry?"

"This is Jill's Bryony," Mad informs Agnes.

"Thank you, Bryony," Agnes says and leans the stack towards her while she removes a chair. "You five come with us."

Two boys scowl. "We aren't little," the squatter of the pair objects.

"Youngsters, then," says Mad. "We'd like to be called that, wouldn't we, Anyes?"

"We aren't them either," says his lanky friend with a sniff like a prelude to spitting.

"You aren't teenagers, are you? You have to be teenagers to be in my quiz."

"Won't you give me and Bryony a hand?" Agnes suggests. "We appreciate young gentlemen, don't we, Bryony?"

The boys ungraciously grab a chair each and tramp after her. She thinks it best to ignore the word one grunts as they see she's leading them to Tiny Texts. Once everyone is seated she hands out pencils and paper. "Ready?" she says with more enthusiasm than any of the contestants except Bryony is displaying. "Listen carefully, then. Number one."

She wonders if Mad gave her the wrong sheet, and then she sees the questions about books are aimed at the age group she's quizzing. There are also questions on bands in the charts, which all the children answer, and sports, which produce a conflict of cheers and boos when the answer has to do with Liverpool or Manchester. Mad's mistake appears to have been too many queries about books, since only Bryony attempts to answer every one. The boys who wanted to be thought older screw up their pages and drop them along with the pencils before stalking into the next alcove. Agnes is repeating the literary questions in case any of Bryony's opponents might make a belated guess when she hears the boys start to compete at loudness. Most of their words have a single syllable, but the longer ones are at least as bad. "Excuse me, could you stop that?" she calls as she hurries around the shelves.

"Don't shout at us," the lanky boy smirks. "We're just reading your book."

It should be in Tiny Texts. "I don't think so," says Agnes. "Will you give it here at once, please."

He's eager she should have it, and in a moment she sees why. Each double page displays a picture and a solitary word for it, but the words have been crossed out and replaced in crude scrawled capitals with the ones she had to hush. Since Bryony has followed her, Agnes makes a swift decision. "Bryony, I'm trusting you to take this to your mummy and not look inside it. Give me your answer sheet to keep safe. Tell your mummy the book's defaced."

Bryony hugs it to her chest as she heads for the counter and Jill, but she's halfway up the Religion aisle when a man accosts her. "That's a bit babyish for you, isn't it? More than a bit. What's the appeal? Come on, you can show me."

"I'm supposed to take it to mummy, dad."

Agnes is confronting the boys. "Tell me the truth, now. You wrote all that, didn't you?"

"We never," the lanky boy protests. "It was on the floor."

"We haven't even got a pen."

"Search us if you don't believe us."

"You're not allowed to touch us. Anyway, he wouldn't have a pen. He can't write."

"Neither can you either."

"Never said I could."

"Give over saying I can't, then."

These are among the words they shout, together with a selection of the ones they were previously uttering. Agnes has told them twice that it's enough when Jake trots over, lowering his broad chubby freckled face and blinking lashes Agnes would be proud to sport. "Let's be polite, lads," he urges. "Ladies present. Other children too."

The duo gape at him. "Why are you talking like that? Are you a queer?" is most of what the lanky boy responds.

"That's what I am and proud of it. Now that'll have to be all, I'm afraid. Out of here till you remember how to behave."

The boys stare at the hands he stretches out to usher them. "Keep your filthy paws off," the squat boy warns, which Agnes suspects he overheard his mother say except for an extra word or perhaps that too.

"We'll say you tried to come up us, you dirty peedo," the lanky boy adds and much else in between.

Agnes slips Bryony's answers into the hip pocket of her dress and grabs the boys by a shoulder each. "There won't be much point in saying that about me, will there? Come along now or—"

The boys duck out of her grasp and dash through Psychology. "You touched us. You've had it now," one cries with embellishments as they fling books from the top shelves in their wake. Jake sprints after them, leaping over Jung, but they've fled the shop. Staff aren't supposed to pursue miscreants once they're out of the exit, since Texts isn't insured against whatever might happen next, and so he trudges back to Agnes. "I'll put them straight," he says.

A nearby mother looks askance at that. While Jake retrieves the books as if they're injured birds and somehow his fault, Agnes picks up the boys' answer sheets. Their sole contents are drawings she would be embarrassed to see on a wall. She stuffs them in the pocket she has taken Bryony's sheet from and collects the rest. Bryony has outdone them by half a dozen answers and returns in time to see it. "This young lady is the winner," Agnes says, displaying the evidence.

The others straggle off to find their parents. She's about to take Bryony to receive her prize when Woody darts out of the exit to the staffroom. "Why were you after those boys, Jake?"

The nearby mother lets her wordless agreement with his doubts be heard as Jake holds up a textbook with a broken spine. "They were being stinky-mouthed," he says. "I chased them out and here's their revenge."

"There's too much damage in this store."

Woody sounds so accusing it's no wonder Jake refrains from exhibiting the other ruined volumes. Agnes is willing the confrontation to finish when the mother steers her young daughter over to Woody. "Are you the manager?" she demands.

"That's me, ma'am. How may I help?"

"We thought there was going to be a competition."

"It's my impression we had one. I'm sorry if you missed it, but I'm sure there'll be—"

An even sterner woman shoves one of her sons at him at the end of either arm. "Aren't you meant not to let staff or their relatives play?"

"I don't believe the store has a specific policy on that, but I'd think—"

"Then you should," she objects, and gives her sons a ventriloquistic shake. "Tell him what you told us."

All three children start to clamour, but the girl's shrillness triumphs. "The one who won's mummy works here."

"And you said the organiser took her answers and hid them, didn't you?" her mother prompts.

It's to protect Bryony as much as herself that Agnes says "I didn't hide the answers. I just looked after them while Bryony was kind enough to take a damaged book to the counter."

"More damage? Good God," Woody says, frowning at Jake while the boys' mother mutters "I'll bet she looked after them."

"I'm sorry if there's been a misunderstanding." Agnes assumes Woody is about to defend her until he adds "If you'd like to take your children to the counter they can all have prizes. That includes anyone who was in this half of the quiz."

As the mothers and their undeserving tribe head for the counter, he motions Jake over. "Maybe you could work on not being quite so obvious around children," he says low.

"Unless you're straight, you mean."

"That's kind of unreasonable, wouldn't you say? You know we're an equal opportunity employer."

"I'll try and be surreptitious all the same, shall I?" As though he's indulging himself one last time, Jake says more loudly "Kids aren't my meat, by the way."

Woody stares at him before following the parade to the counter, and Agnes grows aware of Jill's daughter. "Come with me, Bryony. You're still the winner. Let's make sure you get your prize."

Jill is having some trouble with issuing vouchers while Woody observes. Perhaps she's distracted by the sight of her ex-husband and Connie at the end of Erotica. "Don't tell me, it'll come to me," Connie is saying to him. "Orient/Occident, that's where you work."

"And you were one of the party in leather."

"Keep some of my secrets," she murmurs, touching a finger to his lips and another to her own. "So can I help you with anything?"

"I'm just here to pick up a little girl when she's collected her prize."

"Lucky little girl."

Agnes sees Jill swallow a retort and tries to distract her, but all she can bring to her suddenly sluggish mind is "Don't forget Bryony, Jill."

"You'll have to wait your turn, Bryony. Other people are."

"She was going to," Agnes feels bound to point out as she signs on at a till. She's placating one of the mothers with a voucher when the parent of the set of boys turns on Woody. "Are we going to have to come back?"

"Not unless you care to, ma'am. We hope you will."

"Your assistant doesn't seem to want to give them their prizes."

Jill keeps her glare on the register. "There's something wrong with this."

When Agnes glances along the counter she sees no recognisable symbols on Jill's screen, just fragments like a scattering of flimsy bones. Perhaps that's the fault of the angle she's viewing it from, because Woody cancels the transaction and signs on and swiftly endorses the vouchers. "Can we get videos?" one boy begs.

"Our vouchers are good for anything we sell, ma'am."

"They don't read much," the mother confesses.

"We wouldn't have known that, would we, mummy?" Bryony says not quite under her breath.

Jill scarcely grins, but Woody's silence feels like a sudden fog. He passes Bryony's voucher to her as Connie heads upstairs, leaving Bryony's father to venture to the counter. "I'll take Bry to choose her prize, shall I?" he suggests to Jill.

"I'm sure she's more than capable of choosing for herself."

"I'll tag along anyway. Makes me feel wanted," he says, turning the depths of his brown eyes on Bryony, who takes his hand.

As Jill watches them retreat to the opposite side of the shop, Woody says "If there's anything you need to be reminded of, let me know."

"I can't think of anything."

He takes a breath that sounds like a sigh played backwards. "Not discussing customers in public would be one. We were nearly sued over that in Florida."

It strikes Agnes that he's discussing Jill in public. Presumably he realises, since his voice sinks as if it's being dragged down. "Counter routines," he barely utters out loud.

"The till was playing up."

"I guess we'll know if it happens again. Yes, Agnes, Anyes. Were you waiting for something?"

"I thought you'd want to see this," she says, passing him the defaced book from the Returns shelf behind the counter.

The first page he opens tugs his head down. When he speaks he seems to be casting his voice into some profundity of the book. "We need to be a whole lot more vigilant."

"I wonder if whoever did it wrote in any others."

"Madeleine can check for that while you finish your shelf end."

She didn't intend to give Mad another task. Bryony and her father are returning to the counter, and she beckons them to save Jill from making any more trouble for herself. Bryony presents her with a book of poems from the Tennish section. "You were quick," Agnes remarks.

"My dad's taking me for lunch in Chester and then we're going to the zoo."

"Maybe you'll see some mating routines," says Jill. "It can make you laugh, what animals get up to when they meet."

"I don't think it's the time of year," Bryony's father says.

"Some of them seem to think they're hot all year round."

Woody emits a sound like a grunt that has snagged on a cough, but only Bryony looks at him. The till Agnes is using feels sluggish, or time does. The machine lingers over regurgitating the spent voucher for her to slip in the drawer; the details gather on the screen with all the speed of objects floating up through mud. She's about to draw Woody's attention to this in Jill's defence when the till sticks out a receipt. As Agnes drops it in the Texts bag she hands Bryony, Jill is told "I'll have her back with you for Sunday dinner."

"It'll be waiting for you, Bryony. Sleep well. Dream you're somewhere special," Jill says, and faces Woody as if challenging him to speak.

Agnes is making for her shelf end when he follows her. "Anyes? Any call?"

"For what?"

She turns to find him gazing barely patiently at her. "Did your customer call back?"

"Not yet."

"So long as you've got something for them."

"They won't be disappointed," she's anxious to persuade herself at least as much as him.

Her entire conversation with her father is repeating itself in her head, leaving little room for thoughts. As she stands guidebooks on the brackets under her Winter Breaks notice while Woody helps Mad return the chairs to the staffroom, she realises how sunlit all the places in the books may be. Half her display invites people to visit countries she has never seen, but that's part of her job. When she's home she can reminisce about holidays with her parents. Outside the fog is edging closer to the shop, and sunlight is a memory—one that she decides it's unwise to indulge just now. Memories won't lighten the greyness that is Fenny Meadows. They make it seem eager to grow dark.

# WILF

**"Mist dumber."**

"I beg your pardon?"

"Mist dumber, wasn't it? *A Mist Dumber Night's Dream* by Speak-shape."

"Ah, is it a parody?"

"About as much of one as you. Are you hauling on my chain or do you really not recognise me? That's too sad. You don't want to forget old times."

"Forgive me, I—"

"Slater. I expect you thought it looked like Staler. Fred Slater, and you're Lowell. Wilfred Lowell, only didn't you sign Wildfed Wellow or some such crap once?"

By now Wilf has remembered him. Slater's face hasn't aged much in ten years, but it has ended up on the front of a lump of pallid mottled flesh wider than itself. He still lets his mouth droop until it tugs at the rest of his face while he waits for his victim to catch up with the joke, and Wilf wonders if he'll pinch or poke or punch to gain the reaction he wants, as he used to when their school desks were next to each other. "I must have been having a bit of fun," Wilf says.

"You never seemed to be having much not being able to spell."

"Well, I am now."

"We'd all have had a good laugh if you'd said you wanted to work in a bookshop."

He never read a paragraph more than he had to. It was Wilf who was so hungry to read he felt he was starving until the dyslexia tutor taught him how. "What about you?" says Wilf. "Have you made much of yourself?"

"Maybe you'll hear from me some night soon."

"Sorry, why would I do that?"

"Don't you like hearing from old friends?"

Can he really believe he was ever one of Wilf's? Wilf's politeness is starting to feel like thin ice under entirely too heavy a burden. "If you'll excuse me, I ought to—"

"Hang on. You're helping me, or you will be in a minute. I'm your customer."

Nigel glances at Wilf along the counter from the till he has just arrived at, and Wilf daren't seem unworthy of working at the shop. "How may I help, then?" he makes himself ask.

"Try listening." Slater treats him to a pause that isolates the dwarfish music in the air before he says "Hello there, Mr Lowell. I wonder if you realise how the changes in our climate may be affecting where you live?"

"I really couldn't say. I shouldn't think—"

"The winter's getting wetter every year. Can I ask when you last had your damp course checked?"

"I haven't got one," Wilf says with some triumph. "I'm on the top floor."

"Don't feel too safe. It can still reach you, what's happening. How am I doing so far?"

"I'm afraid I don't think I'd be buying."

"Where would you say I'm going wrong?" Slater says and lets his face droop like a bloodhound's. "What's your secret as a salesman?"

"I don't know if I've got any." At once he's afraid Slater will betray it to Nigel—Wilf's old problem, even if he has solved it for good. He feels as if his teenage self is desperate to burrow out of reach inside him. "Just enjoy it," he suggests.

"Oh, I am. So are you going to show me what I need?"

"What do you think that is?"

"Psychology." Slater lets him start to leave the counter and says "Psychology of cold calling."

Wilf likes no aspect of the job more than leading customers to the books they want and placing their prize in their hands, but he can't go direct to this subject. It will be in either Psychology or Selling. He sets about typing it in the Search box on the Information screen. He hasn't finished when Slater leans across the counter and emits the kind of smothered snigger that used to multiply around Wilf whenever he was forced to read aloud in class. "That isn't how you spell it," Slater announces.

"I know that."

Wilf bruises the word and deletes it, and scrutinises his fingers on the keyboard as they type. P, s, y, c, h, o . . . When it's completed he looks up, to be faced by PYSCOLOGY. "You've done it again," gleeful Slater almost shouts. "Sounds like somebody's taking the piss."

Nigel hands a customer a bag and hurries along the counter. Just now the droll expression his ruddy rotund face tends to wear as if he's hoping for a joke looks rather too like Slater's. "Any trouble, Wilf?"

"The computer's playing stupid games. Look what happens," Wilf says, and goes through the process once more. "That's how it's acting. There aren't even the same number of letters."

"Let me have a crack," Nigel says and ducks his balding shiny head over the keys. "Well, it seems to have righted itself. Was it just psychology?"

Wilf stares at the word as Slater says "I wanted it for cold calls."

"Try sales, Wilf," Nigel advises and makes way for him at the keyboard.

Slater's. A. Loutish. Evil. Sod. Wilf isn't sure how long it takes him to think of the words, but he feels as if he can't type until he has. He raises his eyes at last and sees the second word in the search box: SLAES. "You saw what I put in," he protests.

"I see it plain enough," Nigel says as he takes over at the keyboard. A moment's flurry of his fingers replaces the mistake with SALES. He scrolls through the titles the search words bring up and stops at *Call and Sell*. "Is this the sort of thing you had in mind?" he asks Slater.

"Could be."

"Unfortunately it's not in stock, but we'll be happy to order it for you," Nigel says and returns to the till to serve another customer.

At least he's too busy to hear Wilf mutter "Are you certain you want this? If we order it for you we have to ask you to commit yourself to buying it."

"Let's see you order it, then."

All Wilf can do is perform the routine. "Have you ordered from us before?"

"I didn't know you were here. Now I do you'll be seeing a lot more of me."

Wilf opens the ordering window on the screen and watches while it copies the details of the book into itself. The computer appears to have finished malfunctioning until he enters Slater's name. However appropriate Slyter might be, it's wrong. He overtypes the vowel with a finger that's starting to feel grubby with nervousness. The screen offers him the particulars of another Slater who has ordered from the shop. He drives them away by typing an F, but Slater says "Better put in my whole name in case you get me mixed up. Make it Freddy while you're at it. That's who I am to my friends."

Wilf can think of another word F is for. By now he's typing in the hope that the clatter of plastic will blot out Slater's leaden drone. He can only stare at the word that takes shape. "That's not me," Slater snorts.

Just the same, Feary seems altogether too relevant. Wilf's damp hands feel prickly with grit as he inserts the correct letters. "Just need my address now, do you?" Slater says. "It's Knutsford Road in Grappenhall."

As Wilf jabs at the keys, they sting his fingertips. He has the impression of trying to pin down language that is sinking out of reach. "Not Kuntsford," Slater sniggers. "That isn't where I live."

It sounds right to Wilf, and he almost says so. He transposes the letters and types Road, and confronts the final hurdle. Git, Riff-raff, Arsehole, Ponce, Prick, Excrement . . . The words seem to fit the situation so well he has to concentrate on keeping them to himself, but has the struggle to hush them confused his fingers? What appears onscreen looks too primitive for words: GLPARENPLAH. He deletes letters and types others while Slater's gaze sticks to him like clammy mud. At last the word is corrected, and Wilf is about to ask for the house number when Slater says "Maybe that's not the book I want."

"I thought you did," Wilf protests and then remembers Slater's words.

"Your shop's going to make me buy it even if it isn't right, so I'd better not risk it. Don't worry," he says as much to Nigel as to Wilf. "I'll have plenty to ask you for next time."

Wilf clenches his fists under the counter and hopes Slater's back is aching with his stare. He's glaring at Slater's absence when Nigel joins him. "No sale?"

"I don't think he ever meant to buy it. He was just amusing himself."

Nigel lowers his voice. "Can we be professional?"

Wilf's fists are still hidden, but he's afraid his secret isn't. "What are you . . ." he falters. "What did I . . ."

"You know we mustn't discuss customers in public."

Slater would be overjoyed to know he'd landed his victim in yet more trouble. While Wilf grits his teeth and bruises his tongue against the roof of his mouth to trap words that feel as if they're bulging his skull, Nigel says "Are you comfortable using the computer?"

"I'm fine. I'll be fine. I am now."

Each protestation seems to convince Nigel less. He lingers until Wilf could almost imagine he's averse to returning upstairs. At last he heads none too directly for the exit up to the staffroom, leaving Wilf alone at the counter. It's Wilf's opportunity to prove he can use the computer when he isn't being watched. Any subject will do—old times, since Slater raised them.

He's typing the first letter when a dull glow appears to seep up from the depths of the screen. It must come from headlights, since it casts the silhouette of someone outside the window. The blurred grey body disappears as the head swells up at the bottom of the screen. The shape is so faceless Wilf has the unpleasant notion that the features have been squashed out of existence against the window. He swings around to see nobody outside the smeared glass, just a car leaving a bloody trail with its brake lights across the wet tarmac. Perhaps one of the trio of saplings in front of the backdrop of fog that reduces the tarmac by half managed to project the vague shadow a hundred yards or more onto the screen. That's deserted now except for Wilf's lonely O perched on the shelf of the search box.

Only, let, determination, tell, I, may, affect, spelling . . . That the sentence is clumsy doesn't matter; nobody can hear him muttering it under his breath. All he cares about are the letters on the screen, which are in the right order. Can he type them without putting words to them? He can, and again too. Relief makes him dab his forehead as Greg marches briskly to take up a post alongside him.

Greg inspects the screen and crinkles his reddish beard with a finger and thumb. "Have you finished?" he seems to feel more than entitled to learn.

"Just testing something. It's all yours."

"It wasn't for a customer."

"Not specifically."

"It can be done without." Greg's eyes scarcely indicate this is a question before he deletes the phrase from the search box. "You'll be on your way then, will you?" he says even less uncertainly. "We don't want the next person to be made late for their break."

He must want to be a manager—he sounds like one often enough. "I'm going to Frugo if anyone's looking for me," says Wilf.

He was so eager to finish reading his second novel of the week before he left home that he forgot to grab a meal from the freezer. He hurries out of Texts, to discover that the fog has drifted closer. Fetching his coat will only waste time. He folds his arms hard and strides past Happy Holidays, and the fog backs into the afternoon, leaving a snail's track on the pavement Woody calls a sidewalk. Fat pale lights are wandering about in the murk—headlamps, of course, however quiet the cars are. Overhead the spotlights are elongated toadstools blurred by luminous mould. The fog loiters in the glow of the units that are occupied by shops and smudges their windows while it gathers like a huge breath on parked cars. Figures composed of painted bones lean against the fronts of the unoccupied units: they're graffiti surrounded by scrawls that are barely words, if even. Wilf hastens past them to take refuge in Frugo.

The walls and ceiling of the supermarket are as colourless as the befogged spotlights. Unspecific muffled music hangs in the air while silent personnel unload cartons in the white aisles. Wilf takes a moss-green plastic basket to the rudimentary delicatessen section and bears a pack of sushi to the nearest till. The checkout girl, who wears an overall like a dentist's and has eyes weighed down by mascara, hardly glances at him even when she passes him the sushi in a bag so flimsy it's sibilant. The package thumps his ribs as he folds his arms to breast the automatic doors. For a moment it seems the glass won't move aside in time, and then the fog embraces him.

The quickest route back is through the car park. The fog wobbles backwards as he jogs across the tarmac. Out here the murk seems more solid; it reminds him of tripe, a thick slab of whitish flesh that crawls back to expose its tarry bones. Those are saplings keeping one another company in strips of grassy earth that relieve the barren black. Before long they're his only companions, since the fog has done away with the shops. He feels it trail over his face like wisps of icy cobweb extending themselves from the leafless branches of the saplings he's about to pass between. As he rubs his face with his free hand the supermarket bag blunders rustling against his chest. He treads on grass strewn with fallen leaves, and his other foot follows. The moment all his weight is off the tarmac, a mouth fastens on him.

It feels as if the veiled landscape has puckered to seize him. The cold slimy bloated lips close on his ankles and suck him down. The fog towers over him, and he imagines it muffling his cries for help before the mouth does. Then he flounders out of the mud and hears it smack its lips as he staggers across the tarmac. It was only mud, he almost shouts at his unforgivably silly self, but why was it so deep? Besides his shoes, an inch of his socks and trouser cuffs are black with it. He tramps at the fog until it peels itself away from the bookshop.

He's stamping on READ ON! when Greg strides to the near end of the counter. "Good Lord, what on earth have you been up to?"

"Just trekking back from"—Wilf feels trapped in stupidity until he manages to dredge the word up—"foraging."

"Anyone would think you'd been out in the fields. I don't think you should walk through the shop like that, do you?"

Wilf's mouth is opening before he can think of a polite answer or a quiet one, but he succeeds in saying only "I wasn't going to." He wipes most of the mud off his shoes with the supermarket bag and hands it to Greg. "Can you bin that while I try and get upstairs without being asked to leave?"

As he trudges across the shop his left shoe reiterates a sound rather too reminiscent of the nether fanfare he seems unable to suppress whenever he uses a public toilet. He has to walk with his right toe turned up while he grips the right knee of his trousers to lift the sodden cuff clear of his ankle, so that it's no wonder Greg watches him and two small children giggle at his progress. The cuff moulds itself to his leg as he shows the staffroom exit plaque his badge. Even once he's closed in he still feels watched and stupid. He hauls his trouser leg upstairs and leaves the sushi on the staffroom table before heading for what some of the staff as well as Woody have started calling the men's room.

The light flares on with a stuttering buzz. Who can be responsible for the state of the place? Wads of paper encrusted with mud are strewn about the floor and block the sink. He uses a handful of paper towels to dump them in the toilet, then he takes most of a roll of towels to rub mud off his clothes. He keeps being distracted by the absurd notion that the next time he raises his head, the mirror will show him he isn't alone. Of course behind him there's only the greenish wall as blank as fog. Once he has rid himself of all the mud he can he sits in the staffroom with an old friend, *War and Peace*.

He's feeding himself the first sentence and a Japanese mouthful when he hears voices in the office. "I forgot to tell you I was sitting on something for you, Jill," Connie says.

"Is it very squashed?"

"That might be funnier if you hadn't said very."

"Sorry. Clumsy of me. Is it squashed?"

"Not so funny second time round. I've got your author photos, so if you could put the promotion up today that would be brill. Get your imagination working."

"It's been doing that quite a lot lately."

"Did you want to tell me something?"

"I don't know about want. Let's leave it, shall we."

"No, let's not. Look, Jill, if I'd known you'd been married to Geoff . . ."

"He's nothing to me, so don't give my feelings a thought."

"That's very, sorry, what?"

"I was going to say my daughter's are a different matter."

"Is she likely to be coming to the shop much?"

"Not much, I shouldn't think. Even less if she's banned."

"No call for that, surely. Shall we just try leaving our home lives at home? That's the pro's way. Why the look?"

"I wasn't sure what you meant for a moment."

"Got it now? Super. Here's Brodie Oates for you. I'm giving you a window display. Get me all the custom you can."

"I don't know if I'll be as good at that as you are, Connie."

A silence follows in which Wilf imagines both women pretending they've no idea what Jill means. He's about to make a noise to indicate they aren't alone when Jill opens the door. She and Connie stare at him as though he has been eavesdropping, which he has. He fills his mouth with sushi and tries to take refuge in reading the book.

*"Eh bien, mon prince . . ."* He can't progress past that while the women are staring at him, and even once the door is shut and Jill is dealing the stairs a series of blows with her feet his mind keeps snagging on the words. He knows Tolstoy is demonstrating that French was the second language of the Russian aristocracy in Napoleonic times, but the thought is no help. He reminds himself what a joy it was to be able to read any book, one a day sometimes, but the memory falls short of his feelings: it's as though greyness like a combination of fog and cobwebs has settled over his brain. Abey Ann, mon prance . . . A B Ann . . . A Bloody Awful Nonsensical Nonsense . . . Has Slater done this to him? Blaming his old enemy only wastes time when he needs to regain himself. He shoves a forkful of sushi in his dry mouth and swallows hard as he sees from his watch that he has been rereading the first line for minutes. Can't he entice himself into the story by recalling its scope? The romances, the duel, the society occasions, the hunt, the battles, above all the people? When he turns to the list of characters at the front of the book, the names might as well be lumps of mud.

Bezuhov, Rostov, Bolkonsky, Kuragin . . . They sound like

consonants rasping together—like language groping for itself and failing to take hold. He knows it's his mind that's doing so, which is worse. When he returns to the opening paragraph the names seem to lose shape, filling his head like chunks of a substance too primitive to have meaning. Are they why he can't read more than a phrase at a time and takes so long over each one that its sense has sunk out of reach by the time he drags himself to the end of the sentence? The paragraph is less than eight lines long, yet he hasn't finished it when he scrapes the last forkful out of the plastic container. As his eyes labour back to the first words, Greg's voice appears above him, hushed yet enlarged. "Wilf call twelve, please. Wilf call twelve."

There isn't a phone in the staffroom. Connie gives him a blink that contains a trace of the look he received from her and Jill. As he fumbles with Ray's phone he almost knocks the Manchester United badge off the computer monitor. "What do you want, Greg?"

"Are you about on your way down? Angus is due for his break, but you know Angus. He doesn't want to trouble you himself."

"My time isn't up yet, is it?" Wilf asks Connie.

"I couldn't tell you without looking at the roster. It's up to you to keep an eye on yours."

He was only trying to make peace with her. He glances at his watch so as to tell Greg in her hearing that he's wrong, but he isn't. Wilf has spent the best part of an hour in struggling to read a single paragraph. He feels as if his brain has shrivelled to less than a child's inside his uselessly huge skull and is desperate to hide there without risking another word. "So what shall I say to Angus?" Greg insists.

"You can tell him to make his own calls in future, and here's what I think you should do to yourself." Wilf keeps all that and more inside him, instead blurting "I'll be down."

He's almost out of the office when Connie says "Have you had a chance to sort your section out, Wilf?"

"What sort of, I mean sort what?"

"It was looking neglected last time I found someone a book in it."

It isn't neglected at all. He tidied it last night and still had had time to help Mad tidy Toddlers. He throws his sushi container in the bin and his fork in the sink and runs downstairs. "Just a second," he tells Angus as he detours to check his books.

If they're out of order, he doesn't see how. The Bibles are all together, and the books about them follow them. Anything occult is in Occult, philosophies are in Philosophy, even if he can't fit his mind around the more protractedly abstruse titles just now. Are the books arranged by author within their subjects? As he realises he can't judge, he's overwhelmed by a chill so intense it freezes him where he stands. He's peering helplessly at the mass of books when Greg steps out from behind the counter. He leans towards Wilf like an athlete straining to start a race while Angus looks loath to be the reason. "Wilf . . ." Greg urges.

"Sorry, Angus. I was distracted." Wilf still is, all the more so when he discovers he can't read the spines of his books from behind the counter. That's the fault of the distance. It doesn't mean he's unable to read. He has no problems in serving customers—by now using the till is as instinctive as driving—which gives him back some confidence until he wonders if it makes him little more than an extension of the machine, no brain required. Just now he isn't anxious to test himself at the Information terminal, and he's glad nobody requires him to use it. By the time Jill takes over at the counter, he's yearning to go home to his own books, but won't his doubts follow him?

Pacing up and down his aisles shows him nothing he's certain of. The sodden trouser cuff plants a cold kiss on his ankle at every other step. Is he simply convincing himself the books are out of order by looking too hard, just as he couldn't put a sentence together when he tried to read? He's beginning to feel watched, though he can't see the watcher. Is he in danger of betraying his secret to the monitor in Woody's office? He can overcome his difficulty again if he has to—he's older and wiser now. He makes himself turn his back on his section. His shift ended fifteen minutes ago, and the books that fill his flat in Salford are waiting to welcome him home. Once he's there he can relax, and then he'll be able to read. He'll be able to read.

# JAKE

**Sean brings the Passat to a gentle halt across three parking spaces** outside Texts and lays his warm firm slightly pudgy hand on Jake's knee. Not much louder than the chugging of the engine he murmurs "Be good till tonight."

"What about then, Sean?"

He gives Jake the smile that's all the more of one for challenging him to prove it's there. "Be as bad as you like."

Jake thinks moments like these are why they're still together. He's happy to linger in it while the exhaust fumes play with the fog that dances around the car, but Sean lifts his hand to the steering wheel. "I'll collect you at seven, then. Better be moving before your man in uniform comes and shouts."

The new guard stands like a bouncer in the entrance, emitting smoky dragon breaths. Jake hopes Sean is feeling guilty only about his parking. He plants a hand on Sean's cheek, which is rough with obstinate stubble, and eases Sean's face into position for a kiss that tastes of sweetish pipe tobacco. Beyond him Jake sees the guard stick out his upper lip as if he's trying to catch a moustache to add to his disapproval. He's one reason why Jake pulls his partner closer, but Sean parts them before Jake has had enough. "Will you do something for me if you have the chance?"

"Anything," Jake says, wishing the guard could hear.

"Just see if you've any books I can use next term and buy them if you have."

"I wouldn't be sure which."

"Now, Jake, I thought you were listening at dinner." He's become the playfully severe lecturer Jake fell in love with halfway through Sean's evening class on gay Hollywood, and Jake feels half his age, though they're both thirty. "I told you I'll be teaching fifties melodrama," says Sean.

"Honestly, I'd rather you looked yourself. You aren't lecturing for an hour."

"I do want to see where you work," Sean admits, and swerves the car backwards.

Jake loves his abrupt impulses, but this manoeuvre could be dangerous in the fog that seems heavier in Fenny Meadows with each shrinking day of winter. It lurches to follow them as Sean parks precisely in a space with a single deft twirl of the wheel. He slips out of the car as Jake does, and is striding towards Texts when he grabs his hip-bones as if to mime how suddenly he has stopped. "What am I looking at?"

Three faces with as little colour to them as the fog are staring out of the display window—three of the same round smug hairless face lined up as if awaiting wigs. They're too large for their bodies by half. One body cut out of a magazine wears a man's suit, the middle one exhibits hairy knees beneath a kilt, while the right-hand body sports a dress. Each is perched on a heap of copies of *Dressing Up, Dressing Down*, by Brodie Oates. Beside them a sign says **WHAT DOES HE MEAN? FIND OUT ON FRIDAY**. "Shall we?" says Sean.

He's only proposing they should enter the shop. As they reach the doorway the guard moves into their path. "I hope you're going to behave yourselves in here," he says so low he mightn't want them to be able to prove he spoke.

Jake has faced down bouncers more butch than him. "We couldn't behave anyone else, could we?" he says sweetly and takes Sean's hand.

Sean doesn't try to keep it to himself, but he doesn't quite hold Jake's either. Sometimes he's shy outside the gay patch of Manchester. Jake can feel him growing hot, perhaps with embarrassment or fury at the guard for saying "That's what I mean. We don't need that in here."

"Who's we?" Jake asks more sweetly still.

Sean grips his hand and tells the guard "He's one of you."

The guard's face turns so red it reminds Jake of a traffic light. "He's bloody not. I'm not having that."

"You can't," Sean says, deciding to enjoy himself. "I am."

Jake is wondering how long they're going to test how red the guard's face can become when Lorraine trots past in baggy corduroys. Her ponytail wags and then lifts as she swings around on the READ ON! mat. "He works here," she says.

The guard grimaces as the tip of her hair brushes his flaming cheek. "Who?"

"I wouldn't mind either, but it's this one. Are you coming upstairs, Jake?"

"I ought to." Jake leads Sean past the mat before relinquishing his hand. "Will you be here when I come down?" he hopes aloud.

A jewel of fog trembles on Sean's eyelashes until Sean flicks it away with a fingertip. "I'll make sure I am."

Angus is behind the counter and not quite watching them, but muffled embarrassment seems to be his natural state. Mad's could be tidying the children's section, and as she heads back to it from finding a car-repair manual for a customer, she flashes Jake and Sean a smile. Otherwise the only people to be seen are two men in the armchairs by Erotica, their heads so nearly bald they might almost be monks meditating on how little of the world they've time for. Lorraine slaps the plaque by the door up to the staffroom with her badge and then takes enough time on the stairs for Jake to feel dragged down by the chill the bare walls have trapped. There are voices beyond the door at the top, and Ray is at the head of the staffroom table. "Morning, both," he says as Lorraine opens the door. "Now my team's complete."

That comes with a grin as untidy as his reddish neck-length variously curly hair, but Lorraine won't be charmed. "We aren't on for two minutes."

"No harm in getting started as soon as we can, is there?" When she removes her card from the Out rack but only holds it, Ray sucks his mouth small and wry while he twitches his eyebrows up and down before the vaguely amiable expression returns to his jowly pinkish face. "I hope we all saw the match at the weekend," he says.

"Which was that?" says Wilf.

"Only one it could be, isn't there?" Ray practically shouts, perhaps not realising that Wilf is more polite than interested. "Manchester United giving Liverpool the boot two-nil."

Wilf, Jill and Agnes deliver a muted dutiful cheer, and Ross counters with a boo faint enough to be comical. "Now, now, let's be sporting," Nigel calls from his desk in the office while Greg contents himself with a reproving blink at Gavin's latest yawn. "Aren't you two taking sides?" Ray asks the newcomers.

"Not between men," says Lorraine and slides her card under the clock. "I don't see much difference, I'm afraid."

Jake waits until he's clocking on to say "Why would I want to watch a lot of boys with bare thighs chasing one another?"

Nearly everyone laughs, though he isn't sure how many feel forced into it. Lorraine takes the seat Ross kept for her, and Greg slides his behind slightly away from Jake, who sits between him and Wilf as Ray passes out the Woody's Wheedles sheets. "Looks as if the boss has been putting the old brain to work," Ray comments.

"That's what it's for," Woody says as he strides out of his office. "Okay, let me do the talking. Faster that way."

"Want my seat?"

"I'll stand. Want to hear the bad news first?"

"You're in charge," says Ray.

"There is no good news. First month's sales, the worst for any branch of Texts."

"That'll be because people are still finding out we're here, do you think?"

"Swung on and missed, Ray. Worst sales for anybody's opening month."

"Christmas has to help, won't it?"

"Pre-Christmas sales growth, worst for any store. Figures for last weekend, guess what? The worst." His narrowed eyes might be searching for culprits until he says "Okay, that's what we have to fix. Who has ideas?"

Ray has had enough of playing straight man, and nobody else wants the job. Woody tilts his gaze up as if searching for ideas beneath the flattened black turf of his hair and rubs his face almost expressionless. "Anyone. Anything," he says. "Make me feel we're a team."

To Jake it feels more like being back at school—like being asked a question nobody wants to be the first to answer, especially since Ray seems to think he's entitled to wait on Woody's behalf. At last Lorraine says "Could it be where we are?"

"You need to give me more than that."

"Fenny Meadows. Would anybody want to come here if they didn't work here?"

Several mouths are opening when Woody says "You'll tell me why not."

"Maybe they don't see it till it's too late."

"You're making me do a whole lot of work. Too late for what?"

"I mean, maybe they don't see the signs. When I drove here just now I nearly missed the junction for the fog."

"That'll be what kept you, then," says Ray.

Ross comes to her aid. "It's only if you work round here you know you're close when you hit the fog."

"It wouldn't make much sense for anyone to build here if it was like this all the time, would it?" Woody protests. "I spoke to head office, and there wasn't any fog when they were checking out the site last winter. Yes, come in, don't just listen."

He's staring at the stockroom door behind Jake, who feels a chill like a breath on the back of his neck and turns to find the door is open just enough for someone to peer through. Greg is rising dutifully from his chair when Woody hurries to lean into the stockroom. "Must have been a draught," he mutters, rubbing his upper arms once he has slammed the door. He looks as if he hopes that has wakened everyone as he says "Okay, does anybody think Lorraine identified a problem?"

"Not enough people realise we're here."

"You got it, Ray. So have you all been telling everyone you know?"

The murmur of response is mostly the sound of people trying not to single themselves out. "Come on, team," Woody urges. "You're making me think you don't want to win. Who's going to get us pepped up?"

He's performing such a parody of an American that Jake for one doesn't know where to look. Eventually Jill says "The parents I meet and my little girl's teachers know where I work."

"That's a start. And your friends?"

"They are my friends."

"Sure, and we are too, aren't we? I want us all to be friends here. How about we don't just tell our friends about the store, we tell everyone we even slightly know."

"How about everyone we meet?" Greg proposes.

Gavin lets out a sound like a series of esses. "How do you want us to do that, Greg? Hi, you don't know who I am and you're going to think I'm mad or tripping, but I work at Texts and I'm why you should come and see?"

"We needn't talk. We could wear something."

"You want me to go clubbing with this around my neck," Gavin says, rattling his Texts badge on its chain.

"Any other possibilities?" Woody says to silence it.

"We could carry our things in a Texts bag," Jake suggests and feels exonerated until his name appears overhead. "Jake," Mad's voice calls. "Just letting you know your friend Sean says he has to leave."

"Shall I answer that?" Jake asks Woody.

"Do you have a reason to?"

It's Gavin who saves Jake from any further reproof. "I could leave our flyers in the clubs I go to."

"Why don't you each think of someplace else to leave some," Woody says and calls into the office "Connie, can they get a fistful of events sheets each?"

"They can, but . . ." She takes a leaflet out of the carton she has just slashed open. "You aren't going to like this," she says.

"Hey, I'd rather have misery than mystery."

"A nasty little apostrophe's wormed its way in."

As well as announcing that Brodie Oates will be signing his books, the sheet encourages the public to watch the press or ring up to learn of further events, but the first word anyone is likely to notice is at the top and half as large again as any of the others: **TEXT'S**. Woody stares at it until Connie brings it close enough for him to grasp with a fist. "Call the printers and tell them they need to fix this right now," he says, "and let them know we won't pay for it."

"I don't think we can really do that." Her lips pinch inwards as if they would like to hide their pinkness, but then she has to say "I'm certain I checked the copy before I emailed it, only the computer must have thought it wanted correcting and never asked me. I've just looked and the mistake's on there as well."

"Okay, here's what you do. Correct it and print out say a thousand we can distribute while we're waiting for the real thing. They won't look as professional, but at least we can get them out there."

Connie is retreating into the office when he says "Wait, let's see if we can make this work for us. Before Connie starts, who's got ideas for events for us to run? That's besides Lorraine's reading group."

Jake isn't shrugging off the question; he's moving his shoulders to rid them of a chill—a draught, of course, not the breath of someone who's hiding behind him to enjoy Woody's troubles. Nevertheless Woody stares at him until Ray says "Do we know any writers with local connections?"

Gavin hasn't quite finished a yawn when he says "Isn't there what's his name?"

"I should think there'd have to be," Ray tells Woody like a teacher apologising for a pupil to a headmaster.

"The one who wrote about here," Gavin insists. "Somebody Bottomley."

"Okay, Agnes, Anyes, that's your section. Find out what there is to know and tell Connie," Woody says. "All right, we need to move this along. I'm keeping you guys off the floor. Think promotions and events and give them to Connie by let's say three o'clock, but there's another way I hope you can all help. The chief and her squad will be here from New York to see how we're shaping up in less than two weeks. We're going to show them every book in order on the shelves and as tidy as the day before we opened, and not a single item in the stockroom."

"Can we manage that?" Jill says.

"Good to hear from you again, Jill, and the simple answer is I'm asking everyone to work all night the night before the big day."

"Count me in," Greg says at once.

"I'll have to see who could look after Bryony," says Jill.

"Are we getting double time?" Lorraine asks.

"Time and a half," Woody says. "That's everyone, me included. You know I'll be here."

When nobody responds at once, he clears his throat so sharply Jake imagines it must hurt. "No absolute urgency," Woody says. "I'll put up a sign-up sheet so people can commit once they've cleared their schedules. Ray?"

"I'll be on it, don't worry."

"No, I mean will you assign jobs? Just remember," Woody adds as his gaze snags on each of them, "anything you do to help the store is helping you as well. It's the public that keep us employed."

As he heads for his office at last, Connie takes his place. "Provocative window, Jill," she says. "I think that's the word."

"So long as it gets people's attention, would you say?"

"And brings them in. I haven't seen too many tickets going yet. When I've done my leaflets you could all make sure you give one to every customer, and it wouldn't hurt to start telling them now who they'll be able to meet."

Jake sees Greg struggling on behalf of the shop to overcome his aversion to the idea. A laugh that tastes like a sneeze catches in Jake's nostrils as Ray dispatches him to shelve books. He's the first into the stockroom, where a hollow clapping of cassette boxes on the Returns shelf greets him—his entrance must have disturbed them. The skeletal shadows of the few empty racks twitch almost imperceptibly beneath the fluorescent lights, one of which is unsettled, buzzing like a torpid insect. His shelves are heaped with romances; books all the colours of candied sweets are close to toppling off the edge. He fetches a trolley from outside the lift, which for an instant he fancies he hears uttering a single word, and trundles it to his racks. He grabs the first heap of romances to turn it horizontal on the trolley, and the pile behind it spills backwards, sprawling in all directions wherever there's room. "Don't be damaged," he pleads, and manages not to knock down any more as he reaches for the books. He inches his fingers behind the bulk of them, and his fingertips encounter an object squashed behind them.

It's as cold as the wall it slithers down. It seems to writhe away from his touch as he recoils so hastily that a stack of romances topples onto his chest. It must have been a book, however much larger it felt, as well as too clammy and obese and not even flat enough to begin with. He's already unsure how much he imagined or what sound he emitted that brings Ross into the stockroom. "That was truly camp, Jake," he says. "Were you calling for help?"

"What does it look like?"

"Here's some." As he grabs the topmost books from the pile against Jake's chest he bumps Jake's nipple with his thumb, perhaps to demonstrate he isn't threatened. "How did you end up like that?" he amuses himself by asking.

"Something fell down at the back I couldn't seem to reach."

"Shall I try?"

"That'd be more than sweet of you."

Ross leans across the shelves and gropes blindly about until Jake begins to grow afraid for him. He's breathing fast and shallowly, which appears to disconcert Ross, when Woody hurries in to demand "Who was making that noise?"

"Nobody," Ross objects and renders his voice manlier by half an octave. "We were just talking."

"We had a bit of a panic," says Jake. "Over now."

Ross drops an armful of books on the trolley. "I expect you shouldn't try to handle too much all at once, Jake."

"I'm not sure what I'm seeing here," Woody says. "Ross, you need to deal with your own section before you start lending a hand."

He watches Ross find a trolley and take it and his increasingly red face to the video racks. He doesn't return to the office until both Ross and Jake are busy with their stock. Jake's hands start to feel grimy with apprehension as he reaches further into the gloom in the depths of his shelves. He snatches the last books away from the wall to reveal nothing but concrete, bare except for a faint muddy shapeless stain. Whichever book unnerved him by slipping away from him, he must have retrieved it without knowing.

All four shelves of the trolley are brimming with romances, and more are piled on top. Jake has seen funerals move faster than he dares to wheel them to the lift. He inches the trolley between the doors as soon as they're wide enough. As he steps in and thumbs the grubby button, Ross tries to catch him up. "Lift opening," the mechanical voice promises, only for the doors to close. The cage lumbers downwards and shudders to a halt before it repeats itself in, Jake thinks, not nearly so female a voice. Is the source already wearing out, or the lift itself?

He has pushed less than a foot of trolley clear of the doors when they clamp themselves on it. Bruising his thumb on the button fails to shift them, and when he wrenches at them he feels as though his fingers are sinking into mud, an impression the greyish dimness aggravates. Of course the doors are edged with rubber, and after not much of a struggle they sidle apart. He runs the trolley out so fast that two books with hospital staff on the covers are left behind. As he picks them up he's fearful that the doors will seize the opportunity to shut him in, though why should that make him so apprehensive? He lurches upright and darts out to lay the books on top of the trolley, then pulls open the door to the sales area and trundles his burden out just soon enough to prevent the alarm from squealing about him.

He's hardly begun to sort the contents of the trolley when Ross emerges from the lobby with another full of computer manuals. "Sorry it shut. I didn't mean to keep you out," Jake calls, which brings him a forgiving grin from Ross. It looks uneasy too, perhaps because the new guard is staring at them both with some distrust. As Jake wonders if he should save Ross from any further misunderstanding, Greg marches up to the guard and thrusts out a hand. "I didn't get the chance to introduce myself before. I'm Greg."

"Frank," the guard discloses and shakes the hand while he does.

"You'll have met the boss," Greg says in the tone of a second in command. "Do you know the others here? That's Ross. Angus. Madeleine, she's usually in the children's section. That's Lorraine just joining the rest of us." With a pause to quarantine the information, he adds "That's Jake."

"We've met."

Frank's lack of enthusiasm provokes Jake to shout "We hit it off right away, didn't we? I'm only sorry I didn't get to hold your hand like Greg."

They stare at him with a dislike so identical he thinks it's as dull as the fog. For a moment he even imagines that the advancing murk beyond the doorway behind them has been attracted by the prospect of a quarrel, or something in the fog has; certainly he feels spied upon. Perhaps it's Woody at his office monitor or just the thought of him. It's enough to single Jake out until he turns back to his shelving and forces himself to ignore it, along with Greg and Frank and anyone else who disapproves of him. At seven there'll be Sean, but for now there are the colours of the bunched spines, colours he can almost taste as he wields the alphabet: cherry, orange, lime, lemon . . . It doesn't seem to matter that he's reducing the books to little more than blocks of pastel and himself to the kind of stereotype too many of his colleagues may assume he is, more a decorator than a bookseller. All he knows is that the colours are helping to fend off the greyness that has closed around the shop and, if he let it, around his mind as well.

# ROSS

**When Mad returns from being called away by Woody her face looks** as though it's hiding a mask that's capable of rendering her thoughtful bemusement blank. Ross recalls those layers of expression from when she was deciding to end the relationship. He's no nearer knowing if they mean he's expected to ask a question, but as soon as her gaze happens to encounter his, it draws him over to Teenage Texts. "What did he want?" he murmurs.

"Seems I shouldn't have announced Jake's boyfriend had to go."

Lorraine takes issue with this, though Ross isn't sure if it's Mad's comment that has attracted her from Information or the sight of him with Mad. "Why shouldn't you?" Lorraine demands.

"I was supposed to call Jake to the phone because the message wasn't for the public. I just thought I was saving time."

"If you ask me management won't let you win. I'll bet Woody would have been in a sulk if you'd called anyone away while he was trying to persuade us to lose our sleep."

Lorraine and Mad are regarding each other as though they're competing at sweetness, yet Ross feels they're most aware of him; he feels like a device they're using to communicate. "I don't mind working all night," he says. "Could be an experience."

"Why do men feel they have to prove they can do things there's no need for?"

"I don't think that really fits, does it?" says Mad. "I'm on the sheet with Ross."

"Oh, are you?" says Lorraine as though she couldn't be less interested. "Anyway, if you want anything from me I'm not far."

"I think I've forgotten why I would, Lorraine," Mad says.

"We call it sticking together, those of us that do. We need to when the shop doesn't hold with unions. If we let ourselves put up with even little things they'll just get worse."

"That one wasn't little, it was microscopic. I'd have forgotten it by now if you hadn't joined in. Sticking together has to be good, though. When you're in my section it would be great if you could give it a bit of a tidy if you see anything out of place."

"There's a few of those around the shop," Lorraine says more meaningfully than the words can really bear, and more than Mad bothers to acknowledge. She leaves Lorraine a smile so faint it contradicts itself as she returns to pulling out books that are leaning their spines against the Teenage wall in imitation of their readers. As Lorraine stalks back to Information, whatever she's hoarding up to say seems to trail over Ross like a shadow. No wonder he feels safest shelving his computer books.

Quite a number of the manuals are at least twice the size of most of the rest of the stock, but though that means he has fewer items in a trolleyful, it also needs him to make more space for each. He has to move the contents of three shelves to fit just one guide to Linux in, and once he finishes lugging the books about he has to shift the subject markers. Without the dozens of plastic tags that name systems and languages and applications and every aspect of the Internet, he would have no idea where anything belongs. He's attempting to memorise at least some of the order when the phones begin to ring.

The ten-second rule says that every call should be answered by then. Lorraine is bagging books for a man in a puffy anorak, and so Ross hurries to the phone at Information. "Texts at Fenny Meadows, Ross speaking, how may I help?"

"Chief there?"

Ross seems to have heard the woman's voice before. "May I ask who's calling?"

"He'll know. He'll be seeing me."

He isn't sure if he should take her brevity for rudeness—her voice is oddly stiff. "Still light, is it?" it apparently costs her an effort to ask. "Dark here."

Perhaps she's tired. "I'll just put you on hold," he says, and does so before thumbing the Page button. "Woody call ten, please. Woody call ten."

He has barely replaced the receiver when it shrills. "What can I do for you, Ross?"

"There's a caller on line one for you."

"With a name, maybe?"

"She wouldn't say."

"Always get a name and give yours."

"I told her mine. She said you'd know her. I think she's calling from abroad."

"I believe you could be right. Thanks, Ross."

Ross tramps back to his shelves to find space for another blocky volume. As he rearranges books he hears a muffled fitful panting huge enough to be audible through the delivery lobby. Soon a giant or somebody with ambitions to be as loud as one starts pounding on the outer door. Ross is moving to respond until he hears the door clank open. He has made room for one more manual when Woody appears from the lobby, outside which Ray is loading cartons onto a pallet truck from a lorry that's adding exhaust fumes to the fog. Ross has the impression that the fumes are hardly moving, instead thickening the murk. The inner door shuts as Woody strides over to him. "What did you do to my call?"

"Nothing. Put it through."

"Nothing sounds more like it. There wasn't anybody."

"I said I was putting her on hold. She'd understand that, wouldn't she?"

"She'd have to be kind of stupid not to," Woody says and stares at him as though Ross implied it was the case.

"I meant if she was American." Ross sees Lorraine straining to listen and turns away for fear she'll intervene before he says "Maybe she lost the connection."

"I guess then she'll call back. What did she say to you exactly?"

Ross is going nowhere near Woody's last word. "She'll be seeing you, I think she meant soon."

"Really. That is news." Woody glances from his watch to the phone, and Ross deduces that he's reminding himself that no personal calls should be made from the shop. "Anyway, back to work," Woody says. "I need a hand unloading the new stock. I'll try and find you an extra hour to finish shelving."

Clearing the trolley will take more than an hour, but Woody is already on his way. "Bring that with you," he says over his shoulder and admits them to the lobby as Ray shuts the outer door with a clank. "We'll take over now, Ray," Woody says. "You're busy enough."

He jabs the button by the lift. "You can leave the cart here," he tells Ross as Ray heads upstairs and the lift speaks. "If anyone needs it they'll let you know."

Ross is trying to decide how recently he heard the voice beyond the doors. He's about to risk a question when Woody says "Can you grab that?"

He's leaning on the handle to release the brake and push the pallet truck into the lift that is only a few inches wider, but one of the uppermost of the cartons has started to topple. Ross squeezes between the entrance to the lift and the contents of the truck to clamp the topmost cartons of all four stacks between his arms. He presses his forehead against the insecure carton, which is as cold as the fog it smells of. "Better hold on till we get upstairs," Woody says.

Ross shuffles backwards into the lift as the truck advances until his spine thumps the rear wall. "Okay?" says Woody and pokes the Up button. The voice of the lift still sounds muffled as a laugh somebody is hiding behind a hand; it must be blocked by the cartons that are all Ross can see or feel or smell. When he opens his mouth he tastes cardboard and fog. "Was that . . ."

The lift jerks as it sets about hauling itself upwards. The truck lurches perhaps no more than an inch towards him, enough to pinion him against the wall. "Okay?" Woody says again.

"I should be." A carton has trapped the left side of his face against the icy metal wall, but at least that leaves most of his mouth free to shout "Who did we hear just then?"

"All I heard were you and the elevator. Who do you mean?"

"The lift," Ross yells, though his squashed nose is struggling to breathe. "Whose voice is it?"

"Haven't the foggiest. Came with the elevator."

The lift jerks again, and the carton grinds Ross's face against the metal. "Can you pull it away a bit?" he's barely able to shout.

"No room to let the brake off. Don't worry, nothing can move."

Cartons are crushing Ross's chest now. They're robbing him of the last of his breath and any chance to take another. "Please," he gasps, but it travels no farther than the darkness that's a carton leaning on his face. The announcement that the lift is opening sounds so muffled it might be underground, and he no longer cares how much the voice reminds him of Woody's caller on the phone—they couldn't have been so similar. In a few seconds the lift carries out its promise, and in a few more Woody manages to release the brake. Ross staggers forward, clinging to the stacks of cartons.

"Just drop it," Woody says as he halts the truck at the unloading bin, then peers at Ross. "Everything okay?"

"Will be."

Once Ross has filled his lungs so hard they ache he dumps the carton on top of the bin, which is the size of a table for four and crowned with thick wire mesh. Woody slices through the parcel tape with a knife and inverts the carton. When he lifts it, armfuls of books are left standing on the mesh while the packing falls into the bin with a tinkle of polystyrene. Before Ross has picked up a single book Woody deals at least a dozen onto the stockroom racks. By the time Ross begins placing a handful Woody has grabbed another pile and lets his gaze slump on his assistant's meagre burden. Ross tries to match his speed, heaping books against his bruised chest, which they chafe as he dodges from rack to rack, scarcely glimpsing the titles as he divests himself of them: *Insects Have Rights Too; The Royal Corgi Annual; Collectible Hotel Freebies; Jesus Was a Joker: Puns and Wisecracks of Christ; Chat Shows that Changed the World; To Boldly Split: English as It's Spoke . . .* Ross has helped sort three cartons' worth, though Woody is leaving him even further behind, when Connie wanders into the stockroom. "Help," she remarks. "More books."

"That's what Christmas means." Woody slashes a carton and tips it up. "Coming to help, did you say?"

"Still working on events. I'm afraid Adrian Bottomley won't be one. I asked him if he'd like to do a signing, and he seemed fine with it till I mentioned where we are."

"Don't stop," Woody tells Ross, who has halted to listen. "What's wrong with that?" he says just as sharply to Connie.

"I got the impression he didn't think enough people would turn up to make it worth his while."

"Screw him and anyone that doesn't want to be part of the team. Okay, see what else you can put on our leaflets." When she hesitates, Woody says "You can leave us alone. I guess we're both safe."

Connie grins in case she's meant to but looks puzzled as she exits. Woody is recalling how he fancies he caught Ross and Jake together, of course. Ross can't think how to deal with this; his mind seems entirely occupied by the process of sorting books. Indeed, it doesn't occur to him to check the time until Woody opens the last carton but one. "Getting tired?" Woody enquires as Ross consults his wristwatch.

"It's supposed to be my break."

"Want to finish this first? Shouldn't take more than a couple of minutes."

Ross imagines Lorraine's reaction if she even suspected him of agreeing to that. He does so mutely nonetheless, and the task is finished not too long after Woody said it would be. "I guess that won't have hurt your appetite," Woody tells him.

Does he eat in his office? Ross has never seen him do so in the staffroom or even help himself from the percolator, which presents Ross with a gush of coffee so strong that an inch of milk still leaves it resembling mud. As Woody returns to his office Ross fetches from his locker the ham sandwiches he made last night while his father loitered in the kitchen as if he was close to finding a way to help. He drops them on the table and opens the crinkled foil they're wrapped in before flattening a cybergaming magazine beside them. If Mad saw him now she might emit a single tut and bring a plate to slip under the sandwiches; Lorraine would shake her head and her ponytail at the sight of the kind of magazine she says only men read. He finds himself willing them both to stay downstairs. He should have realised asking Lorraine out would lead to problems.

Enjoy your episodes, his father says. They're what life's made of. Don't expect to spend it all with one person; that's not natural. He sees this is his father's method of dealing with the way his wife left him with three-year-old Ross and never came back from a holiday with girlfriends that was meant to be just a break—it justifies how his father has never lived with anyone except him for longer than a few months since—but it feels right to Ross too. It was why he took his chance with Lorraine when she surprised him with friendliness, but should he have been no more than friendly? Is he bound to antagonise either her or Mad? Struggling to think about them reduces him to gazing at pictures of computerised fights while he sticks food in his mouth. When he hears Woody utter a sound too savage to have time for words, for a moment it seems to be expressing his own frustration. "What is it?" Connie cries.

"Little—" Whatever else Woody might have said he leaves behind as he flings the door to the stairs wide and bounds down them, missing every other one. Connie's startled gaze catches Ross's as she swivels her desk chair and peers into Woody's office. "We've been invaded," she says as though she doesn't understand what she's seeing.

She's watching the security monitor. Ross joins her in time to observe Woody rushing through the top left-hand quadrant while Frank the guard tramps across the sector diagonally opposite. The rest of the screen shows a pair of deserted aisles until two figures dart into the lower left-hand section, throwing books off shelves as they run. There must be a fault with the monitor, because the figures are trailing grey strands of themselves—but a fault can't explain why their faces look as though they've left all their skin and flesh somewhere else.

If they're made up or wearing masks, how reassuring is that? Ross feels as though he's less watching than dreaming the sight of two prancing dwarfish shapes with faces so basic they resemble primitive images. He has to see what they really look like. He runs downstairs almost as fast as Woody did and hauls the door open, to be met by two skulls topped with hair.

He sees the boys are wearing masks left over from Halloween before the wearers dodge out of reach, masks so cheap they couldn't be more rudimentary. As he starts after them the boys sprint past the counter and out of the shop. "Leave them to it, Frank," says Woody as they merge with the fog. "Just so they don't get back in."

"I think we may already have had to chase them once," Agnes says from the counter.

"Nobody told me. When?"

"The day we had the quiz. I think they're the ones that were being a nuisance."

"Explains the masks. If any more of those show up we'd better see their faces."

Woody stalks into Homecrafts, where his angry head ducks and reappears like a bird's as he picks up cookery books. When Ross starts to retrieve medical volumes from the adjoining aisle, this only seems to aggravate Woody's rage. "Go finish your break," he mutters. "We don't need anybody saying you were cheated out of it."

No doubt he means Lorraine. Ross thinks she has approached to keep an eye on how he's being treated until she says "I haven't had my coffee break yet. Can I take it now?"

"Sure, why not. Leave me to fix these."

Ross shelves the books he picked up and is heading for the staffroom when Lorraine takes hold of his arm. "Let's talk outside."

She lets go once he follows, and hugs herself as they step out of the entrance. The fog beyond the three scrawny trees has soaked up all the heat and light of the sun, transforming it into a sourceless greyish diffused presence. The murk retreats a pace as though acknowledging or mocking Lorraine and Ross, then drifts back, leeching colour from a few parked cars. Ross wonders if the boys could be hiding nearby in it as Lorraine trots along the shopfront and waits for him to catch up. "Did he make you come down with him?" she demands.

"Of course he didn't, Lorraine."

"Then why do you have to jump to his defence?"

"I didn't think I was. I didn't know he needed it."

"Men don't, you mean."

Though Ross keeps his sigh quiet, he sees it swell in front of his face like a thought balloon in a comic. "I don't, no. I mean, I don't mean that. Why do you . . ."

"Go on, tell me it's my fault somehow."

"I'm not saying it's anyone's fault. It just seems sometimes you don't like working here at all."

"I expect I'll like running my reading group. I like talking to people about books. That's why I thought I'd like a job that was all about them, but it isn't, is it? Do you know what I'd love to do?"

"Is it something for Connie?"

"For God's sake, Ross, there's more to my life than this place." Lorraine glares at the fog as if it has dared to contradict her and says "I'd like to teach riding."

"Can you?"

"I've taught my little cousin Georgie on her pony. You should see her bouncing up and down on it all proud of herself. There was a job at the riding school, but I didn't know then I was that good at it, so I applied here instead."

"There'll be other riding jobs round where you live, will there?"

"Not often. I don't think the girl the school took on has settled in too well, though."

"Maybe you'll be able to take over, and you've got to like more than your reading group while you're here, have you?" When her eyebrows rise a slow quarter of an inch, perhaps to let the possibility in, Ross says "At least that's something to thank Woody for."

"I put myself forward. He didn't choose me," Lorraine objects and twists around as if to confront Woody through the window. As he straightens up, tenderly smoothing the corners of a paperback, his gaze snags on Ross's and his lips move. "What does he mean, you're busy?" Lorraine requires to be told.

"Maybe you should ask him."

"Fair enough, I will."

The fog seems to greet her intention with a dance, trailing its hem over the tarmac. "Hang on," Ross blurts. "He'll be thinking of me and Jake."

"Well, that is unexpected. Why would he do that?"

"I think he thought I was giving Jake the wrong kind of hand in the stockroom. I hope you don't need me to tell you I wasn't."

"No reason to get defensive if you were, Ross. That's half the problem with the world, men not accepting their feminine side."

"The other half is women not owning up to their male part, you mean."

He knows she doesn't before he has finished speaking. His attempt at wit seems nothing more than automatic now that it's exposed; he feels as though he's being forced to perform a script for an unseen audience—the boys in the masks, perhaps? When Lorraine turns towards the fog he thinks she has the same impression, but she says "I'm going for a walk."

"Shall I come with you?"

"I wish I were riding." She mustn't intend him to hear any wistfulness; none is left in her voice as she says "There's really no need."

"I just thought you mightn't want to be alone in this."

"I won't be going far." Apparently deciding that's too much of a concession, she adds "Unless I want to."

She marches along the side of Texts to the staff car park and disappears into the fog without a backward glance. Her rapid footsteps grow muffled as if she's walking into mud. Ross can hear no other sound except the unresolved thunder of the motorway, but suppose the boys are lurking in the fog, waiting for Lorraine to see their skulls bob up from it? When her footsteps shrink to the size of pins being tapped into a board and then dwindle into silence, Ross wanders back past the bleary display window, rubbing his arms hard. He has just trodden on the READ ON! mat when the alarm begins to shrill like a bird gone blind and insane.

Woody is the first to reach him, trying while he sprints to rub creases out of the pages of a book on puddings. "Who went out?" he's eager Ross should tell him.

"I think it was me coming in. I don't know why. I didn't touch anything."

Woody types the code only the managers know on the keypad to gag the alarm. As he resets it Ross produces the comb that's all his shirt pocket contains, then empties his trouser pockets of a handkerchief and some change, not to mention a stone that reminds him of an eye asleep, which Mad picked up last week in the car park. Frank the guard watches Ross's pockets hang their tongues out and continues to look suspicious even when Woody says "Okay, Ross, we trust you. Put your stuff away and walk back through."

Ross is pocketing the stone that feels coated with fog as he ventures between the security pillars. He snatches out his hand as the alarm pipes up. A woman in a fawn coat and matching scarf and hat, who is wheeling a toddler lagged in a hooded one-piece suit of the same colour, pulls the push-chair back from entering the shop. "Please, ma'am, step right in," Woody urges and informs the toddler "I guess a goblin got into the works."

The child starts wailing either at the noise or at Woody's explanation. It sounds as if the alarm has taken on an extra note, a siren that persists once Woody finishes retyping the combination. "It's gone now," the mother mumbles through her scarf, but the puffed-up bundle of a boy or girl arches its back in an attempt to escape its bonds as she wheels it between the security posts. "Sorry," she says more indistinctly still.

"That's perfectly all right, ma'am," Woody says. "Any time you're ready, Ross."

Somewhere in the fog a woman is coughing as she runs, and someone is driving a car. There's no reason why these sounds should make Ross nervous, though the antics of the alarm do. The moment he advances between the posts it begins to screech. The toddler enters the competition, and Mad ambles over to give the child a grin of amused reassurance. "What's your secret, Ross?"

"Nothing that I know of. I don't see how I can be doing it."

"Then show me who is." Woody frowns at the keypad as the mother unwraps her mouth to tell the toddler "It's only a silly machine, look. The gentleman who sounds like the funny men in your cartoons can switch it on and off."

"Let's hope so, ma'am." Woody has to raise his voice to be heard over the toddler's solo. Yet louder and a good deal more sharply he says "Hold it, Ross. I want a few seconds before I reset it."

The step Ross was about to take hovers above the mat. What's happening in the car park? The coughs sound almost starved of breath, and he feels anxious for whoever is running about in the fog. Perhaps she's breathing the fumes of the car as well. He steps towards Woody instead of through the posts. "Can't I just—"

"In a minute." Woody doesn't glance away from peering over the hand he's using to ensure nobody can read the combination. "Try it now," he says. "On second thoughts you try, Madeleine. See if it likes girls better."

"Watch," Mad says to the toddler. "It isn't going to hurt me. There's nothing round here to hurt anyone." She takes the longest stride she can between the posts, and the alarm commences yammering at once.

As she turns to offer the toddler a laugh, the running footsteps and the breathless coughs that sound entangled in them veer towards the shop, and so does the snarl of the car. Lorraine staggers out of the fog beyond the nearest trees so fast she almost falls. Her arms are outstretched as if she's trying to dive clear of the murk. Perhaps she's wishing the shop closer than the two hundred yards or so she has to cross. Her eyes and mouth are wrenched wide, and her face is almost as grey as its background. Whatever she might want to cry out collapses into another spasm of coughs. Ross is struggling to understand why she looks backlit when the fog behind her shines more fiercely and emits a rising snarl. "That's never—" Mad says as if she hardly knows she's speaking. "That's my car."

Before Ross can shout a useless warning the car rushes at Lorraine. The windscreen is coated with fog through which he glimpses a blurred figure that looks too small to be in charge of a vehicle. He has distinguished nothing more except a swollen shapeless grey mass that must be a head when the left-hand headlamp slams into the backs of Lorraine's knees.

Something breaks—the lens or Lorraine or both. The impact flings her over the windscreen, clearing a swathe of the glass. Ross still can't make out the shape hunched over the steering wheel; the inside of the car looks clogged with fog. Lorraine sprawls on the metal roof and then, as the car swerves back the way it came, slithers off. The first part of her to hit the tarmac with a slap that sounds flattened and somehow empty is her head.

Ross feels as if everything has been stretched thin and brittle and unreal as a film: the toddler shouting "Fell down" and beginning to giggle, the mother so desperate to put a stop to this she snatches off her scarf and winds it round the child's mouth before supporting herself on the push-chair and hustling it away into the shop, Woody cursing under his breath as the numbers he types fail to hush the alarm, Mad running to kneel by Lorraine only to recoil from an expanding stain darker than the condensation on the tarmac. Then the car slews into view, its driver's door flapping wide, and Ross is terrified for both women until it rams the left-hand tree and stands nuzzling the broken stump.

As the alarm falls silent he seems to hear a huge sluggish wallowing movement so muffled it sounds buried, and then there's only the discord of Mad's abandoned car. He's no longer paralysed by the clamour of the alarm. He dashes out of the shop, and the chill of the day gathers in his stomach before shivering through him from head to foot. He has no idea how his voice will sound if he calls to Mad not to move Lorraine—not when her head is at such an awkward angle he doesn't see how she can bear it. Lorraine's body jerks with a cough, and greyness rises from her lips before they settle into a slack grimace. He wants to think she's trying to expel the fog she had to breathe in as she ran. Then her eyes appear to fill with it, and the low dismayed cry that escapes Mad turns into it as well.

# RAY

**When the Punto coasts towards the back of Texts a pale mass as** wide as a coffin is long seems to swell out of the concrete wall. As the car noses closer and the headlamp beams squeeze the fog brighter, the mass shrinks and splits in two like an amoeba. The halves glare at Ray like great flat blank eyes until he switches off the lights. A glow the red of diluted blood vanishes behind the car as though the fog has swallowed it in the process of catching up with him. The key rasps out of the ignition, and the cooling engine starts to tick like a clock that's growing slower by the moment. He retrieves from the passenger seat the lunch Sandra insists is the least he needs to eat, and the Mothercare bag it's wrapped in crackles as he steps onto the slippery tarmac.

Four cars are already huddled under the last two letters of the shop's name. As he sets the car alarm he stays well clear of the adjacent vehicle in case he might wake it up. He's pinching his overcoat shut—no point in buttoning it for the sake of a few hundred yards—when he has to snatch his hand away. Of course the shrill chirping is only his phone; he knows that before it finishes the first phrase of the Manchester United anthem, and why should he feel it is drawing attention to him? He perches his lunch on the car roof and drags the phone out of his pocket, together with a wad of paper tissue he used the other day to wipe little Sheryl's mouth. Dried chocolate has turned the wad hard as a pebble, which skitters across the tarmac as he interrupts the tune. "Is that you?" Sandra says.

"Who else are you expecting?"

"I thought for a moment I heard someone else. What's making you sound like that?"

In the year and a half since Sheryl was born he has grown used to being told he's doing things he's not aware of. "Like what?"

"As if you're in a basement. Deep down somewhere, anyway."

"No basement here," he says as a shiver sets him buttoning up after all. "You know you're welcome any time you want to come and see."

"When the baby's finished teething. You don't want her making a fuss when people are trying to read."

Ray wishes she would stop acting embarrassed whenever anyone hears Sheryl cry, as if she thinks it means she has failed somehow. "You still haven't said where you are," she reminds him.

"Out at the back of the shop."

"Where that poor girl was?"

The murk lurches at him as Sandra's voice does, and he wonders if he could be standing where Lorraine began to be chased by whoever stole Mad's car. The notion makes him feel as though fog has gathered in his stomach. "It's all right," he tells himself as well as Sandra. "I'm just going in."

"Have you time to drive over to Frugo for me?"

"Not much at the moment. What do you need?"

"More support tights. I've put my big fat toe through the ones I bought at the weekend. Don't bother if it doesn't matter how I look. I don't want my legs to end up like my mother's after she had me, that's all."

"You know it matters to me, and you've never looked better."

"I'd love to have seen your face when you said that, Ray."

What's wrong with having a bit more of the woman he fell in love with? He has lost count of how often he has kept that comment to himself lest she think it's a substitute for a compliment. All that matters to him is that she's still Sandra under no more padding than he has put on himself and under layers of moods that are surely just a phase of having Sheryl. "You'll see it next time," he says. "I'll go over in my lunch break. Nearly time for work."

"I don't like to think of you rushing your lunch."

"You haven't given me an hour's worth, nothing like." As he realises she could take that for a complaint, however inappropriate, he hears Sheryl start to wail. "Listen, I really have to go, and it sounds like you do as well," he says. "Give her a kiss from me and yourself one."

How is she going to do the latter? His turn of phrase leaves him feeling stupid. He slips the phone into his pocket and takes hold of his lunch bag, which is colder and wetter than he would have imagined he gave it time to be. As he hurries around the bookshop, a restless insect rustling accompanies him down the alley—the blank walls have trapped the fidgets of his package, a sound that flutters across the car park into the mass of fog. Woody is waiting in the entrance of the shop and just about raises a thumb to greet him. When Ray consults his watch he finds he's minutes later than he realised, though at least not late. "My wife called," he feels required to explain.

"Okay, well, fine." It clearly isn't even before Woody says "Sure it was your wife?"

"As sure as I am the sun's up there somewhere."

"Somewhere is right. Well, I guess you know your own wife."

Ray is about to enquire, possibly politely, what this implies when Woody says "Me, I get calls from people who aren't even there."

"I expect everyone's a bit shaken up."

"This was yesterday, before the tragedy." Woody stares into the fog as if he sees Lorraine and says "Ross convinced me I'd been called by a lady I knew."

"I take it she hadn't."

"She was pretty fierce about making sure I got that when I rang her last night. We won't be talking any more after some of the stuff we both said. I can live without feeling I've been tricked in the middle of everything else."

"You don't think Ross did that, do you?"

"He says not, and I have to believe him. It wasn't New York on the phone either, though, and I didn't do us any favours calling them to ask if it was. I guess now they think I'm worried about their visit."

As Ray steps into the building his stomach tightens at the threat of the alarm. When it doesn't pounce he glances over his shoulder to discover Woody isn't following. "Looking for someone?" Ray asks.

"May as well make sure people are on time while I've been moved out of my office."

"The bosses have never done that, have they?"

"Right, they haven't," Woody says, turning his back on the fog. "Are you thinking maybe they should because I'm not doing enough?"

"Not a bit. If anything I'd say you try and do too much."

"Like where, Ray?"

"I'm saying I hope you know me and Connie and Nigel won't let you down. We're on top of our jobs."

"You mean you've all got your territories and you don't like me invading them." Woody's gaze, which looks as though it's crying out for sleep, lingers on him. "You didn't appreciate me taking over your staff meeting yesterday, right?" Woody says. "One thing jobs are about is saving all the time we can."

"I understand that. I did quite a lot of it while I was working at the stationers before I came to Texts."

"Okay, good. Then you have to know why we need it, the way things are shaping up. Two of us running your meeting would have taken twice as long," Woody says and raises his voice. "Wilf."

Ray is glad of the interruption. He wasn't comfortable with arguing so close to what happened to Lorraine and where it did. As Wilf turns from hastening into the shop, Woody says "Can I ask you to take something over for us, Wilf?"

"I should think."

"I know you're the man for it. Maybe you already realised we need someone to run Lorraine's reading group."

Wilf presses one forefinger against the length of his lips so hard they're still pale when he releases them. "Wasn't that supposed to be tomorrow?"

"Still is. Too late to tell everyone who's coming that we've cancelled, even if we knew who they were. You're working late anyway, and I remembered how you said at your interview you love nothing more than reading."

"I don't know which book she chose. I may not have read it."

"Planning anything tonight?" When Wilf only lifts a cupped hand as if he's trying to catch words to feed into his mouth, Woody says "See, I knew I picked the right guy. Remember how you told me you can get through a book in an evening. Lorraine chose the Brodie Oates novel. Shows she was doing her best to be part of the team. Shouldn't give you any trouble, that size of book."

Ray sees Wilf decide against responding and Woody take this for agreement. "Thanks, Wilf," he says, and even more briskly "Anything to add, Ray?"

It's less a question than a dismissal. "Can you let us in, Wilf?" Ray says so as to feel in some kind of charge, and has to point out that Wilf is presenting the wrong side of his badge to the plaque on the wall. As they reach the staffroom Nigel looks up from the latest Woody's Wheedles sheet. He seems uncertain how bright he should allow his eyes to grow. "Ray," he says, not so much a greeting as an expression of sympathy, and in the same tone "Wilf."

"Nigel," Ray feels bound to respond in as similar a manner as he can produce, though he thinks Nigel may be overdoing it a little. He runs his card under the clock and stuffs his rustling package into his locker, then heads for his desk. He hasn't switched on his computer when Mad emerges from Woody's room, followed by a policeman and a policewoman with expressions as identically sombre as their uniforms. "Thank you," the woman says without acknowledging that Mad is close to tears. As the pair tramp out through the staffroom, Mad mumbles with her back to Ray "Can I stay in here a few minutes?"

"Have your break if you like."

Apparently she doesn't. She sits behind him in Nigel's chair, facing the wall and Nigel's dead computer. Ray feels shut in, as though the emotion she's trying to restrain has merged with the windowless concrete. A muffled sniff he assumes he's meant to notice escapes her, prompting him to ask "Would it help to talk?"

"They said I couldn't have locked my car."

"You think you did."

"I more than think." She swings around to stare not quite at him with a fierceness that almost dries her eyes. "They said there wasn't any sign it had been broken into, but that just means whoever did knew how to, mustn't it?"

"A child would be able to do that, you think."

"It's only Ross who says it was a child, and he didn't see what they looked like. I didn't even see anybody in the car." She turns her stare on Ray without toning it down much. "Besides, I'll bet some children these days know how to do that and worse."

"I expect that's possible."

"Saying it's my fault the car was stolen is like saying I wanted, I wanted Lorraine dead."

"Good heavens, I shouldn't think so. I'm certain nobody—"

"Somebody wanted it," Mad says and glares through Woody's door at the security monitor, where grey figures foreshortened to dwarfishness are roaming the maze of the screen. "Maybe when the police have finished with my car they'll be able to hunt them down."

"Let's hope so. How did you get here today?"

"My father had to change his hours to bring me. My parents

wanted me to take a couple of days off, but I don't think I've got the right. It's like saying I was harmed as well."

Ray meant to entice her away from her pain, but she seems unwilling to renounce it. "I think that's very—" he's compelled to start to say with no idea how to continue. He's glad that Woody gives him an excuse to interrupt himself. "Oh, you're still here," Woody says to Mad as he strides towards his office. "Any problem?"

She dabs her eyes with the back of her hand so swiftly she might almost just be glancing at her watch. "Only getting over being interviewed."

"Is that going to take much longer?"

"Ray said I could have my break."

"Did he? I guess you'd better be taking it, then." As if she can't or shouldn't hear, Woody tells Ray "At least she came into work."

"Did someone not?"

"Ross called in sick. The police are having to go to his home."

"I hope they won't be too rough on him." Ray wishes Mad weren't hearing him ask "Did they know he and, well, Lorraine had started going round together?"

"Not from me they don't. Did I miss something? Did you know about it, Madeleine?"

"Yes," she just about admits.

"Really? Pity, then. Kind of proves what I've come to think."

Since she doesn't respond, Ray says "What's that?"

"It's my experience it doesn't help the store if personnel get too close."

"Oh," says Mad.

"That's my experience," Woody says as if he didn't grasp or doesn't care that she meant she could do without hearing. "The girl I was telling you I phoned, Ray, I don't believe having her here would have helped me keep my mind on the job."

With enough dignity for the person referred to as well as herself, Mad stands up and walks out through the staffroom, where Nigel is intoning "Gavin. Greg. Jake. Agnes. Jill."

"Don't sound like that or you'll have me in tears," Jake pleads.

"You're starting me off too," Agnes warns him or Nigel.

"The hardest part was telling Bryony last night why I was weepy," says Jill. "And you may all think this is stupid, but I felt guilty because she couldn't remember who Lorraine was."

"I'd like to see anyone call you stupid for that," Agnes challenges.

When Greg clears his throat Ray thinks he means to answer her until, presumably to Nigel, he says "We don't want customers seeing anyone's upset, do we? It could put them off."

"We can't afford that." Woody has been watching two dwarf police leave the shop, but now he makes for the staffroom. "Give me the floor a moment, Nigel."

"Take as long as you need. It's your time, after all."

"No, it's the store's." Woody lets more than a second of it gather mutely before he says "Okay, I know everybody's shocked and grieved about our loss. We wouldn't be human otherwise. Does anybody want to take a moment to say anything?"

"We ought to send flowers," Jill says.

"Already ordered. On their way."

"When's the . . ." Agnes has to start again. "When's the funeral?"

"I believe next week."

"Maybe some of us should go," Gavin says without a trace of a yawn.

"Sure, if it's your day off or you can swap with someone, but I've thought of another way we can remember her. Each of you and everyone that isn't here just now get to take charge of half an aisle of Lorraine's. That way we don't need to hire anyone else and it's like saying she can't be replaced, which she can't be, am I right? And I guess you all know what else that means."

"Do we?" Greg asks as though his colleagues may not have grasped it.

"Everyone will need to work the overnight shift," says Woody to a silence Ray imagines full of shrugs and other expressions of unenlightenment. "Why don't we think of it as a tribute to Lorraine."

Greg makes an enthusiastic sound, Nigel slightly less of one until he increases it to match, as Ray becomes aware of listening and that Woody may have finished his oration. The risk of being caught idle digs its claws into Ray's stomach. He switches his computer on and wills the blank grey screen to show some life. The opening icons gradually surface, and their colours seep up to fill them. What's the significance of the thin rectangular icon halfway down the middle column? He can't recall having seen it before, and it's unidentified by any word. He's tempted to open the program to discover what it is, but clicks on Staff instead.

The time clock feeds its details to the computer for him to check before forwarding the information to head office. He brings up the November staff record onscreen and scrolls in search of Lorraine's name. He's copying the details of each of her last days into a separate file when he notices there's a stranger on the screen. It isn't a name. It could be a smaller version of the unfamiliar icon, so blurred that he can't be certain where its outline ends and the slightly paler background starts. Peering closer makes his eyes feel drawn out of focus. It appears among the entries for every day he has examined so far: just the minute after midnight is attributed to it on the first day of November, while it has three minutes to its credit on the next afternoon, and five the following day. It must be showing the times when some error crept into the system. As it rises yet again to meet his scrolling it puts him in mind of a grub. Seven minutes on the afternoon of the fourth, eleven the next night, thirteen early on the sixth . . . He hears footsteps behind him and twists around. "Calm down, Ray," Woody says, displaying his palms. "It's only me."

"Do you mind glancing at this? There's something I don't understand."

"Show me."

He sounds more edgy now than he implied Ray was. Ray turns his back on him and is scrolling upwards through the document when he glimpses at the foot of the screen a movement that makes him think of a worm retreating into mud. The line that credited the stubby lump with thirteen minutes in the shop has disappeared, not even leaving a space. When he scrolls through the days he has dealt with, and then down as far as the latest shift, he can't find any sign of the trespasser. "Am I seeing it yet?" Woody says.

"It isn't here, but I'll show you where I think it's coming from." This seems so urgent that Ray closes the program without saving any changes. He's bewildered when it closes as if there weren't any, and still more bemused to see that the nameless icon has vanished from the desktop. "It's buried itself," he protests.

"Was it crucial?"

"I don't know. I hope not." As he reopens the time clock program he's afraid the entries may have been corrupted, but they look unaffected. "It must have been one of those things computers do for no reason," he decides aloud.

"We can do without that. I'll leave you to get on with it, then."

The staff meeting has come to a muted end. Even the dispersal of footsteps is subdued and wordless. Woody's pallid flattened reflection dwindles into the computer screen, and then its depths swallow him. His office chair squeals on its axis and releases a creak, but Ray still feels watched; he could almost imagine that he's being spied upon from wherever the unknown icon and its smaller version hid. He makes himself concentrate on his task, and has arrived at the twelfth of the month without encountering any intruder when the building seems to quiver. Only his eardrums and perhaps the image on the screen are doing so as someone pounds on the back door of the shop. "Always more stock. That's what we're here for," Woody cries and dashes through the stockroom.

Very soon Ray hears the muffled clank of the bar on the delivery door, and thinks the trundling of the pallet truck is just audible too, a noise like an underground restlessness. It seems to descend and eventually to rise again, followed by a second clank. Perhaps that sounds so final because he's copying the details of Lorraine's last day, which appears never to have ended, since she didn't return to the clock. The notion catches in his throat, and he has to hold a long not quite steady breath, then swallow. He's closing the program when Jill says overhead "Manager to counter, please. Manager to counter."

Her voice is ominously controlled. Ray glances at the security monitor and sees her boxed in by a pair of tills, one forefinger resting in the middle of her upper lip as though it's holding her pensiveness in place. She doesn't lower it until he's nearly at the counter. "What's the situation, Jill?" he's just not too breathless to ask.

"It's Lorraine's father. He wants to know where . . ."

"Where is he?"

"He said he'd wait outside. Shall I page Woody?"

"He's busy as usual. I'll deal with it," Ray says, only to find nobody outside the shop.

The fog is hulking less than a hundred yards away. A single floodlight is visible, a drowned dripping sun raised like a trophy on a pole. The late November sun has been reduced to a greyish glow with no identity apart from the murk. The ruminations of the motorway seem enmeshed in the fog; the constant suffocated murmur sounds as though the obscured landscape is struggling to breathe. As Ray steps onto the tarmac that glistens like mud he remembers the ambulance crawling into view, its approach heralded by the fireworks of its pulsing lights, altogether too festive a spectacle. When he opens his mouth the chill of the fog he's tasting shivers through him. He can't quite shout or even say "Mr Carey." Instead he forces a cough.

He's wondering whether the murk has smothered the sound when he hears a tentative footstep, followed by several more assured or at least more rapid, and a figure blunders into sight opposite the travel agency next door. Ray sucks in a harsh breath that tastes like grief, because the face above the muddy shoes and grey trousers and padded grey coat—a face squeezed smaller by a fat grey hood—is Lorraine's. Of course it's only a version, one bearing a moustache like a couple of yellowing brushes. Its skin is so pale and loose and wrinkled that Ray senses the man has lost a good deal of strength, but as he veers towards Ray his tired eyes try to brighten. "Are you from the shop?"

"I'm a manager. Ray," Ray says, stretching out a hand as he steps forward.

"Just one?" When Ray uses both hands to clasp his right, which he offers as though he has almost forgotten how, Mr Carey peers at Ray's gesture before submitting the faintest of smiles. "Just one manager," he amplifies.

Ray isn't sure if the smile is volunteered as an apology or a plea that Mr Carey is entitled by his situation to make feeble jokes. As Ray feels his lips shifting to imitate it, Mr Carey lets the smile drop. "Where was she?"

Ray relinquishes the cold slack hand. He mustn't point; he cups his fingers to indicate the mass of fog beyond the splintered tree-stump. "Over there," he murmurs with all the regret and gentleness the words have room for.

"Can't you remember exactly?"

"I should be able." Whether Ray would prefer not to be is another matter, but Mr Carey's melancholy feels like a suppressed accusation. As Ray glances back from heading for the scrawny grove he sees the fog thicken and close with a hungry eagerness over the shopfront. The shop has been erased by the time he's past the tree that's farthest from the one Mad's car felled; even the glow from the display windows is indistinguishable from the murk. "About here," he says, he hopes no louder than enough.

Lorraine's father is pitiably keen to join him. As Ray bows his head towards the black surface, Mr Carey paces away and halts about six feet from him. "Here?"

"About, I think, I'm afraid, yes."

"So close."

Mr Carey is gazing past him. Ray turns to see the outlines of the shop entrance and the windows drifting in and out of visibility like a mirage. Could some illusion of the kind have mocked Lorraine in her last moments? He hopes the idea hasn't occurred to Mr Carey, who says only "Did you leave her out here in this?"

"I think we thought it could be worse to move her."

"Worse," Mr Carey echoes as though sadness won't let his voice rise to a question.

"We put a coat over her and someone was with her all the time."

"Even though she'd already left us. I do know that. Thank them for me and her mother all the same."

"Won't you come inside?"

"Will I feel closer to her there?"

How can Ray answer? He shifts uneasily, aggravating an impression that the tarmac is so thin underfoot he can sense the cold dark earth beneath it. "I should," Mr Carey decides. "I'll be meeting her friends."

The sound Ray makes is neutral. Perhaps Mr Carey doesn't hear it as he heads for the shop, talking volubly now. "We kept meaning to surprise her at work. We'd have liked to watch her when she didn't know we were. Never put anything off if you can, isn't that what they say? I never understood why till now. Her mother's being looked after by her sister in case you were wondering. She'll be asleep for a while on the sedatives, that's why she isn't with me."

Ray would like some of this to mean Lorraine has a sister. Mr Carey reaches the pavement in front of Texts and halts with one foot on the tarmac. "Have you children yourself?" he seems to hope.

"A little daughter."

"Just one?"

He seems unaware of echoing his previous attempt at a joke, and Ray thinks better of drawing attention to the similarity. "She's our only child so far."

"Ours too. They grow up before you can catch your breath, you ought to realise. They're meant to, that is." His gaze slips past Ray as though to lose itself in the fog, and then he drags it back. "Would you care to see?"

"Of course, if you'd like me to."

Though Ray is unsure what he's inviting, he has sensed too much of a plea to refuse. He takes a pace towards the shop entrance to encourage Mr Carey to follow, but Lorraine's father lingers as if the tarmac has caught his shoe while he unzips a pocket and takes out his wallet. He uses a shivering finger and thumb to widen a slit in the leather and extract a photograph the size of a credit card, which he displays on his outstretched palm. It shows a small Lorraine in a white blouse and striped tie and with her hair in not quite symmetrical pigtails. Her eyebrows couldn't be higher, nor her grin wider or prouder of itself. "It was her first school photograph," Mr Carey says. "She was five."

The fog flaps closer behind him, as though the photograph has attracted it or something it conceals or is exhaling. Ray can only think he's imagining this nonsense to prevent himself from being too distressed by the photograph. "They'll all want to see it, I expect," Lorraine's father says abruptly and hurries into the shop.

Ray is afraid the alarm will play its trick. Only Frank the guard greets Mr Carey, however, by frowning at the photograph as though it's being proffered as identification. Mr Carey is too intent on heading for the counter to notice. "Were you friends of my daughter's?" he asks Agnes and Jill.

The women draw together as he holds the photograph out to them. Having blinked at it, they raise their eyes with such care that they look wary of spilling the contents of the lower lids. After a pause during which tiny violins chirp overhead like birds trapped in the shop, Jill says "That's . . ."

"My little Lorraine before she grew up, well, nearly did. At least now I can see she must have been with people she liked. She never told us much about her time here, but her mother was right, you don't need to say you're happy if you are. We were never that demonstrative a family." He rests his tired gaze on the photograph long enough to be making a silent wish before he asks "Was she a credit to you?"

The violins have chirped a relentlessly cheerful bar or several by the time Ray grasps that the question was aimed at him. "To the shop, I should think she was," he exclaims. "We'd all say so, wouldn't we, girls?"

"I would," Agnes says with more than a hint of Lorraine's defiance.

"And me," says Jill, then drops her gaze as though it has been tugged down by her teeth on her lower lip.

"Would you even if it wasn't true? Don't worry, it would only prove you were her friends. I'm glad her mother will be meeting you."

Jill releases her bitten lip to say "Is Lorraine's mother here?"

"She didn't want to come now she can't see Lorraine. You'll meet at the church."

"Oh yes. Sorry. And I'm really sorry about . . ." Each of Jill's words seems to be harder to articulate, as if they're catching on the emotion behind them, but when she says "Could you excuse me?" it rushes out like a single word.

"I'll go with her, can I?" Agnes blurts and races after her to the staffroom.

As Ray retreats behind the counter so that it doesn't appear unattended, Mr Carey says "Ladies. They're better off than us in some ways, aren't they? They don't care if they see each other having a good cry."

Ray feels as though Lorraine's father and the women have delegated him to suppress emotion on behalf of all of them. He could imagine fog has lodged behind his eyes, blurring the far ends of the aisles. Even once he has risked a blink, Mad's section still looks vaguely befogged. Mr Carey peels back his hood, releasing tuft after grey tousled tuft of hair, and turns the photograph on the counter towards himself. He might be addressing it as he murmurs "I hope it was a child, don't you?"

"Forgive me, you hope which?"

"The police said a child was supposed to be driving the car.

I wouldn't like to think anyone else could be so thoughtless."

"We've had to chase a few little savages, but I pray they're not that bad."

"Are you a praying man? I used to be." Mr Carey lifts a corner of the photograph with a fingernail bitten to the quick and returns the picture of Lorraine like a stigma to his palm. "Anyway, I'd best let you get on," he says. "I'm not a customer."

Three women with a handful of romances each have arrived at the end of the rope that leads to the sign requesting people to queue there. As Ray serves them he's distracted by the sight of Mr Carey's hunt for anybody wearing a Texts badge. Each of them is shown the photograph, which is starting to put Ray in mind of a membership card that gives admission to their hearts, an unforgivable idea but one he can't entirely dismiss. More than once he hears Mr Carey murmur "church". He's bagging a wrestler's ghost-written autobiography for a track-suited man with rusty sunlamped skin and a stubby neck that looks electrical with veins when Mr Carey returns to the counter. He waits until they're alone to ask Ray "Have I met everyone?"

"Some won't be in till after lunch. The manager's in the stock-room."

"You'll have had enough of me by then. Be honest, you have now."

"Not at all," Ray says, performing a vigorous shake of his head.

"May I let you know once we've settled where and when so you can tell the rest of Lorraine's friends? I'll leave her picture if you like and you can give it back to me at the church."

"I'm sure that won't be necessary."

Mr Carey seems to grow belatedly aware of Frank the guard or of his significance. "Were you here when it happened?" he asks, brandishing the photograph at him.

Frank turns such a slow frown on it that Ray fears his lack of recognition will distress Lorraine's father. He's about to abandon his post at the counter and explain when Frank says "I was in here. Ronnie and them that came with the park, they was on patrol."

"Where would I find them?"

"In their hut, only I'd think twice."

"Why that?"

"He heard her running and the car and never went to try and stop it. He wasn't that slow when I worked with him in Manchester."

"Out of condition, do you mean?" Mr Carey wants to believe.

"Stupid and takes forever to get where he's going. Thinks he's so impressive he doesn't need to run. Maybe it's beneath him, I shouldn't wonder."

"I think perhaps I don't want to meet him." Mr Carey lays the photograph to rest in his wallet, only for his pocket to stay clear of his increasingly shaky hand. At last he manages to lodge the wallet and zip the pocket shut, and says to Ray "Could I ask you one last favour?"

"I didn't think you'd asked me any yet."

"It's kind of you to say so." Mr Carey tries for a smile that his lips shake off. "Would you mind showing me where Lorraine left her car?"

Jill reappears from the direction of the staffroom, and a moment later Agnes wheels a trolley through the exit near the lift. "I'll let you have the counter back, Jill," Ray says. "If anyone wants me I won't be out long."

The fog has closed in. The retail park resembles a photograph blurred almost blank by sunlight or by chemicals gone wrong, with just the shopfront and its strip of pavement and a bite-shaped arc of tarmac left in focus. "I believe the car is over by the supermarket," Ray murmurs.

"Why so far away?"

"We aren't really supposed to park at the front. I expect she didn't want it to be noticed."

"By you, do you mean?"

This sounds like a sad accusation, all the harder to deal with because of its vagueness. Mr Carey leaves it behind as he hurries past Happy Holidays, where handwritten offers of travel are peeling away from condensation on the inside of the window. Perhaps he doesn't hear Ray protest "I did."

Ray catches up with him alongside TVid, where a couple are screaming at each other on the daily *Relate* show on at least a dozen televisions. Next door in Teenstuff a pregnant but otherwise skinny teenager is fingering scraps of cloth that are either skirts or blouses. In the Baby Bunting window ranks of cloth dolls with perfunctory faces seem to be watching for a spectacle to begin, while inside Stay in Touch the staff appear dissatisfied with all the mobile phones they're testing. Beyond the unoccupied properties covered with boards that are crawling with graffiti—primitive shapes and brief yet illegible words—an alley leads to the guards' long low boxy hut, in which a radio commentator's voice sounds frantic to escape a mouth stuffed with fur. Mr Carey hesitates beside the alley for a moment and then trudges onward. As the front of the supermarket looms into view, its windows displaying special offers in letters so large only the fog can defeat them, he disentangles his key-ring from a pocket and uses both hands to point the fob at a red Shogun, which acknowledges him with a beep of its horn and a wink of its lights. "It used to be the family car. Lorraine wanted it, so we gave it to her," he seems to feel required to explain, "though we thought there was too much room."

Ray's afraid Mr Carey may add that there is now, but he only climbs into the vehicle. "Thank you for looking after me," he says. "I'm glad Lorraine had you for a manager."

Ray turns his hands up in a gesture he hopes is self-deprecating rather than dismissive. He watches fog redden and grow pale as the Shogun backs away from the kerb. The headlamps appear to draw tendrils of murk while the car dawdles towards the exit from the retail park. The rear lights swell before their redness vanishes as if the place is trying to pretend a stain was never there. The drone of the engine is shrinking towards the motorway when Ray dodges into Frugo. All at once the errand Sandra sent him on feels like a re-assurance that nothing has threatened their and Sheryl's lives.

He finds tights in the Household section and carries two packets united like Siamese twins to a checkout staffed by a severely cropped young blonde with TRISH pinned to the left breast of her pink overall. Clutching a Frugo bag, he hurries out to confront the fog. Can it have grown colder? He does his best to hug himself while maintaining his grasp on the carrier. The grey mass drags itself ahead of him along the pavement and lurches at him from the car park. As he passes the graffiti, a drop of condensation traces the outline of a squat discoloured figure with a smeary blob for a face. He could almost imagine that the frenzied jabbering from the guards' hut is using the daubed mouth. The unappealing notion makes him feel pursued, and once he's alongside Stay in Touch he can't help glancing back. He's in time to glimpse movement beyond a lonely parked Toyota, over which the edge of the fog is lapping—a blurred huddle of shapes ducking out of sight. They're no taller than the bonnet of the car.

They're children, then. He mustn't assume they are in any way connected with Lorraine's death, but he wants a word with them. "Hold on there," he calls and sprints towards the car. He hears a retreating commotion that sounds oddly unlike footsteps. He's abreast of the Toyota when he sees the fog embrace three small blurred shapes out on the deserted tarmac.

He has no idea why he hesitates before dashing in pursuit. They're only children, despite the tricks the murk and his nerves are eager to play. When the fog puts an end to an indistinct glimpse of the trio, it makes them appear to merge not only with it but also momentarily with each other. As he veers across the car park after them he catches sight of the audience of dolls in Baby Bunting, which explains why the notion of unfinished identical faces has lodged in his brain. The three small figures seem to be shuffling rather than running—that has to be why their movements sound barefoot, if not softer—and yet they're outdistancing him. He's unable to identify how they're dressed; the grey tatters that smudge their outlines must be fog, which has also steeped them in its colour. Then he's distracted by silhouettes of trees that drift into focus beside them, two saplings and the broken stump of a third. He thought he was heading for the buildings that are still to be completed, but somehow he has strayed back towards Texts. "Where are you wandering off to, Ray?" Woody calls behind him.

He turns to see Woody gripping his hips with his splayed fingers in the shop entrance. Ray jerks his free hand at the saplings. "You can see I'm—"

The hand hovers in the air with nothing else to do, because the tarmac is deserted. "Say what?" Woody shouts.

Ray backs towards him, squinting at the fog in case the children resurface. "Did you see where they went?"

"I don't talk to anybody's back, Ray." When Ray faces him Woody says "We saw you charging about and that's all. You just looked lost to me."

"Some children are hiding out there. I thought . . ."

"Did you? Maybe you want to check that out, Frank." As the guard heads for the splintered stump, Woody says "The way I heard it you were supposed to be taking care of Lorraine's father."

"I did that. I took him to her car."

"Did he give you that for your trouble?"

He's gazing at the Frugo bag, which rustles as though indicating Ray can't keep still for guiltiness. "The car was by the supermarket and I thought I might as well nip in while I was there," Ray explains. "Women's things, you know, for my wife."

"Nothing like efficiency, Ray."

"We can call it my break."

"Good idea," Woody says, and his gaze lets go of Ray. "Anything?" he shouts.

"Can't see nobody," Frank's flattened voice responds.

"Were they doing much, Ray?"

"I told you, hiding."

"Looks like they hid. I guess they might with someone chasing them. No need to assume they're bad just because they're kids, am

I right? They're potential customers. Or did you recognise them?"

Ray has had enough. He's struggling not to shiver, and his shirt is beginning to glue itself to him like chilly wallpaper. "No," he says and makes for Texts with a rustle of the supermarket bag.

Perhaps the word or the plastic sounds defiant, because Woody's stare seems to rise from some depth Ray would rather not encounter. "Next time you run a staff meeting, tell them not to leave the store in future without they check with me first," he says, and then his gaze sinks inwards but doesn't lose its hold on Ray. "No," he decides. "Forget it. I'll deal with everyone myself. That's my job."

# CONNIE

**She didn't go to bed with Geoff to spite Jill. It wasn't her idea to have** a post-cinema drink at Orient/Occident, it was Rhoda's and another girl's who Connie met at university. She didn't object to the venue, however, and once she saw Geoff behind the bar she didn't mind admitting to herself she'd hoped he would be. When it was time for Rhoda and her friend to leave, Connie gave up her lift home so that she could carry on talking to him, and everything after that felt like already having made her choice. That doesn't mean she wasn't in control, and she's not about to lose it: even as a child she couldn't bear it when other children made a fuss, and the few times her parents started arguing in public she wished she could shrink.

There's no reason for Jill to know about her night with Geoff, especially when they're distressed about Lorraine. Why was she so harsh to Jill about her window display, though? Perhaps she's nervous about how their first author's visit will turn out, but that's no excuse. Controversy is publicity, and surely the best way to promote

Brodie Oates. She'll say as much to Jill when she sees her, she promises herself as she drives away from her snug little two-bedroomed house in Prestwich.

Five minutes later she's on the motorway. In another ten she would be at Texts if it weren't for the fog. Once she sees it crawling onto the road she knows she's close to Fenny Meadows, though the retail park and the sign for it have been blotted out, together with the sun. The wet green fields on either side of her turn grey and diminish to large verges walled in by nothingness, and she feels as if her brain is dwindling too, as if while it's robbed of sunlight the space is plugged by fog. She's in second gear by the time she coasts past Frugo; she could almost imagine the patch of tarmac the fog doles out has given way to waterlogged earth that is dragging the wheels down. She parks behind Texts and hurries down the oppressively blank alley to the front of the shop.

A breath of fog seems to have caught in her head to grow more stagnant than it already smelled. Clearing her throat doesn't shift it, but makes Gavin cut a yawn short and busy himself at tidying the events leaflets on the counter. All the customers have one; at least a dozen men and women are at large among the shelves. Woody ought to be pleased, but he isn't working today. Connie runs upstairs to the restroom, as he prefers to call it, and blows her nose so hard on several tissues her skull feels pumped up. Her vigour must be why she seems to glimpse a grey mass quivering into view at the foot of the mirror; she's annoyed by having to turn to confirm she's alone in the room. When she has rid herself of enough of the residue of fog to ignore any that remains, she clocks on and flashes a smile at Nigel's shift meeting, Jill included but not singled out, on the way to her desk. She's about to check her email when she hears the meeting scatter and the office door inch open. "Connie?" says Jill.

Her voice is low and guarded but determined, and her grin looks shy of being noticed. "What's the joke, Jill?" Connie prompts.

"I don't know if you'd want to call it that," Jill says, snapping open her handbag. "Have you realised what you did, if it was you?"

Has she deduced somehow that Connie spent the night with Geoff? Why should Connie react as though it has anything to do with Jill? She's suppressing her resentment at being made to feel defensive when Woody jerks his door open. "Something else wrong?"

"Isn't this your day off?" Connie blurts.

"Why, would you like it to be?"

"Only for your sake. You need time off like the rest of us."

"Time enough for that when we're on top of everything. I'm still dreaming of a stockroom with nothing in it waiting to go down, except that isn't going to be just a dream." He pauses long enough for Connie to wonder if behind his murky eyes he has indeed drifted close to sleep, and then he says "We interrupted you, Jill."

He's aggravated Connie's defensiveness so much that she's ready to deny whatever the letter Jill produces from her bag is accusing her of. When Jill unfolds it, however, it proves to be an events leaflet. "I was saying to Connie, sorry, Connie, I don't think you could have spotted this."

Woody lurches out of the doorway to twist his face towards the leaflet. "Hey, that's new."

For a moment as she peers at it Connie is able to believe that nothing obvious has befallen it, and then she rereads the top line: EVENT'S AT TEXTS. The apostrophe is almost small enough to be mistaken for a crumb of mud—just not quite. "I don't believe it," she hears herself say, which makes her feel even stupider. "I checked it onscreen and when I printed it out as well."

"Still looks to me like we're screwed, then."

"Sometimes you read what you expect to be there, don't you?" Jill says. "I didn't see it at first myself. It was when I took a bunch to school to give people, my little daughter asked if there wasn't a mistake."

Her grin is fiddling with her lips again. It may mean to be wry and sympathetic, but is she really unaware of worsening Connie's situation? "Maybe people will think it's right and just a bit original, like you," she tells Connie. "It could be saying event is at Texts, you know, there's an event at Texts, though I suppose it should really be events are."

Connie's almost certain Jill is slyly taunting her. Perhaps she thinks Connie won't challenge her in front of Woody, in which case she's about to learn that she's a presumptuous bitch. Did Connie think something else about her earlier? It's nowhere to be found in her mind now. She opens her mouth, only to feel as though Greg is using it for ventriloquism and to make her look more of a fool. "Connie call six, please. Connie call six."

"Better do that," Woody says. "And thanks for the publicity, Jill, even if it doesn't give the impression we want."

She didn't say she gave anything to anyone. Connie would take time to point that out except that Woody is staring at her phone to urge her to use it. "Yes, Greg," she says, having snatched it up.

"The reading group is asking where they're supposed to be."

Why doesn't he transfer the call? She knows he's anxious for promotion, but she doesn't care for the way he behaves as though he's already a manager. "Put whoever it is through," she says, "and I'll speak to them."

"They aren't on the phone, they're here. They're due to start in a few minutes."

"I doubt it, Greg. Somebody's lost track of time."

"That's what it says on your handout."

"Who told you that? Jill?" Perhaps the name sounds like an accusation rather than a request for the leaflet, because Jill hesitates before passing it to her. "I'm not seeing this," Connie says only just aloud.

"Can't be there then, can it?" Woody says as his eyes demand an explanation.

"I know I put eighteen hundred, not eleven. I'll swear I did."

"Swear all you like, just not in front of the customers."

His voice is so lacking in encouragement that returning to the phone is almost a relief. "Is Wilf about?" she asks.

"He's on his way to the stockroom."

"I'll catch him."

As Connie stands up, Woody lifts an open hand so fast she could take it for the threat of a slap. "Before you hustle, have we finished finding problems with the stuff you wrote?"

"I hope so."

"Better make sure, huh?"

What infuriates her most is that he's saying this in front of Jill. Rage must be blinding her; she can hardly distinguish what she's labouring to read, let alone whether it contains any further mistakes. "Didn't you check it?" she sees no reason not to ask. "I thought you liked to keep an eye on everything."

"I guess I must have figured we could trust you to fix it this time."

The nearest to a response she feels able to risk is "Jill, are you hanging around here for anything in particular?"

Jill reaches for the leaflet and then lets it lie on the desk. "You keep it, I've still got some. What should I do with them?"

"Connie will give you some with no mistakes in them, won't you, Connie? Let's make certain we don't waste any more paper." Woody adds a stare to that and strides through the staffroom to throw the far door open. "Wilf, you're in demand."

"I was going to put my books out and the ones you said I had to of Lorraine's."

"Time for those later. Right now Connie has a surprise for you. Your fan club's waiting down below."

Wilf is struggling to keep an expression to himself. "Who is?"

"Your reading group. I know they were meant to be here this evening, but we can't send them away when they've been told it's now."

This seems not to strike Wilf as any kind of an improvement on whatever he was expecting. "You read the book, didn't you?" Woody urges.

"I nearly finished it last night at home. I fell asleep at the end."

"We're talking about how many pages?"

"At least a chapter."

Connie senses he hopes that will disqualify him, but Woody

says "That's going to take you what, five minutes at your speed? We'll carry the seats down and you follow as soon as you're done. Gonna help me, Connie? Jill needs to be shelving."

"You go first, Jill." Connie feels absurd for saying this as they reach the doorway, because she's too aware of trying to establish she's still a manager. She stacks four chairs to Woody's seven as Wilf sinks into the last one with the Brodie Oates book. "Lots of new books for you, Jill, and don't forget Lorraine's," she can't or at any rate doesn't resist saying on her six-legged way through the stockroom.

"I'm not about to forget her."

Woody plants his stack before the lift and knuckles the button. "See to these while I tell the group everything's on its way, can you?" he says. "I'll catch you at the bottom."

The rapid trapped staccato of his footfalls on the stairs is brought to an end by the clank of the bar on the door, and then Connie hears the lift hauling itself upwards. Beneath its creaks there's another sound: a woman's muffled voice. Whoever she's addressing seems unable to get a word in, or is she the voice of the lift? If Connie pressed her ear against the door she might hear what's being said, but before she can bring herself to do so the lift announces that it's opening and twitches wide.

She isn't sure why she doesn't quite trust it. She props a chair against the double thickness of the door and transfers the stacks by degrees into the lift: four, three, three. As she ventures in to push the button, she's poised to dodge out again. The lift tells her it's closing and is meant to wait a few seconds for anyone who's entering. Instead the eager door shoves the chair at her, and there isn't room for her to sidle past it. As she flings the chair aside she realises she ought to have used it to force the lift open. She's certain she has trapped herself, but she scrambles out and almost falls headlong as the door snaps shut at her back.

She stares as if that may convince Jill she either didn't stumble or intended to. Did she hear the briefest pause, almost like a stifled giggle, between the syllables of the second word the lift pronounced? It must have been a fault in the mechanism. She trots downstairs as Woody reappears from the sales floor. "Should be a lively discussion," he says. "They aren't just readers, they're a writers' group."

Connie refrains from imagining that he receives a muffled answer from within the lift. It must have said it was opening, because after a pause that makes him click his tongue as though summoning an animal, it does. "Oh, I thought someone was in here," he says.

She assumes that's a rebuke for leaving the chairs unattended. The one she threw aside has fallen over. He plants it on the heap of three and loads them with three more, and strides out with his arms locked under them while she dashes to retrieve the others. Woody must think she wants to match his speed. He holds the door to the shop open just long enough for her to slip through. "Here we are, everyone," he calls. "Please take a seat."

As Connie follows him into the Teenage alcove, the people she saw wandering the aisles and lingering over books converge. Most of them are old enough to travel free of charge, apart from two young women who succeed in looking both intense and timid. Once the chairs are arranged in an oval the oldest of the group, a short stout woman with hair plaited like a greying cake, who's wearing voluminous green slacks and a cardigan so multicoloured it borders on the biblical, remains standing. "Are you both talking to us?" she elects herself to ask.

"Our volunteer's on his way, ma'am." Woody is staring at the door as if this may conjure Wilf when Agnes calls overhead "Manager to counter, please. Manager to counter."

She needs someone to authorise a refund to a teenager with stubbly pimples who has returned a concert video by Single Mothers on Drugs. As Connie initials the voucher, Wilf emerges from hiding. "Here's our champion reader," Woody announces, which seems not to appeal to Wilf, and makes for the tills as the customer, having crowned himself with a motorcycle helmet, tramps out of the shop. "What happened there?" Woody demands.

"What did he say was wrong, Anyes?"

"No music on it, and it didn't look like a concert either."

Woody frowns as if he thinks Connie should have learned at least that much before authorising any refund, and then he grabs the tape. "I'm going down to the video store to look at this."

As soon as he's out of the shop, Agnes says "Connie, don't you think we should all go to the funeral?"

"We can't, can we? Somebody needs to be here."

"Couldn't we close for it would only be a couple of hours or so? Don't you think Lorraine is worth that much?"

"There's no use saying that to me, Anyes. It's Woody you'd have to persuade."

"I thought you might ask him if you thought it was important."

"I'm sure you can. You seem capable enough," Connie says while she tries to hear what's happening in the Teenage alcove. The woman with the greyish mass of plaits has folded her arms so fiercely she appears to have no breasts and is pointing one forefinger at Wilf. "What's your interpretation?" she's saying in a teacher's schoolyard voice. "It's your choice of book."

"It isn't really. The girl who chose it isn't, isn't here."

"It's your shop's choice, and you're the shop. We only bought it because we were told. Hands up anyone who would have otherwise." She rubs her lips together for the instant during which she shakes her head at the tentative gestures of the two young women. "So explain why you set it if it wasn't just someone's idea of a joke," she challenges Wilf.

"It could have been the author's, some of it anyway, do you think? He'll be here next week in person if you want to ask him."

"We're asking you. Your boss says nobody reads like you. What do we all want to know?"

"What the ending's meant to mean," says one young woman, and the other nods.

"The ending," their spokeswoman cries decisively and jerks her open hands at Wilf, paroling her breasts. "We'd all like to hear what he makes of that, wouldn't we?"

A murmur of general agreement is combined with laughter bereft of mirth. Wilf sits forward on his chair and lifts his gaze clear of his audience, only to catch Connie's eye across the sales floor. He glances hastily away and blinks at nobody in particular as he mumbles "Maybe it depends how you understand the rest of the book."

"How do you?" the second young woman is eager to discover, but is overruled. "We'll come to that," the organiser says. "We want to know what we're expected to get out of the very last paragraph."

"What did you all think? Did you have different ideas?"

"Let's hear yours first. Your boss said if anybody could make sense of it you could."

Connie has stayed behind the counter so as not to embarrass him, but she needs to deal with the events leaflets. She's pacing sidelong when his eyes meet hers again. His trapped stare feels as if it's desperate to clutch at her. "I can't," he says and lurches to his feet like a puppet hoisted by its mottled head. He stumbles between the chairs and seems about to flee behind the scenes, then abruptly veers towards Connie. "Could someone else possibly do this?" he pleads.

"What is it, Wilf?"

"I'm . . ." He wags his fingers in front of his face and pinches the air as if he's trying to drag something out of his brain. "I've . . ."

"It'll be a migraine, will it?" Agnes tells him.

"I don't know, I've never had one," he says, then peers at her with something like gratitude. "Before," he adds.

Connie wonders if Agnes means to adopt Lorraine's role of speaking up for her colleagues even if they haven't asked her to. "Are you really not going to be able to carry on, Wilf?"

His eyes glisten like the shrouded tarmac outside. "I'm sorry. I'm letting everyone down."

Presumably that's a yes. Connie would take charge of the reading group herself, but she has only leafed through the book. She lifts the nearest phone and sends her voice into the air in search of Jill. "Let your people know we're sending a substitute," she says to Wilf, "and then what will you do?"

"There's nowhere you can lie down, is there?" Agnes says. "Try sitting with your eyes shut. You won't be able to drive home."

"Can you leave your shelving for later, Jill," Connie doesn't ask. "Apparently Wilf has a migraine and we need someone to talk to his group about the Brodie Oates book."

"I don't know if I liked it."

"Then don't lie about it. Get them talking, that's your job. They're in Teenage. Come straight down," Connie says and cuts her off.

Wilf has trudged to give the readers' group the news. The plaited woman throws up her hands and her gaze as he retreats to the armchair nearest to his section and sinks into it, closing his eyes. He opens them almost at once and stares at the books ahead of him before covering his eyes with a hand and sinking deeper into the chair. Connie is about to offer him some paracetamol when Jill appears with a glass of water and a brace of aspirin. Once she has ministered to him he hides his eyes again as she marches to the Teenage alcove without glancing at Connie. She perches on the edge of the empty chair and says "I'm Jill. Who liked the book?"

Connie has to hold her mouth straight as Jill is met by silence. Eventually the young women admit they rather did. Connie would linger to hear how Jill deals with the plaited woman, but that won't repair the leaflets. She leaves the counter as Woody stalks into the shop. "Let me know if this guy returns anything else," he says, dropping the cassette on the Returns shelf. "It's been taped over."

"What with?"

"Some old historical movie. One of your battles, it looks like. It isn't even tuned in right. No wonder he didn't want to keep it." By now Woody's staring at Wilf and Jill. "What's been going on while I was out?"

"Wilf's got a migraine," says Agnes. "Jill's read the book."

"Tell him to sit upstairs till he recovers, for God's sake," Woody tells Connie.

She's taking a resentful hot-faced step towards Wilf when Agnes says "Connie said I had to ask you about closing for the afternoon so we can all go to Lorraine's funeral."

"Woody wants you to sit upstairs so the public doesn't see you." Having hurried to tell Wilf that, Connie strays back towards the counter to hear Woody say "Why all? Some of you didn't get on with her too well is how I remember it."

"I'm certain her parents would like everyone to go."

"They won't know how many staff there are, will they? It makes no sense to shut down for any length of time when we're already a person short. And I'm going to need anyone who wants to attend the funeral if it isn't their day off to commit themselves to working overnight next week. I hope everyone will anyway when they'll be helping to get her section the way she'd want it."

As Agnes stares at Woody in disbelief, Wilf makes for the staffroom. Connie follows him in case he can't see to line up his badge with the plaque on the wall, but he unites them deftly enough. Halfway up the stairs he twists his head around to blink at her as if he feels hunted. "Sit at Ray's desk so people can take their breaks," she says. "It's his day off."

Wilf grips the arms of Ray's chair and lowers himself in front of the blank computer screen. As Connie switches on her monitor he flattens a hand across his eyes. She deletes the unwelcome apostrophe and is rereading the document when she notices that he's spying through his fingers. "Anything else you can see I should do?" she asks.

He shuts his fingers so fast and hard she's afraid he'll pinch his eyes between them. "No," he mutters.

The image on the monitor shifts like fog. As she scowls at it to convince herself it hasn't played another trick, Angus hastens into the staffroom and fills his mug with coffee from the percolator. She knows he won't refuse anyone a favour. She's about to ask him to glance at the document until Agnes darts out of the stockroom. "Angus, are you working overnight next week?"

"I was going to. I've put my name down."

"I wasn't saying you shouldn't, only Woody says anyone that does is free to go to the funeral. I still think we all should be. I think we would be if we stood together."

She has raised her eyes and her voice towards Connie, who tries to ignore her by studying the screen. The harder she concentrates, the less meaningful the words on it appear, even once Agnes returns to the stockroom. As Connie decides to print out a leaflet in case any errors will be more obvious on paper, Woody sprints upstairs, humming the tune the overhead speakers inflicted on everyone for weeks before the shop opened: "Goshwow, gee and whee, keen-o-peachy . . ." "Got to keep our spirits up," he remarks to Angus. "Here's the man we need."

"Nearly finished my break," Angus assures him and gulps half a mugful.

"Hey, no need to choke yourself. I'm going to ask you to help me out next week. You didn't hang out with Lorraine much, did you? You weren't one of her particular crowd if she had one."

An angry clatter of books on a trolley in the stockroom is followed by a silence like a held breath. "I only knew her to work with," Angus admits.

"So you won't mind giving her funeral a miss, will you? You'll be releasing somebody who cares."

"Won't her parents wonder why I stayed away?"

"You ever meet them?"

"Not yet, but . . ."

"Then I guess they don't know you exist. It'd only stir them up if anyone made an issue of it, and they don't need that right now, do they? That's settled then, yes? I can count on you."

"I expect so," Angus says, and Connie senses he's hoping this will somehow placate Agnes. "I mean, you can," he has to add for Woody's benefit, provoking a furious onslaught on the trolley in the stockroom. He drains his mug and dumps it amid its predecessors in the stagnant sink before fleeing downstairs while Woody examines Connie's screen. "How's it looking now?" he enquires.

"I can't see a problem, can you?"

"I'm always seeing those," he says and glances towards the security monitor in his office. "I'm afraid the writers weren't too fond of your buddy Jill."

"I wouldn't call her that exactly."

"Is that so? Something between you I should know about?"

"As far as I'm concerned there's nothing between us at all."

Only some of his watchfulness drains into the stare he has turned on Connie. "She wasn't too successful at selling them on your book," he says. "Most of them went away wondering why we recommended it."

"Why, have they gone already? How long have we been up here, Wilf?"

As Wilf shakes his head without letting go of his eyes with his hand, Woody says "Half an hour at least by my watch."

Has she been at the screen all that time? Through the clinging mass of her confusion she hears Woody say "I'm afraid they weren't all that impressed with you either."

She's starting to feel as she imagines Wilf does. "I can't remember ever speaking to them."

"With your leaflet. I let them think it was some printer's fault, but I don't like having to hide things on behalf of the store. Will I have to again?"

"Don't you know? You're looking at the same thing I am."

"I'm looking at you, Connie," he says and lowers his gaze to the screen. "Print it as soon as you're happy with it, and then you can shelve a bunch of Lorraine's books so people have a chance to buy them."

She has to assume he's seeing no more mistakes than she is—none at all—but as he veers into his office she wonders if he and her brain could be conspiring to play a trick. She glares at the screen until the words revert to marks utterly devoid of meaning. As she starts the printer on the basis of nothing except desperation, Wilf releases a low groan that she could take to be voicing her helplessness.

For a moment she wants to confess it, and then she takes her mouth in a firm hand. She's just tense after what happened to Lorraine, she tells herself. They all must be, and it will ease eventually. She isn't about to talk herself out of a job.

# ANGUS

**As his mother steers the Vectra onto the Fenny Meadows slip road** she says "You don't want to drive us the rest of the way, do you?"

Is she telling him so or that she would prefer it if he did? "Do you want me to?" he counters as the roundabout dredges itself up from the fog at the foot of the ramp.

"That has to be up to you, doesn't it, Angums?"

He's so intent on concealing his wince at the nickname he keeps hoping she will let him leave behind that he hasn't replied by the time they arrive at the roundabout. The motorway rears over them, exposing its wet greyish pockmarked underside above concrete pillars snared by graffiti like vegetation too primitive to have defined its species. "It isn't far," he says, feeling trapped in a conversational game where the loser is whoever makes an unqualified statement, which is how he feels most of the time with his parents. "I mean, I could give it a try."

"You'd like to be able to get yourself about, wouldn't you,

though don't think for an instant your father and I mind bringing you and collecting you. You're on our route."

"Maybe I shouldn't risk driving in this."

"I'm sure that's sensible if you don't feel confident enough. I only thought you'll have to learn sooner or later to cope with conditions like these, and there shouldn't be much on the move in your car park."

When he doesn't respond she drives under the motorway again. The fog lumbers after them through the gloomy dripping passage while it disentangles itself from the graffiti ahead, and then it seems to stagnate in the retail park, replacing the sky and denying the mid-morning sun and reducing the buildings to pallid blocks of mould. The Vectra crosses the car park, passing random strips of turf guarded by lank trees fattened by the fog. Tyre marks gape like glistening mouths on either side of the tree Mad's car felled; they're already overgrown with new grass. Beyond them Texts heaves up from the murk that clings to the display window and obscures patches of the Brodie Oates promotion. "Your father will pick you up tonight then, Angums," says his mother.

"Thanks. I'll drive us to the motorway tomorrow if I can."

She tilts her head an inch away from him, and her eyes farther. "Don't be so anxious to please everyone or you'll end up pleasing nobody, especially yourself."

He feels as if he's being urged to turn on her—by a part of himself he would rather not acknowledge, not an audience that's skulking in the fog. He clenches his teeth to shut up his tongue while she pats his cheek, a gesture that suggests a yearning for all the kisses he couldn't avoid outside the school gates, and murmurs "Go on then, Angums, make us proud."

He clutches his packed lunch and waves to her as the car bears away the L-plate like a badge of every time he has stalled the engine or accelerated instead of braking or skinned a tyre against the kerb. At least he's not that bad at work, he thinks as the fog swallows a last tinge of red. He hurries into Texts, and Woody's giant voice goes off like an alarm. "Keep smiling. Nobody likes a grouch."

The corners of his mouth haul themselves to attention before he realises Woody is addressing Agnes. As she observes his reaction her blank expression twists into a scowl. "That's worse. We don't want to see that again," Woody's voice descends to say, and as she ducks behind the counter so fast she appears to have been seized by a cramp "Any time you'd like to join us, Angus, we can start."

Angus is glad she's too busy hiding her grimace to watch him scurry to obey. The only customers are two studiedly bald men who seem to have marked out a pair of armchairs as their territory. Perhaps they intend to buy presents for children; each of them is leafing through a book with very few words to a page. Their dull eyes barely flicker as Angus hastens past with a rattle of containers in his lunch box.

Everybody at the staffroom table does indeed appear to be waiting for him. Ross looks relieved he has appeared. Jill seems ready to defend herself, surely not against him. Gavin opens his mouth, but the nearest to a greeting he produces is a yawn he mostly swallows. Jake says "Here's the boy" more enthusiastically than Angus is certain he likes. He's saved from having to respond by Woody, who darts out of his office. "Okay, let's get you up to speed," he says not much more quietly than he sounded overhead. "I'll take this, Nigel. Maybe part of the problem is Brits managing Brits."

Nigel shrugs and meets nobody's eyes as he tramps into the stockroom. He doesn't hesitate or glance back when Gavin says "That's a bit racist, isn't it?"

"Hey, we don't need that word round here. We don't need anything that stirs up trouble. If we don't admit we're different we can't learn from whoever's got it more together, am I right? Take a seat whenever you're through there, Angus."

Angus is trying to clock on but has the impression that the card isn't registering; it feels as if the slot is clogged with mud, though when he peers in, it looks clear. He swipes the card once more and drops it in the In rack and hurries to sit down, not soon enough to prevent Woody from saying "There's a small example of the stuff we need to get rid of."

Angus feels Jill is transferring her defensiveness onto him by demanding "What is?"

"Some of you don't seem to be used to our routines yet. The more things you can do without having to think about them the better."

"I don't know if that's ever a good idea, doing things without thinking. I can't imagine telling my daughter to."

"Round here it's essential. Let's keep discussion for another time, shall we? I need what I have to tell you to sink in."

"God, that sounds masterful," says Jake.

Angus wonders if he's deliberately exaggerating himself, and hopes Woody is. Jill lets out a giggle, most of it chopped off by shock, and Gavin emits a laugh that's even shorter and more mirthless. "Any more comments anyone needs to get out of the way?" Woody asks and stares at them.

Angus can't help feeling forced to shake his head and offer what he hopes isn't too much of a smile or too little either, though everybody else keeps their response to themselves. "Okay, then," Woody says. "I wish I could take all of you to see how we do it back home."

"How do you?"

"Glad you asked, Angus. When you walk into a shop you want to feel the staff are eager to do everything they can for you, don't you? That's what I'm not always getting from some of you, and I don't only mean the ones around this table right now."

"Some of us Brits, you mean," says Gavin.

"That's exactly right. Maybe it's the British class thing, you feel serving is beneath you, but it isn't if you want to work for Texts. I'm starting to think it's one reason we aren't seeing enough customers. We need to make them feel this is the best bookstore they were ever in, which by God it is from what I've seen of the competition. We have to make sure they keep coming back and tell all their friends."

Angus doesn't want to feel delegated to ask, but the silence tugs his mouth open. "How do we?"

"I know why you guys are feeling blue, but we don't want the customers to be. For a start you smile whenever you see a customer. Remind yourself they're the people that are keeping you employed and maybe that'll help. Go ahead. Like this."

He jerks his fingers up on either side of his face as if to urge the corners of his mouth higher. His eyes are wide and ready to answer any question, his lips are parted to expose his gleaming teeth. All this might look more welcoming if his eyes weren't so red. His face puts Angus in mind of a clown's helpless mask, especially when it doesn't relent until everyone has attempted to match it. "You all need to work on that," Woody says as the expression sinks into his face. "Okay, let's try what goes with it. From now on we greet every customer. Will anyone be uncomfortable saying welcome to Texts?"

It's him Angus can't say he's comfortable with, and so he says nothing. Woody's either happy or determined to take the silence for general agreement; certainly his smile is close to surfacing again. "So I'm a customer," he declares. "Who's going to welcome me?"

He isn't gazing only at Angus, but Angus is unable to ignore the urgency that seems to be turning Woody's eyes even redder. He clears his throat, and the end of the noise catches on his first word. "Welcome to Texts."

"Couldn't hear you."

"Welcome to Texts," Angus nearly shouts as his hot face swells around his mouth.

"Hey, I'm in the store, not out there in the fog. That's more enthusiastic, anyway, but what am I not seeing?"

Failing to grasp what he means gives Angus the impression that his brain is steeped in fog. Woody's eyes widen like wounds, and he jabs a chewed thumbnail at his face. Instantly the smile is back and toothier than ever. "It's nothing without this," it hardly wavers while he tells Angus.

Angus stretches his eyes and mouth wide and hauls the corners of his lips so high they start to tremble. "Welcome to Texts," he says, but so much of it is caught by the smile that he feels like a ventriloquist's doll.

"Not too bad. Practice every chance you get. You can rehearse whenever you're not on the sales floor," Woody says not just to Angus. "Now who's going to try to top him?"

Angus wonders if he's expected to maintain the smile while everyone else competes. When nobody volunteers he lets it go, and feels his face shrink as Woody says "Hey, it won't mean we're any less of a team. Helping each other improve makes you more of one."

Jake stretches his arms wide as if he's about to embrace Woody. "Welcome to Texts," he says in a voice he might use to seduce or be seduced, and simpers enough for both.

"You may want to tone it down a shade, but it wasn't that funny, Gavin. Let's see yours."

Gavin doesn't alter his smirk as he says "Welcome to Texts" with no emotion at all. Before Woody can comment, Jill says it as if she's offering a child a treat and follows it with an expectant smile she turns on Ross. She must want to encourage him, but when he repeats the formula his smile looks not too far from tears; Angus suspects he's remembering Lorraine. "Okay, it all needs work, especially the smiles," Woody says. "And once you've got it you need to have that attitude every moment of your day to every customer."

He searches their faces for it or mutiny before adding "I need one of you to take leaflets to all the stores. Who'll be fastest?"

Gavin opens his mouth, but Woody mustn't like his speed. "You can do it, Angus. Go now before we start losing people."

He means to the funeral. As Angus picks up a heap of leaflets from Connie's desk, Woody says "Why don't you leave them on the cars out there too. Okay, your time starts now."

Angus grabs his coat and struggles to struggle into it without putting down the leaflets. A notion that the smile is threatening to resurface on Woody's face makes him clumsier still. He drops the leaflets and dresses himself and gathers them again before fleeing to the stairs. He's emerging onto the sales floor when Agnes says from the ceiling "Assistance to counter, please. Assistance to counter."

She's issuing a gift voucher to a large woman with a small head balanced on several chins above the ruff of a chunky sweater. A man whose grey ponytail sprawls over the fur collar of his shabby astrakhan overcoat is waiting at Information. As Angus dodges behind the counter the man swings his wrinkled face to him, fingering the dimple in his chin. "Don't blame you wearing a coat in here, or were you getting out while the going's good?"

"Is it?" Angus says without knowing why.

"Fog's lifted a bit. Don't expect it's for long. Before you run, I'm Bob Sole. You've got a book for me at last."

As Angus ducks to the Customer Orders shelf he's aware of having forgotten to smile at Mr Sole, let alone welcome him. None of the tags the half a dozen books are sprouting bears Mr Sole's name. "Sorry, what was the book called?"

"It's *Commons and Canals of Cheshire*. Feller by the name of Bottomley wrote it. Adrian, if that's a help."

It doesn't seem to be. "Did someone say it was here?"

"You sent me a card." Mr Sole pulls it and a scattering of tobacco out of his pocket. "You won't mind me asking, but are you having a joke? This is the second time I've ordered it, and your mate I asked for it last time seemed to think something was a laugh."

Angus remembers Gavin saying in the staffroom that they had a customer called R. Sole. At once he hopes he won't smile after all or unleash a sound to go with it. He hides as much of his face as he can by leaning over the card Mr Sole deals with a snap onto the counter. Seizing the phone lets Angus keep his face averted. He's about to summon help when Woody says in his ear "Not on your mission yet? What's the problem?"

"We're supposed to have an order but I can't find it." Angus is suddenly terrified of how he may react if he's asked for the customer's name, until Woody says "I'm guessing it's *Commons and Canals of Cheshire*."

"That's it, but how—"

"I have it here in my office. Tell the customer I'm bringing it right now."

Angus feels safe in hitching up his lips as he turns to Mr Sole. "The manager's on his way with it for you."

He has scarcely replaced the receiver when Woody darts out of the exit to the staffroom. Mr Sole swings around in the midst of a smell of stale astrakhan to peer at the thin drab book in Woody's hand. "Making sure it wouldn't stray this time, were you?"

"Just glancing through it while we had it," Woody smiles.

"Much about this neck of the woods?"

"Nothing I'd call important," Woody says and turns so fast that Angus is uncertain whether his smile had already begun to vanish. "I'm handling this. You shouldn't still be here."

"Oh, right, that's right," Angus gabbles, which brings to an end the sympathetic look Agnes was considering on his behalf. He fumbles the leaflets off the counter and clutches them to his bosom as he dashes out of the shop.

The sun has made no headway against the fog. If anything, a sourceless dazzle aggravates the blindness that has erased most of the retail park. Vague folds of it waver on the tarmac like the skirts of a vast sluggish dancer. They must be why Angus feels he's being paced when he leaves Woody's stare through the window behind. As he dodges into Happy Holidays, a sodden grey veil is drawn over the far end of Texts.

Two girls in yellow sweaters with a large H on each breast are playing noughts and crosses behind the counter. Both raise their heads with eagerness that looks not unlike surprise, and the even blonder and slimmer girl says "Where can we fly you off to?"

"I'm not going anywhere just now. We wondered next door if you'd mind taking some of our leaflets."

"Don't bother wasting many." As he drops about a dozen on the counter she says "That's more customers than we've had all week."

Angus leaves the girls with a version of Woody's smile as he backs out, but it seems not to impress them much. The fog has beaten a mindlessly mocking retreat far enough to reveal an old Skoda out beyond the splintered tree-stump. He makes for the car in case Woody notices it hasn't been leafleted. He lifts one creaky windscreen wiper and plants a leaflet under it, and is retreating towards the fog that has descended on the pavement when a voice behind him calls "What's that you've stuck on my car?"

He skids around to glimpse a tall figure through the undamaged pair of trees. The figure blurs and almost vanishes on the way to tramping past the stretch of grass. The man is wearing white trainers, green trousers, a scraped leather jacket dangling several tatters, a black woollen hat from beneath which tufts of white hair are in the process of escaping. His small mottled face does its best to draw together around its swollen pockmarked nose as he bends his lanky form towards the car. "Oh, it's you," he says even more flatly than his Lancashire accent entails. "You were after me."

"Who was?"

"Your lot here. Texts. Doesn't look as if it would have been worth the effort."

"Why wouldn't it?" Angus is provoked into demanding.

The man peels off the leaflet and squeezes it into a dripping wad that he shies onto the grass, where it lands with a plop. "What's a readin group?"

"A . . ." A glance at the topmost leaflet in his hand shows Angus what the man has in mind. "It's, it's like a read-in. Where you read."

"Nice try, son, but too late. Carry on then, spread the mistake around. That's how the language we've spent all these centuries building gets pulled down."

Angus can't think of a retort or a defence. "Why did you say we were after you?"

"I've written a few books. Part of one's the story of this place. Maybe that's why you thought I was worth having."

The fog wavers, and Angus feels as if the world has. "I think we've just sold one of your books, if you're . . ."

"Adrian Bottomley, that's me, for all it signifies. Not what you expected, eh?"

Is his attitude why he refused Connie's invitation? "Why didn't you want to sign books for us?"

"Nothing against your shop in particular. It's this whole place I can do without."

"So why are you here now?"

"Maybe selling a book was such an event I thought I'd better be here," Bottomley says, then relents. "Didn't like what I heard happened."

"What was that?" Angus asks and feels worse than stupid. "Lorraine, you mean?"

"If she's the girl that was run over. Don't like to think of anyone dying here."

Angus stares about and sees nothing except two and a quarter trees in a strip of sodden grass surrounded by a walled-in patch of tarmac. "Why specially here?"

Bottomley lowers his head and butts the air in the direction of Angus's leaflets. "Aren't you supposed to be spreading the word?"

Angus considers taking them back to point out the error, but he doesn't want to make trouble for Connie. Since nobody else has noticed the omission of a letter, it seems best not to draw attention to it—can't they pretend it was intentional if they need to? "Will you come round with me while I do?" he asks Bottomley.

"Don't you want to be out here on your own? Can't say I'm surprised after everything that's gone on."

"I was hoping you'd tell me."

"Someone ought to know," Bottomley admits, and abruptly heads for the pavement. "Come to think," he mutters, "someone has to."

His tone leaves Angus unsure how to take that or even whether it was addressed to him. Bottomley says nothing more on the way to TVid, where a bloated woman and a thin unshaven man with blistered arms are screaming at each other in a turned-down murmur on a therapy show. As the audience jeers and boos, one of the pair of staff who are laughing at the spectacle glances at Angus, who asks "Can I put some of these on your counter?"

"Do what you like with them," he says as he sees where they've come from. "Did you sort out your hooligan tape?"

"Which was that?"

"Some mob fighting on a video that was meant to be music. Your manager looked like he could kill whoever messed it up."

Angus is dropping a handful of leaflets on the counter when Bottomley enquires "Don't you want to read what he's leaving in your shop?"

The assistant who seems to do all the talking grabs one and examines it for a few seconds before slapping it back on the heap. "Looks all right to me."

"Will it have to do, then?" Bottomley might as well not have said. As he tramps out and Angus follows him the televisions raise a derisive cheer, a blurred inarticulate voice emerging from more than a dozen mindless orifices. Outside he turns on Angus. "So what do you know about this place?"

"Not really anything except my job."

Angus adds the latter half in the hope that will give Bottomley less reason to scowl, but the author's expression doesn't soften as he says "You didn't get anything out of my book."

"I never had a chance to read it."

"You and the world, son." Without relinquishing his bitterness he says "Only you might think you'd want to know where you're giving so much of your life to. Do you know why it's called what it's called at least?"

"I don't."

The apologetic answer fails to win him over. Angus doesn't understand why he brought up the name of the shop, but Bottomley finds nothing else to say as they continue their trek. In Teenstuff a manager is overseeing two assistants as they change displays around. In Baby Bunting the mob of dolls with identical sketches of faces in the window have begun to look dusty, and the two visible members of staff are playing My First Computer Game, while next door in Stay in Touch the workers seem to be having difficulty using mobile phones. Bottomley rests an increasingly dissatisfied stare on Angus whenever he repeats "Can I put some of these on your counter?" He must think changing the words of his formula makes him more literate and superior to Angus—"Aren't you going to see what they say?" and "I'd check what he's giving you" and "Have a read first"—though the variety seems to afford him little pleasure. As they emerge yet again into the fog, which appears to have gained more substance from the energy it's sucking down from the unseen sun, he strides at it as though he's bent on confronting it or driving it off. He reminds Angus of a grandfather trying to chase a bad child. After several paces he stumbles to a halt and gasps "Keeping the gangs away now, is it?"

"I expect one did this." Angus points at the graffiti that have grown like deformed ivy over the unoccupied shopfronts. "And we've had children messing up the shop. Maybe it was one who stole the car and did what you heard about."

"Not the same." Bottomley's impatience leaves sympathy behind. "I'm talking about gangs that used to meet here for a fight till the buildings went up. You'd wonder what brought them here from miles round, wouldn't you? Or maybe you wouldn't, not being from round here."

"I can't say I'm as local as you," Angus retorts.

"You might have learned a bit of history at school, all the same. Do you know how many battles there've been here, not just fights?" When Angus shakes his head in what feels like an unsuccessful attempt to stir his brain, Bottomley wags two fingers at him. "Civil War and before that with the Romans," he says and returns the fingers to a fist he continues to brandish. "And between them there were villages here, in the Middle Ages and a couple of centuries later they had another go. Make you wonder anything?"

Angus feels shut into his dullness by the interrogation and the walls on both sides of him, crawling with moisture and graffiti to his right, quivering sky-high on his left. "Such as . . ." he says in case that hides his ignorance.

"Fair dos, maybe you're not wondering. Maybe you've worked out what happened to the villages."

"Fog like this?" Angus suggests as if he's a child desperate to please a teacher.

"Keep going. We were speaking about it before."

"Battles, you mean."

"If you want to call them that," says Bottomley, but Angus has somehow forfeited his patience. "There was plenty of violence, that's for definite."

"Let's hope we've seen the end of it."

"Hopeful type, are you? You look around the world and see us all getting on with one another."

"I thought we were talking about here."

"You're not telling me your lot don't have any differences. You can't believe there's no tribes any more."

"That doesn't mean there's violence."

"Said you weren't from round here," Bottomley declares and surges forward as though he can't bear him any longer. Angus has to follow him past the guards' hut, where a radio voice that sounds blurred beyond words is shouting through the sightless window, and into Frugo. As Angus makes for the nearest checkout girl, Bottomley lurches into the liquor aisle. "Can I put some of these on your counter, well, everyone's?" Angus asks.

"Never drink on an empty stomach," Bottomley seems to be advising anybody within earshot, and waves a finger at her. "Don't you want a look at those first?"

"What are you trying to give us?" She's halfway through peering at the topmost leaflet before her suspicion fades into indifference. "It's about some bookshop," she informs her colleagues. "Writers and reading and that kind of stuff."

"Put them with the papers," the adjacent girl suggests. "People read them."

From the supermarket entrance Bottomley takes time to include Angus in a despairing stare as the girl takes half his leaflets. Angus trails him to the last occupied property, Stack o' Steak. He's already seated at a table red as a plastic toy, and greets Angus with a cry of "Hey up, here comes literacy."

Neither of the staff outside the kitchen, both of whom sport orange T-shirts with So'S printed across their chests, appear to welcome this any more than Angus does, or Bottomley's question. "Can he put some of those on your counter?"

By now it has become such a ritual that Angus feels bound to produce the response. "Do you want to look them over first?"

The man he asked lowers his cropped skull so close to them that Angus is reminded of a feeding animal. "Don't see why not," he eventually tells Angus in a tone that also contains the opposite.

Angus isn't sure whom Bottomley's applause is meant for until the author asks him "Got the point at last?"

"I don't think so."

Bottomley gives up and turns to the second waiter, who is hairy only by the standards of the job. "How much do I need to eat to get a bottle of your house?"

"He can just have the bottle, can't he?" the man says in a voice like a shrug rendered vocal.

The author squints at a plastic menu half the size of the table he lets it drop on. "Tell you what, I'll have the white and a plate of Chunks o' Chicken."

Angus grows aware of being watched. No doubt the diner staff wonder why he's lingering. He can't leave until he has at least begun to understand. He hurries to the table and sits opposite Bottomley. "What point?" he pleads.

"Any chance of the bottle while I'm waiting? Just one glass." Having called that, he says nothing to Angus in the interim. He scowls at the glassful of wine he's brought and downs half of it before grumbling "A bottle and one glass, I meant." When he mutters after the waiter "Too many apostrophes round here" Angus takes the chance to respond. "Not only mine this time."

Bottomley peers at him. "Do they expect you to have any qualifications where you work?"

That sounds so insulting that Angus raises his voice to be heard by the staff of the diner. "I did three years at university."

"Well, bring on the trumpets. Three more than me then, son, and you still don't get the point. Go away and think about it. I mean go right away. Maybe that'll help."

Angus feels his spine pressing against the chair to push it back. He struggles not to give in to somebody for once. "You keep refusing to tell me things," he protests. "You said someone had to know."

"That's right, and they will. Whoever bought my book from you." With even more weary indifference he adds "That's if they can be bothered to read that far."

Angus watches him sink into his bitterness and imagines him pulling it over his head like a stale blanket. He can see no point in talking further to the author. He leaves him to the bottle the waiter has brought and hurries out. Swapping all the colours for the monochrome of fog and tarmac feels like starting to go blind. As he hurries back along the pavement, the window displays past the graffiti look faded by the murk. Nobody seems aware of him, yet he feels observed, a sensation at least as oppressive as the fog. He must be nervous of encountering Woody, he thinks as Woody emerges from the shop to say "Did you have enough for all the cars?"

"All the ones I saw."

The trick makes Angus feel the reverse of clever. He would mention Bottomley if he thought he'd learned anything worth telling. Instead he asks "What did you say was in that book about here?"

Woody stares at him while he comprehends the question or decides how to answer. "Just some history."

"Such as . . ." Angus forces himself to prompt.

"It was settled a couple of times."

Angus doesn't know why he feels Woody has managed to pay him back with a trick, unless it's guilt that he's experiencing. He hasn't thought of any further question when Woody says "Better scoot off to your shelving now. But listen, thanks for going out there and thanks for staying here this afternoon. Hey, that's exactly what we need to see. Keep that up."

"Keep what, sorry?"

"The smile."

Angus feels it cling to his lips and writhe like an insect. "That's nearly it," says Woody. "Work on it while you're in the stockroom."

Angus is retreating in that direction when Woody adds "Let's get through this afternoon and then we'll be back to normal." As Angus flees along one of Lorraine's aisles he wonders what Woody regards as normal. He's almost sure that he hears Woody's parting murmur, which seems to freeze to the nape of his neck, unless that's a breath of the fog. "Smile," Angus fancies Woody is repeating to him or to himself, and feels as if something has stretched an arm at least the length of the shop and closed its reptilian grasp around his mouth.

# GREG

**He has taken the fog into account, of course. It used to be a** leisurely twenty minutes' drive from Warrington to where the slip road for the retail park is now, but since his first visit to Texts, when he almost let himself down by arriving late for his interview, he has added seven—two more than five, to be safe. He brakes as soon as he sees fog basking in the afternoon sun on the motorway ahead. Some of the cars in front don't slow until the fog is almost thick enough to put their lights out, and none of them heads down to Fenny Meadows. He knows management couldn't have predicted how fog would settle in the area—it never did last winter when he used to drive past en route to work at the library in Manchester—but the world is changing to nobody's benefit. He'll keep that in mind if he's ever called upon to judge a location for a branch of Texts.

He's travelling at under thirty by the time he reaches the slip road. As he steers the Rover onto it a car on the motorway swings out to overtake, blurred both by speed and the murk. Greg braces himself to hear a screeching skid and an impact, and when neither penetrates the upholstered whitish air he nevertheless drops his speed to compensate. He coasts off the roundabout and cruises behind the unfinished buildings to Stack o' Steak, beside which a large grey dog or some wild creature about as tall is digging its face into a garbage bin. He would stop to focus on it and, more to the point, to suggest to whoever's in charge of the diner that they should make their rubbish secure from animals, but he has come to work early to release his colleagues for Lorraine's funeral. If they're going to insist on attending, it's only right that they should be punctual. It would be hypocritical of Greg to join them when Lorraine's attitude to the job couldn't have been more unlike his own. If he were a manager he might have felt required to put in an appearance, though he understands that Woody doesn't feel comfortable with leaving Greg's colleagues unsupervised in the shop. Greg did consider pointing out that he'll be there but doesn't want Woody to think him presumptuous.

Beyond Frugo he lets the fog dictate his pace, which gives him a chance to observe who's parked where. He doesn't recognise any of the very few cars in front of the shops as belonging to a workmate. He'd refrain from telling Woody if he did. Not only does Woody have enough to deal with, but Greg believes in giving people the opportunity to mend their ways; he always did when he was a school prefect, for minor offences at any rate. He drives behind Texts and parks alongside several vehicles beneath the name the fog has rendered invisible from the motorway. Briefcase in hand, he locks the steering wheel and then the Rover before marching around the shop.

Though the inside of the window is patched with grey, the patches aren't where he would like them to be. They don't obscure the three faces of Brodie Oates, three round smooth self-satisfied faces bunched like balloons on strings of bodies that aren't small enough, not when the one that isn't wearing a suit or a kilt is done up in a dress. All this isn't even Jake's doing, which might be understandable if certainly no more palatable. People like him can flaunt themselves all they want now, and nobody else is permitted to comment; it's the same sort of unfairness as Greg's father keeps objecting to—as he says, a fellow can't call a black fellow a black fellow any longer, but the black fellow can call a fellow any kind of fellow he likes. At least they aren't bound to have any on the staff at Texts, not like the library where Greg's parents work and he did. All it does is make people feel uncomfortable, robbed of words, because they no longer know what they're allowed to say. There again, what's to be said to Jill? Did she mean to shock people with her window or indulge in a sly joke? Greg wouldn't think anyone loyal to the shop would want to do either, and you ought to be as proud of your place of work as you were of your school. He is, and he means to keep it that way, even if that entails not always being liked by everyone. He got used to that at school.

As Greg passes between the security pillars the guard looks uncertain how to greet him. Was that a simper that's swallowed up by his flattened pugnacious face? "Good afternoon, Frank," Greg says to put him at his ease, and receives a grunt for his trouble. He strides under the false ceiling of music towards the staffroom and encounters Agnes pushing a trolley at no great speed into the Travel section. "Better put a smile on if you want to keep people happy," she tells him.

"None of us can do too much of that."

Her mouth takes on a shape like a smile reflected in stagnant water. "You sound just like him."

"If you're referring to Woody I'd call that a compliment."

The water Greg imagined seems to drag her mouth down further. "What are you doing here, anyway? You aren't due for nearly an hour."

"I thought I'd make sure you could do your duty by the funeral, those that are going. We don't want you being late when you're representing the shop."

"It isn't a duty, it's anything but. My God, she's only been dead a week." Agnes leaves her mouth open for a moment before adding "She was worth quite a few of some people here."

All she's achieving is to remind Greg how quarrelsome Lorraine was—indeed, Agnes is demonstrating how that has infected her—but he won't allow himself to be provoked. "Well," he says instead, "I think we'd both better be getting on with our work."

She seems ready to argue even about that, though he was careful to include himself. He almost fancies she has managed to incite the staffroom entrance to rebel; he has to show the plaque his badge twice to convince it he's authorised to enter. As the door clanks shut he runs upstairs to entrust his briefcase to his locker. He's sliding his staff card under the clock when Woody steps out of his office. "I thought someone was pretending to be you on the monitor," he says. "Why, you're nearly as early as me."

"I thought you might need me if we've got staff going off."

"That's the kind of guy we want," Woody tells Angus, who is crouching over the table and the remains of his lunch as though hoping not to be noticed. "Would you do anything for this place, Greg?"

"I'd like to think so."

"It isn't asking much, is it, Angus? Why don't you show him. You're top dog so far."

For a moment Angus seems worse than reluctant. Greg is wondering if he has caught the attitude Lorraine appears to have bequeathed to Agnes when Angus twists around to face him. The sides of his mouth strain upwards as if they've been pierced by invisible hooks. "Welcome to Texts," he mumbles.

His expression is more desperate than welcoming, and his voice falls short of both. "Hey, you did better before," Woody cries. "See how special you can make me feel, Greg."

Greg would do his best for him and Texts even if Woody's eyes didn't look raw with pressure. "Welcome to Texts," he says with his biggest smile and holds out his hand as well.

"You need to match that, Angus. We don't want anyone taking

the lead, do we? You can show the others how it's done, Greg, and that's how you greet every customer that comes through the door. The hand too, I like that. Just one more thing—whenever you talk to a customer, recommend a book."

"Any in particular?" Greg asks, since Angus has found some lunch to duck towards.

"Whichever excites you. Everything's good or we wouldn't sell it. I shouldn't tell you what to like."

Greg thinks Woody might guide people to the heights more than the depths; surely as a manager he has to have taste. Perhaps Greg can bring that up next time they're alone—it isn't for any of the other staff to hear. He's wondering whether he should remind Angus that his lunchtime must be close to over when Woody says "Okay, Greg, so long as you're extra right now, will you be Lorraine?"

Angus clears his throat so loud that he silences everyone. Greg suspects it's only because that's drawn attention to him that Angus mutters "Nobody can. There's just one of everyone."

"You must know Woody's asking me to shelve her books."

"Glad at least one of you understands what I'm saying."

Greg hurries into the stockroom, not least to avoid watching Woody rub his eyeballs redder still. Nevertheless he would be tempted to fetch him if it weren't obvious that Woody has more than enough on his mind. Whoever sorts new stock onto the racks is supposed to deposit each person's share of Lorraine's books on their lowest shelf—Nigel wrote tags to help them—but not only has somebody dumped them in any space they could find in Greg's storage, they've given him books on sculpture that are Jake's responsibility, naked smooth male figures Greg is certain will delight him. Here's an armful of photography collections too, which are up to Wilf to file once he recovers from the headache he claimed Brodie Oates' novel gave him until it was time to go home, as if being made to feel sick by the affront the book represents were an excuse for anyone to fall behind in their work. Whoever dumped the stock on Greg's racks seems to have needed a wash; when he's finished wiping the books as he transfers them, his handkerchief looks grubby as a schoolboy's. The volumes that belong on his racks appear to be cleaner, but that doesn't mean he's in favour of all of them: what kind of customer would want an anthology of paintings called *Even Monsters Dream* that's wrapped in a picture of Hitler asleep? As Greg sorts the books onto a trolley he tries to find some he can recommend. Nudes could be embarrassing, abstract art means less than nothing to him, surrealism always strikes him as a symptom of a mental state that can be treated nowadays—a pity the painters couldn't apply their technique to a better end. He settles on a book of English landscape paintings. Landscapes never harmed anyone, he reflects as he rushes the trolley out of the stockroom.

The lift wastes time by crawling upwards and then murmuring about opening before it does. He commits the trolley to it and hurries downstairs to await it rather than risk tracking mud into the shop from the shapeless footprints someone was inconsiderate enough to leave in the lift, such a tangle of marks they suggest some kind of dance. Either the offender or someone more dependable must have wiped the lobby clean of the rest of the footprints. Greg hauls the trolley forth as soon as the lift sets it free. He's guiding it onto the sales floor when the phones begin to ring.

Nobody else seems eager to respond. Ross is behind the counter, but he's staring at the fog. The others are shelving—at least, Jill is, though she could be quicker. Gavin is busy stifling yet another of the yawns Greg thinks management should take up with him, and Agnes hasn't even finished putting the books on her trolley in order. Greg speeds his to the phone next to the Teenage alcove. "Welcome to Texts at Fenny Meadows," he says for his colleagues to hear as well. "Greg speaking. How may I help?"

"Is Annie there?"

For a moment Greg wonders if somebody has infiltrated the shop, and then he understands. "May I ask who's calling?"

"Her father."

"And could you tell me what it's concerning?"

"We just want to know she's safe."

"Perfectly. I'm looking at her."

"Only a friend of the family drove past there earlier and he says the fog's worse than ever."

"He ought to have paid us a visit and seen how much we have to offer. Don't worry, the fog hasn't prevented any of us from coming to work."

"Could I have a swift word with Annie?"

"Is it something I can deal with? I don't know whether she'll have told you personal calls aren't really on except in an emergency."

Greg should have thought to look away from her. As her father says "Forgive me. If you could tell her—" she deserts her trolley and stalks over. "Who's that? Is it for me?"

"Excuse me one moment," Greg says into the mouthpiece, which he covers with his palm. "It's your father. As you're aware, the shop doesn't like us to—"

"It can't like or dislike anything. It's just a place, you silly prat." While snarling this she grabs the phone. "Give it to me. Let go," she says even more harshly and digs her nails into the back of his hand.

Her violence does more than shock him; it makes him want to hurt her worse. If she can't behave like a lady she shouldn't expect to be treated like one. He's about to seize her fingers and twist them against one another until she cries, the way he used to deal with juniors he didn't take to the headmaster, when he realises Woody may be watching. "You'll regret that," he murmurs with a smile into her face before yielding the phone to her.

She's already pretending to be unaware of him. As he wheels the trolley into Lorraine's section, Agnes says "Yes, daddy, I'm here." Once she can't see what he's doing he presses the back of his hand against the end of the trolley. The wood is cold, but is it also moist or is that Greg? It doesn't squeeze much of the sting out of his hand. The recurring discomfort slows him down, which means he hasn't shelved nearly as many books as he would like by the time Agnes finishes whispering into the phone and comes for him. "Don't you ever do that again," she says as low.

"I rather think I'm the one who should be issuing a warning."

"If you interfere between me and my family ever again I'll do a whole lot worse. Who the hell do you think you are?"

"Someone who believes the shop's entitled to expect the standard of behaviour it's paying us for."

"For once we're agreed about something. The amount they pay us, they needn't expect much."

"If management could hear you they'd think"—he glances away from shelving to underline his words with a look—"you're soliciting on behalf of a union."

"They wouldn't want one knowing about our pay and conditions, you mean? Maybe you wouldn't either."

"We knew what we were offered when we signed up. We don't need a union to set people against one another and undermine the shop."

"Have you any idea what a prig you sound, Greg? Don't you realise it just makes people laugh at you?"

"I wonder which those might be. I'd think more might be laughing at how you pronounce yourself."

Greg is hardly conscious of his words by now. Only the flares of pain on the back of his hand keep him volleying retorts at her. He's concentrating on the shelves so hard he doesn't notice they have company until Woody speaks. "What's the situation here? I don't see any smiles."

Greg produces one and has to remind himself not to welcome Woody aloud. Agnes persists in most of the grimace with which she acknowledged Woody's presence and mutters "Don't see any customers either."

"I guess that ought to change now Angus has spread the word." Woody heightens his eyebrows to swell his eyes, exposing yet more red, and to turn his smile interrogative. "I still need to hear why you were arguing."

Agnes glares a challenge at Greg, which proves she's foolish not to know him better. "My colleague thinks we ought to join a union," he tells Woody.

"How's that going to help the store?"

"You want us smiling, don't you?" Agnes demands. "Maybe then we'd have more reason."

"Isn't working here enough? It is for me."

Woody's smile has grown wistful enough to be pleading. Greg is about to conclude that it has succeeded in quelling the rebellion when Agnes turns on him. "Finished snitching?"

"Since you bring it up, perhaps you should let Woody hear what I had to remind you about."

"I don't care who tells me but they better make it quick."

Greg is disappointed that Woody seems to be classing him with Agnes. "I'm afraid I had to point out you don't approve of personal phone calls to the shop."

"The store doesn't, sure enough."

Greg senses that any number of objections are competing to be first out of her mouth but doesn't anticipate hearing Agnes protest "What gives him the right to tell me? He's just one of the staff like me."

"Could be he'll be over you not too far into the future if he carries on the way he is. What was the call?"

Greg thinks her rage has silenced her, but she declares "My father."

"Was it urgent? Something that couldn't wait till you were home?"

"I don't suppose you'd think so."

"I'd appreciate you making sure it stays there from now on, then."

That strikes Greg as an amicable way of phrasing it, but Agnes confronts Woody with a wordless stare until he says "Are we killing time here or do you have more for me?"

"You're right, I oughtn't to be wasting time. You wouldn't want anyone from the shop to be late for the funeral, would you?"

She marches away without giving him a chance to answer. She's pushing her trolley towards the lift with more enthusiasm than she showed her books when Angus opens the door to the lobby. "Are you certain you don't want to say goodbye to Lorraine?" she asks, staring past him at Woody and Greg. "I'm sure management can hold the fort till we get back. It doesn't look as if there's going to be much for them to deal with."

"I think I'd better stay if you don't mind, just in case."

He hasn't finished speaking when she presents her back to him. "Time for everyone to go that's coming," she calls. "We don't want to rush in the fog."

Two men whose scalps appear to have engulfed most of their hair glance up from their armchairs and the children's book each is holding open in his lap. They seem to wonder if Agnes is including them. "I'm driving everyone," she informs Woody.

"Sounds like you are, sure enough."

Greg smiles to indicate he understands the quip. As Agnes disappears into the lobby he returns to his shelving. Woody approaches the seated men to ascertain what kinds of books they like, but has elicited only "Don't know" and "No" by the time Agnes leads her troop through the shop. "We'll be back as soon as we can," Jill assures Woody while Agnes remains defiantly mute.

Once Ross and the women nobody's allowed to call girls any longer have passed the window, Greg strains his ears to judge where Agnes is parked. He sees the same question has occurred to Woody, who darts out of the shop. Four car doors slam, muffled by the fog, and as he becomes part of the murk the vehicle outdistances him. A grey breath precedes him into the shop as though he's full of fog. "That wasn't in back," he announces, Greg assumes more to him than to Angus, to whom Woody then turns. "And you missed one."

He snatches a handful of leaflets from the counter and hurries out once more. Greg takes himself to be left in charge and does his best to stay aware of his surroundings while he works. Is one of the seated men muttering, or are both of them making a surreptitious noise? As well as the thin wintry chatter of Vivaldi overhead Greg is convinced he hears an underlying motif, voices that keep collapsing into a single voice and then parting while they struggle to speak or chant or produce some other sound. He would ask the men to be quiet if there were any other customers, though Angus seems unaware of what they're doing and of a good deal else. He has abandoned the counter to tidy his shelves, and Greg is about to remind him that the tills always have to be manned during opening hours when the phone saves Angus. He sets out for the counter, but Greg is faster to the extension by Teenage. "Welcome to Texts at Fenny Meadows. Greg speaking. How—"

"Is the boss about?"

Greg doesn't know if it's ruder of the man to interrupt or to imply that Greg sounds nothing like a manager. "May I ask—"

"It's his landlord."

That does rather change the situation. "Angus, can you see Woody?" Greg calls.

Angus sidles to the end of the window display and leans towards the glass, to be met by a grey swelling wider than his head—his breath. The seated men swivel their dull eyes as if they think Greg spoke to them, and Frank goes as far as peering out of the entrance. "No," Angus admits, echoed by the guard.

"Do you think you might consider going a bit further, Frank?" When the guard takes him literally, if he even does that, Greg manages to contain his frustration. "He doesn't seem to be available at the moment," he tells the phone. "May I take a message?"

"I'd just love to be able to find him in."

"He should be here for hours once he gets back."

"In the house he's meant to be renting from me."

Greg hesitates for only a second; it's surely his duty to ask. "Is there some problem with payment?"

"None of that. His bank's not let me down. I like to see my tenants are comfy, that's all."

"Shall I ask him to ring you?"

"That'd be a start."

Presumably the landlord has no further comment to make before static that sounds like an uprush of water sweeps away his voice. When the static sinks into the dialling tone Greg reverts to shelving. He repatriates a pair of stray books—a guide to sketching, with a scribble on the cover for a face, a watercolour manual that falls open at daubs hardly more than graffiti—and tries to make up the time they cost. At least now he hears only the pinched twittering of violins, and he won't let Angus distract him by keeping a watch on the fog. Is he looking out for customers or Woody? The rest of the staff will have gone straight to the funeral. Greg falls to speculating which of them the shop could manage without: Connie and her brittle insistence on treating everything lightly, Nigel and his faint grin that seems to invite every situation to amuse him, Ray with his football emblems that have no place in the shop, Madeleine acting as if her section is the only one that matters . . . Greg has unloaded one side of the trolley by the time Woody reappears. "Was I long?" he says with a smile that hopes not.

"I shouldn't think so," Angus says.

Perhaps Woody senses as Greg does that Angus is too eager to please. "I guess more cars must have shown up since you were out."

"That'll be it," Angus says quicker still.

Greg waits until Woody turns his smile aside from Angus. "There was a call for you."

"Nothing like feeling wanted, huh? What do I need to do?"

Greg assumes he'd prefer Angus and the men not to hear about his business. "Should we talk privately?"

"Do you think? Okay, sure." Woody's smile seems to urge them both towards the delivery lobby, and grows wider and fiercer as he has to slap the plaque on the wall twice with his badge. When the exit defers to him he mutters "It wasn't her again, was it?"

"It wasn't a lady."

"I wouldn't call her that any longer." He jabs a fist at the door to help it shut and faces Greg. "So who's after me?"

"Your landlord."

"Is that right?" For a moment his smile appears uncertain of its own meaning. "What did he say to you?"

"Just that he's kept missing you at your house. He only wants to check you've got everything you'd like."

"That isn't much. I believe I have, sure enough. I must have been here when he came visiting."

Greg's aware that Woody works longer hours than anyone else at the shop. He's wondering if it would be presumptuous of him to say so when a question leaves his mouth instead. "Has someone come back?"

There's movement in the stockroom; it sounds as if books are being fumbled off the shelves. "Somebody's upstairs," he hisses.

"Think so? We'll soon see," Woody says and shoves past him to dash up the stairs. Greg is so thrown by his rudeness that he doesn't know whether to follow, and then he sees that if anyone has sneaked in, his job is to head off their escape. He sprints out of the lobby and past the children's section to the door up to the staffroom. He releases it with his badge and closes it even more softly before tiptoeing upstairs.

Someone must have decided they owed more loyalty to the shop than to the funeral, because Greg can hear a shuffling of books. How did the person manage to return unobserved by him or Woody? By the time he gives up stealth and hurries into the stockroom nobody is to be seen, not even Woody. A rack jangles faintly and settles down, but Greg isn't about to imagine that anybody has squeezed into hiding behind the books. He's tiptoeing again while he strains to identify a noise, a repetitious mutter—a voice chanting somewhere ahead. It isn't in the empty staffroom, nor the office Ray and Nigel and Connie share. It's in Woody's room.

As Greg crosses the shared office he ignores the sight of himself shrinking into the blank screens, a manikin multiplied by three and sucked down into murk. Woody's door is carelessly ajar, and he's sitting with his back to it. All four quarters of the security monitor appear to be occupied by the same image, a close-up of part of a face, unless the face is so large that just a fraction of its loose swollen-lipped grey-toothed grin fills the screen in fragments. It must be a reflection of the fluorescent tube overhead, because as soon as Greg steps into the office the image resolves into four views of the sales floor. One shows Angus gazing morosely across the shop at the seated men, and at last Greg hears what Woody's muttering. "Keep smiling," he repeats. "Keep smiling."

"Shall I tell him when I go down?"

"You bet," Woody says, and his smile twirls to face Greg as his chair swings round. "You're the man to remind him."

"I couldn't find anyone in the stockroom."

"You and me both. Just some books fell down."

Very occasionally, such as now, Greg might feel Woody's smile is inappropriate. "Not shelved properly, you mean?" he feels he should emphasise.

"Couldn't have been."

"Do we know whose fault it was?"

"Couldn't say."

"So long as they weren't damaged."

"You're my kind of guy, Greg. You make me feel I'm doing it the way it should be done. Don't worry, everything's going to be perfectly fine once we're all shut in for the night tomorrow."

He sends his smile after Greg and then pivots to watch the monitor. Greg wishes he could think of more to say, but perhaps Woody meant to assure him that he has said enough. He feels as if he has been favoured with a hint of the pressure Woody's under, which is tantamount to a mute appeal for support. Woody doesn't need to ask aloud. As Greg heads back to his shelving and to remind Angus how to look, he needn't remember to keep smiling, because he already is. That comes from being clear in his own mind. He won't allow Agnes or anything else to muddy his motives, and he'll be keeping what he's learned about Woody to himself. He's here for Woody and the shop.

# GAVIN

As the earliest bus out of Manchester for Liverpool drags the last of its glow across Gavin, the night gathers on him like ice. There's no sign of civilisation around the bus shelter in the lay-by except a mile of road in three directions. The one he needs is the winding lane boxed in by hedges behind the shelter. He has tramped less than a hundred yards when the spiky twigs close around the illuminated refuge, and he's alone with the charcoal dusk before dawn.

He's coming down from E, and the speed it must have been cut with hasn't quite worn off. It's lending him energy and toying with the possibility that his mind and everything around him are about to flicker into a different state. Nobody is hammering a lump of metal; that's the sound of his feet in the lane. He isn't hemmed in by tangles of grey ice, they're hedges creaking like it on either side of him. Is he really glimpsing a muted twinkle of frost on the road? The chittering mixed with a shrill clatter is a bird flying out of undergrowth. The stale cold breaths that keep finding his face aren't emerging from a mouth that's waiting to swallow the sun, they're winds impregnated with fog. It, more than his progress, is delaying the bloodshot dawn ahead, which is one reason why he knows he's approaching Fenny Meadows. He might tell someone if there was anyone he thought he could that the fog tastes different around the retail park, not just stagnant and faintly decaying but with an indefinable underlying flavour so sly as to be virtually imperceptible. In that case, how can he be sure it's there? All he knows is that it seems a fraction more apparent every day he comes to work and that it puts him in mind of an extra drug in a tab that's supposed to be pure. He doesn't even know which drug, if any that he has ever sampled. Perhaps it's mostly the stubborn fog that makes his exposed skin grow clammy and begin to crawl as he comes in sight of the entrance to the retail park.

Someone has been walking a dog on the grass around the edge of Fenny Meadows, or several dogs. The prints must have frozen and melted and frozen again; they might as well be shapeless, despite conveying the impression that they're determined to take shape. Do they lead all the way around the outside of the retail park? He can't see why it should matter, except that as he crosses the hardened mud bristling with tufts of grass behind Frugo he realises the mistake he made. The marks he thought a pet or pets had left are the size of human footprints, if not nearly the shape, and the ones he took for the owner's are several times as large. They must have been made by some machinery while the shops were being built, and have become misshapen since. The undertaste of the fog seems to rise from his sore jaw to fasten something like electricity on his brain until he stops staring at the prints and heads past Frugo onto the car park.

He knows his way across, however foggy it becomes. If the tarmac feels soft and not entirely stable underfoot, that's because hours of dancing under the jagged light at the club and his tramp along the lane haven't entirely worn off. He just has to dodge from one stand of trees to the next, four token plantations before he should be in sight of Texts. His lack of sleep must be catching up with him: the trees nearest Frugo look swollen, only very gradually losing weight as the fog that blurs them appears to drain into them rather than retreating. The trees beyond them start out even greyer and fatter, and their fleshy appearance seems to sink into the patch of grass. Gavin doesn't like that much, thought it's preferable to the sight of the third clump shuddering as if they're ridding themselves of a jellyish greyness that vanishes into the mud. They must be shifting in the wind that urges fog at him as he sprints towards the last excuse for a grove. A few dead leaves fly to meet him as well, a couple landing on his sleeve while the rest settle on the tarmac so stealthily he peers at them. They're clenched empty spiders, or is he hallucinating? To end up that size they would have been bigger than his hand when they were alive. The taste of the fog wavers through his head as he shakes off whatever's clinging to his sleeve. He hurries past the tree Mad's car cut down, but why is he hurrying? His watch shows that nobody is due at Texts for a quarter of an hour. Then a layer of fog peels away from the shopfront, letting him see through the bleary window a figure scurrying down an aisle and brandishing a weapon.

Even when he identifies Woody, Gavin thinks he's chasing someone and about to club them unconscious or worse. It's only after Woody has wagged the object gleefully above his head as he parts two books with his free hand and inserts his burden into the space on the shelf that Gavin understands it's a book. By then Woody has caught sight of him. His smile is beyond magnification, but his eyes bulge with a greeting as he runs to open the door. "Hey, Gavin," he cries through the glass. "Thinking you could beat me?"

"Beat you at what?"

"Say again?"

Now that the door is open the question doesn't seem worth repeating, but Woody smiles at him until he mutters "Beat you at what?"

"At nothing. To the worm. Anyone behind you?"

Once Gavin grasps that he's being asked if he has arrived by himself he says "Nobody I know of."

All the same, Woody turns his smile on the fog for several breaths that resemble drifts of it before he shuts the door, which tolls like an underground bell. Gavin is beginning to wish he'd taken more time on the road but feels compelled to ask "Did you say something about a worm?"

"The one the early bird gets. You have to eat a few worms if you're going to fly."

Gavin is making for the staffroom in the hope he'll be leaving that idea behind when Woody says "Take a moment. You can be the first to see."

Gavin swings around to be confronted by Woody's smile and his breath, which is continuing to mimic fog. "See what?"

"Don't you notice any difference?"

He's staring past Gavin, who has to turn his back on him. At the far end of the aisles the children's section looks almost imperceptibly drained of its colours and possibly not quite in focus, as though a trace of the fog he can still taste has reached it. He doesn't think this is what Woody is eager for him to notice—so eager that he senses Woody's expression like a hint of teeth resting on the nape of his neck. He squints harder at the children's books and at the aisles that lead to them. "It's all tidy."

"Nearly all. I'll be through by the time we open. I wanted to show you guys how the store can look, how it needs to every morning from now on. If I can fix it by myself a bunch of you sure can."

"How long did it take you?"

"Twice as long as a pair of you, three times as long as a whatever you want to call it, what do you, doesn't matter, three. You do the math."

Gavin doesn't care about the answer but will feel stupid if he doesn't make his point clear. "How much sleep have you had?"

"Enough or I wouldn't be standing here, right? Once we're through tonight we'll all have a chance to sleep."

Does he think Gavin needs to be told that? Gavin feels close to overdosing on Woody's intensity—he doesn't know if the man looks more like an evangelist or a clown. When Woody pounces on another book to relocate with smiling vehemence, Gavin heads for the staffroom. He's just here to do the job he's paid for and to have some fun if he can find it along the way.

The plaque by the exit insists on being shown his badge twice. The delay gathers like a storm cloud in his head. Frustration or the last of the speed sends him up the stairs without treading on half of them. He shoves the staffroom door aside and snatches his card from the Out rack. He slides the card under the clock and drops it in In, and is considering awakening the percolator when he hears a flurry of activity. Footsteps are hurrying upstairs, though for a second he thinks their approach has blotted out another movement, softer and of no shape he can define. Was it in the stockroom? It has gone now, and he tells himself it couldn't have been there as the door by the clock admits Nigel and Mad. To his bewilderment, both the clock and his watch show they're on time, and Woody is following as if he has herded them upstairs. "No need to sit down," he says. "This won't take long."

Nigel's mouth droops open as though having his shift meeting hijacked is no joke. "Here's how we do it starting now," says Woody. "Why doesn't everyone try to be the best at something to do with the store, your choice." His smile barely slackens while he adds "Come up with it while you're working. Gavin, you man the. counter for an hour unless Madeleine wants to woman it."

"He can have it," Mad says without humour. "I expect my section's needing me as usual."

Gavin feels as if he has inadvertently antagonised her. He heads for the stairs as much to escape a sense of being trapped as to start work. He hasn't reached the bottom when Woody darts after him. "Okay, I'm not hounding you," Woody says.

He's hurrying to open the shop. His haste seems pointless, since he lets in nothing but a surge of fog that immediately vanishes. The absence of customers may be why Mad doesn't restrain herself at the sight of the children's section. "Well, thank you, whoever you were," she cries close to the top of her voice.

"That would have been me," Woody calls.

"I doubt it. I hope not."

"Where are you seeing a problem?"

"Where aren't I? Take a look."

Gavin doesn't see why that shouldn't include him; there are no customers for the counter to be guarded from. He follows Woody to the Teenage bay, where Mad is staring at the books and gripping her hipbones with her splayed fingers. When Woody swings around he seems ready to order Gavin back to the counter, but then he says "See anything out of place? If you do you're a better man than me."

Gavin finds his having to take sides makes his skin tingle while his mouth recalls the stagnant taste of the fog. "Sorry, Mad," he's forced to admit. "It looks fine to me."

"Maybe it's something men can't see," Woody offers, and a smile as well.

Mad isn't won over by either. "What's that meant to mean, I'm seeing things?"

"Maybe it's the time."

"I don't know about anyone else, but I'm wide awake."

Woody tilts his head leftward and slits his eyes, a pose that he appears to think renders his smile apologetic. "Time of the month. The girl I used to be with—"

"Keep it to yourself," Mad says so fiercely and unblinkingly that he retreats a step. "Looks like men aren't welcome right now," he murmurs.

Gavin is even less inclined to side with him, but Mad turns her back as if he has. He leaves Woody observing her and retreats to the counter. At least the shop has attracted customers; two squat figures are plodding across the car park. They're past the splintered stump, which grows mouldy with fog and then merges with it, before

Gavin is certain they're the two men who have spent he doesn't know how many days in armchairs in the shop. As they shamble through the entrance he dons his wildest grin. "Welcome to Texts," he enthuses. "Can I recommend *Dance Till You Drop* by D J E?"

He couldn't do this if he didn't find it hilarious, but Woody can't object to the recommendation, since they do stock the disc jockey's memoirs. Gavin's grin is threatening to own up to a giggle by the time the men finish frowning wordlessly at him and stump off to Tiny Texts. Mad doesn't conceal her distrust as she watches them. When they each select a copy of the same picture book for infants without disarranging its neighbours she shakes her head, perhaps at herself. As the men sink into armchairs, which emit creaks like frogs exchanging calls, she raises her hands beside her shoulders, though Gavin doesn't think she's blessing anyone. "All right, maybe it's me," she says and heads for the stockroom.

It sounds less like an admission than some kind of accusation of whatever has confused her. Gavin used to think she took the same attitude as he does to the job—have fun wherever you can find it and make fun of the rest to yourself—but she hasn't shown much of that lately. When Woody dodges through the gap as the door closes after her, Gavin wishes he'd taken the chance to let her know he's on her side. At least she has to realise he's not like Woody's pet Greg.

He leans on the counter to watch how long it takes either of the seated men to turn a page. One rouses Gavin's hopes by pinching a corner crablike between a finger and thumb, but then he releases it. In perhaps no more than a couple of minutes his friend takes hold of a corner so as to let it drop. Gavin doesn't notice that their lethargy is dictating his pace until Mad reappears with a trolley full of books. He's about to find some way of appearing to be busy, in case Woody is observing him from upstairs and doesn't think Gavin looks as though he's pondering how he can excel, when Woody emerges from the delivery lobby and pushes a loaded trolley over to Animals. "Here's half your stock that's waiting to be put out," he tells

Gavin through a smile his words leave behind. "You'll be close enough to the counter."

Is it his lack of sleep that's compelling Gavin to examine every cover before he shelves the book? By the time he has finished in Pets he feels as if his head is full of eyes gazing up in stupid worship. In Zoology he has the notion of reorganising the volumes in the order opposite to evolution, but why? It's a good job he has no books on amoebas, or he might. Before he has unburdened the trolley of many more volumes he doesn't know if he's filing them or supporting himself on them. He has never been so glad to see the next shift arrive.

Greg bows Connie and Agnes in, though there's room between the security pillars for all three, then sends his voice after at least one of them. "Glad to see I'm not the only person who's eager."

"What are you saying you're eager for, Greg?" Connie wants to know, unless she's pretending.

"Work, of course." He seems genuinely—Gavin would say stupidly—unaware that she could have meant anything else. "You'll have given yourself time for parking, Agnes."

"My car's not in my handbag if that's what you're asking."

"You know what I'm getting at. It's where we're supposed to park."

"It's where it is right enough."

"I'm asking if it's round the back. I'm putting you on your honour."

"I'm not even going to answer you, Greg."

Her stare does that. When she glances at Connie for agreement with her disbelief, however, Connie says "He is right really. No point in arguing over something this silly."

Agnes looks betrayed. "I'm parked where I feel safe and that's where I'm staying," she tells anyone who cares to hear, and stalks off to the staffroom.

Gavin wants to giggle to himself at the pompous pettiness of it, but the confrontation has revived an unwelcome taste in his mouth.

Greg and Connie follow her upstairs, but Greg reappears almost at once. "I'll take over at the counter, Gavin," he says as if Gavin should have stayed there. "I'm sure you'll need to catch up on your sleep for tonight."

Gavin presents him with a yawn even huger than it has to be. Once he has seen Greg's jaw work like a camel's to contain a responsive gape, he pushes the lightened trolley to the lift and sends it upwards. Hearing the cheery but decayed voice of the lift sets off the lingering taste in his mouth. He collects the trolley when it arrives at the stockroom and unloads the books that will have to wait until later to see—he was about to confuse himself by thinking daylight, but since when has that entered the shop? As he clocks off he observes Agnes and Connie not speaking to each other, sitting as far apart as they can manage at the staffroom table while Woody watches for the rest of the shift on his screen. The hostile atmosphere feels yet more suffocating for the lack of windows, but Gavin veers into the office to ask Nigel "When are those videos you're sending back going?"

"They'll have to be tomorrow now."

"Could I take a couple home and bring them back tonight?"

"They've all been returned faulty, you know. That's why they're on my rack."

"There'll still be stuff on some of them, won't there? I just wanted to see if there's anything I'd like to buy a copy of."

"I shouldn't think our lord and master would object to that," Nigel says, having glanced at Woody's closed door. "Show me downstairs what you're taking."

Presumably he doesn't want to linger near the mute confrontation in the staffroom. As Gavin hurries through, the rest of the shift arrives and Connie and Agnes compete at greeting everyone. Gavin dodges into the stockroom to grab tapes of concerts by Cuddly Murderers and Pillar of Flesh. Nigel is down by Games and Puzzles, and favours the cassettes with a nod before saying "I hope you'll be shutting your eyes as well."

Gavin resists explaining that he only means to watch them until the speed wears off. He's making his temporary escape from the shop when something insubstantial yet ominously vast swells out of the blind fog to meet him. His mind takes longer than he appreciates to grasp that it's a sound—an unyielding thunder that drags itself across the sky to sink into the shrill whisper of the motorway. When the airliner falls silent beyond the unseen horizon he feels as if the world has shrunk to the size of Fenny Meadows. He hopes he can leave that impression behind well in advance of reaching the bus stop.

As he passes the splintered remains of the tree, a car crawls out of the fog behind Texts. He recognises Mad's green Mazda before it cruises over to pace him and Mad lowers her window an inch. "Am I going your way, Gavin?"

"I'm walking to the bus."

"That's miles. You're Cheetham Hill, aren't you? Not too far away from me at all," she says and halts the car. "I wouldn't mind company if I'm going to tell the truth."

He grows aware of the left-hand headlamp lens, which is splintered like a dragonfly's wing. It's hardly surprising if Mad doesn't want to be alone just now. He thought he might be able to walk off some of the speed, but he climbs in. She doesn't speak again until they're driving up the ramp to the motorway overlooked by a sky that's indistinguishable from the fog except for an ill-defined paler blob of sun, and then she says "What did you think about the funeral?"

"I thought it was sad. What was I going to think?"

"It was lots of kinds of sad all right," Mad says, poising the car on the starting line at the top of the ramp. "The priest trying to convince everyone she'd achieved so much in her life and not being able to think of much, and if he was just trying to convince her parents that's worse. Do you know what he reminded me of?"

Gavin remembers how the priest droned through the eulogy and the prayers that followed as if there was no difference between them and kept singing "Aaah-men" on exactly the same two rising notes. "He reminded me of a priest."

"I was thinking more of one of those letters you get where a computer's filled your name in. I bet he says most of what he said whoever's funeral he's taking. Like a singing telegram except he goes on a lot longer and doesn't sing as much."

Gavin wonders if this is what she expected him to think, and also whether she is ever going to risk driving onto the motorway. She leans towards the side window, where her breath blooms in imitation of the fog before she sends the Mazda forward so abruptly that Gavin's seat thumps the back of his head. "The saddest part," she says, "the saddest part was how her parents kept insisting it wasn't my fault and I mustn't blame myself."

Gavin has begun to feel he may as well stay quiet, having been enlisted simply as a listener. The fog is retreating ahead of the car, but Mad's eyes are glistening as if they've blurred to compensate. "No, that wasn't the saddest," she says.

She has to blink at Gavin to prompt him to ask "What was, then?"

"Didn't you hear what her mother wanted the priest to tell them when he was trying to get away for the next funeral?"

"Saw him trying. Didn't hear."

"She was saying there had to be a reason for Lorraine to die, otherwise nothing makes sense."

"Did he say what he was supposed to?"

"That's just about exactly what he did. It had to be God's will, and we've got to accept it even if we don't understand it yet, that's what he said. He only made her wonder what kind of god would want that to happen to Lorraine."

Gavin assumes Mad has left off the big G now. "You would."

"I wished I could have told her. That's when I went to find out how Wilf was."

"He seemed better than when he was here last."

"I know," Mad says impatiently and throws Gavin a look that shakes the car. "What would you have said to her?"

When he says "The same as she asked" she stares at him as if he's refusing to think. Ahead the fog has dissipated into mist in which the outskirts of Manchester are regaining their shape, churches and chain stores sparkling like images of a renewed clarity that falls short of his intellect. He's beginning to nod off or to lose seconds of his consciousness, maybe longer, so that the sight of a high-pitched primary school class spilling out of the gates of Granada Studios is followed at once by a tram pacing its reflection in a canal a mile later. Then the chimney of Strangeways Prison pokes over the towering wall, which means another mile has fallen through a gap in his mind. "Nearly there," he says at least as much for his own benefit as Mad's, and props one eye open with a finger and thumb until he can announce "Here's fine."

"Do you want me to pick you up tonight?"

"Thanks, but I'm not sure where I'll be. I'll see you at work."

More than likely he'll be starting off from home. He doesn't like to give up his options, that's all, which is one reason why girlfriends end up arguing with him and then leaving him to himself. As the Mazda chugs away towards Chadderton he turns along the side street under trees that lean out of the overgrown gardens to drip jewels on him.

He lets himself into his flat beyond the senile porch and drops the videotapes on his parents' old sofa on the way to tossing his coat on the bed across the room. He holds up the rickety toilet seat with one hand while he directs himself with the other, then leaves the bathroom for the even smaller kitchen to discover what he left himself for breakfast. There aren't too many pimples in half a carton of milk, and it isn't so sour that he's unable to use it to wash down the cold remains of last night's second hamburger. He dumps the carton in the pedal bin and the plate in the sink, and shoves Cuddly Murderers into the video recorder before he lands on the quarter of the sofa that isn't occupied by clothes or compact discs or magazines or books.

Cuddly Murderers dance onto the stage like forks of lightning, and the forest of an audience starts to sway as though it has been caught by a wind. The band launches into screaming "My Sweet Uzi", but they're less than halfway through the song when the screen turns grey and swallows them. They're replaced by a film of two gangs of men in armour fighting, and then some more wearing another kind in combat with a group clad in none. Gavin speeds them up, only to have to watch a further mob dressed in nothing much clubbing one another to the earth. He wouldn't even call this a battle; it's a contest for who'll be left alive. Eventually a single hulking figure survives to be raised high on some kind of triumphal platform, though not for long while Gavin's pressing the fast-forward button. Then a crowd of squat shapes hold one of their number down on a mound and slash at her with a knife or a sharp stone. What kind of film is this supposed to be? Was someone copying a video of death scenes and did they put the Cuddly Murderers tape in the machine by mistake? The victim swiftly twitches her last and vanishes into renewed greyness. Gavin keeps speeding the tape, but when five minutes' worth has shown him nothing more he lurches off the sofa to substitute Pillar of Flesh.

As the spotlight finds Pierre Peter onstage he begins to sing "Seeds Like A Pumpkin" while the audience finishes cheering and whistling. Another light settles on Riccardo Dick, but no sooner does he start his guitar riff than the image shivers, letting greyness in. The concert has been ousted by a blurred monochrome film or one so poorly copied it has turned black and white. Gavin is reaching for the control, though he feels as if he's trying to move while struggling to awaken, when he sees what else is wrong. More accurately, it's the same thing: it's the same film.

He races through the battle footage before his grasp slackens on the control. Why would anybody want to copy this material over a second tape they'd bought? He opens the cassette boxes to peer at the name on the Return slips. He squeezes his eyes shut and stretches them wide and looks again. The tapes were bought by different customers, one from Liverpool, one from Manchester.

He feels incapable of understanding what this could imply until he has been to sleep. He might as well be dreaming the images on the screen; he can't judge whether the savages clubbing one another are bathed in gore or mud. Now that the tape isn't speeded up he sees that the victor is elevated by an object like a huge rudimentary limb. Having brandished him, it plunges him into the earth or the fog, whichever it sprouted from, perhaps both. The screen is overwhelmed by grey before it shows what happened next, or was it earlier? The stunted shapes dragging their victim to the mound that appears to form itself out of the mud look even more primitive than the combatants did, and the object they use to open her up is worse than crude, hardly even sharp. When at last she stops writhing and silently screaming, does Gavin really see the mound sink into the earth and bear her gaping corpse with it? Fog or blankness engulfs everything, and the featureless tape continues to run until he fumbles to switch it off. Perhaps he'll watch it again later, but just now he has no idea how much he may have only imagined he saw. Nevertheless as he pulls off his clothes and trips over his trouser cuffs as he flounders towards the bed, he tries to hold onto an impression that he has been given the answer to something he was recently asked. Once he has slept, perhaps he'll be able to remember both.

# WILF

**He switches off the headlights and stares at the rear wall of Texts** until his mind begins to grow as blank. That's no use. It may feel peaceful, but he isn't here for peace; he's here to work. He wants this job—he loves books and being able to take customers to exactly what they're looking for—and there's no reason he can't do it unless he lets himself believe there is. The shop is only like his flat with even more books, and if he can put them in order at home he has to be able here too. He climbs out of the Micra and slams the door, which echoes somewhere in the fog like a single giant heartbeat. Though the afternoon shift doesn't start for ten minutes, he hurries round the corner so fast that he could imagine he's fleeing his own lonely footsteps or how isolated they make him feel.

A black Audi is parked across three spaces in front of the shop. As Woody strides to meet him in the entrance, Wilf hears people leaving the car behind him. "Welcome to Texts," Woody smiles.

He isn't talking to Wilf. He's staring past him, lower than Wilf's eyes. Then his gaze flicks up to them, and he smiles harder still and hoists his eyebrows. What's wrong with him? Wilf swings around to see who's being greeted and to release himself from the disconcerting sight of Woody's distorted face.

Two people are standing behind Wilf. The man is half a head shorter than he is, and wearing a suit of some red and white checked material bright enough for a dress. Above his white shirt and black cravat his round smooth face is pursing thin lips so nearly invisible they look in need of lipstick. His young companion is taller than Wilf but slimmer than the dumpy man to compensate. She's dressed in a grey suit pinstriped with black. Both of them appear to think themselves significant; could they be Woody's bosses from America? Wilf risks another glance at him, which provokes a fiercer smile and a silent repetition of his greeting. This time Wilf understands, though not why Woody took it to be anything like obvious. He moves to stand by Woody and face the newcomers and raise an expression suggested by Woody's as a preamble to saying "Welcome to Texts."

"And what do you think we're recommending to customers today?" Woody cries. "Nothing but *Dressing Up, Dressing Down*."

"Two minds with just a thought between them, eh?" the man says in a Scottish accent thicker than Wilf is sure is genuine. "Whose was that, then?"

He's jabbing a stubby thumb at Jill's window display, which largely consists of a bunch of his face. "She's not here right now," Woody says without letting his smile down. "Can I give her a message?"

"Shall I bring the colour to her cheeks, Fiona?" says Brodie Oates. "Fiona's my personal girl from the publishers."

Wilf is glad Agnes isn't there, especially since Fiona is eyeing the author as a mother might regard a brilliant but wilful child she can't resist indulging. "You won't upset her like you did the lady in the shop in Norwich, will you?" she appeals to him.

"She shouldn't have let the wine run out." As Woody stiffens almost imperceptibly at that, Oates grants the display another glance. "Saw me as three persons, did she? I won't argue with that. Tell her, how do you Yanks put it? Tell her she done good."

Woody's smile widens like a split in a tree about to fall. Before he can respond aloud, if indeed the expression would allow it, Oates says "Is that supposed to do me?"

He's gazing across the shop at a table piled with copies of his novel. "Your publishers didn't tell us you needed anything else," Woody apologises for them or the shop.

"Bad Fiona. What do you deserve?" Oates watches her blush while he says to Woody "You'll be keeping the alcohol behind the scenes, then."

"I just have to scoot over to the supermarket for it."

"They'll have stuff worth drinking there, will they? Chateauneuf will pass at a pinch." Oates stares at the space in front of the table of books. "Don't be stingy with my audience either," he says. "Nothing beats a few glasses to put them in a buying mood."

Wilf can only imagine why Woody's smile is stretching even wider. "I'll take you up to the VIP lounge till they arrive," Woody says, covering the plaque on the wall with his badge. "Sesame. Sesame," he mutters, shoving at the door.

He leads the way, leaving Wilf to trail after Fiona behind Oates. Wilf is on the lowest stair when the author says "So what did you make of my wee tale?"

"I'm looking forward to reading a signed copy," Woody says at once.

"Just so you'll be paying for it."

"Sure I am. The store's entitled to expect it and so are your publishers. I don't believe in taking any gravy. I'm just a member of the team. The guy below you, now, he's read your book."

"Aye?" Oates says and turns to Wilf. "What's the verdict, then?"

Everyone has halted. Even Fiona is gazing at Wilf. In books

people often wish the ground would swallow them, but he has always thought that was an exaggeration until now. "Truthfully . . ." he instantly wishes he hadn't said.

"That's what we're waiting for fine right. Nothing less."

"It gave me a migraine."

Woody emits a startled laugh that doesn't quite go with his smile. "Och, the poor bairn's brain," wails Oates.

Wilf tells himself that Oates isn't like Freddy Slater, however mocking he sounds. It had to have been Slater's fault that Wilf couldn't read the ending of the novel when he was under so much pressure to finish it, just as Slater gave him problems with *War and Peace,* which he was subsequently able to read with no trouble at home. Perhaps Slater has found someone else to torment or grown bored with it; Wilf hasn't seen him since. "Will you tell us what gave you the head?" says Oates.

Woody looks so taken aback he almost drops his smile. Perhaps the question has a different significance for Americans. "The ending," Wilf admits.

"Which was that?"

Perhaps Oates isn't so unlike Slater as Wilf wanted to believe. Certainly he's making Wilf feel the way the final pages of the book did: incapable of reading or of understanding what he'd struggled to read. Wilf is grateful to Woody for saying "Shall we continue upstairs? Our events manager is anxious to meet you."

Once he has held the staffroom door wide for Oates and Fiona he darts to call into the office "Connie, here's your celebrity."

As she hurries out to offer her hand and spread her pink lips, Oates says "Is it you that's responsible for my show in the window?"

"Would you like it to be?" When he bows over her hand and kisses it she says "Then I'm happy to be."

"Jill made the window up, didn't she?" Wilf can't help blurting.

"You don't know what Jill and I say to each other."

Connie has forgotten to smile, but Woody turns his up. "Are you with us yet, Wilf?"

Presumably he's asking if Wilf's working. Since it will reassure him that he can and remove him from present company, Wilf doesn't mind. "May as well be," he says, running his card along the slot beneath the clock.

"Okay, take some chairs down and set them up. Connie, I'm just driving over to Frugo so we can be hospitable."

Wilf props the staffroom door open with a chair and stacks five more on it and lumbers downstairs with them. He's halfway when the door shuts behind Woody and six chairs. "Something wrong with the elevator?" Woody says with no smile in his voice.

"I thought this would be quicker."

"So long as you're thinking of the store. Can we take it you're fully recovered?"

"From the migraine, you mean."

"Is anything else wrong with you?"

He's descending faster than Wilf, who mumbles "Nothing to speak of."

"First time you've suffered?"

"I've never been that bad before," Wilf says, which at least is true enough.

"So make sure you see Ray and fill in a sick form. Are we waiting for something?"

The top chair jerks nervously close to Wilf's eyes at each step down, but he reaches the exit to the sales floor without dropping the chairs or tripping over them. As soon as Wilf hauls the door open Woody darts past, leaving him to struggle through the dwindling gap, beyond which he almost collides with the chairs Woody has abandoned. "Okay, you set these up," Woody says rapidly. "That's one thing I need to order in for occasions like this, more chairs. If anyone needs to stand this time they'll have to not mind."

Wilf wonders how determined Woody is to hope. Just now the shop has fewer customers than chairs. "As long as we've got all night tonight," Woody murmurs, "why don't you stick around when you've finished setting up. It'll be good for him to know there's someone here from the store who's read his work. You can fill in with questions if you need to."

Wilf can think of hardly anything he needs less; the situation brings an unidentifiable stale taste into his mouth. He takes his time over unstacking the chairs, as though this may somehow postpone the author's appearance. He has finished arranging them in rows of four in front of the table when two men with pates scraped almost bald, who have been sitting as still as their armchairs, drag those over to swell the back row. They resume their seats and revert to staring at the covers of the picture books each has propped on his lap. He's wondering whether they'll feel patronised if he tells them what the other chairs are for when the voice he would least like to hear accosts him from behind. "Have they promoted you already?"

Wilf turns as slowly as he can, though it's childish to assume that will make Slater vanish. More than ever Slater's face resembles a moist translucent mask stuck on a wider lump of ruddy flesh. His mouth droops open as if encouraging Wilf to catch the joke or miming how cloddish he thinks Wilf is to miss it. "What do you mean?" Wilf almost manages not to ask.

"Looks like they've made you chairman."

He follows this with several times the mirth the joke deserves while he stands so close Wilf feels the laughter is being thrust in his face. He can't breathe until Slater has finished, by which point Wilf's mouth tastes clogged with fog. "Want to look something up for me?" Slater says then.

"You'll have to ask at Information. I'm busy here."

Slater lets his mouth fall open in such contemptuous disbelief that Wilf sets about rearranging the books on the table to prove him wrong. "That looks like the job for you all right," says Slater. "Shouldn't think even you could get those out of order."

"I thought you wanted information. This is where people are coming to hear an author talk."

"That's why I'm here. I was sure you'd be pleased I'm supporting your shop." Once he has left his mouth open for a while Slater adds "Your boss ought to be."

Wilf's hands have begun to tingle and draw into fists as his mouth turns sourer. He fumbles with the books, but his fingers are so unwieldy that one copy sprawls off the table onto the floor. When he retrieves it, the open pages are smeared with mud. It will have to go to Nigel as a damaged copy. Wilf is staring at Slater to place the blame when people start to converge on the chairs.

He would be grateful for the distraction if they weren't the writers' group he had to abandon. Before he can move away from Slater their spokeswoman, chosen or otherwise, marches over to him. Her grey hair is piled snakelike on top of her head, and she's wearing more colours than ever. "Have you made any sense of it?" she enquires.

"What can't he make sense out of now?" Slater is avid to hear.

"He has problems with the ending like the rest of us."

She has taken an instinctive dislike to Slater, who turns his retort on Wilf. "Got the rest of it though, did you?"

"I'd have said so."

"What's it all about, then?"

For once Wilf feels as if Slater's handing him punch lines. "You'll have to read it and decide for yourself." Wilf hesitates, but not long enough to resist saying "If you can."

"Don't you be giving anybody the idea I'm the one that can't read, Wiffle."

"You aren't suggesting this gentleman can't," the woman in the rainbow garb objects. "He wouldn't be working here."

Slater is only starting to dangle his lower jaw when she presents him with her considerable back. Wilf doesn't know what Slater might be capable of calling after her about him or telling him for everyone to hear if there weren't an interruption. Woody has returned quicker than Wilf could have expected the fog to allow anyone to be. "Buying that? Good for you," he says of the book in Wilf's hand.

Wilf is suddenly afraid that Slater will accuse him of damaging it, but Woody gives nobody a chance to speak. "Welcome to our first Fenny Meadows author appearance," he smiles as he clears a space on the table for six bottles of wine and a pillar of plastic cups. "Our famous guest will be with you momentarily," he says more jubilantly still, uncorking a red and a white. "Please have a drink on the store. That's everybody except staff."

He keeps his smile towards the gathering until he's well on his way to the staffroom, but Wilf wonders if he's concealing disappointment at the size of the audience. Two more people—a man in a creaky yellow oilskin jacket and a woman in denim, even her feet—join it, perhaps attracted by the wine. Most of the writers approach the table for Wilf to serve them too. Slater grabs the red and fills a cup almost to the brim for himself, then sits on the front row as Connie ushers Oates and his publicist onto the sales floor. The author halts at once and jabs an upturned hand at the audience as though testing for rain. "Are they it?"

"I think we may have to blame the fog," says Connie.

"Fog's fault, is it?" he says and stares at Fiona. "Not the publicity by any chance."

"We leafleted everywhere we could think of," Connie assures him.

A murmur passes through the audience, making Wilf nervous for her sake in case anyone mentions the misprint. Perhaps it sounds to Oates as though the audience is supporting her. "Don't I rate a chair?" he growls at Wilf.

As Wilf picks up the solitary unoccupied seat from the front row, Slater comments "You wouldn't expect him to know how to deal with a writer."

Wilf plants the chair behind the table and retreats to hide as much of his embarrassment on the back row as he can while Connie stands next to Oates. When she describes him as the author of one of the year's most talked-about novels he gives her a dissatisfied scowl and himself a second cupful of wine that earns a scowl too. "Are we pissed enough for this yet? Dunno if I am," he says once she has finished, and empties the last of the bottle into his cup. "I hear some of you didn't get my ending."

"Make that all," the rainbow woman says from the front row.

"Well," Connie just about protests at her back, but Oates ignores both of them. He opens a copy of *Dressing Up, Dressing Down* and then another, and props the latter up in front of him. "Let's test if you've room in your wee heads for this."

Wilf ought to be able to relax while being read to. No doubt Woody is addressing the rest of the afternoon shift, even if that should be Nigel's job. Surely Woody isn't spying on the sales floor from his office, and so Wilf has no reason to feel observed while hearing how a Victorian detective takes his clothes off to reveal he's a jewel thief who removes hers and proves to be an army sergeant, except that beneath her uniform she's a chanteuse who is really a detective or rather, once stripped, simply a naked man at a computer in a room overlooking Edinburgh. He lifts his gaze to his audience—he does, and so does Oates, if there's any difference—and indicates the various costumes. "Your turn now," he says. "Your choice. Try it on."

He feeds himself more wine before Wilf can judge from his expression whether the last phrase is intended as a joke and if so on whom. When the writers start to mutter, Wilf takes them to be sharing his suspicion until the rainbow woman gives them more of a voice. "That's not what it says in the book."

"It is in this one."

She elevates her eyebrows until they resemble quotation marks framing a silent question. As Oates busies himself with uncorking another bottle of red wine, she asks almost loud enough to be heard upstairs "Are you telling us there's more than one ending?"

"Different final pages, aye. The rest of the book won't show you which you've got. It's my belief you shouldn't know where you're bound till you arrive, any more than I did. I expect you agree, being writers."

"Sounds more like you want to make people buy two copies."

"Wouldn't you?"

She's gazing at him as though she doesn't care for either meaning of his query when Slater peers over his shoulder at Wilf. "Which one have you got?"

"I couldn't tell you offhand."

"I'd be interested to hear," Oates says, draining his cup to make room for a refill. "Which is it?"

Wilf feels as though the author is siding with Slater against him. He glances at the last page of the damaged copy and shuts the book. "The one you just read to us."

"I've never seen you read that fast or anything like," Slater objects. "Are you sure you did?"

"Of course he did," says Connie, and turns a puzzled smile to Wilf. "What's this about?"

"Go on, Lowell, you show us. Show us all how you read."

What's making him behave this way? Wilf wouldn't have believed he could at his age. He has a suffocating impression that by reverting Slater is forcing him to return to childhood too. He wills Connie to confront his tormentor, but she only looks bemused. "Nobody's come to hear me," Wilf succeeds in protesting. "I'm not the author."

"Maybe the author would like to hear one of his readers do it," Slater says.

"Now you mention it, I might," says Oates, raising his half-empty cup to encourage Wilf. "Go on, do me the favour. Let's hear what it means to you."

Some of the writers, not to mention the denimed woman and the oilskinned man, are staring at Wilf by now, the rainbow woman hardest of all. It feels exactly like being forced to stand up in class, though he's crouching over the book as though it's a pain in his knotted guts. Are they the source of the unpleasant stagnant taste? As he lowers his eyes to the novel he finds himself praying that it will somehow offer him a refuge. He glares at the last page and tries to free himself from the sight of it by speaking. "I told you," he says, and as clearly as he's able "Your turn now. Your choice. Try it on."

"That isn't the whole page, is it?" When Oates shakes his head so vigorously his jowls have trouble catching up, Slater says "You could have memorised that, Lowell. Give us the rest."

It's only because Wilf can't face the spectators that his gaze is dragged down to the page. The prospect is worse than ever. The paper is strewn with black marks, bunches of symbols that he tells himself are letters without being capable of naming even one. Isn't e the commonest? Perhaps if he spots which mark occurs most often, that will unlock his recognition of the others, the way cryptographers break codes—but he's still counting frantically under his breath when Connie says "I really think I need to know what's going on."

"Let's see," says Slater, and sits next to Wilf before he can think of shutting the book. "Thought as much. Will you tell her, Lowell, or shall I?"

His mouth sags wide as if this is his best joke, and Wilf can think of only one response. "I'm buying this," he informs whoever ought to know as he rips a handful of pages out of the novel and stuffs them in Slater's mouth.

He wishes he'd thought of such a retort years ago, but it's worth having waited to see his enemy's eyes bulge with shock. Either that or Wilf's vehemence sends Slater over backwards. As he and the chair thump the floor Wilf follows him down and kneels on his chest. "Want the rest?" Wilf enquires with a smile he thinks Woody might be proud of. "My pleasure. Swallow this."

He's surrounded by noises—gasps from women, Connie repeating his name increasingly loud and sharp, the men in the armchairs grunting with laughter or approval—but he's mostly aware of a choked sodden mumble, Slater's stopped-up words. He has even less to say for himself now than Wilf used to have in class, which is so satisfying that Wilf doesn't immediately relent when Woody's voice rushes out of the staffroom exit. "Stop that," he

shouts more than once on the way to stooping close enough to confront Wilf with saliva glistening within his smile. "Enough,"
Woody urges. "Enough."

Wilf thinks there might be room for another chapter in Slater's
mouth, but there's no doubt he has made his point. He leaves the remains of the novel spread-eagled on Slater's chest and levers himself
to his feet by propping his fists on his enemy's shoulders. As Slater
lurches off the floor less gracefully than a drunk and flounders about
in search of somewhere to eject the contents of his mouth, Woody
gives Wilf another close view of his teeth. "Wait in my office."

All at once Wilf's legs feel flabby and unstable, as though whatever drove him has drained away through them, leaving his skull
hollow above a stale taste. He reminds himself that Slater's mouth
will be flavoured with paper and ink, a notion that helps him walk
almost steadily to the exit to the staffroom. As it decides his badge
is valid he sees Connie pass Slater the Frugo bag that contained the
wine. Some of the women emit maternal noises while he spits ex-
travagantly into the bag, and some cast Wilf out with their eyes until the door shuts behind him.

He supports himself on the banister all the way to the staffroom.
Without its chairs the table puts him in mind of an abandoned altar.
Books are clattering on racks in the stockroom while Ray frowns at
his computer screen in the office. Even if Ray didn't look preoccupied Wilf wouldn't feel able to discuss his sick leave. He retreats
into Woody's office, where the monitor shows Woody presenting
Slater with a gift voucher and a smile of supplication. In the opposite quadrant the audience has settled down for Oates to answer a
question about his book or Wilf. As Wilf leans against the clammy
concrete wall and watches Woody usher Slater out of the shop, he's
tempted to take the single chair until Woody darts across the sales
floor as if he's aware of Wilf's presumption. Before Wilf is even
close to prepared for the onslaught, Woody's in the room.

He spins his chair away from the monitor and plants himself on
it to face Wilf. "Well, that cost the store."

It's Woody's unrelenting smile that encourages, if that's the word, Wilf to ask "How much?"

"A whole lot more than you're going to be able to afford."

"I'm sorry." Wilf doesn't know what to add except "I shouldn't have done that here."

"Hey, where else are you going to do it?" This sounds like an endorsement or at least a parody of one until Woody says "Who else don't you want to hear the truth about you?"

A surge of renewed fury makes Wilf blurt "What did he say about me?"

"How you fooled the store. I'm going to need to make sure you're the only one that's lying low here, aren't I, God damn it? The only guy that can't read."

"That isn't true. It's nowhere near."

"Hey, is that a fact? Okay then, show me." Woody smiles savagely at the lack of books in the room and pulls out the drawers of his desk until he finds a pile of official forms, one of which he thrusts at Wilf. "Go ahead, let me hear you read this."

At first the reason Wilf can't concentrate on the task is that he's thrown by what he thinks he glimpsed. When Woody opened the right-hand bottom drawer a crack, was it really full of socks and underwear? Every second Wilf spends wondering makes him appear more illiterate, and so he peers at the form. He recognises it as an application to work at Texts, but that isn't the same as putting the swarm of marks on the page into words. When he strains to force some meaning out of them his body starts to quiver, inwardly to begin with. "I can't just now," he says and feels even stupider for trying to explain. "It's Slater's fault. He used to get me like this when we were at school."

"I haven't time for this," Woody says, snatching the form and returning it to the drawer. "I'm only glad we found out about you before New York got here. Let's have your badge."

This sounds so reminiscent of a Western or a crime film that Wilf almost thinks Woody and his smile are jesting. "You can't believe I was never able to read," Wilf says. "How did I manage to shelve all my books?"

"I checked your section," Woody tells him and demonstrates the look he must have given it. "Thank God we'll have time to fix it before tomorrow. I don't have your badge yet."

Wilf takes it off and drops it on the desk. He feels as if there's nothing left of him worth having—as if whatever was worthwhile has been draining out of him unnoticed since he started work at Texts. He's turning to bear his dull empty shame away when Woody demands "Did you fill out your sick form?"

A last feeble uprush of pride incites Wilf to admit "I don't need to. I've never had a migraine."

"Fooled us there as well, huh?"

"You made me rush the ending of that book so I could talk to the writers and I couldn't finish it. That's what all this has been about, not being able to finish a book."

"I should be taking some of the blame, should I?" Woody says with a smile that seems to bleed into his eyes. "I believed you when you said you were a reader. It never occurred to me to check."

"I can read. It's what I like most. I've just kept not being able to read here."

"Well, here's your chance to do it someplace else," Woody says as if Wilf has insulted him or the shop or both. "Did you card yourself out?"

"I didn't think."

"Hey, let me do it for you." He springs out of his chair and heads for the door so fast Wilf barely has time to dodge out of his way. He grabs Wilf's card out of the rack and skims it under the clock, then snaps it in two and plants the halves on Ray's desk. "All yours, Ray. Mr Lowell is quitting as of right now."

"Good Lord." Ray gives him and Wilf an unhappy puzzled blink each. "Why on earth is that?"

"I'd call it getting rid of an invader," Woody says, levelling his smile at Wilf. "Still here? You shouldn't be. Maybe you forgot it says staff only on the door downstairs."

Surely it can be nothing except contentiousness that goads Wilf into saying "I haven't paid for that book yet."

"Ray will stop it out of the salary we wouldn't be paying you if it were up to me. Just leave."

Wilf sees Ray trying to decide how sympathetic to him he should look. "It's all right," Wilf feels bound to assure him while failing to convince himself, and then he can't face either of them. He grabs his coat from his locker and struggles into it as he plods unsteadily downstairs and heaves the door open for the last time. Since nobody appears to be watching him, he sneaks over to his section. The harder he peers at the books, the less he's certain whether they're in order; the titles and the authors' names might as well be in a foreign language or none at all. He's growing dizzy with straining his eyes and his mind when Woody's voice proclaims overhead "Mr Lowell is no longer with the store."

Brodie Oates' gaze finds Wilf as the author finishes saying that it takes him a year to imagine a novel and six weeks to write it. As the listeners turn to stare at Wilf he wonders if they're treating him to the disapproval they would otherwise have kept for Oates. In any case it makes Wilf feel even more ostracised than Woody's announcement did. Connie lifts one hand in a wave that scarcely admits to itself as Wilf flees towards the exit, beside which Greg offers him a pursed reproving smile and a shake of the head from behind the counter. It doesn't matter how rude Wilf is to him now, but the only words he can bring to mind are terse as grunts. They grow stale and sour in his mouth as he leaves the shop for good.

Suppose Slater is waiting outside for him? Wilf hopes so: he's welcome to all the words Wilf kept to himself and maybe more than words. The fog that's suppressing even the time of day falls back for a breath, and he thinks it let him glimpse a watcher until he realises he saw only the pair of trees and their stunted companion.

Nevertheless, as he retreats around the corner of the shop he has a distinct sense of being followed, however invisibly and silently. "Why don't you show yourself?" he calls, though it makes his mouth taste worse. "You've got what you wanted. Come on, let's see your face."

He hasn't tempted Slater out of hiding by the time he reaches the Micra. He slams the door as hard as he would have liked to have done on some part of his tormentor. Once he has succeeded in inserting the tag of his seat belt in the slot he rests his shaky hands on the wheel. The chill of the fog and his reaction to the events of the afternoon have seized him with a fit of shivering. He gazes at the meaningless blank of the rear wall of Texts until he regains enough control of himself to line up the key with the ignition.

Because of the fog he drives slowly out from behind the shop, but it feels as though he's skulking, afraid to be noticed. The light from the windows recedes into the nebulous glow, trees slither past in the murk, and then there's only an inexact patch of tarmac crawling ahead. What if the headlamps lit on Slater? How would he behave if he saw Wilf grinning over them as they gathered speed towards him? The corners of Wilf's mouth are starting to raise themselves when he remembers Lorraine. His hands clench on the wheel as he's overtaken by a shudder of self-loathing. He doesn't know how even Slater could have rendered him so thoughtless. Perhaps he didn't deserve to work at Texts after all.

The supermarket drags itself into focus before sinking into the grey depths of the mirror. If that's the last sight he will ever have of Fenny Meadows, he can't decide how that makes him feel. He cruises to the roundabout and up the motorway ramp. Though it's raising him towards the sun, he has a sense of being held back by the unstable pallid blankness and its chill. When he reaches the edge of the motorway he lowers his window to listen for oncoming traffic. By the time he's convinced he can risk a sprint, a mouldy taste of fog has lodged in his mouth.

The motorway is reluctant to unveil itself. He slackens his speed almost at once until the fog ahead more or less matches his pace. Before long it shows signs of drawing away, and he glimpses the sun like a silver token someone keeps breathing on. Soon he'll be able to see his way clear, a prospect that feels like being free of Fenny Meadows. That's hardly going to be possible unless he comes to terms with what he did. He doesn't want to brood over it while he needs to concentrate on driving, and it isn't quite the reason why he takes a firmer grip on the wheel. His mind is so weighed down by his encounter with Slater and the aftermath that he hasn't thought about the things he saw and said.

The sun gleams as though it has been polished, then it dulls and vanishes while he tries not to let his mind cloud over. Is Woody living in the shop? Why has Wilf been unable to read only there? The questions seem incapable of raising themselves quite far enough for him to grasp them; he needs to be out under the sun. He even has an odd impression that he shouldn't risk thinking them until he has escaped the fog—absurd, but it rouses his nerves. He presses the accelerator as the fog bares a quarter of a mile of road. Though he has no sense of travelling fast, the needle of the speedometer is swinging towards vertical when the fog takes an abrupt stand ahead. As he brakes, greyness floods the mirror. All at once the murk is so close on every side that despite the heater its chill seeps into the car and into him. He's fighting not to let his shivers reach the wheel when the fog behind him blazes icy white and unleashes the sound of an enormous trumpet. There's a lorry at his back, and it can't or won't slow down.

He tramps on the accelerator. The fog surges eagerly to cut him off, but it's more than fog. He's racing towards the wide high whitish backside of a lorry that's travelling at less than half his speed. He brakes, only for the deafening horn and the blinding light in the mirror to lurch closer. He jerks his foot clear of the pedal and twists the quivering wheel. He has forgotten to indicate.

The car is veering into the middle lane when the lorry behind him swings out to overtake.

He can't return to the inner lane. He's too close to the vehicle ahead. He catches the indicator lever with the side of his hand and shoves it down as he swerves into the outer lane. The glare of the following lorry is still in his mirror. It's only trying to pass him, he isn't prey that it's determined to run down, it isn't in league with the fog that in any case can't be determined to trap him, but the thoughts are no use: they don't prevent the lorry from bearing down on him faster than he can gain speed. He grips the wheel and flees into the middle lane, and hears a vast gasp that suggests he has shocked his pursuer. It and a huge spasmodic panting are emitted by the brakes the driver has applied at last, but there's no longer any need. Wilf brakes and steers into the inner lane behind the foremost lorry so as to feel entirely safe.

He hasn't skidded. He hasn't come up too fast behind the vehicle, even given the poor visibility. When he hears a gigantic tortured screech of metal he tells himself it has nothing to do with him—and then a wave of fog at least as wide as all three lanes rushes at him in the mirror. He's put in mind of a breath expelled by a vast silent gleeful laugh until he sees it isn't fog, because a word taller than the car is printed on the flat pale surface. For an instant he's most concerned to know why he can't read the word. The letters are reversed, of course—the letters on the side of the lorry. The entire rear section of the vehicle is swinging towards him on the hinge of the cab.

The fog shrinks away across the lanes, and he sees the cab scraping along the central barrier, striking sparks from it and buckling it out of shape. A seizure of trembling spreads through his arms into the rest of him as he grapples with the wheel to speed the car into the middle lane—to outdistance the object that's swinging towards him like a colossal scythe. He's pulling out when the rear of the lorry catches the Micra and slews it side on towards the lorry ahead. The next moment everything collides, and the car caves in so fast that he scarcely has time to understand what's being crushed besides shattered glass and groaning metal. It's him. It's his head, which fills with noise and whiteness that sinks into a flood of black.

# JILL

**"Mummy, have you really got to work all night?"**

"Don't worry, Bryony. I'll be fine. I had a sleep while you were at school."

"But have you really really got to go?"

"We're all working. We've got an inspection tomorrow, I told you, like you have at school. You know how your teachers try and make sure everything's looking its best. So long as it isn't just about putting on appearances it isn't wrong, do you think?"

"I thought you liked helping me with my work for school. I like it when you tell me better words."

"I will again. Honestly, love, I won't be gone for long, and you know I'm not going far. What's the problem?"

"I like it when you read to me in bed."

"Don't you when daddy does? I thought you used to."

"I do still. Have you got to work because he isn't giving us enough money?"

"Bryony, I don't know if you're old enough to understand this—"

"I am. Miss Dickens says I'm old for my age."

"Well then, try and understand I don't want to depend on your father or anyone else any more than I absolutely have to. The more I earn myself the happier I am."

"I want you to be happy."

"You don't need me to tell you that's what I want for you, and you will be if I can buy us more things, won't you? The more committed I am to the job the more likely I am to be promoted. That's how it works."

"You told me that."

"Is there something else before your father comes, then? What's actually bothering you?"

"Maybe I won't be able to sleep."

"Why not? Is there some reason you don't like sleeping at your father's? If there's anything at all I should know you mustn't be afraid to tell me. Is there, Bryony?"

"I might have a dream."

"Why should you? Why only there?"

"I had it last night."

"Did it wake you? I'm sorry, Bryony. I must have been too asleep to hear. What was it about, love?"

"Me and daddy couldn't find you at the shop."

"Perhaps it was my day off."

"No, it was tonight and I was worried about you because it was so dark."

"It won't be. The shop's always lit and if you remember there are big lamps outside as well."

"We couldn't see. I'm sure it was dark. I could hear you calling out but I couldn't get to you, and then I couldn't find daddy either."

"It would have been the fog, was it? That's what must have got into your head. I expect daddy found you and I did as well, but you'd already woken up."

"No, he was looking for the other lady."

"Which other one?"

"The one who dresses up in leather."

"Do you mean Connie? What do you know about her?"

"I heard her talking to daddy when I was at your shop for the competition."

"And have you bumped into her elsewhere?"

"No, mummy. Only that time."

"I wonder why she made such an impression, then," Jill says, and the doorbell seems to respond with a ring as terse as a four-letter word.

Bryony swings her unshod feet off the creaky cane sofa and jumps up. "I'm just going to the toilet," she says as she always does when leaving is imminent, and runs upstairs.

Jill is inclined to take her time over answering the bell, which sounded more peremptory than it has any right to be, but she wants a private word with Geoff. She hurries down the short hall that's decorated with Bryony's paintings and crayonings of girls on ponies, which she keeps assuring Jill she doesn't want to own or hire even if they could afford it, and twists the latch. The front door snags halfway as usual on some undetectable obstruction, then swings wide to show Geoff stooping to tug a clump of dandelions out of a crack in the path. "No need for that," she tells him.

"They're making the place look untidy."

"So let them. Bryony likes scattering the seeds." His eyebrows stir just enough to provoke her to add "I should think you'd sympathise with that."

"I didn't realise you still cared where mine end up."

"Are you saying I should have while we were together? Don't tell me. I don't want to hear," Jill says, only to infuriate herself further by having to amend it. "Not unless it's somebody I know."

"Why would you imagine that, Jill? You're making it sound as if I'd want to hurt you."

His deep brown eyes have produced a faintly injured look, but it no longer works. "Bryony seems to think there's someone we both know."

"She's completely mistaken. You can't believe I would ever introduce her to any—" A thought snags his gaze, which tries not to admit as much. "I've done my best to keep her away from my private life," he insists.

"Not much point in that if you bring it where I work while Bryony's there as well."

"I didn't know, did I? I mean, nothing had happened. I won't come near the shop again if that's what you prefer."

"You mean things have happened since, not that it's any affair of mine."

"It isn't really, is it, but well, yes."

"I wonder if you've the slightest idea what difficulties you may have made for me. Presumably you can't have, not that I'd call that an excuse."

"I'm not sure I see the problem. We're all adults and I should have thought we could act like it."

"You're going to start then, are you?" This leaves enough of Jill's anger unexpressed that she blurts "I wish my parents weren't on their winter break. I'd rather Bryony stayed with them."

Upstairs the toilet flushes as if it's washing away Jill's remark. Geoff looks close to giving her an understanding look, which makes her angrier still. She's tempted to forbid him to show up at Bryony's Christmas play at school—to threaten to walk out if he disobeys. Instead she shouts "Hurry up, Bryony. I want to put the alarm on."

She's ashamed of her sharpness when Bryony appears clutching her overnight bag, from which her teddy bear is poking out his battered head to see where he's going on the way to keeping her bed warm. She waits with her father on the path while Jill types the date she and Geoff split up. Jill has barely shut the door when Bryony drops the bag and runs to hug her so hard it feels as though she wants to root them to the path. "It'll be fine. It'll be an adventure," Jill says and strokes Bryony's head until the hug slackens enough to let her disengage herself. "I'll see you tomorrow after school."

Bryony stands next to the Golf as Geoff climbs in while Jill starts the Nova. As Jill eases the car away from the kerb, Bryony lifts her free hand in a timid wave that Jill tells herself isn't really a hopeless attempt to arrest her. Bryony must still be more upset to be reminded that her parents aren't together than Jill realised. Once they're home again and Jill has slept off the night at the shop they'll have a proper talk.

Ten minutes take her through Bury and onto the motorway. She has sped past several exits when she encounters a slow herd of traffic. Eventually it takes her to the elevated section that gives her a distant view of the stretch past Fenny Meadows. While the fog emits only the faintest tinge of red, an elongated shining wound leads there—the brake lights of hundreds of stationary cars. Jill switches on the radio and tunes it to a local station. The Nova has crawled for some minutes to the accompaniment of a folk song about the lone survivor of a battle when the radio issues a travel bulletin. "The M62 eastbound of junction 11 is closed due to a series of accidents. Police do not expect it to be reopened for some hours. Drivers are asked to find an alternative route."

That's where Fenny Meadows is. Jill is tempted to use this as an excuse to stay away from Texts tonight and let Bryony know, but it wouldn't be fair to the rest of the staff. When she arrives at the next junction she heads for the East Lancashire Road so that she can come up behind the retail park. Less than ten minutes later she's on the dual carriageway, but misses the turn for Fenny Meadows. If there's a signpost from either direction, it certainly isn't prominent. Once she reaches a gap in the central reservation she swings back so as to cross to the first side road she's able to locate, which is marked only by an illuminated bus shelter. The lane doesn't even seem to have a name.

It's the route to Fenny Meadows, however. Before long the fog makes that clear as well as the opposite. The tall thorny hedges that enclose the road, their spikes glinting as the headlights sharpen them, appear to be liquefying rather than shaping themselves from the murk. Occasionally a shiver passes through the tangles of black twigs, and they exude greyness like a mass of cobwebs. There must be a wind, because the fog keeps lurching eagerly closer both behind and ahead of the car. By the time she has guided the Nova around all the curves and crooks of the narrow lane, she's more anxious to reach Fenny Meadows than she could have imagined. She lets out a relieved breath that glimmers for an instant in the air as a pale surface framed by the hedges proves to be more solid than fog.

It's the rear wall of Frugo. She drives past the shops, some of which are already closed for the night. The glow from their windows lies inert in the murk, which seems to snag on the livid graffiti that swarm over the unoccupied properties. Not a hint of Christmas is visible in Texts; the shop feels mired in the October that first gave rise to the fog. At the back her headlamp beams expand into a white stain that vanishes into the wall. She locks the car, and as the keys finish jingling she discovers she's holding her breath.

Why is the retail park so quiet? She feels as if the fog has swamped every sound until she realises what's missing: the noise of the motorway. When she heads for the front of the shop her footsteps seem shrunken by their isolation and yet too loud. She could fancy that something dwarfish is scuttling after her down the alley—her echoes, of course. She's glad to have left the dim passage until she sees Connie in the window.

The three photographs of Brodie Oates lie at Connie's feet. Jill won't miss the display—presumably it's redundant now that he has visited the shop—and she won't let herself feel as though it's her face Connie seems about to wipe her shoes on. She's hurrying past Frank the guard, who looks preoccupied with the fog, when Connie calls "I put these on a trolley for you, Jill."

Jill has half a mind to pretend she didn't hear. She wasn't expecting Connie's voice to render her body so stiff it feels crippled and shrivelled, and to bring such an unwelcome taste to her mouth. She turns to see Connie pointing at the books she has taken out of the window. "That's kind of you," Jill says with a sweetness that can't quite overcome the taste.

"It is rather, isn't it? You can put them and the signed ones on a shelf end. Maybe they'll move faster once people can get their hands on them."

"You've got some left over from your show, you mean. Didn't it go as well as you were planning?"

Connie parts her full pink lips to lure her closer. The gesture sickens Jill, but she can't resist approaching for Connie to murmur "Not as well as our star kept telling us it should. He blamed everything except the fog and his book. Your display, I'm afraid."

"I do apologise. I'll just have to try even harder, won't I."

"I'm not criticising you, Jill. I'm only saying what he said. I don't think we could have done any more for him than we did, any of us."

"Well then," Jill mutters, and is about to head for the staffroom when Connie says "You've got ready for the marathon, have you?"

"I expect I'm as ready as anyone."

"Someone's looking after your little girl, what's her name, Bryony, isn't it? Someone's taking care of her."

"Her father." Jill feels as if she's spitting out the stale taste of the phrase as she adds "He's very good at taking care of people for a while."

Connie either has no answer to that or doesn't feel any is advisable, but the sight of her lips nestling together to conceal an expression goads Jill to enquire "May I ask where you got my daughter's name from?"

"Didn't I hear it the day you brought her along?"

Jill can't remember. She only knows she feels that Connie has bested her. As she turns away, her mouth filling up with dirty words and their taste, she hears Connie promise "They'll be waiting for you when you come down."

She means the books—the excess of them that she ordered and dumped on Jill. Two men who seem to have occupied a pair of armchairs ever since Jill can remember watch her stalking away. She brandishes her badge at the plaque on the wall and comes close to kicking the door. Eventually it gives way, and she chases her faint breaths upstairs to the staffroom.

Ross and Mad are sitting at either end of the table with Agnes between them. She's wearing a prim frown like a reluctant chaperone and saying no more than they are. All three seem glad to see Jill, though perhaps only because she's somewhere to look. As she runs her card under the clock, Woody darts out of the lair of his office. "There you are. I thought we'd lost another of the team."

Jill doesn't know if his red-eyed smile makes his thoughtlessness more shocking or suggests he's too tired to think. Ross grows rigid so as not to wince, and Agnes lets her jaw drop on his behalf, while Mad looks as though she might give him a comforting pat if she could reach. Jill can only try to lessen the tension by saying "The motorway's closed. I had to use the old road."

"Connie told me," Woody says, presumably about the motorway, but the name sours Jill's mouth. "Want to hear the good news?"

His smile is fierce enough to prompt all his listeners. It's Ross who mumbles "If there's some."

"Hey, why am I not seeing smiles round here? What is this, a wake?" When everyone but Agnes has been forced to placate him, Woody says "Okay, the good news. You just heard it. Your expressway's blocked."

Mad breaks the bewildered silence. "That's good?"

"Right now it is. Just this one time we can live without customers coming in the store and screwing up the order. I guess we may need till tomorrow to clear the stockroom. We had a big delivery this afternoon and we're short of a member of staff."

"You keep bringing that up," Agnes protests. "Don't you realise Ross—"

"Gee, I'm sorry. I didn't tell you yet. We had to get rid of Wilf."

"Wilf," Agnes says, not unlike a bark. "How do you mean get rid?"

"Let go. Can. Fire."

"How can that be? He said at the funeral, sorry, Ross, he'd be in today."

"He was here sure enough. That's why he isn't any longer."

"But you can't just dismiss someone like that. What was he supposed to have done?"

"Attacked a customer and did his best to choke him. I guess even you wouldn't hire a guy who did that."

"Who says Wilf did what you said?" Mad intervenes.

"I do. Everybody that was here for our author signing does. The security tapes will too."

"I'd like to see them," says Agnes.

"When you have some authority you can. That's if they aren't out of date by then."

Agnes opens her mouth, only for Angus to play the ventriloquist. "Manager call thirteen, please. Manager call thirteen."

"I've tidied the stock on the racks so you can get straight to it. Shelve your own books first and then we'll sort out who takes which of Wilf's," Woody says and sprints into his office.

Agnes plants her forearms on the table with a thump. "I don't know what he thinks he can expect of us after talking to us like that."

"I didn't think he said anything too bad to me," says Mad.

"Oh, are we only a team when it suits us?" Once she has glared so hard at everyone that nobody ventures to answer, Agnes says "I don't see why we should carry on working here if he can scrap whoever he feels like whenever he feels like it."

"It's not that simple, is it?" Ross says. "Sounds like he did have a reason."

"You ought to be the last person who'd want us to lose someone else. What do the rest of us say?"

Jill has to finish being shocked by what Agnes said to Ross before she can respond. "We're here now. You say we're a team. You don't want to let us down."

She has lowered her voice. At first she assumes she's trying to keep the discussion secret from Woody, but is he likely to hear while he's repeating "Who is it" to the phone? All at once she has the notion that the argument has attracted an eavesdropper in the stockroom; she even imagines she hears the side of someone's face rubbing against the door, except that the sound is so close to the floor that the listener would have to be on all fours. She starts when someone comes into the room, although it's Ray emerging from the office. "Jill's right," he murmurs. "Let's get this night done with and show the bosses how reliable we are, and then I'll talk to Woody about anything you want me to, I promise. If you want I'll have a word with them while they're here if I get the chance."

"That should do it, shouldn't it?" Mad says to Agnes, who stares at her as if Mad has no right to speak. Jill is about to agree with Mad, not least because she feels as if they're all stuck up to their necks in a morass of stagnant emotion, when Connie's voice produces itself out of the air. "Jill to window, please. Jill to window."

This reminds Jill that there are none in the upstairs walls. No wonder she feels close to suffocated. She's relieved to escape the room, even to join Connie, at least until she does. Connie is standing in front of the window, drumming her nails of one hand on the apex of the trolley in a childish rhythm blotted out by Vivaldi overhead. "I thought you'd be down by now," she says. "Better just stack these books on the floor at the end of a shelf for the moment. We're going to need every trolley in the place tonight."

"Pity you waited for me to do it, then." Jill's on the edge of saying something of the kind when Connie asks "Will you want these?"

She's pointing at the three versions of Brodie Oates with the toe of her expensive multicoloured trainer. "I'll let you decide where you ought to put them," Jill says with her sweetest smile.

For a moment she expects Woody's voice to appear in praise of her expression, and then she's distracted by a blemish on the outside of the window. Something has trailed along the glass at knee height, no doubt a child marking its territory with a greyish discolouration like the track of an overgrown slug. The irregular swath is punctuated with imprints that resemble kisses from a large wide sloppy mouth. She isn't about to direct Connie's attention to it—Connie might send her to clean it off. As Jill unloads the trolley at the end of the shelf for Oates, Connie peels the images of him off the carpet and takes visible pleasure in crumpling them before dropping them daintily into the bin behind the counter. She's rubbing her hands together, either wiping them or in some kind of triumph, when the phones ring throughout the shop.

She's closer to one than Jill is. Jill interests herself in arranging books until Connie answers it. When she says "Sorry?" and repeats it after a pause, Jill glances up to meet her eyes. Something like amusement surfaces in them, and she holds out the receiver. "Is this for you, I wonder, Jill?"

If it is, Jill resents her having got in its way. She doesn't quite snatch the phone, but she waits until Connie is bound for the stockroom before speaking. "Hello?"

At first she can't hear anyone. She's about to return the phone to its stand when a voice seems to form out of the emission of static. Is it attempting to tell her what it wants or saying that somebody or something was little once? As Jill strains to distinguish the sluggish mutter she feels as though it is rising towards her. If it's repeating a phrase like a chant, even once her ears start to ache with effort she's uncertain what the message is supposed to be. "Little ones" or "Little one" perhaps? The voice sounds like a recording blurred by age and close to slowing to a halt. It must be a prank, but aimed at whom by whom? She grows furious with herself for being held there by it, focusing the whole of herself on it as though it means anything at all. "Hello?" she demands. "Who's really there?"

The chant seems to be disintegrating, sinking back into the ooze of static. The words sound softened, half digested by the whitish noise. "If I don't hear something else right now I'm putting down this phone," she says as if she's addressing a child, maybe less than a child. When her threat has no audible effect she waves the receiver at Angus to bring him along the counter. "What can you hear?"

"I don't know." Having listened for a few more seconds, he offers "Nothing much."

She takes back the receiver to find nothing but a hiss that could only pass for a voice if the mouth it belonged to was liquefying. "I wish you'd try to be a bit more definite now and then," she tells Angus as she silences the phone with its stand.

He isn't the one she should be angry with. She hurries upstairs to catch Connie wheeling the trolley into the stockroom; the lift must have taken its time. "Why did you give me that call?" Jill is determined to learn.

"Ross, you grab this trolley while it's free." Once he has, Connie turns to her. "I thought it was about some child."

"I'm not the only person here with one of those."

"No need to look at me."

"I wouldn't dream of it. You still aren't giving me a reason why you passed the call to me."

"Some child was supposed to have done something wrong, wasn't that it? Doesn't yours ever? What an angel."

"Of course she does sometimes. Don't we all, Connie? That doesn't mean the call had anything to do with her. You'd no right to assume it did."

"All right then, maybe it was about those kids we had trouble with over the quiz. You won't say you weren't mixed up in that."

"Mad was too, and Wilf."

"They weren't around. You were. Couldn't you deal with the caller? I didn't realise I needed to stay in case you couldn't handle it."

"There wasn't anything to deal with by the time you gave up. I don't believe there ever was. It was just a stupid pointless joke."

Does that sound as though she's accusing Connie? She's simply trying to convince herself. Either the call or Connie's interpretation, if not both, has made Jill anxious about Bryony, all the more so for being unable to define why. As she wonders how to move away from the argument, she hears the lift begin to talk. It sounds lower than the bottom of the shaft—so distant that the words rising at her back seem too close to the phrase she heard over the phone. It's a childish idea, and hasn't the squabble been childish too? "Shall we both stop?" she suggests. "We're acting like kids in a playground."

Connie's lips grow straight and thin before she speaks. "I'll behave like a manager by all means. Maybe you can remember how that means you should behave."

The lift announces that it's opening and then lives up to its words, revealing an empty trolley. "Load all the books you can and leave them by the shelves they're for and let someone else have the trolley," Connie says and marches away to the office.

Jill seizes the trolley as the lift begins to creep shut. As she races into the stockroom she fancies running Connie down in what would after all be an accident, but the room is deserted. A book topples off a pile out of sight on a rack, and then the silence holds itself still and thick. It must have been a book, though it sounded oddly soft as well as large. No wonder her nerves are distorting her impressions when she's worried about Bryony. She flings armfuls of novels onto the trolley until it's full and plods behind it to the lift, which opens as soon as it has raised its crumbling voice. She shoves the trolley in and thumbs the button, then dodges out and runs downstairs to the phone by the Teenage alcove. For a moment— God, longer—there's only a featureless patch in her mind where Geoff's number should be, and then she dredges it up to dial.

"Hi there. Geoff here or maybe not, which is why you're listening to a tape. Whatever I'm doing I hope you're having as good a time as I am. Talk to me about anything you like and don't forget to say who you are at least and where I can get in touch."

"It's Jill. It's mummy, Bryony, if you're listening," Jill adds, which brings her no answer either. "I thought you two might be there by now. I expect you've gone somewhere for dinner, have you? Don't bother telling me I'm silly for asking when you can't answer. I just wanted to say I'm here at work and I'm fine, Bryony, so you make sure you sleep all night for me. If you feel like saying good night you can always ring this number," she's desperate enough to suggest, and reads it off the plastic stand. "You ought to put your mobile number on the machine, Geoff, and then I could speak to her right now."

This isn't just for him to hear. Connie has trundled a load of books onto the sales floor and is waiting with monolithic patience to be noticed. When Jill turns to her, having finished with the phone, Connie unfolds a fist towards the trolley. "I found this in the lift. Are you already calling it a day?"

"Of course not. I was coming back for my books. I was only trying to have a little word with my daughter. I didn't manage, maybe you heard."

"I don't know what you think I can do about that."

She knows perfectly well, which is why she's saying the opposite. Nothing but anxiety for Bryony could force Jill to ask "You'll have Geoff's mobile number, will you? I would have but he's changed it recently."

"It's possible I've got it somewhere."

"Then could you let me have it?"

"I don't believe so."

Jill's appeal sounds as puerile as she finds Connie's behaviour. "Why not?"

"You should know why."

"Because you're enjoying keeping it from me."

"No, Jill," she says so stiffly that Jill is almost convinced she's telling the truth. "Because nobody's allowed to make personal calls except in an emergency, and it doesn't sound to me as if we've got one of those, not to mention how much it costs to call a mobile. I'm surprised you need telling, but you wouldn't expect me not to, would you? Just a few minutes ago you were wanting me to act like a manager."

"I wouldn't think you'd take what I want into account."

"That's right, it should be what the shop wants, and I hope that's what we all do."

Before Jill can think of a retort or withhold it so as to renew her plea in whatever way she has to that will reach Connie, Woody's voice descends on them. "Hey, let's see some smiles. No reason why we can't have fun tonight."

"Are you going to tell him different?" Connie says, exhibiting a smile Jill's sure is manufactured for the cameras. "Just put your daughter out of your mind for a while. As you said before, she's being looked after."

She inches the trolley at Jill and pushes herself away from it. Words crowd into Jill's mouth, but she's just able to restrain herself from shouting that perhaps one day Connie will know how it feels to have a child. Instead she trudges with the trolley to her shelves.

The books might as well be cartons full of nothing she can use, unless they're simply empty. That's how little they seem to mean, both while she's putting them in order and once she has stacked them in front of the appropriate shelves. How can she feel like this when she loves books and came to work at Texts because she did? Perhaps the Brodie Oates novel has turned her against reading, except that she doesn't seem to have done much of it since she started at the bookshop; in fact, she can't recall any of her colleagues reading much. Just now that's an oddity she hasn't time for, because she knows what's intervening between her and all the books: her misgivings about Bryony. As she returns from parking the trolley by the lift she sees the fog under the floodlights is heavy as rotten velvet, a giant discoloured greyish curtain that sways sluggishly back from the window at her approach. Suppose there were an emergency? How long would it take her to drive through the murk to wherever Bryony is? She has to believe that Bryony is safe, that she has no reason to think otherwise. She shelves books and moves books along shelves and from shelf to shelf to shelve more books with thuds that seem as dull and repetitive as her thoughts. Woody has unloaded a trolley in Wilf's section and is filing books with rapid terse precise flat impacts that she can't help taking as an apparently endless series of criticisms of her pace. Bryony must be home soon—at Geoff's, rather—and when they hear Jill's message, surely they'll call. Nevertheless when a car coasts out of the fog and halts outside the entrance she hopes it has brought them.

It isn't even a Golf. It's a Passat, and Jake climbs out of the passenger seat. The last of the staff are arriving: here comes Greg along the smeared window. Jill can't be sure if he's one reason why Jake leans down to give the man in the driver's seat a lingering kiss. Greg twists his entire torso away from the sight, only to be confronted through the glass by Jill's lack of disapproval. He marches as far as the security posts and stands by them as if he means to reinforce their vigilance. Jake hasn't reached them when Greg says "There's no excuse for behaviour some people might find offensive."

"Who are you calling people besides you, Greg?"

Frank the guard tramps scowling out of the Erotica section. "There's me for second."

Jill doesn't like seeing anyone outnumbered, in the schoolyard or anywhere else. "Nothing wrong with showing a bit of affection," she calls with a smile at the three of them even Woody might be proud of, except he's intent on his shelving.

"Maybe you'll both know what it feels like sometime," Jake says to Frank and Greg. "Maybe you'll show up at the Juicy Fruit some night, you protest that much."

That's more combative than Jill cares to be. She confines herself to smiling at him as he struts in the direction of the staffroom once he has blown a kiss and waved the car away. Greg and Frank shake their heads at each other in disgust before Greg strides after Jake. Jill doesn't imagine he realises how this looks in the context, but she has to smother a giggle. Seconds later her amusement leaves her alone with her multitude of books.

Is she starting a fever? Either the ones she picks up or her arms are growing heavier as she finds space for another book, another book, another book. Unbelievably and unbearably, Woody has finished his shelving and gone to find more. She's unable to judge if she's hot or cold or alternately both, which may be an effect of the fog that must be sneaking unseen through the open doorway. Can't she use her feelings as a pretext to leave? Is she really so worried that she would make for Geoff's flat and have to wait outside if nobody is there? What on earth is there to be nervous about beyond her own state of mind? All she knows is that when the phones shrill, the sound feels like a hook that has lodged deep in her brain. She dashes to snatch up the phone at Information before anyone else can reach one. "Hello?" she hopes aloud.

"Who's that?"

She wants to believe the blurred voice is Geoff's, but there's no point in deluding herself. "It's Jill," she says, and has time to add "Jill at Texts at Fenny Meadows."

"Hi, Jill." This is followed by a stifled yawn that means he hardly needs to say "It's Gavin."

"Where are you? You sound odd."

More specifically, his voice sounds in danger of being engulfed by static. Indeed, she thinks it has been overcome until he says "I don't know. That's why I'm phoning."

"You don't know where you are? Oh, Gavin." She has often suspected that he uses drugs, and now she feels fiercely maternal. "What have you done to yourself?"

"Nothing. It's the fog." His voice fades, so that she isn't certain that he says "It's worse than fog."

She still thinks drugs could be involved. "Gavin, you must be able to tell where you're phoning from."

"My mobile."

His resentfulness gives way to a yawn that must be sucking fog into his lungs. "But how have you got wherever you are?" she persists.

"Took the bus and came down the usual road, but I've been walking a lot longer than I ever do. Must have wandered off along a side road and never realised. I don't wonder in this."

"Would you like someone to drive and see if they can find you?"

"Not a good idea, not in this crap. Thanks, though. I'm turning back and I expect I'll find my way. I just don't know how late I'll be."

"Shall I tell Woody?"

"I wouldn't mind a word with him."

Jill has to remind herself which buttons to press to put Gavin on hold and move onto the public address. "Woody call twelve, please. Woody—"

The interruption leaps at her through the receiver. "Hey, I'm nearly as fast to the phone as you are, Jill. What's up?"

"Gavin's got lost somewhere and he doesn't know when he'll be here."

"We're surely finding out who can be relied on, aren't we. Didn't he dare to tell me himself?"

"He wants to. He's on the line."

"Okay, I'll take him."

Woody sounds capable of blaming Gavin not just for absence but for being the third absentee. Jill would come to his defence if she could think how, but before there's a word in her head the phone excludes her from the conversation. A clamour of books on shelves accompanies her back to hers. Practically everyone is shelving; the only other people in the shop are two resolutely bald men in armchairs, who are clutching picture books as if, like children, they're afraid their treasures will be snatched away from them, though neither seems to be in a reading mood. As Jill returns to her task she feels like part of a machine the size of the shop, a machine devoted to producing thud upon thud so dull they might be pounding out of the books any intelligence they contain. She must be depressed to think that way; certainly her mind feels grey and stagnant. Perhaps that's another sign of whatever is refusing to let her stay either hot or cold and weighing down her arms even in the tiny intervals when they're free of books. All the same, she isn't so hampered that she can't run to Information when the phones burst into a chorus. "Hello?" she gasps.

"It's me again."

"Oh, Gavin." She tries to conceal her frustration. "Do you want Woody?"

"Not this time. You'll do."

She would respond with amused resentment, or perhaps less than amused, if his voice didn't sound so distant, in danger of being engulfed by nothingness. "What for?"

"I've already tried to tell him. I just think someone ought to listen."

"I am, but where have you got to?"

"I still don't know. That's why I thought I'd better call while I can. The fog's not doing my battery any favours."

"Shouldn't you save it in case you need someone to find you?"

"I don't know what sort of person could find me in this." She thinks a swelling wave of static has carried off his voice until he says "What's that?"

Though she presumes he's asking himself, she blurts "What, Gavin?"

"I'm going to see. Listen, while I am I'll tell you—" He stifles a yawn, unless he sucks in a breath. "Hold on."

"That's what I am doing."

"I'm either nearly there or back at the bus shelter. There's a light, only it's odd."

"How odd?"

"It shouldn't be doing that. Anyway, when I got home this morning I started looking at—"

"Hello? Gavin? Hello?"

Only static responds. When Jill presses the receiver against her ear she seems to catch the faintest trace of his voice, but it's no longer talking to her. That's all she gathers from its tone before it sinks deep into the static, which she could imagine is surging up in triumph. Then the phone is a dead lump of plastic, which she's lowering when Woody uses it to ask "Was that a customer?"

"It was Gavin again."

"No wonder you weren't smiling. What's his problem this time?"

"He's still trying to find his way." Woody's watchfulness is making her nervous, but she won't be daunted from remarking "He said he was talking to you about something he saw this morning."

"That would be how I tidied up the store while I was waiting for you guys to arrive."

"Are you certain that's it? I had the impression it was urgent."

"What are you suggesting it was, then?"

"I've no idea. I thought you might have."

"I just told you mine. Maybe you should trust me on this, huh? Don't let me keep you away from your shelves if there's nothing else you want to run past me."

Jill imagines him watching her face as she gives up the phone. She imagines that he's smiling down at her, though in fact he must be smiling upwards; either way, the thought stiffens her mouth. She feels as if he's hovering invisibly over her while she retires to her section. As she slams books into place she's repeatedly drawn to glance out of the window, but it's never Gavin that she has glimpsed. The furtive approaches and withdrawals must be of patches of fog, not of figures peering slyly out of it. She can only assume Gavin saw the bus shelter ahead or, if the light was moving, headlamps on the road he started from. When the phones renew their summons, however, she feels she has an extra motive to dash to the nearest. "Jill," she pants into the receiver. "Jill at Fenny Meadows."

"It's me, Mummy."

Of course Jill is relieved. She tries not to be even slightly disappointed that it isn't Gavin to reassure her he's safe and to answer the question she's eager to revive. "Are you at your father's, Bryony?" she asks instead.

"We just are now. We had a lovely dinner."

"I'm glad. What did you have?"

"Burgers. I had a giant one and daddy had to help me finish it."

"I hope it won't keep you awake. You ought to be in bed with school tomorrow."

"I'm going in a moment. I only wanted to say good night like you said. I'm sure I'll sleep."

"That's what I wanted to hear."

Jill smiles, and then her expression falls awry as she wonders if Woody is assuming he's responsible for it. "Are there lots of people there?" Bryony says.

"Just about everyone that should be."

"Daddy said there were. You'll be safe then with everyone together."

It's barely a query, if even that. Perhaps Jill feels it should be one because she doesn't want her ex-husband speaking for her. "I'm sure we all will," she says. "You have the best sleep ever and I will tomorrow."

"Good night, only it won't be for you, will it?"

"Because it'll be good morning, you mean. So long as it's that, and it will be, and you can wake me when you come home from school."

"I will very gently."

"I know."

They seem to have run out of reasons to continue talking. All at once Jill is wary of being asked if she wants to speak to Bryony's father, which she doesn't. "Good night then. Good night," she says, and cuts herself off before any further repetition makes her feel stupid. At once the phone demands "Was that our stray again?"

"It was my daughter checking up on me."

"She's through for the night, is she?"

"I believe so. She's off to bed."

"So long as she stays there. So long as everyone leaves us alone that hasn't any business here tonight."

Jill has no answer to that. She stifles the receiver with its stand and follows the habitual route back to her shelves. The books are waiting; her arms already feel burdened. At least she knows Bryony is safe. Surely that ought to lighten her mind—and yet for a moment, until she succeeds in dismissing the unwelcome notion, she fancies that Bryony has robbed her of her last excuse to escape.

# WOODY

**Who is he not seeing in his aquarium? That's how the staff look: like** creatures behind glass and swimming through a greyish medium that the images on the monitor sometimes make adhere to them in streaks. Jake is the creature that gives a wriggle now and then, Greg is the deliberate one that moves only for a purpose. From up here Woody's able to observe the patterns they describe, Greg staying well clear of Jake while Angus avoids Agnes as though the similarities of their names are driving them apart, not that Woody can pretend he blames him. Ross is the creature that seems to need Woody to prod it into life; it's moving slower than the others and holding its head low. That may be partly to avoid any eye contact across the shop with Mad, who retreats limpet-like into her nearest alcove whenever he wades close. On the other hand, Jill raises herself as though she's capable of striking out to defend her territory if Connie floats anywhere near her. The staff are most themselves when they've forgotten that they're being watched; Woody wishes someone had thought to mount security cameras in the outer office and the other upstairs areas. He hears Ray or Nigel at a computer out of sight beyond the open door, and a muffled clank of books on a rack in the stockroom. In a moment, however, Ray appears out of the exit from the stairs to the staffroom and drifts about to encourage everyone who's shelving, ducking to dredge up lump after grey rectangular lump as if they're immersed in a ritual. Whoever is left can't be in both the office and the stockroom, and when Woody looks out of his door he finds all the computer screens blank as the walls, if greyer. The office is deserted. He's about to locate Nigel in the stockroom to confirm he has just shut down his computer when Jill puts on a big voice. "Woody call twelve, please. Woody call twelve."

Woody sprints back to his desk so as to observe her while they speak. She's behind the counter yet again and gazing not quite up at him as though she wonders where his eyes are. "You're fond of the phone today, Jill," he remarks.

"I thought it would be quicker than coming to find you."

"I'm easily found. You can't lose me. I'm always here." Instead of telling her any of this he says "So what's taken you away from your shelves this time?"

"I was wondering if we have Gavin's mobile number."

"Why do you need it?"

"In case we can find out where he is now. His phone cut him off, but he may be able to take calls even if he can't make them."

"We already have a job tonight, and that isn't searching for him."

"I'd like to know he's safe, wouldn't you?"

"I like to know where all my staff are, sure enough." Mouthing this feels like the smile he sends her as he says aloud "Okay, leave it to me."

She takes her time and, more to the point, the store's. Once she lets go of the phone she surveys the ceiling as if she doesn't think she has said enough. As she returns to her section by no means as eagerly as he would like, he's close to calling down that she should find a smile, but there are no customers except two seated men whose grey pates look smooth as weathered rocks. Suppose the public is absent tomorrow as well? Then at least everything will be tidy for the visit. Perhaps he should be glad if Gavin isn't there to undermine the image of the store, not just with his constant doziness but the nonsense he at least hasn't passed on to Jill. If the same material has been recorded over more than one cassette, that has to mean the same customer faked the fault twice and perhaps used someone else to return the second tape, unless the customer return slips were mixed up. If Gavin intends to keep on making more of it, perhaps Woody ought to find out where he is. He switches on the computer.

The desktop seems to be in no hurry to appear. Too many seconds elapse before the blank screen breaks out in rudimentary symbols that twitch and darken. A shiver passes through the surface under the glass as though it's wakening or about to waken, and Woody thinks he glimpses a similar disturbance on the security monitor; he almost thinks that the floor shifts underfoot too. If he's tired it's no wonder, though he'll never let his staff see it. He did manage to drowse intermittently in his office last night, and that's all he will need until tomorrow is over. He wouldn't be asking the team to stay up all night if he hadn't proved he could do it himself. He shuts his eyes for surely only a few moments, and when he looks again the screen is swarming with icons waiting to be called up.

He opens the staff list and blinks stickily at it. Aren't there too many names? The idea makes his eyes and brain feel hot and swollen until he notices that Ray has added Frank to the column and left Lorraine on it, where he supposes she'll have to remain for her parents to be paid her last salary cheque. Once Woody has convinced himself that there are no other lurking names he clicks on Gavin's to bring up his details. The store has both his mobile and his home number.

The mobile doesn't ring. Presumably it's out of power, unless

Gavin has switched it off. Suppose he wasn't telling the truth and is actually catching up on his sleep at home? Woody lets that phone ring until he loses count of its repetitions, but there's no answer, not even from a machine. On the whole he hopes Gavin is on his way home: they can do without his infecting any of his colleagues with his yawns while everyone is bound to be susceptible to them or with his irrelevant preoccupations. If this means the rest of the team has to work harder, shouldn't that bring them closer together? They have all night to make up for his absence. Extra work is a small price to pay for an improved workforce without him or Lorraine or Wilf.

Woody is relinquishing the phone when he hears movement in the outer office. A glance at the grey figures ducking like animals to food tells him who it has to be. "Nigel," he calls.

"I'm here. I'm not there," Nigel's head says around the door as though it's making a joke of itself.

Woody's skin is growing clammy with the notion that Nigel has joined Gavin in causing confusion when he realises Nigel thinks the phone was being used to summon him. Woody waves it at him before hanging it up. "I've just spoken to Gavin," he tells Nigel. "Not trying any too hard to join us by the sound of it. Could be he'd rather stay home watching tapes."

"Why that in particular?"

"He tells me you gave him a couple of tapes to play with. I guess you forgot they're the property of the store."

"They were brought back faulty. You don't want anyone to take a look at them, then."

"I can do that at the video store if I think it's necessary. Why the expression? Don't you trust me?"

"I'm sure everybody has to. Why would you ask that? It's just you shouldn't load so much on yourself, if you'll allow me to say so." When Woody continues smiling Nigel withdraws, and Woody thinks he has backed off until Nigel enquires "Isn't that right, Ray? Don't you think Woody's attempting too much by himself?"

222 · Ramsey Campbell

"I must say you're looking a bit stretched, Woody," Ray says, having appeared beside Nigel. "Do remember you've got us and Connie if you want to unload anything."

"There's plenty to unload," Woody says, feeling his smile widen. "Looks like there may be Gavin's stock as well as Lorraine's and Wilf's."

"We were thinking more of pressures of management," says Nigel.

"Were you? I was thinking of what's best for the store, and that's getting every book and video and compact disc downstairs and in order. Or do you expect me to do your share of that? I thought you just told me I'm doing enough as it is."

Ray and Nigel exchange glances that seem not to want Woody to notice them and that remind him of schoolboys obliged to stand outside the principal's office. "We can do it, can't we?" Nigel says to Ray. "Call it a match if you like. I'll shelve for the Scouse team if you will for the Manks."

Ray stares at him and makes his breath heard. "I never took you for the sporting type."

"That's a shade harsh, isn't it, Ray? We had cricket at my school, and I didn't let the side down."

"We're footballers, us lot from Manchester. We got a bit rougher and dirtier."

"Pardon me if I shouldn't have used the term I did. Mancunians, is that more the style?"

"You can use all the words you like, love. The main thing is now we know what you think."

Woody has no idea where any of this is coming from. "If you can't get rid of your differences maybe you can keep them out of the workplace."

At first they seem ready to prolong their disagreement, and then Nigel spins on his heel. Ray follows him and so, having shut down the computer, does Woody. Ray and Nigel are loading trolleys amid a thunder of books on wood. He finds a trolley by the elevator and fills it with armfuls of Gavin's books, then sends it down and has the exit to the sales floor open by the time the elevator arrives. As he parks in Wild Life, Jill strays over to ask "Did you manage to raise Gavin?"

"I tried both his numbers. Nobody at home and nothing at the other."

Woody has begun to sort the trolleyful as an indication that she should return to work when Agnes adds herself to the interrogation. "What's happened to Gavin?" she apparently thinks she's entitled to know.

"Jill? You're the one it seems to be an issue for."

"He rang in to say he was lost in the fog, and now are you saying his mobile's dead, Woody?"

"Someone ought to phone the police, shouldn't they, Jill? We don't know what could have happened to him."

"I would feel happier."

"Hey, getting your shelves right should do that for you. I thought you Brits were supposed to have your emotions under control. I wouldn't have expected you to want to send the cops to track down some guy who's just gotten turned around in the fog."

"Some guy," Agnes repeats. "That's all he means to you. That's how much the shop cares for the staff."

She's confronting him with a stare, and Jill has produced a somewhat sadder toned-down version. He's about to inform them that it depends how much the staff care about the store when the phones intervene. "Hey, maybe that's him now," Woody says as he makes for the nearest. "Maybe you summoned him."

Grasping the phone gives him back to himself. "Texts at Fenny Meadows," he takes pleasure in announcing. "Woody speaking."

"Thought for a moment there you were in Yankee land."

Is he meant to know the caller? The man sounds as if he expects to be recognised. "I'm where I'm supposed to be," Woody tells him. "I'm the manager."

"Brought you over to take charge, did they?" The man's local accent is growing flatter than ever, or his voice is. "Let's hope you can."

Woody is close to wondering aloud whether this is someone else who wants to undermine the store or him. Instead he says "May I help you?"

"Me, no, I shouldn't think. More like it's the other way round."

"Go ahead. We can always use input from our customers."

"I'm a bit more than one of them. You thought so, any rate," the man says with a pride that sounds ashamed to own up to itself. "You invited me there, or one of your crew did. Sorry I turned you down, but I'm glad."

"Should I know why? I believe I've read something of yours."

"That wouldn't tell you." Apparently he doesn't intend to either, since he asks "Is the feller there that was putting notices about? He stuck one on my car and dumped the rest in all the shops by you, as if that's going to do any good."

"Why shouldn't it?"

"Show a bit of sense, lad. Have you looked around you lately? I'd be surprised if you've got any customers at all."

"That's because the expressway's blocked just now."

"I forgot I shouldn't be expecting sense." Before Woody can deal with this, Bottomley—that's his name, Woody has remembered—says "Any road, is he available?"

Woody is gazing straight at Angus, but there's no question of letting him or any of the staff hear from the writer. "I'm afraid you'll have to leave a message."

"Tell him I must have sounded rude."

"I'm sure he'll know that without being told."

"Clever," says Bottomley in a tone that means the opposite. "What I'm driving at, I should have made myself clearer while I had the chance. That place was getting to me, and that's the truth."

"You must have to imagine all sorts of stuff to be a writer."

"That's the last spot I'd imagine anything. It's not the sort of book I wrote about it, is it?"

"I couldn't honestly say."

"There's plenty more like you. You're in the vast majority, no arguing with that." His pride has sunk to the level of resentment, and Woody is hoping his indifference has brought the call to an end until Bottomley says "I wanted the lad with the notices to know I wasn't trying to insult him."

It's only because Woody needs to learn all he can about the incident before confronting Angus that he asks "Why should he have thought you were?"

"I didn't mean he wasn't up to the job. I was saying just the contrary. You'll have got even more qualifications, won't you?"

Woody can't see the point of the question but is provoked to retort "A bunch."

"And you never noticed the mistake either."

Woody's furious to seem to be confirming this by saying "Which mistake?"

"Good God, have you not still? It's got to be worse than I reckoned. You didn't know there was a word wrong on your notices."

"Of course we did. We fixed it."

"Not on the ones you left round that place."

"Yes, those. There was a rogue apostrophe we got rid of."

"Lots of them about these days, but it wasn't one of those. I'm talking about how you said there was a readin group."

"Reading, you mean."

"You did, but it's not what your notices said."

Woody snatches one off the stack beside the phone and narrows his eyes at it. For a moment he's unable to locate the word—he could imagine he has forgotten how to read—and then the misprint swells into his vision as though he has rescued it from being submerged. His rage seems to make the floor quiver underfoot; no doubt that's how it feels to be so undermined. His fist is crumpling the leaflet into a hard spiky lump when Bottomley comments "Sounds like you've got it now."

"It'll be dealt with," Woody promises through his fiercest smile.

"How are you going to do that? If you're blaming anybody you've missed the point."

Woody knows he's going to dislike the answer but can't refrain from saying "Who else would you suggest I blame?"

"Try where you are."

"If you've any complaints about my store I'm listening."

"Not the shop." Bottomley fills a pause with a clink of glass and a generous amount of pouring before he says "That's another thing I could have been clearer about. He may have thought I meant the shop as well."

"I wasn't told you said anything about it."

"I expect he didn't think it was worth mentioning. He'd have thought I was asking where it got its name."

"Pretty obvious, I'd say."

"That would be, right enough, but I meant your business park."

Why should Woody care? The man's drunk and embittered and most unlikely to tell him anything he would like to hear. It's only in order to speed the conversation to its end that he says "What about it?"

"Haven't you Yanks got the word over there?"

"We have a whole bunch you don't. Which in particular?"

"You're losing it now. You're getting disputatious. You're starting to sound like your lad that couldn't see the mistake he was spreading about."

Woody flings the wad of paper into the nearest bin so as to stop bruising his palm. "Have you finished trying to be clearer?"

"Fair comment. I'm behaving like I'm there myself. Must be the drink." Nevertheless Woody hears him take one before asking "Would you call it fenny in the States?"

"I don't believe so, not where I come from. Why?"

"If it was a marsh."

"But it isn't."

The writer is silent long enough that Woody expects him to say more than "It was."

"When?"

"After they built a village there in the sixteen hundreds. If you believe the tales, after they did in the fourteen hundreds too."

In case he needs to be prepared to counter any of them Woody has to ask "What tales?"

"The one you can be sure of is how the second lot went mad. Supposed to have been from drinking bad water. By the time they'd finished fighting or whatever they did to one another there wasn't even a child left alive."

That's in his book, but Woody had almost succeeded in putting it out of his mind. He would wonder aloud if the story has been published anywhere else, except that there's something he doesn't understand. "So what are you saying happened to the first village?"

"Sank, and the other one too."

"You mean the land had to be drained. Why would they go to all that trouble to build a village in the middle of nowhere much?"

"They didn't have to. The land changed by itself."

"Hold on. I know it didn't have to be drained to build the retail park. You aren't telling me it drained itself twice."

"At least."

Is that in his book as well? It adds no credibility, and Woody is about to make this plain when Bottomley says "You got one thing right. It was nowhere much at all, so you'd wonder what led anyone to build on it."

"As far as the stores are concerned it's the expressway, obviously."

"That wouldn't be enough."

Not enough to justify the retail park? Woody can't see what else he could mean. The writer mustn't know much about business; maybe that's why his books have failed to sell. The fog can scarcely persist all year round, and once it lifts, the stores will come into their own—Texts will, anyway. Woody assumes the man is sinking deeper into the effects of his drink; he hasn't said anything that Woody needs to keep in mind or put in anyone else's. When Woody says "So are you through giving me your message?" he's smiling mostly at the joke.

"Seems like I've got to be. Did my best." Woody hears the phone fall away from the writer's mouth to be replaced by a glass that immediately sounds emptier, and then Bottomley's voice fumbles its way back to the receiver. "Here's a thought," he insists. "Here's a good one. Try telling the feller I met and the rest of them when you're clear of that place. See what they think then."

"Why would I want to do that?"

"Think about it when you're somewhere else."

This has to be the worst sort of undermining, so indefinite that it's almost too insidious to be fought off. "Here's just fine for everyone," Woody says and cuts him off.

He's about to start dealing with the people Bottomley exposed when Agnes straightens up with a book. More than ever he's reminded of an animal feeding, not least by her sullen almost bovine expression. "That wasn't Gavin," she says.

"Hey, you noticed."

"I thought we were going to try and make sure he's safe."

"No need to think except about your stock." This doesn't seem to please her, but he doesn't see why he should. "I won't be phoning from down here," he says for her to interpret how she chooses. He's on his way to order Angus upstairs when the phones rouse themselves again.

Is the outside world determined to interrupt their work? The mouthpiece of the phone is clammy with a lingering trace of his breath. "Yes?" he says, sharp as a knife with a hiss for a point.

"Is that the bookshop?"

"It is, ma'am." He softens his voice and his smile, because she sounds like an eager customer. "Woody speaking. How may I be of assistance?"

"Is our daughter there? Is she all right?"

"Everybody here is all right. Who did you want to talk to?"

"She likes to be called Anyes."

"It wasn't your idea, then. Kind of rebellious, huh." Why is he not surprised that the latest unnecessary intrusion has to do with Agnes? "Anyway, yes, she's here and as okay as ever."

"She wasn't involved in the dreadful accident on the motorway, then. We've only just heard about it. We thought she might have rung to say she was safe."

"That wouldn't be possible, sorry."

"Why not?"

The woman's voice is exposing its nerves while Agnes frowns at him as though she hears her mother. He does his best not to use words Agnes can fasten on. "Store policy. Nothing out unless it's for business."

"Don't you think that's a little too inflexible? It's like shutting everybody up in there."

He sees where Agnes has learned her attitude. "Not my rule, ma'am," he restricts himself to saying. "Applies to me just as much."

"Then you're agreeing with me, aren't you? You ought to be able to do something as the manager. I'll have a word with Agnes if I may."

"Can't do, I'm afraid."

"What have you got against that? You just said—"

"Busy. Will be all night. The whole store to prepare for an occasion, and people that ought to be helping aren't. Don't worry, you can trust me. Everyone's safe while I'm in charge."

Neither this nor his smile seems to reach the woman, who says "I'd still like to speak to my daughter."

"As I said, not possible. Please don't try again. I'll be taking all the calls."

He feels more overheard than ever. He feels as if by lowering his voice he has drawn an audience closer, one he can't even see. Agnes scowls sidelong at him as she stoops as little as she has to for a book. When her mother emits a gasp of outrage or incredulity he dispenses with the phone. "I want to see you in my office now, Angus," he shouts as the exit to the staffroom gives way to his badge.

He can see Agnes from the office too. As he watches sluggish downcast stunted Angus cross the floor he observes her resting a hand on the phone at the counter. He sends his voice down to her and the rest of the staff. "Let's keep our minds on why we're here tonight, shall we? Talk to me if you have to talk to someone. Right now we don't need anyone except who's here."

He's gratified to see Agnes snatch her hand away as if the phone itself has accused her. When she glares about the ceiling he feels the corners of his mouth lift, inverting the expression she takes to her shelves. He would invite her to find a smile if he hadn't to deal with Angus, who ventures into the office with a very tentative grin. It wavers between lessening and turning puzzled as Woody says "You don't believe in sharing your encounters with the store, then."

"Encounters with the store." If possible even more dully Angus says "What kind?"

"Not with the store." Woody finds it difficult to credit that anyone working for Texts could be so stupid. "With the man you met," he says through his smiling teeth, "while you were supposed to be publicising us."

"You mean the, what would you call it." Angus devotes altogether too many seconds to coming up with "The historian."

"I wouldn't call him that, no. More like an interfering son of a bitch, and maybe you can tell me why he was hanging round here."

"I got the feeling it was because of Lorraine."

"Sick as well as interfering, it sounds like. Looking for material he can use in his next book, or maybe in the one with Fenny Meadows in it if he ever sells enough to reprint it."

"He wasn't just talking about Lorraine. He wanted to tell someone about Fenny Meadows."

"Yeah, I heard that stuff from him. Some of it I wouldn't be surprised if he made up. You know what's a whole lot more important? The one thing he said that was any use, you didn't post our advertising on the cars like you were told to."

"I did some. I thought most of the leaflets were for the shops."

"You thought you knew more about how to push the store than me, did you? There's too much thinking getting in the way around here." The comment makes Woody feel asinine, especially since he isn't sure what he means by it. "In future," he tells Angus, "I guess you'll know just do what you're told."

"I ran out."

By God, now even he's arguing. Woody thought he was one of the people who could be relied upon to commit themselves to the team. "Okay, why don't you do that," Woody rather more than suggests, but Angus only blinks a dumb question at him. "Run out of here. Run down to your shelving."

Having to explain his point seems to rob it of wit. He turns his back on Angus so as to be ready to catch him on the monitor. He has a good idea of what will follow, and it does. Angus has scarcely returned to the sales floor when Agnes swoops to question him about the interview. As Woody spies on their unsmiling conversation he mouths the words he thinks they're using, and then he realises they're wasting not just their time but his and, worse, the store's. "Can we keep chat for our breaks tonight," he directs through all the speakers. When Angus retreats guiltily to his shelves while Agnes gazes in frustration after him, Woody adds "Connie, join me in my office."

Perhaps it's apparent from his tone that he isn't inviting her out of friendliness, but he doesn't understand why Jill should observe her departure with more of a smile than she has displayed since arriving for work. He watches Connie sink out of sight beyond the bottom right-hand corner of the screen. When he hears footsteps on the stairs he can't help being confused by their upward progress; he's close to imagining that someone unidentifiable is being drawn towards the room. He jumps up, leaving his chair in a spin, and hurries into the staffroom as the door reveals Connie after all. She looks taken aback by his appearance—surely by finding him so near. "I'm shelving," she says somewhat defensively. "Do you want me to carry on?"

"You don't think that would take too much readin."

She looks ready to smile at this; in fact, she begins to. "How's that again?"

"It just came to me that I don't know how much readin you do."

"Quite a lot whenever I've the time. I don't talk like that, do I?"

"Working for the store has to need readin, right? Or maybe you'd call it workin."

"To be honest with you, Woody, if there's a joke I'm not getting it."

"Not gettin it either, I guess. Hey, that makes the both of us. Why don't we take a look at your leaflet together."

She holds her hands and her pink lips slightly open in a fashion he suspects she has meant to seem appealing ever since she was a child. "They're all out there. Shall I go down and get one?"

"No need. It's here waitin to be seen." When she responds with a frown like a twitch of a nerve in her forehead Woody wrenches his smile wider. "You can bring it up on your computer. Go ahead, cough it up on the screen."

She moves to her section of the office desk barely fast enough to keep him from telling her not to waste time. A greyish surface patched with symbols so vague as to be meaningless swells into view on her monitor and forms into the desktop screen. She snaps at it with the mouse, on which she has inked whiskers, then employs the pallid smooth limbless object to dig into her files. As the publicity text quivers into sight and steadies itself she murmurs "What did you want to look at?"

"Take a good look."

She takes at least that before releasing a gasp that sounds like the reverse of the breath she just sucked in. "Oh Lord. Oh no. You're joking."

"I'm not, no. Were you?"

"What could have stopped me seeing that?"

"Do you know, I'd have asked the same question."

"I'm serious. What could have? I've never been that careless. I don't believe anyone could have had a reason before to say I was at all. Scatty maybe, but that's how I like to be with people." With the briefest pause for agreement or encouragement, not that Woody is minded to provide either, she adds "There's something about this place I'm starting not to care for much."

"You know what, I feel the same way about staff that aren't loyal to the store."

"Loyal how? Doesn't it include saying if you see things are wrong?" It isn't conscientiousness Woody hears but nervous triumph as she demands "What's that?"

Her gaze appears to be trying to sidle behind the computer. "Try a shadow," he says impatiently enough to tug his smile awry.

She pushes the keyboard aside and drags the monitor away from the wall. Woody is reminded of someone turning over a rock to reveal what's underneath. Is she trying to distract him from the incomplete word on the screen? He wishes he'd conducted the interview downstairs, however embarrassing that might have been for Connie; she's wasting time he could have filled with shelving. She has indeed exposed a mark on the wall, but he's far less than impressed. "So somebody needed to wash their hands."

"It's here as well."

The back of the monitor bears the imprint of another hand, or perhaps the same one. In both cases the lengths and sizes of the fingers are a good deal more various than the digits of any hand should be. Woody's on his way to frowning when the explanation becomes clear. "The guy who brought the computers up must have been wearing gloves."

"Was he? Did you see him?" Before Woody can assure her without remembering that he did, she makes to lift the monitor back into position, only for her hand to flinch away. "It's still damp," she protests.

Woody plants his hand on the mark to feel nothing except plastic and perhaps a hint of grit. "It isn't now," he says and shoves the monitor close to the wall.

"Did we decide you wanted me to shelve?" Connie seems to hope.

"Sure, once you've fixed your mistake, and why don't you print out a few copies I can show to our visitors tomorrow."

She looks afraid that something may squeeze up from behind her desk and fumble at the computer. "Jesus, I'll do it," Woody says so harshly his teeth ache.

He types the extra g and, having saved the document, sets the printer to emit fifty copies while he watches grey figures genuflect and rise up on the security monitor. He's heading for the stairs at a rate that's intended to make Connie follow when she picks up a leaflet instead. "Are we sure this is how it should be? I don't seem to be able to tell any more."

"Who are you saying is responsible for that?"

She shakes her head and waves her hands on either side of it to signify her brain or the surroundings. Woody grabs the topmost of the leaflets the printer has churned out. By the time he has finished scanning the clammy page it has grown chill, though surely not moist, in his hand. "I don't see a problem," he informs her.

"Shall we ask someone else?"

"Why would I want to do that?"

"In case there's anything neither of us is seeing."

"I'm seeing plenty. Mainly how the night is going to be wasted if I don't stay on top of some people."

Her lips part, either to object or because she realises she's in-cluded, only to press themselves an even paler pink. "Okay, let's get back to shelving," Woody says and holds the door open so that she obeys. He hurries downstairs behind her to speed her up and sprints back to Wild Life, where he sorts the books and unloads the trolley so fast that a book falls open at a photograph of chimpanzees in the jungle beating one of their number to death. He scoots the trolley to the elevator and is slamming books into place when Agnes approaches him. "Isn't it time we started taking our breaks?"

"Has anyone been here that long?" When he glances at his watch he's by no means entirely pleased to find that the store will be closing in less than half an hour. "I take it by we you mean you," he says.

"Someone has to be first."

"Someone has to set an example, sure enough. Hey, I hope there's a smile in there somewhere. Okay, the sooner you break the sooner you can be back at work. Let's make certain we keep it to ten minutes."

She ought to realise that starts now, especially since she was so impatient for it, but she lingers to demand "Have you called some-one about Gavin?"

"I've done everything that's necessary."

"And?"

"I expect we'll hear more in due course."

Even she can't quite bring herself to accuse him of lying. In any case it's presumably the truth. She contents, if that's the word, her-self with a challenging look, no match for his smile. When she makes for the staffroom he doubts she has time for the coffee he as-sumed she would use to liven herself up. Perhaps he can allow her the extra minute or two if it helps her work harder—but then her voice erupts beneath the ceiling. "Has anybody got a mobile I can borrow? I'll pay for the call."

He dashes up to the office to find her watching the security mon-itor through his doorway. Is it possible she even dared to use his extension? "What gives you the idea you can use the PA for that kind of message?" he feels profoundly restrained for enquiring.

"It's quicker than going round everyone. I thought you'd want me to save time."

"And who are you proposing to call?"

"My parents to tell them how I am so they can get some sleep. I don't think anyone can object to that when I'm on my break and not using any of the phones the shop wants to keep all to itself."

He feels alternately hot and cold from his dash or with anger. Can he believe her? Suppose she plans to call the police about Gavin and bring more inconvenience? He's considering whether he should put her on her honour, if that still means anything to Brits like her, when Ray's voice booms through the speakers. "If it's not a very long call, Anyes, you can pinch mine."

"There you are, Ray thinks he's allowed to use the PA," Agnes is pleased to inform Woody as she hurries to the stairs.

Woody's stinging eyes feel so swollen he could almost fancy that an insect bit him. He seizes the receiver in his office and sends his voice to say "Will everyone be aware that the phones are only to be used for the good of the store."

This appears to rekindle Ray's interest in the books heaped at his feet as Agnes lets herself down off the bottom of the screen and then bobs up close to him in the top left-hand quadrant. Ray slips a mobile phone out of his jacket and hands it to her with a swiftness Woody finds surreptitious. Woody takes the stairs in twos, to recommence shelving and ensure she doesn't overstay her break. She has stepped outside to phone, but is back well in time. It's only when she loiters next to Ray that Woody feels he has to interest himself in their conversation. They aren't discussing Gavin; Ray is complaining "I wanted my wife to be able to get in touch. More than likely she'll be up half the night with the baby."

"I honestly don't know what could have gone wrong. All I did was switch on and dial."

"I charged it this morning." Ray pokes a button, but nothing responds. "Still dead as mud," he takes time to notify her.

"I can't understand it. I wouldn't have left you phoneless, I hope you know." She raises her voice to call "Has anyone else got a phone?"

"Why, so you can kill theirs as well?"

"So we don't have to depend on the shop."

"I guess that's exactly what you should be doing," Woody tells everyone.

Nigel has raised his head at her appeal but has second thoughts about any offer he was proposing to make. "I left mine at home," Ross admits. "I don't know anyone who'd want to call me now."

"My boyfriend's got hold of mine," Jake is eager everyone should hear.

Greg stares hard at him and then not much more gently at Agnes. "I'm surprised you haven't got one of your own."

"I didn't bring it. I thought I could rely on the shop like we were just told. Are you saying you can lend me one?"

"I can't imagine why you'd think I would be, under any of the circumstances."

Woody sees that neither of them means to look away before the other does. He's suddenly aware of two shaven-headed men in armchairs—of how the books propped on their laps remind him of the placards contest judges hold up. "You have just a couple of minutes, Agnes," he says.

"Maybe I should stop trying to get on with people I don't. Maybe I should call it a day before you lock up."

"Can't call it a day when it isn't one," Mad remarks as she snatches a book off a Teenage shelf.

He would like to believe she intends to jolly Agnes out of her sullenness, but Woody could have managed without the interruption and without Greg's. "So long as you're aware you'll be letting every single one of your colleagues down, Agnes."

"Okay, Greg, I'm handling this."

"Greg wants you to think he only cares about this place," says Agnes. "Cares a lot more than he does about the people in it, anyway."

"I'm sure he cares about some of us deep down," says Jake.

A splutter that the shelves he's kneeling behind don't quite muffle escapes Nigel. Greg gives Woody a look that's on the way to holding him responsible and unprepared to wait long for him to intervene. He isn't entitled to confront Woody like that. Nobody here is, and the way to remind them is to deal with the actual culprit. "Agnes? Your time's up."

"You're telling me you want me to go."

Can she really think he means that? He's being made to feel as if his words have to struggle up from some unsuspected medium, emerging blurred almost beyond recognition. "Right," he says. "To go and shelve."

"You're asking me to stay."

If she's trying to convince herself or any of the listeners that she has won the skirmish, she isn't clever enough. "I'm sure everyone here wants you to," Woody says for them to hear.

He realises he should have put it differently when the seated men raise their eyes to her—eyes drained of all expression. It doesn't help that nobody else is looking at her. After a pause that makes his smile twitch, she says "Maybe there are people I oughtn't to land with more work."

Once she deigns to resume shelving he returns to Gavin's. The confrontation has left his skull feeling stuffed with mud and grit. The books the seated men are holding on their laps have started to put him in mind of identity plaques in a police photograph, especially when he thinks how they must appear on the security monitor. He's beginning to wonder if the immobility of the men is distracting or infecting his staff. Aren't their movements too sluggish? He does his best to set them an example with a shelf's worth of new books before he glances at his watch. "Texts will be closing in fifteen minutes," he shouts. "Please take any final purchases to the counter."

The seated men seem unaware that the announcement has any relevance to them. Woody shelves loudly and rapidly for most of five minutes. Since this fails to stir them, he uses the phone next to Reptiles to declare "Texts will be closing in ten minutes." This has no apparent result either, nor does filing books so vigorously that he cuts a knuckle on the edge of a shelf. Well before his next proclamation is due, he's obliged to consult his watch while he sucks his rusty finger. The second hand crawls like an insect tethered on a thread around the dial, and when at last it grows vertical again he feels released to breathe. "Texts will be closing in five minutes," he and the overhead speakers say. "Would customers please make their way to the exit. The store will be open tomorrow at eight."

The seated pair could pass for statues in a museum, complete with descriptions of themselves. He's wondering how long to give them before he updates the broadcast when Nigel goes over to murmur to them. Their heads may rise an inch or so, but that's all. Before long Ray joins his colleague to no effect beyond more murmuring. Far too many of the staff are more interested in eavesdropping than shelving, which is another reason why Woody hurries to intervene. "Look, we've told you it's nothing personal," Nigel is saying. "We have to shut for the night now, that's all."

"He said you lot aren't going home," one of the men objects.

"He shouldn't have told you. I don't know why he did."

"You calling him a liar?" one says with sudden enthusiasm.

"I'm not calling him anything. I'm simply asking you politely to let us shut, and so's he."

"Shut it whenever you like."

The other seated man laughs or grunts at this before adding "Let's see who's the most politest, you or your mate."

Ray and Nigel turn to Woody with some relief instead, prompting the men to twist their heads an inch or so in his direction. Their faces are stagnant, their eyes expressionless as fog. "They've brought another of their mates," the left-hand man informs nobody or everyone.

"Reckon he's the leader of their gang."

He feels as though they have draped their inertia over him like a thickening grimy web. "My staff have asked you nicely," he says with a smile that needs some conscious maintenance. "Can you leave now, please."

"We're in no bugger's way," the right-hand man says.

"We're comfy, us," his crony adds.

"We're closed to the public now. We aren't insured for anyone but staff."

Woody's almost certain that's the case, but the men look as if they know he isn't. "Never mind saying we're public," one somewhat obscurely complains.

"We've been here every day. We deserve a bit of credit."

"Have you bought anything?" enquires Nigel.

Woody has the impression Nigel wants to make up to him for failing to eject the men, and Ray also tries by remarking "You don't seem to read much."

"Who says you've got to read to be here?"

"You lot don't all. The one that tore the book up and stuffed it in the other bugger's gob, he couldn't and he works here."

"Not any more," Woody immediately feels he had no need to say.

"You could all be like him, far as we know." Ignoring Woody, the left-hand man says to Nigel "Let's hear you read a goodnight story and maybe we'll give you some peace."

"And you read us one as well," his comrade says to Ray.

Ray and Nigel swing around from avoiding each other's eyes to meet Frank's arrival. The guard has taken long enough to quit defending the entrance from nothing except fog. "Look out, here's reinforcements," the left-hand man remarks.

"More if they're needed," Greg vows, slamming a book onto a shelf and marching over.

The men tilt their heads as if they're enjoying their slowness. "We having a fight?" one hopes, enthusiastically for them.

"If you insist," Woody says before anyone else can speak. "With the law if you don't move right now."

Perhaps the last phrase is too ambitious. Even the sense of the rest appears to take time to seep through. "You really want us going out there," the right-hand man eventually has to have confirmed.

"You got it. We really do."

"You'll be stuck all night with just them that's here," his companion points out.

"I guess we'll live."

"All right, we know where we're not wanted." An unnecessary number of seconds make themselves felt before he follows his words out of the left-hand chair. His associate heaves himself up with the same sticky gasp of moist leather, muttering "That's what we know all right."

Frank tramps after them down the Poetry aisle with Woody in his wake, and Greg stays in Woody's, leaving Ray and then Nigel to bring up the rear. They're herding the men out of the store, not being led towards the blank wall of fog that towers above the floodlights and embraces the dark. As the men shuffle off the READ ON! mat and onto the sidewalk one says "Don't reckon the bluebottles would get here too quick in this."

"He means the police," Nigel murmurs to Woody.

"There won't be a reason for me to call them now, will there? Good night," Woody bids the sullen backs as he secures the door.

The men swivel their torsos and stare at the clicking of the keypad. They haven't finished staring when their feet begin to carry them into the fog. Soon it dilutes the figures, then flattens them and fills their outlines with a shifting pallor before it absorbs them. As Woody watches to be certain they're gone for the night, he hears Nigel murmur "You rather landed us in that, didn't you, Ray?"

"Like to tell me how?"

"You didn't have to give them quite so much information just because they asked if we were leaving too."

"It's called being friendly, Nigel. That's how we are up this end of the road, and aren't we supposed to be welcoming everyone? That's the routine, isn't it, Woody?"

"I guess I can't argue with that."

"If anyone did any landing, Nigel, maybe it was you getting their backs up."

"I've had no complaints about how I handle people. I'm not expecting any either."

"Maybe it was you not being from round here did it."

"I'd say they'd have to be rather stupid, anyone who reacted that way."

"Why, aren't we allowed to notice any more if someone talks different from us?"

"More grammatically, you mean."

"Next you'll be saying I'm another thickie like someone else turned out to be."

"Hey, I talk more different than any of you," Woody intervenes. "Let's just make sure we're on our own at last with no distractions." That brings the argument to an end without his having to chide them in front of the rest of the team. He's still in control, and he raises his voice until it sounds as big as the interior. "Okay, everyone go to the edge."

Nobody does so, not even Greg. Ray and Connie look as though they want to exchange glances. "Go to the walls as far apart as you can," Woody says, grabbing the nearest phone from the counter to give himself more of a voice. "Get it now? Take a good look on the way that there's nobody else here."

Is Agnes deliberately lagging because she can claim she's only doing as she was told? As he watches her his skin crawls hot and cold, and his eyes prickle like patches of a rash. When she reaches the video section at last he succeeds in relaxing his grip on the phone, which has been creaking in his ear like a structure about to collapse. "Fine, everyone stay where you are and look around. Clear?"

He doesn't immediately understand why several of them seem close to insulted, and then he smiles at himself and, more importantly, at them. "I'm saying is the store clear?" he amplifies, and the phone does.

"Clear," Greg calls, followed by a chorus of everyone else; Woody sees their mouths move, at any rate.

"Fine, fine. Now give everyone you can see a smile." Woody lets his linger on each member of the team in turn before asking "Anyone had less than they think they deserve? Then let's be sure to keep that up for the night."

Frank emits a cough from beside the security posts. "We've all got a smile for you too, right, guys?" Woody says, and the store does in his voice.

The guard begins to turn towards the exit before at least one of them has finished smiling. "I'll be getting home, then," he mumbles, rubbing one reddened cheek.

"Thanks for your help today. Travel safe."

As Woody unbuttons the door Frank takes a heavy pace away from it; he might almost be recoiling from the prospect of the fog. "Good luck," he says too loud to be speaking only to Woody, who could almost imagine he isn't being addressed at all.

Woody doesn't respond until the door is locked. "We don't need it, do we?" he shouts as Frank tramps past the window, dragging his blurred swollen shadow across the fog. The shadow slithers down it and vanishes into the glistening sidewalk as he turns the corner of the store. Soon a giant muffled cough is audible behind the building, and then the motorcycle chugs out of the retail park.

244 · Ramsey Campbell

Before too long the harsh clogged throaty sound is no louder than the miniature violins overhead, which seem to scurry off with it and silence it. "Okay, now it's just the team," Woody shouts. "Everyone back where you were. Let's find out what we're capable of tonight."

# MADELEINE

**"Mad." The word seems to hang in the air until she glances up,** when Woody's disembodied voice says "Take your break now, please."

She has finished shelving her books at last, and tidying her section too. She knows it isn't the way to think, but she's tempted to welcome the fog if it keeps grubby little hands away from making a mess of her shelves. As she gives her alcoves a satisfied inspection, Woody adds "Ross, you break as well."

Nobody could mistake Ross's reaction for eagerness. Once he raises his head above his aisle, where she could imagine he was doing his best to hide, he takes longer still to risk eyeing Mad. When she flashes him a neutral smile she feels as if Woody's invisible stare is trying to pull her lips into the shape he favours. "You look as if you could do with a coffee," she calls across the shop to Ross. "I don't mind telling you I could."

That's more than true. As she holds her badge against the plaque beside the door up to the staffroom she shuts her eyes for what she assumes is a moment, only to open them to find Ross next to her. The door yields to his shove, and he holds it open for her even when she's well through it. "Don't worry, Ross," she murmurs. "You know I don't bite."

His mouth struggles to hold back an expression, and she remembers that he knows the opposite. She almost thinks she glimpses the faintest lingering mark of her teeth on his neck. As she hurries upstairs she feels as though she's trying to outrun her remark, which she would never have made if she were more awake, but neither the staircase nor the equally windowless staffroom offers any escape. All she can do is lift his mug and hers down from the wall cupboard. Whoever put them away seems not to have cared about how, since several others topple forward with them. Ross saves those by reaching up behind Mad but almost drops them when her shoulders meet his chest. By the time she shuts the cupboard he's on the far side of the table and pretending that they didn't touch. "Ross," she rebukes him.

"Sorry," he mumbles, blinking about for somewhere safe to look.

"For what?" For touching her or for recoiling? Rather than embarrass him by appearing to wait for an answer, she says "Shall we just try and get on together? There are too many people round here at each other's throats."

She's speaking quietly to ensure Woody doesn't hear over the clatter of books on at least the third trolley he has loaded so far. When her choice of words catches up with her she hopes Ross didn't hear either. She turns away to pour the coffee and to avoid imagining any vestige of her bites, which she can almost taste. The percolator bubbles with a muddy sound as she plants the mugs on the table and says "I mean, shall we agree to forget the past? It doesn't have to affect us, does it? No reason we can't still be friends."

Ross ducks to gaze into his coffee and then ventures to glance up. "I thought we were."

"That's good." A sense that his eyes aren't revealing all he feels prompts her to add "Don't you think?"

"I said. Only forgetting might be harder."

There's no doubt where his memory has lodged. "I wouldn't ask you to forget Lorraine."

"I'm glad." He looks rather less than that for a pause before he says "I should have gone out there. She might still be alive."

"It wasn't your fault. Nobody could say it was. You were stopped."

"I should have anyway. It's only cowards that blame other people when they could have done something themselves."

His unhappy contemplation settles on her until she blurts "Are you saying I could have?"

"No, of course not. Absolutely not. Well . . ."

"Let me have it. You just told me you weren't a coward."

"Maybe if you'd parked out in front like Agnes . . ."

"Yes, if I had, what, Ross?"

"Maybe whoever stole your car wouldn't have had the chance to."

"You think we'd have seen them in all this fog?" Her hand that was reaching for her coffee jerks as though she's indicating the walls. His suggestion isn't new to her; she's kept herself awake at night with it. When she says "Even Agnes doesn't park close enough to be noticed" she wants to convince them both.

"About time everybody did." He feeds himself a gulp of coffee and almost spouts it back into the mug. "God, this is strong."

Mad takes a sip, which is at the very least enough. "Ouch, you're right. Who made it?"

"I did."

Woody's voice is so loud that for a moment she thinks he's using the speakers. She sees Ross realise as she does that everything they've said may have been heard in the stockroom. He cups a hand to send a whisper at her. "Does it taste stale to you?"

The coffee flavour is so overwhelming that she can't distinguish whether there's more to it. She's about to risk another sip when the thunder of books on wood ceases and Woody appears in the stockroom doorway. "I figured I'd help the team stay awake."

He looks like insomnia embodied, though his lips are peeled back from his teeth in a smile that seems bent on denying he's anything but fresh. His dark blue shirt is so rumpled he might have slept in it, and the last time he shaved he missed an inch of stubble around the left hinge of his jaw. His wide eyes glisten like raw wounds. Mad thinks he's going to urge them to drink up his brew, but he says "Who's at whose throats?"

How long is her careless use of words likely to haunt her? She wants nothing more than to be rid of them, which is partly why she says "I wasn't thinking of anyone in particular."

"That sounds like you were thinking of everyone."

It occurs to her that this isn't far from the truth, but it's surely up to him to notice; she isn't about to get anybody into trouble. "No, I was exaggerating," she says, hoping it's true.

"I need to be careful who I put together, though, right?"

"That's up to you."

"At least you guys are good together. Of course, you used—" His smile wobbles and his gaze appears to sink into his eyes. "But then you—" There's another interlude for his smile to grow uncertain whether to look contrite or amused or both. "Gee, I do apologise. I couldn't have been thinking. Would you like me to stick around while you're up here together?"

"No need at all," Mad says, the first word in chorus with Ross.

"I guess I've managed to unite you, huh?" Woody's presence is making the room feel yet more enclosed by the time he says "You've another few minutes. I'll leave you to it."

As soon as they hear the trolley rumbling towards the lift, Ross murmurs "I've had enough."

She assumes he doesn't mean only the coffee he pours down the sink. She isn't sure if she's included, but can't help feeling that she is, since he hurries downstairs without leaving her even a glance. She certainly won't care. She sips her coffee and wishes she had a book to read, though she's unable to call a single one to mind. There's none in the staffroom; she doesn't know when she last saw anybody reading in here. She could look in the stockroom except for having had enough of Woody. "If you're up for books, Nigel, take these," she hears him saying by the lift. "I'll grab some more."

Instead he wanders back into the staffroom. "I guess I'm entitled to a break," he says. "When you're through here you can help Nigel shelve."

She braces herself for his company, but he heads for his office. She's attempting once again to taste the coffee when he begins to speak. Is he telling her to finish her break? It's clear from his tone that he's talking to someone. Mad's effort to distinguish his words makes the walls appear to flicker and shift like fog, unless that's a symptom of her lack of sleep. Her skull feels brittle and teeming with static by the time she grasps he's saying "That's how we like it, guys. Keep on moving down there."

He must be addressing the security monitor, but she doesn't enjoy being alone with his voice. "Let's get lively or I'll have to call you up," he says. "That's it, keep on bobbing up out of that stuff." Obviously this is how the images on the screen look to him, and no wonder if he's had as little sleep as she suspects, but that's hardly reassuring either. She's sipping coffee quicker than her body welcomes when she hears him say "Hey, you're ahead. You're the man."

This time it isn't just his utterance that bothers her. Why didn't she notice the echo before? It seemed to repeat only his last three words, and sounded more than muffled: buried, she's tempted to think. Perhaps Woody has become aware of it and turned towards whichever section of his office is producing the effect, because when he says "You're the one, sure enough" the low dull thick voice doesn't follow his words so much as underlie them. If he's no longer facing the screen, whom is the remark intended for? She has to assume he's talking to himself, not an idea that encourages her to linger. She downs rather less than a mouthful of coffee and empties the rest into the sink. She rinses the mug and leaves it on the draining-board, and hears Woody speak again as she heads for the stairs. Is he talking in his sleep now? She could imagine that the echo, which sounds more subterranean than ever, is close to absorbing his low voice, but the idea makes no sense. She's wondering as she returns to the sales floor whether she ought to mention his behaviour to Connie or Nigel or Ray, until she notices what she overlooked. She needs to tidy away the books the men who occupied the armchairs left behind.

Both the large thin books are Tiny Texts. One is called *A Is For Ant*; the other says it's for *Angel*. Might little readers end up confused if they saw both? No doubt they would be young enough to accept a smile from the ant as well as from the angel, especially since the ant is such a simplified cartoon. At least they would be too young to know other words the letter stands for: abyss, accuse, agony, alien, ambush . . . Mad has no idea why these and more are floating up in her head. She holds the books against her chest and makes to plant them on the top shelf in her first alcove, but nearly drops them as she sees the bottom shelf.

Rather than cry out, she traps her lips between her teeth. Some of the picture books are the wrong way up, several are the wrong way out, and two are sprawling on top of the others. She knows she didn't leave any of her shelves like that; she never would have. She slams the *A* books into place at the very start of her section before she calls out "Who's the helpful person?"

Heads swivel to gaze or blink at her. Because she doesn't know who the culprit is, they all look brainless as busts perched on shelves. When other heads rise into view she thinks of puppets hauled up on strings or with a hand stuck inside them. "Tell us that again, Mad," Connie says. "Are you wanting help?"

"Not from whoever was in my section while I was upstairs."

Connie is raising her eyebrows at the same pace as she broaches her pink lips when Woody's voice flies out of its nests beneath the ceiling. "Connie and Jill break now, please. I guess that can't involve any problems." The remark is spoken lower, presumably to himself, and then he returns to the attack. "Connie and Jill."

"Go along, Jill. I'll be up when I've sorted this out." Connie turns back to Mad less than halfway through saying this. "I don't think we're with you, Mad. Nobody's been there. We've all been too busy."

"Too busy to see what someone did, you mean. Just take a look."

Has any more of her section been disarrayed? Mad stalks in and out of her alcoves to examine them, only to become frustrated by failing to detect any more chaos. It feels like an anticlimax to have to return to the beginning, however fiercely she says "Look at this."

Only Jill advances to do so, and that's on her way to the staffroom. "Oh, Mad, after all your work," she says, but also "I didn't do it and I honestly didn't see anyone."

Connie waits for the door to shut before she says "For a change I've got to agree with Jill. I think she was speaking for all of us."

Everyone nods, and it doesn't improve matters that some of them appear not to want to. They gaze at Mad until she blurts "What are you suggesting?"

"I thought it was you that's doing that." Connie advances to frown at the shelf and to murmur "Just put it right and don't make such a fuss. I expect the time caught up with you for a few moments, that's all."

Mad feels as if her brain is shrinking as small as the argument. A wave of mingled heat and chill that may also be tiredness surges over her as she refrains from speaking until Connie has gone upstairs. "If it wasn't any of us that must mean there's someone here that shouldn't be."

She's confronted by too many stares and by guarded expressions she likes even less as Ross says "What do you want people to do?"

"We need to search again. Really search and not just stand about grinning like clowns at each other. Start at the sides and meet in the middle and if anyone's here they'll be trapped."

Ross seems to feel bound to support her. He retreats to the video and compact disc shelves against the wall, and then Angus moves to stand in front of the counter. The next moment Agnes marches to the literature section alongside the window. "Well, if that's the consensus," Nigel says. "Let's get it over with if it'll put any minds at rest."

"They aren't meant to be resting," Ray objects. "We don't want them dozing off."

"I don't see where there's any chance of that."

Greg strides to a wall as far away from Jake as he can manage. "I'm ready," he announces in a tone close to a rebuke.

Ray and Nigel turn their backs on each other and pace away like duellists. Nigel is the first to reach a wall, and swings around at once. "Off we trot, then," he says. "Let's make certain nobody can say anywhere was overlooked this time."

Mad assumes this is aimed at her and whoever sided with her. All at once she feels both nervous and stupid. What is she expecting anyone to find? If a child were lurking in the shop it would surely have failed to keep silent by now, and who else would have hidden so as to disarrange her books except a child? If by any chance an unnaturally noiseless little intruder has succeeded in remaining unseen—if perhaps it's crawling on all fours towards the exit and too lacking in intelligence to realise there's no escape that way—the impression makes her uneasier than she can comprehend. She begins to sidle alongside the rear wall as Angus does along the counter so that nobody can dodge unnoticed out of the aisles between them. Tiny violins provide a relentless accompaniment that feels as though a swarm of strings is embedding itself in her brain. She tries to remember to breathe while swallowing a sour upsurge of coffee that tastes far too stale. She can't help growing tense in case a shape darts out of the next aisle, but when she almost lets a cry loose it's because Jake has. "What was that?"

"Good God, don't squeal so loud," Greg tells him. "You'll give everyone a headache."

"There, quick." Jake is waving a hand at a nearby aisle. "It went along there. Head it off."

At first Greg seems too busy displaying his aversion to Jake's gesture, but he marches to the far end of the aisle Jake blocks. "Where is it?" Jake cries. "It wasn't moving fast. It didn't come out here."

"What are you trying to say you saw?"

"Some kind of grey, grey thing low down. It poked out and went back in when I saw it like a slug when you touch it."

"I shouldn't think anyone's surprised there's no sign of anything like that."

"I'm telling you I saw something," Jake insists more shrilly.

"Then tell us where it went."

Mad isn't sure if Jake intends to answer by demanding "What's that stain?"

"I can't imagine. Maybe you know more about such things than I do."

Mad is less than eager to see, but she's the next to look once she has checked the intervening aisles with Angus. In the middle of the space between Jake and Greg is an irregular greyish discolouration about a foot across. No doubt because Jake has lodged the image in her head, she's reminded of the mark a slug or rather a mass of them might leave. "So what are you dreaming up now, Jake?" Greg enquires. "It melted? Went through the floor?"

"It was there," Jake contends. "You'd have seen it if you hadn't been complaining about your poor little delicate ears that can't cope with anybody showing any feelings."

"It's men not sounding like men I don't care for."

"I'm not surprised if people have started imagining things," Agnes says behind Greg before he has finished speaking. "I expect more of us may from missing our sleep."

Mad assumes Agnes is offering her as well as Jake the excuse. The rest of the staff have converged on the aisle, having searched the extent of the shop without result. Is Mad going to persist in the belief that there's an intruder? What possible point would there have been in disorganising a shelf's worth of books? All it has achieved is to set her and Jake apart from the others, if either of them lets that happen. "Everybody happy now?" Nigel hopes aloud.

"Everybody satisfied?" Ray adds or translates.

Jake looks at Mad but withholds his expression. She must have forgotten to tidy that one shelf; nothing else makes sense. "Got to be," she says for both of them.

Jake is turning away as though his vigorous shrug has spun him round when Woody's voice flies out of its various lairs. "Someone needs to let me know what you're playing at down there."

Ray and Nigel both head for phones, and Nigel is the winner. "Some of us thought we could have had a better look around before we locked up," he informs the phone.

"You mean I could have," Woody says throughout the shop.

"All of us. You keep saying we're a team."

"So what did the team decide?"

"We're on our own in here."

"Okay, I don't mind if everybody smiles about it this one time. What does it take to cheer you up? Hey, I'll tell you something that ought to—it's nearly Christmas. That has to start bringing us some more custom soon."

Mad thinks that should have begun happening weeks ago, and perhaps Nigel is keeping the same thought quiet. "Still no smiles?" Woody booms from everywhere. "What we need is a truckload of good will."

Nigel shuffles on the spot as if he regrets he was so keen to reach the phone, until Woody says "Ross, grab a disc of some Christmas music. It can go on my tab."

Ross spends so long at the compact disc shelves that Mad grows edgy with impatience. At last he brings Nigel a copy of *Santa's Disco*, which wouldn't have been her choice. It hardly matters; when Nigel ousts Vivaldi with it, there's no sound. "Let's try something else," he urges.

This time Ross eventually selects *Carnival of Carols*, which Mad would have chosen in the first place. The trouble is that it doesn't play either, and when Nigel replaces it with Vivaldi, that too is as silent as the swaying of the fog outside the window. As he jabs the buttons again, Woody demands "What's the holdup now?"

Nigel grabs the receiver and keeps poking the controls of the player as if he's on a leash that's the telephone cord. "Something's gone wrong. Nothing will play any more."

"So don't waste any more time on it. Why don't you all vote on some Christmas songs and sing while you work."

"Like the slaves we're expected to be," Agnes remarks.

"What was that? What did she say, Nigel?"

Nigel hesitates before mumbling "I don't think I quite caught it."

Greg clears his throat with an eloquence he may be hoping will communicate itself to Woody. It must have fallen short of the phone, since Woody says "I guess maybe she's thinking I should join in and not just tell everyone else what to do, am I right? Here's a tune to get us in the mood."

Mad doubts that she's alone in growing apprehensive as he draws an amplified breath. Once he begins to sing she wouldn't be surprised if nobody knows where to look. He's performing either at the top of his voice or with his mouth against the mouthpiece; the huge blurred song audibly trembles the speakers. Among the less appealing aspects of his performance is his inability to remember most of the words, largely confining himself to an exhortation to let it snow. Mad is wondering if he would prefer that to fog when he interrupts himself. "Hey, this wasn't meant to be a solo. Don't tell me you don't know that song. It was in a movie some of you have to have watched."

"To be honest, and I don't know how alone I am in this," Nigel says, "I think we'd work better without singing."

Everyone but Greg makes their agreement visible at once. "Don't nod so much or you'll be nodding off," Woody says, with what kind of a smile isn't clear. "Maybe I ought to serenade you instead."

The nervous silence this provokes is interrupted by the clank of a bar on a door. Connie hurries out of the exit from the staffroom, followed by Jill. Both seem to be trying not to betray how Woody's voice has driven them downstairs. In a moment he cuts himself off with a magnified clatter that prompts Ray to shout "Time to get back to work."

Nigel clearly thinks either that he doesn't need to be told or that he should have done the telling. He trudges back to Humour as the rest of the staff move away from the stain on the floor. Is everyone determined to ignore Woody's behaviour? Mad doesn't want to lose the chance to bring it up. "Did you hear anything odd while you were upstairs?" she calls.

"That isn't much of a joke," says Connie.

"I mean apart from what we've all been hearing."

"I didn't," Ross apparently thinks worth establishing.

"It was after you left me alone up there. Woody . . ." The only words Mad feels able to use convey less than she wants them to. "Woody talking to himself."

"Maybe he's decided that's the best way to avoid arguments round here," says Nigel.

As Ray stares hard and sharply at him across the floor, Jill says "I think we'd have heard him if he had been. There wasn't any other talking going on up there."

Mad has the impression that Angus intends to prevent a quarrel by remarking "I'm glad he's stopped singing at least. That song didn't make me feel much like Christmas."

"He was only trying to get us smiling," Greg objects. "What's the matter with the song? Too American for you?"

"Too mixed up with that Bruce Willis film with all the mindless violence."

"I thought the film was bloody terrific," Ray says. "Must have left my mind at home."

This time it's Nigel who sends a look too eloquent for words across the shop. Meanwhile Jake enquires "What did you think of it, Greg?"

"Nothing wrong with heroism. He's only trying to save his wife and her workmates."

"Wasn't it the one where he's in his vest all the time? And you nearly had us believing that wasn't your kind of thing."

Greg's face stiffens and grows mottled, and Mad finds herself wishing for an interruption; even Woody calling for more smiles might do. All the altercations have made the air feel thickened, prickly, close to suffocating. She can't judge whether the shop is hot as rage or cold as loathing. Once Greg ends the confrontation by planting a book on a shelf with a sound like a blow with a club, Mad sets about putting her chaotic books in order. She's hoping everyone is preoccupied enough with work to gain some inner calm when Ross complains "Hang on, don't put anything on my shelves. I've got no room."

"I need space too," Angus protests. "Anyway, they aren't your shelves or mine. They're Gavin's when he comes back to work."

"Don't say that's an angry Angus," Ray calls, apparently to Nigel. "We're never going to have a bit of mindless violence, are we? Seriously, now, you lads want to shake and make up."

Ross pretends to ignore him, only to seem provoked by him. "If you don't give me some room," he mutters at Angus, "I'll have to move books all the way to the end of the aisle."

"Same here if you start crowding me. Sorry, you've got to stay out of my patch."

"Children," Jill says, raising her head above her shelves to shake it at the pair. "It can't be worth falling out over, can it? Shall I help one of you and somebody else help the other?"

The sole immediate response is Connie's. "You're awfully fond of telling people they're like children, aren't you, Jill."

"Maybe it takes someone that's had one to see it," says Ray.

At first Nigel confines himself to eyeing him, and then he lets his thought out. "The rest of us are blind, is that it? Those of us who wish we could have one and can't must be the worst."

"I don't know why you had to share that with us, Nigel. It's the first any of us heard you had a problem, am I right?"

Mad hears a wordless grunt, not necessarily of agreement, that she can't locate. "In that case I'd better apologise to anyone I've upset, had I?" says Nigel. "Lock our home lives up at home, that's how we work at Texts."

"It ought to be, shouldn't it?" Greg somewhat more than murmurs.

"Give it a rest, Greg," Ray says. "We don't need to hear from you every other bloody minute."

A mass of unspoken agreement seems to clot the air and turn it as uncomfortably warm as Mad imagines Greg's face if not the whole of him has grown. Rather than glance at him, she continues pulling books off the messy shelf. "My offer's still on if someone else would like to match it," says Jill.

"Just let me put these right and I will."

"Never mind, Mad. We know your section has to be perfect before you'll help anyone else."

She's the last person on the staff Mad would have expected to fall out with her. Is she really saying what everyone thinks? If Mad swung around, would she see all of them resenting her before they could don their false smiles? As she crouches on her knees, she feels as if she's both hiding from scrutiny and being dragged down by it; she's certain she is being watched. It must be Woody at his monitor. Perhaps he's about to enquire what the latest problem is, in which case Mad wouldn't be surprised if whoever answers blames her—but it's Jake who brings the pause that feels silenced by fog to a finish. "I'll give you a hand. Where do you want it, Angus?"

"You could start at the far end and give me all the space you can."

"I bet you're not the only man here who'd prefer that. Don't fret, I'll do my best to open up your end."

Greg clears his throat so fiercely it's little short of spitting, and then the shop fills with a clamour of handfuls of volumes being reshelved. The resonance seems to extend under Mad's knees; she could imagine that the floor is being shaken by an enormous knocking from beneath. Either the coffee has failed to wake her as much as she hoped or the wakefulness is affecting her nerves. She tries to ignore the staccato uproar as she pushes the last of her books into place. They only just fit; indeed, they're so snug that she wonders if little children would have the strength to remove them. She's reaching for the first book on the shelf to move it to the one above when she's distracted by the shadow at the foot of the bookcase.

It reminds her of the stain Jake found, except that it's moving. It's spreading, because it isn't a shadow but moisture that's seeping off the lowest shelf. She drags half a dozen books free to reveal that the moisture is underneath them. It's under all the books—no, it's been squeezed out of them. She opens the topmost of the books she has stacked on the floor, and a clown's face meets her with a grin as wide as its baggy mottled cheeks. Its colours are starting to run, its outline is melting, and the first two letters of the solitary word for it on the left-hand page have merged into a single character like an illiterate capital D.

She leafs through the rest of the book and a scattering of the others. All the pictures are even further on the way to shapelessness. She wobbles to her feet, brandishing the first volume, though she doesn't like touching any of them; they feel softened by the furtive damp, close to disintegrating in her grasp. Nobody spares her a glance as she straightens up. The inside of her skull seems to grow jagged with the incessant clatter of handfuls of books, and there's a stale taste in her mouth. She's trying to decide whom she would least dislike to approach—who is least likely to react as though she's indulging her finicky self—when Woody's swollen buzzing voice is added to the din, which sinks beneath it. "Can a couple of you bring your muscles up here? Something's wrong with my door."

# RAY

**What's the matter with them all? Do they behave like this whenever**
they've missed some sleep? It isn't even one in the morning yet,
however much later it feels. God knows how they'll be acting by the
time the sun comes up, if it can ever be said to do so round here. At
least he has a reason to be edgy, having been up most of last night
as well. Every time he cuddled the baby to sleep her teeth set her
off like an alarm. He wanted to give Sandra a chance to rest because
he knew she could be kept awake tonight, but then she started trying
to take over and let him have some peace. By four o'clock they were
arguing about that, and when Sheryl was quiet at last they had to
kiss and make up, not something he fancies is likely to happen between anybody at Texts tonight. Now Sandra can't even get in
touch for a chat if she's feeling isolated, because she knows the
shop phones aren't for personal calls, and Agnes has disabled his.
That wasn't an excuse for him to lose his temper with Greg, even if
some people might think Greg was enough of one. All the staff
have a right to expect managers to treat them fairly. Though Ray

262 · Ramsey Campbell

wouldn't call what he said exactly unfair, it has left an unpleasant stale taste in his mouth. He's wondering if he should find an opportunity to apologise to Greg when Woody's voice subdues the thunder of books on shelves. "Can a couple of you bring your muscles up here? Something's wrong with my door."

His lips must be against the mouthpiece, he's so blurred. As a book drops into place with a sound like the fall of a lid, Greg says "I'll be one."

It could pass as nothing worse than eagerness if he weren't frowning at Jake, either as a challenge or to warn him off. "Stay with your shelving, Greg," Ray begins to tell him, and then there's no reason not to finish. "Leave managing to management for once."

He's allowed Greg to provoke him again. It seems best to remove himself from the situation, and he's heading for the exit to the staffroom when Mad moves to cut him off. She's holding a picture book between one finger and thumb. "What's the trouble this time?" he has to ask.

"You can see for yourself."

"I'll follow you up, Nigel," Ray calls across the shop.

"I wasn't aware I was on my way."

"Woody wanted two of us."

Nigel stalks to the door and claps his badge against the plaque, actions that feel to Ray like an argument Nigel wants to have. "Wretched thing," he snarls, and is slapping the plaque again as Ray remarks "Looks like there's some damaged goods for you, Nigel."

Can Mad think Ray means her? Certainly she gives him a displeased blink. She has shaken the book open, and the discoloured pages droop like autumn leaves in a fog. The misshapen pictures on them remind him of the blots psychiatrists use as tests, though he wouldn't care to imagine what any of them resembles. "Good God," Nigel complains, "how did that happen?"

"It was like that on the shelf," Mad says more than defensively.

"No need for that tone, is there? Just bring the book up and I'll deal with it."

"It's all these. I think it may be the whole shelf."

"Why didn't you notice before?" Nigel picks at the books Mad has piled on the floor, and then he lifts the others off the shelf, breathing furiously through his nose and blowing air out of his mouth and clucking his tongue. Once he has exhausted his methods of expressing disgust and the shelf is empty, he runs his hand over it and the wall behind it. "There's no leak here," he declares.

"I didn't say there was," Mad points out.

"Then whatever's been happening must have taken a while, mustn't it? We might have expected you to notice when you're always so concerned about your section."

"It didn't show up till I put the books in tight."

"So you're admitting you're responsible."

Her face tautens, stretching her lips even straighter than they were. As she glances at Agnes, Ray asks "Are you sure it's just that shelf?"

Nigel scowls at him as though it has become Ray's fault. "Leave the others," he tells Mad. "You can come back to them if there's time, or perhaps that should wait till after the visit. No need to make the place look bad if nobody's going to see there's a problem."

Ray is about to suggest that it could be worse for her if the visitors discover anything she has been told to hide when Woody's voice escapes from upstairs with an amplified clatter of plastic. "I don't see anybody on the way yet. Who's the rescue party?"

Ray points at himself and jerks a thumb at Nigel. "Two solid guys," says Woody. "Okay, you should be up to it. How about right now?"

As Nigel gathers the spoiled books, Ray presses his badge to the plaque and can't help congratulating himself on a petty victory when the badge works first time. He holds the door open for Nigel, but doesn't mean him to sprint upstairs and beat Ray to the office. "Here's the calvary, the cavalry, I mean," Nigel shouts.

"What kept you?" Woody's muffled voice responds.

Nigel veers into the stockroom to dump the books. Ray glances at his watch as he heads for Woody's door but is unable to grasp how much time has elapsed since he last gave in to the temptation to check. "We came straight up, didn't we?" he calls.

"I'm asking what the problem is down there."

"We haven't pinned it down exactly. Water's got into some of the children's books somehow. Best if you take a look for yourself."

"You bet I will. What's the delay now? Give the goddamn door a push."

When Ray grips the handle it feels rough with grit or rust. He twists it as near as it will turn to vertical and shoves hard. Even when he throws his weight against the door, it stands its ground. He grabs his fist with his other hand and leans on the handle while he braces his feet wide apart and thumps the door with his shoulder to as little effect. "What's happened, do you know?" he feels foolish for asking.

"You tell me. When I tried to get out it was stuck."

Ray is bruising his fingers on the handle and his shoulder against the door when Nigel emerges from the stockroom. "Struggling?" he says. "Fear not, here comes the solution."

"Can't wait. Let's see how Scousers use their head."

Nigel ducks so violently that Ray wonders if he's thinking of using it on him. He'll find Ray's forehead waiting for his eyebrows if he does—Ray learned that trick at school. What is he imagining? Nigel's only trying to pretend he didn't hear the remark, and that makes him a weakling, not a fighter. Ray watches him drag the handle almost ninety degrees and incline his body away from it so as to slam himself against the door. When he has failed three times to stir it, he stops to wipe his brow hard enough to be backhanding it. "I already tried that," Ray tells him.

"It wasn't much use then, was it?" Nigel retorts and raises his voice. "Woody?"

"You know what, I haven't gone anywhere."

"The obstruction must be on your side. Can't you identify it?"

"Don't you think I'd have fixed it if I could?"

Ray is feeling amused that it was Nigel who attracted the surge of irritation when Woody adds "Are both of you trying at once? I didn't bring you up here for a contest."

Nigel keeps hold of the handle as if he's claiming ownership and performs another butt, this time in the direction of the door. "Whenever you're ready," he tells Ray.

"That's always," Ray assures him and runs at the door.

His shoulder assaults it and so does Ray's, not quite in unison. That's why it feels as though Ray has budged the door; it's quivering from Nigel's lesser effort. "Try again," says Nigel.

He seems to think it's Ray's fault at least as much as his. A wave of heat leaves Ray close to shivering. He steps back and launches himself at the door, but again Nigel's impact is a fraction later than his. "It isn't working, is it?" Nigel admits. "It must have warped, that's all I can suggest."

"Something's warped around here right enough."

Why did he say that? It must have promised to sound clever, but it's so meaningless as to be worse than stupid, which only makes Ray angrier for letting it into his head. "We aren't doing it right," he restrains himself to saying. "We need to be together."

Nigel gives him a look not unlike the ones Greg turns on Jake. "Together how?"

"How do you reckon? On second thoughts, keep it to yourself. Hit the bugger at the same time, that's what I'm saying."

"Nothing simpler. On three, then. One, two, three."

Ray is still running at the door when Nigel deals it what Ray would describe as a bump with his shoulder. Ray's throbs as he staggers back, and another rush of clammy heat draws a chill in its wake. He's glaring at the door and Nigel as Woody enquires "Everybody busy?"

"Can't you tell?" Ray bellows.

"That's for the team downstairs. Do I see someone that's finished shelving, Agnes?"

Ray feels stupider and more enraged than ever for not understanding that Woody's amplified voice was directed at the sales floor. Presumably Agnes responds in some fashion, since Woody says "Why don't you award yourself a trolleyful of Gavin's." A sigh that sounds thinned by his teeth finds its way into corners stained by dimness under the ceiling, and then he says "I don't hear anything out there. What's holding up the release team?"

Ray is infuriated that Woody's broadcasting the situation. "Some of us haven't worked out how to do it," he yells so loud he hopes the phone transmits it. He's almost sure he hears something like his voice imitating him more or less in chorus.

"Some? I guess that has to be both."

Ray swallows a sour harsh stale taste and waits for the latest clammy wave to finish with him, and then he faces Nigel. "Let's swap. I'll be the man with the handle."

"Of course, if it keeps you happy."

"Don't know about keeps. I'll count as well."

"I wouldn't want to be the chap who stops you."

As soon as Nigel moves aside Ray clutches the handle, which feels grubbier than ever. "Ready?" he barely asks.

"No less than you are."

"One," Ray announces, and an echo does. He thinks it's returning to him through the speakers until he realises Nigel is chanting just not low enough. "What are you playing at now?" Ray growls. "I said I'd count."

"You said as well. I thought you meant we'd what's the word, from clocks, it's Greek, at least it comes from there."

"No idea what you're on about."

"Synchronise," Nigel says more irritably still. "From time, isn't it, not clocks. I thought you meant we'd count and synchronise ourselves."

"Just me. It wasn't much help when you did, was it?"

"Fine, just me. Just you, I mean, that's what I'm saying. Just one of us. You've got your way, Ray."

Ray is sucking in a breath while he vows to utter nothing but the count when Woody asks the whole shop "Why aren't I seeing any movement here? Do you need reinforcements out there?"

"Someone else might be welcome," Nigel shouts.

The slam of a door sends footsteps hurrying upstairs and into the office. "I'll do, will I?" Agnes makes sure Woody hears.

"No offence, Agnes, but I believe we're talking men here."

She's clearly even less pleased by his transmitting this to the entire shop. "What do you two say?" she halves her volume to ask. "You ought to know more about it than him."

"I don't think I'd take issue with him," says Nigel.

"That isn't you though, is it, Ray? Don't say you never disagree with anything you're told."

He might admit to that if he didn't feel she's as determined to cause an argument as to justify her presence, although it's beyond him what would put her in such a mood. "Not this time," he says.

"Agnes isn't still with the rescue party, is she? Shouldn't be. Seems to me I sent her to fetch books from the stockroom."

Agnes confronts the enormous voice with a scowl she lowers to include Ray and Nigel. "Are you being managers or just men? You'd think there wasn't any difference round here."

"Oh, we have our differences all right," says Nigel, but perhaps she doesn't catch it as she stalks out of the office.

"Well, that took time and got us no place," Woody says, and even louder "Angus, why don't you join the team at my door. You look like you're closest to finished down there."

His call seems to render Agnes' footfalls yet more vigorously discontented as they stomp downstairs. The rumble of a trolley grows hollow as it's wheeled into the lift, at which point Nigel says "Do you want to have another bash while we're waiting?"

"I don't. You can if you like."

When Ray keeps hold of the handle Nigel steps back, only to stare at him as if that may compel him to let go. Ray turns to watch the doorway to the staffroom but feels the stare clinging like stagnant moisture to his face. By the time the downstairs door shuts with a clank, words he would like to spit out are growing stale in his mouth. He forces his gaze to stay fixed on the view of plates and mugs heaped in the sink on the far side of a length of table attended by a third of one chair and two-thirds of another. As an escalation of footsteps produces Angus, Woody demands "Is he there yet?"

Ray is disconcerted by a muffled echo of at least some of this. Of course he must be hearing Woody through the door as well as overhead, though the lower voice sounds oddly unlike Woody's and a shade belated. Before Ray can answer, Nigel calls "He is now."

"Gee, I wish I knew what's happening to time around here. He's what you need, right?"

"Should be."

Ray is less gratified to have beaten Nigel to that answer when he hears an outburst of angry clattering from the stockroom. Agnes is hurling books onto a trolley as a retort to what she has just overheard. He wonders if he ought to intervene on their behalf but decides that damaged books are Nigel's job as Woody says "Maybe I should solve your other problem too."

"Which one's that?"

Ray is about to add his question to Nigel's when Woody says "As long as you can't agree who's counting, why don't you leave it to me."

"Or I could if you like," Angus ventures to offer.

"We don't," at least three voices chorus.

A grin jerks at Ray's lips, but he tries to keep it down so that Angus won't feel any more rebuffed than he already looks. "Hey, that doesn't mean we don't need your body, am I right, guys?" Woody adds.

"Absolutely," Nigel says, and Ray mutters most of a yes.

"No call to look that way, Greg. We aren't doing anything up here you wouldn't do. Okay, are you all on your marks?"

"I am," Ray declares as he puts the handle at arm's length, and Nigel shouts his readiness while Angus says his.

"One," Woody warns them, and then his voice falls out of the air and hides beyond the door. "Say, it wouldn't hurt someone to remind me what I'm doing here."

As Ray wonders whether the intercom system has failed, Nigel asks "Sorry, what are you?"

"I'm only meant to be counting for you three. All of them down there looked like they were waiting for the signal too. You can all still hear me, right? Then let's do it. One. Two. Three."

Angus and Nigel hurl themselves at the door. As Ray drubs it with his shoulder Nigel knocks Angus against him and collides at least partly with the wall. "Oh, blast it. Damned stupidity," he cries.

"Whose are we talking about?" Ray wouldn't mind knowing.

"The whole idea. There isn't room for all of us."

"Just say the word and I'll leave you two together."

"That didn't do shit, did it?" Woody complains. "What went wrong this time?"

"Too many people getting in each other's way," says Nigel.

"How many stooges do we have out there? Three sounds like it ought to work."

A chill shiver travels through Ray before anger heats him up again. He feels as if their antics have attracted an eavesdropper. He must be mistaken; Agnes and her trolley have reached the lift, which informs her that it's closing. He even thinks he hears her give it a startled reply that the doors enclose as Woody calls "Okay, this is it. This is when it opens up. Let's make sure it happens this time. Are you all ready for it?"

Ray barely hears his own mutter, never mind anyone else's. "I didn't catch that," Woody shouts. "Let's try it again. Are you ready?"

Ray imagines Woody smiling wildly as if he's urging reluctant children to join in a Christmas game. "Yes," he responds with a good deal more enthusiasm than he's feeling, and can tell the same is true of Angus and Nigel.

"Here it comes, then. One Fenny Meadows . . . Two Fenny Meadows . . . Wait for it . . . Three!"

Ray assumes Woody means to build up everybody's tension and ensure they attack the door with all their strength, but the pauses are so extended that he starts to feel they're rendering time stagnant, just as lying awake in the worst of the dark can. As the final number arrives at last he tries to stay clear of Angus while shoving the handle down and heaving himself at the door. This time he's aware of a concerted impact that shudders through his entire body. At once he is utterly blind.

He's terrified his effort has severed some connection inside him until Angus stammers "What did we do?"

"You didn't get me out of here," Woody calls, "that's for sure."

"I mean the lights have gone out."

"Yeah, I did notice that. Can't you guys see at all?"

"No, not at all," Nigel says in a stiff pinched voice.

"Then I guess it's easier for someone downstairs to fix it." Out of the absolute blackness overhead Woody says "Connie, can you check the fuses? They're under the stairs."

At least the phones are functioning, then. Ray hopes they won't be assailed by too much of Woody's distended commentary, since it adds to the oppressive weight of the dark. He senses that Angus is trying to stand completely still beside him, perhaps so as not to risk brushing against him. He doesn't know if the waves of heat that keep coming into conflict with the chill that has gathered in the dark have anything to do with Angus. Somewhere past Angus he can hear Nigel's breathing, his lips parting with each breath, some of which sound like groans he's increasingly less concerned to stifle. Ray is about to warn him to take control of himself and stop bothering the rest of them when Woody's immense voice and its accompanying mutter say "Keep trying, Connie. Your badge still ought to work."

Ray imagines her groping blindly for the plaque, and then he realises that the sales floor must be floodlit from outside the shop, a notion that feels like a promise of regaining his sight. He assumes the unhappy distant female voice he hears is Connie's, or is he hearing Agnes in the lift? Has its power failed too? Before he can ask his companions whether they've recognised who is in distress, Nigel blurts "You've got a mobile, haven't you, Ray?"

"Did have."

"You aren't saying you've left it downstairs. What's the point of having one if you don't keep it with you?"

"It's in my pocket, but it's useless. Agnes took it in the fog and did for it."

"Have you tried it since?" Nigel's voice sounds rigid with struggling not to grow shrill. "Couldn't you now?"

"Who do you think I should call, Nigel? The leccy company to come and mend the fuses?"

"Nobody."

"Tell you what then, Nigel. That's exactly what I'll do."

"I think I know what Nigel means," Angus admits.

It isn't only his hot moist breath too close to Ray's face that provokes Ray to demand "So who's going to let me into your little secret?"

"Won't it light up if it's working?" says Nigel.

His insistent tone makes Ray want to lash out at him. Ray feels so stupid for not realising the phone could provide them with illumination that as he fumbles it out of his pocket he wants it to prove Nigel wrong, which is even stupider. As he feels for the On key, Woody says hugely "Connie isn't getting in. One of you in the office will have to go down."

Ray presses the key, and the keypad lights up green. He sees Angus begin to smile as the glow pastes his distorted greyish shadow to the door beyond his glaucous face. Nigel leans around him, his panicky expression starting to relax from the mask it must have become in the dark. The next moment the light flickers and dies, and no amount of poking at the keypad will revive it. Ray hears Nigel moaning under his breath like someone unable to waken from a nightmare, and this time he has to fend off Nigel's despair. He knows it's irrational, which ought to save him from being infected, but even once he has stuffed the lump of lifeless plastic into his pocket he feels cut off from Sandra and their baby in a way he has never felt before. Until he drives the notion out of his head he starts to believe that the blind dark means he will never see them again—that the spark of energy remaining in the mobile was his last chance to reach them.

# NIGEL

**It's only dark. It isn't solid, however heavily it presses on his eyes. It** can't stop him breathing; there are yards and yards of air all the way across the office and the other rooms, even if no more can replace the air through the windowless walls once it's used up. There's enough for him and Ray and Angus and Woody. He ought to be glad he's not alone as well as sightless; he oughtn't to be wishing that he could have chosen his companions. Woody is hardly one, given the immovable door, and Ray seems even less of one after having offered Nigel the flare of the mobile phone, the mocking light Nigel's eyes tried to cling to until it and they were swallowed by the redoubled blackness. As for Angus, he seems to be doing his best to stay unnoticed, surely not by the dark—Nigel mustn't let such fancies stray into his mind. All the same, it takes him a while to recognise that the insect clicking somewhere close is Ray's attempt to regain some light. Then it stops, and Nigel is grinding his lips together so as not to plead with him to give it just another try when Ray says "Looks like it's you or me, Nigel. Which?"

The dark appears to respond to the question with a sluggish flurry of greyness, but it's surely only in Nigel's eyes. "What are you talking about?" he has to ask.

"Don't say you never heard him. He wants one of us to go down to the fuses."

Nigel feels as if the dark almost managed to crowd the memory out of his head, along with most of his ability to think. "Would you mind?"

"I might. I've worn myself out for a while."

Nigel's shoulder is still aching from colliding with the wall rather than the door, but he rests it against the wood in case that helps him feel less threatened by losing himself in the blackness. "To be honest, I don't know if I can."

"Had I better go?" says Angus.

"No, you better hadn't. It's just as hard for you as Nigel, or have you got a special problem, Nigel?"

"Perhaps I have."

"Go on, share it with us."

"I wish I could give it to you, believe me," Nigel mutters as Woody shouts "Has anybody gone yet?"

Nigel's feelings speak up without giving him time to think. "Ray is."

"You're trying to order me about now, are you, Nigel?"

"No, I'm saying I won't be going. I'm no use in this."

"Glad there's one thing we can agree about."

The next moment Angus bumps against Nigel and recoils. Has Ray deliberately pushed him at Nigel? Nigel's stance wavers as if he's about to be sent floundering helplessly into the blackness, and he glances down at the feet he can't see as he plants them apart to steady himself. Though he doesn't immediately understand what's there or why it should matter, he blurts "Ray, wait."

"Changed your mind? Don't you want to be left alone with Angus?"

"Of course not. I do, that is, I don't mind. Only what am I seeing?"

"Can't imagine, can you, Angus?"

"Look," Nigel insists and feels idiotic for pointing. "Look down."

When they're silent he begins to grow afraid that he isn't really seeing the faintest trace of grey underlining the door until Ray grumbles "So Woody's got some kind of a light. What bloody use is that to the rest of us?"

"I think we may be able to get some out here too."

"How do you reckon we'll do that, Nigel? Is he going to poke it under the door?"

"Is it the security thing?" Angus blurts as if he hopes to stop the argument.

"That's it exactly, the monitor. It must be on a different circuit, and the computers will be too. If we switch them all on we'll have plenty of light in here."

"That'll solve everything, then," Ray scoffs.

"It certainly should help, wouldn't you agree?"

"Won't help me see the fuses."

Nigel is well on the way to feeling Ray is as mindlessly immovable as the dark. "Maybe once we're able to see what we're doing," he says just short of losing his temper, "we can plug some of the computers in nearer the stairs."

"Good on you, Nigel. You've convinced us. Go ahead."

"You aren't expecting me to do all that by myself."

"Did I say that, Angus? We just want you to switch one on, Nigel, so we can see to do the rest. No point in us all falling over each other and bugger knows what else in the dark. If I'm dealing with the fuses, the light's your job."

"What's the holdup now?" Woody shouts and deals some item of furniture a thump.

"Nigel's going to switch on a computer."

"What in Christ for?"

"To light up the place," Nigel feels slowed down almost to inertia by having to explain.

"So do it, then. What are you waiting for?"

"Yes, what are you, Nigel?" Ray murmurs. "You heard the boss."

The heat that floods over Nigel is anger, and the chill that follows it is apprehension, which he tries to convince himself makes no sense. He relinquishes the handle and slides his right hand off the door, over the shallow frame, onto the wall. He inches his hand over the slippery surface and shuffles to keep up with it, but doesn't care at all for the sensation of offering his face to the dark. Instead he turns towards the wall and presses both hands against it on either side of him. He begins to sidle along it, though its presence so close to his face makes him feel walled in with very little air. His hands progress over it with a series of halting sticky creaks irregularly echoed by the dragging of his feet across the linoleum. He assumes the noises are apparent only to him, since he can barely hear them for his short harsh breaths and the thudding of his heart, until Ray enquires "Are you really going as slow as you sound?"

"I've got to find my way," Nigel protests, or most of it before the fingertips of his left hand recoil from what they've encountered. It's the wall at right angles to the one he's tracing, and it must feel damp because his fingers are. There's certainly no excuse for him to imagine that anything moist has trailed over it to await him in the blackness. For quite a few seconds manoeuvring around the corner is enough to make him nervous—feeling the walls and the darkness they've trapped closing around his face. Then he has to grope along the second wall, moving yet more slowly for fear of sprawling over some item low on the floor. What would it be? A wastebin, of course, but the obstruction he meets in the blackness jabs his hip. He confines his reaction to a gasp, still enough to make Angus demand "What's wrong?"

"Nothing. I'm at the desk," says Nigel, though that's too grand a term for the shelf at which he and Ray and Connie work. He flattens his hands on it and reaches leftwards until his little finger bumps against the edge of Connie's keyboard. He brushes his hand across the keys, which feel like stones unsteadily embedded in a medium as soft as mud and emit an agitated plastic chatter. As the keys grow dormant his fingertips graze the computer monitor, dislodging an object like a dead insect. Just in time not to gasp again he remembers she has decorated the monitor with a metal butterfly. He gropes farther left and knuckles the tower that houses the computer. He runs his hand over the front of the tower until he locates the power button. With his shaky forefinger he presses the button in as deep as it will sink.

There's a loud click, but the darkness doesn't even twitch. "Was that it?" says Ray.

When Nigel peers towards the question he can no longer be sure that he's seeing a hint of a glow under Woody's door. "Apparently," he has to admit.

"It couldn't . . ." Angus pauses to think, unless he dislikes hearing his voice surrounded by the dark. "It couldn't be switched off at the plug, could it?"

"It could. Thanks, Angus," Nigel says, only to feel significantly less grateful as he realises he'll have to crawl under the desk. He grasps its edge with both hands and lowers himself to his knees on the cold linoleum. Rather than risk banging his forehead against the desk he ducks beneath it, though he has to fend off the idea that it's forcing him towards some presence lurking underneath. He feels as if he's thrusting his hand into a lair. There's danger enough; his fingertips almost dig into the holes of the wall socket. His fingers retreat to the linoleum and light upon the flex that straggles from the plug. He's attempting to line up its prongs with the holes in the socket when Ray says "What's that?"

Nigel's nerves almost jerk the plug out of his grasp before he manages to relax. "Just me trying to insert this."

"Not you for a change. Is it Agnes, Anyes, whoever?"

Nigel can't hear her. When he lifts his head to try, the rough underside of the desk claws at the back of his neck. He crouches lower and scrabbles at the socket with the prongs until they snag the triangle of holes. He thrusts them home so hard his shoulder redoubles its throbbing. As he extends a finger to the switch he mouths "Please" before pressing it down.

Dimness springs into view in front of him. Three wastebins stand guard near three plugs in sockets, while two further sockets are unattended even by plugs. He backs out from under the working surface, and a blurred distorted shape crawls after him: just his shadow. As he seizes the edge of the desk and hauls himself to his feet, Ray hurries across the lividly illuminated office to the stockroom door and opens it on blackness. "Agnes," he shouts, "was that you?"

Nigel is about to conclude that it wasn't when she answers. Perhaps she was deciding whether to respond to the mispronunciation of her name. "I'm in the lift. It's stuck."

Her shout is muffled and shrunken by distance. If the lift stopped when the power failed, Nigel wonders why she's appealing so belatedly for help. "I'll go to her while you see to the fuses, Ray," he offers. "Let's move the computers and spread some light around."

"Someone's coming in a minute, Agnes," Ray yells as Woody bellows "What's the situation now?"

"We can see and we're getting some more light," Angus tells him.

"That shouldn't take much time, should it?"

"I'd hope not," Nigel says without striving too hard to be audible as he turns to the desk. Now he understands why the dim glow that clings to everything in the office is grey as fog: the computer screen is. The icons on it look drained of all colour, in danger of losing their outlines and sinking into the depths. He's afraid that if he tries to improve its appearance the terminal may crash. Instead he moves along to his own computer. He's stooping to unplug it when he freezes in a crouch, and the throbbing of his shoulder is imitated by his skull. "Oh, for the love of—"

Ray pokes his greyish face out of the gloom next door. "What's up now, Nigel?"

Is he ensuring Woody hears? He's loud enough that Woody demands "Right, what is?"

Nigel isn't to blame. The holes between the desk and the wall are—holes just large enough for the wires from the computers to pass through. "We aren't going to be able to move these unless we take the plugs off."

"Who's got a screwdriver? I've not, have you?"

Nigel owns up to the lack and Angus gestures it while his ill-defined shadow wags its swollen hands behind him. As Nigel pulls out drawer after drawer under the work shelf Ray says "Better try switching them on."

Nigel presses the button on his computer and more viciously on Ray's. The greyness of the screens turns luminous, and two sets of icons bob sluggishly up. They look too tentative for Nigel's liking. "What's happened to the computers?" he's increasingly anxious to know.

"The main thing is they're lit up, isn't it?" says Ray. "I can stand how it is."

The office must be three times as well lit as previously. More to the point, the staffroom has grown brighter, and Nigel can even distinguish the faint outlines of racks in the stockroom. However difficult he may find the next few minutes, Agnes is in a far worse situation. How ashamed would he deserve to be if he neglected to help? "I'll have to," he tells the others and especially himself.

"Maybe I won't leave you in the dark too long."

Surely Ray is undertaking not to rather than saying he'll consider it. He props the stairway door open with a chair and leaves the staffroom at a trot before his footsteps start losing their momentum on their journey downwards. Nigel is tempted to wait until Ray arrives at the fuses or even deals with them, but that's too cowardly for him to bear. He hurries through the staffroom, past the table that looks coated with glimmering greyish plastic, into the stockroom.

The moment he steps through the doorway he's flanked by blocks of darkness that feel solid as earth. He can just distinguish the ends of the shelves they've buried, bony outlines the colour of fog at night and not much less inclined to shift. Perhaps being re-lieved of most of their stock has left the shelves more capable of movement; as he ventures between the next pair, whose edges re-semble ash both in greyness and a tendency to crawl, they begin to jangle as though whatever contents they still hold are inching to-wards him. He tries to concentrate on seeing ahead, though there's a distraction in that part of the dark as well. The nearly shapeless blotch that's slithering along the aisle to beat him to his goal has to be his shadow, especially since it hesitates whenever he does, but he's surprised that he can even glimpse it in the suffocating dim-ness. He's unable to make out the third set of racks, but he knows by their stealthy jangling that he has passed between them.

Now that they're behind him he would expect them to stop vi-brating with his footfalls. Once they fall silent he attempts to gain some control over his swift unsteady breaths. He senses as well as remembers that he has reached the space largely occupied by the wooden bin topped with wire mesh where all the cartons of new stock are unloaded. The shelves beyond it are fixed to the walls, and it's surely impossible that he's hearing any movement from them. However surreptitious it sounds, the noise must be under the wire mesh—the feeble squealing of bits of polystyrene that his footsteps have disturbed, though it makes him feel he's roused a nest of insects in the blackness. At least by keeping well clear of it and to the left of it he knows he's within an arm's length of the bare wall. He's stretching out his hand in that direction when he almost drops into an inadvertent crouch, though the dark hasn't seized him and Woody's voice wasn't intending to. "No need to call it quits down there," it says. "No need to call it a day. You can see better than us."

He's addressing the staff on the sales floor, of course. Until Nigel divests himself of the impression he even thinks he hears a muffled underlying echo, but he's certainly too far from the office. As his splayed fingertips locate the wall, Woody reduces himself to inter-rogating Angus through the door about the latest situation. Nigel's fingers slide over the chill slippery plaster and then, sooner than he was expecting, lurch off its edge to encounter metal. It's the more recessed of the two doors to the lift shaft. He raps on it with his knuckles and calls "Agnes, can you hear me?"

She gives no indication that she can. He presses his ear against the door, which is so cold it feels like the threat of an earache. If there's any response beyond the door it's blotted out by the savage drumming of his pulse. He runs his fingertips over the door and digs them between it and the frame, where he succeeds in hauling open a gap of a few inches, through which he shouts "Agnes, it's Nigel. Are you all right?"

He hears his flattened dull voice plummet down far too deep a well, which he hopes is as much of an illusion as the chilly damp it seems to breathe at him. He's wondering if Agnes is refusing to answer because of the way he pronounced her name when she says "I don't know where I am."

"You're below me somewhere. I'm at the top doors. I'll come down." It's Agnes that he mostly means to reassure by adding "Down the stairs, that is."

"Can you see where I am?"

"I can't see a thing, to be honest. Ray's gone to operate on the fuses," he says, only to realise Ray should be more than there by now.

"Will you be able to find your way?"

Presumably that's intended as concern, but his nerves don't welcome it. "No question of it. I'm coming immediately," he says, and rather more than that, because the last two words burst into a flurry of extra syllables that bloat them shapeless. "I'm coming now."

He lets go of the door, which meets the frame with a clunk. As he runs his fingers over the metal a fingernail catches on the edge of the second door. Once he has found the wall again he shuffles sideways until he arrives at the corner. Now he's facing the stairway, and it feels as if the blackness of the lift shaft has been tilted to receive him. He reaches into it with his left hand, lower and lower. At last he touches an object like a stick that someone's holding up for him to find: the banister. He restrains himself to grasping it with only one hand and takes the first step down.

He doesn't like wobbling on one leg while he gropes for the stair with the other foot. It must be the blind dark that makes him seem to have to stretch farther than he ought to need. He plants his heel as far back on the tread as there's space for, and slides his sweaty prickling hand down the banister, and lifts his other foot to hover above the oppressive depthless dark. It's just the night, he tries to tell himself—the same night in which Laura will be asleep, her face calm and still on the pillow, perhaps unconscious of a lock of hair that's tickling her cheek. The thought nerves him to shout at or into the dark. "I'm on the stairs now, Agnes. I won't be long."

"Don't be."

Her response sounds more distant than ever. Of course it's muffled by the wall. He wishes he could think how many steps lead to the delivery lobby: surely less than a couple of dozen. Since he's performing the identical action each time he clings to the banister and lets a foot sink into the blackness until it meets a stair, why isn't the process growing easier instead of seeming ever more dangerous? Perhaps that's because he didn't count the steps he has already taken, thus losing all sense of how far he has yet to descend. He could shout again to Agnes, but he's wary of discovering how remote she may sound. The edges of stairs scrape the backs of his ankles, and whenever a foot settles on a tread he feels as though he's leaning out too far over the blackness. He takes another wavering pace downwards that only the banister renders slightly less perilous—and then his fist closes on emptiness. Before he can catch his balance he flounders off the stair on which his left foot was supporting all his weight.

He's staggering across the lobby to crash into a wall, unless he sprawls headlong on the concrete. He flings out his right hand so violently in search of anything to grab that the action throws him against the doors to the lift shaft, dealing his shoulder a bruise that may even outdo its twin. "It's me," the darkness suggests he ought to call. "It's Nigel. I'm here."

"Where?"

He almost wonders that himself, because her voice is farther beneath him than seems possible. She must be sitting down—on the pallet truck, no doubt. "Very close," he assures her as he feels for the edge from which the doors open on the shaft. He drags a gap wide enough to insert his fingers; at least, he struggles to. His fingers won't penetrate even as far as their nails. The doors might as well be a solid block of metal embedded in the wall.

He hauls at them until the throbbing of his shoulders unites across his neck while waves of grey light surge into his eyes. He has the irrational notion that his inability to see what he's doing is the reason he's so useless. Why hasn't Ray fixed the fuses by now? How much longer will it take him? Nigel is wondering if he can shout loud enough for Ray to hear when he realises he shouldn't have to. He has nearly allowed the dark to get the better of his brain. There ought to be plenty of light within reach.

He lets go of the unyielding door and closes his eyes until the waves of false illumination fade, and then he opens his eyelids a slit to peer across the blackness that's the lobby. There is indeed the thread of a glow under the delivery doors opposite the lift, although it's so thin he is barely convinced he's seeing it. "Hold on," he calls. "I've seen something I can do and then I'll be back."

Agnes is silent. Perhaps she thinks it was stupid of him to tell her to hold on, which he supposes it was. He paces through the unseen lobby towards the promise of light and fastens his hands on the bar across the doors. It can't be as rusty as it feels; that must be the prickling of his fists. He flings all his weight against it and hears a shifting that someone less in control of himself might imagine was the sound of an eavesdropper retreating outside. Then the bar splits in two with an emphatic clank, and the doors swing so immediately wide that Nigel reels out of the building.

He has let the light in. This should be all that matters, but he can't help wondering why it doesn't appear to be shining from above him. He turns to squint at the rear wall of the shops. The source of the illumination isn't above the giant X; the spotlight is smashed, and so is the one behind Happy Holidays. The whitish glow is at his back, and creeping closer, to judge by how his shadow that lies face down in the lobby is shrinking and blackening—shrinking as though it's desperate to conceal itself.

He swings around to confront the luminous fog. A glow about the size of his head and more shapeless than globular blunders almost into the open before it either merges with the fog or sinks into the glistening tarmac. At once the lobby doors are pulled shut by their metal arms and lock with a triumphant clank, shutting him in not much more than darkness.

He stumbles through the clinging chilly murk to fetch up against the doors. They're just as unresponsive as he feared. No amount of bruising alternate shoulders on them will move them. He could pound on them, but what effect would that have beyond distressing Agnes? It would take Angus far too long to find his way down to them. The fog or rather its inertia must be gathering in Nigel's brain, because he has to make an effort to remind himself that he can head for the front of the building. There'll be light as well as a way in.

He has taken only a couple of steps between the dim walls—one of concrete, one of fog—when he notices there's light behind the bookshop too. It's more of the kind he encountered as he left the building. It dances lazily through the fog, making his shadow prance on the wall of the shop to keep him company. It would be more welcome if there weren't other signs of life in the fog. He can hear something else on the move, shuffling towards him while dragging a package that sounds worse than waterlogged. Indeed, the noise makes clear that there are two of whatever is approaching.

He peers into the fog and glimpses movements. Although they're low on the tarmac, he doesn't think the intruders are crawling on hands and knees. They could owe their glistening greyness to the murk, but he can't maintain this as an explanation for their lack of shape. He stares at them until he distinguishes that the unstable packages they're dragging are themselves, and then he bolts for the alley between Texts and the holiday agency. The sight that greets him jerks him to a halt as though he has stepped deep in a marsh.

Fog radiant with floodlights blocks the far end of the alley, but that isn't why his mind feels near to paralysis. He's no longer even slightly glad of the light. His shadow has thrown itself face down in the alley, and it's no longer alone. On either side of it a squat lumpy silhouette is expanding like a misshapen balloon, either creeping closer at his back or swelling up from the tarmac, unless they're doing both. For the moment they have nothing he would want to call heads, but they have at least one arm each, altogether too long in both cases, that they're stretching out to him.

He daren't look. He can't even bear to see their increasingly malformed shadows. As he dashes into the alley he shuts his eyes tight, feeling like a child who's trying to believe he can hide in his personal dark. He has fled just a couple of steps when the shuffling converges swiftly on him. In a moment his fists are captured by appendages too cold and soft and uncertain of their shape to pass for hands.

He can make no sound beyond a low choked wordless moan. His fingers writhe in a desperate attempt to pull free but only embed themselves up to their knuckles in the oozy substance. The sensation makes him unable to open his eyes; he squeezes them tighter as if that can drive away what feels like a nightmare born of his sleeplessness. He's trapped in his own night, where he no longer has a sense that Laura is anywhere he can reach. All he seems able to do is strive to retreat into it as digits or tendrils of various thicknesses slither like worms between his fingers. He's held fast by their engulfing clutch as his captors whirl him vertiginously round and round before scuffling away from the shop with him, into the pitiless dark. A solitary hope is left in his whirling brain, and he's past caring how desperate it is. It occupies so much of his mind that surely it has to be true. He hopes that by the time whatever is going to happen takes place, he will no longer be able to think.

# AGNES

**"Gee, I wish I knew what's happening to time around here,"** **Woody** uses the speakers to remark, as if his voice isn't already overbearing enough. "He's what you need, right?"

"Should be," Ray shouts.

Of course he must be. He's a man, and on top of that he's Angus, than whom nobody on the staff is more anxious to please, however little self-respect it leaves him. If all they want to apply to the problem of Woody's door is brute force, no doubt he'll do as well as anyone. Agnes only wishes she could believe that the exchange wasn't meant for her to hear. If management have turned so petty and vindictive, she needn't let it affect her. She grabs handfuls of Gavin's books off the racks and slams them onto the trolley to deafen herself.

It doesn't work. She can hear Woody saying "Maybe I should solve your other problem too"—the whole shop can. She isn't sure that isn't addressed to or aimed at her until he offers to count, and then she feels stupid for wondering. Now he's saying he needs someone's body, and she's glad to be out of reach of the suggestion, though he'd better realise he shouldn't dare make it to her. Perhaps on balance she's grateful to have been sent off by herself; she can't bring to mind anybody on the staff whose company she would welcome. If they aren't trying to prove they're entitled to tell people what to do, they're showing how small they are in some other way. Perhaps the best course for everyone would be to spend time by themselves.

"One," Woody's pointlessly exaggerated voice announces, and Agnes is ready to propose that he might like to do without the phone when he does. She hears the start of an argument of some kind in the office, but amusing as it could well be, she won't indulge in eavesdropping. She loads the last few books there's space for onto the trolley and wheels it through the stockroom, past a muffled squeaking that she takes at first for mice. Polystyrene fragments are rubbing together under the mesh on the bin, she realises as she arrives at the lift and thumbs the button.

"Lift opening," she's told at once as if it was waiting for her. The doors shrink aside, revealing the empty pallet truck, which barely leaves room for her and her cargo. Having manoeuvred the trolley in sideways, she squeezes between its end and the wall of the lift to poke the Down button. There's no point in struggling out again; at least Woody won't be audible in here. The lift gives her notice of its intentions and shuts her in just as she blurts "What did you say?"

She's glad there's nobody to observe her being idiotic. The tape or whatever the lift uses to speak must be growing worn, however premature that seems. Of course it said "Lift closing," not "Still hoping." She finds it less easy to dismiss the impression that the lift itself feels worn out—that it's descending more slowly than usual. Perhaps she's fancying this because she's wedged in a space that would barely let her turn around if she had any reason to. She resents having to borrow an idea from Woody, but nobody will know.

"One," she murmurs, and "Two" after pausing for a second, though she isn't sure whether she's timing the lift or occupying her mind so as not to feel at the mercy of the time the descent takes. "Three," she adds, "f—" Whatever word she might gasp retreats into her mouth, because the lift has jerked to a halt as though it has run out of cable. Instantly it fills with blackness.

For rather more than a moment, during which she's unable to breathe, she begins to imagine that she has been engulfed by a medium more solid than a simple absence of light—that the lift has been flooded with black water. No doubt that's how quite a few of the staff would expect her and any of the women to react, which is why she isn't going to panic. Once she succeeds in drawing a breath she repeats it until it comes naturally, and then she runs her fingers over the cold metal wall to her left and level with her head. In certainly no more than a handful of seconds her forefinger locates the door to the compartment that houses the emergency phone. It must work even if the power to the lift has failed, otherwise what would be the point of it? She snaps the door open and gropes into the recess to find the receiver clinging to the wall. As she lifts it out, a worm as cold as midnight fog squirms over her bare forearm. It's only the cord of the phone, but her arm recoils and she almost drops the receiver. She seizes it with her other hand as well and is bearing it carefully towards her face when it says "Hello."

It sounds almost too welcoming under the circumstances, and not unlike the voice of the lift. Both must have been chosen for their reassuring quality, of course. "Hello," Agnes feels bound to respond.

"Hello."

Her tone is more welcoming still; Agnes could almost find that mocking. She's close to being prompted to echo the greeting once more but understands how stupid that would be. Instead she says "I'm stuck in the lift."

"We know."

Did Agnes expect the phone to be answered from within the shop? She can't decide whether the opposite makes more sense or less. "The lift at Texts the bookshop," she says. "Where are you?"

"Not far."

"Can you let me out?"

"Won't be long."

Isn't the voice unnecessarily odd? Agnes could almost think it's on a tape that is slowing down. Certainly its pitch is dropping as if staying high involves too much effort. She tries to ignore the transformation, not least because she's alone in the blackness with it, and asks "What will you do?"

"Doing it now."

It can't be the same voice. The operator or whoever took the call must have transferred it to an engineer. While Agnes is sure a woman could perform his function quite as well, that isn't as important to her just now as it should be. "Don't you need to be here?" she protests.

"What do you think?"

"I wouldn't know, would I? I can't do your job."

"You want me there."

She won't pretend she's tempted. Either he has a frog in his throat, in which case it must be an especially monstrous specimen, or he believes that the lower he pitches his voice the more masculine he sounds. The most she cares to venture as a response is "Whatever it takes."

"Done."

He must be saying it is, even if he makes it sound as though they've reached some kind of agreement. "What is?" she feels she has more than the right to ask.

"Wait."

"There isn't much else I can do, is there? Maybe you don't realise I'm stuck in here in the dark."

"Oh yes."

She doesn't want to think she hears relish in that. "I want you to tell me what you're doing," she says. "I still don't know where I'm speaking to. I don't even know your name."

For a moment she imagines that the earpiece has become clogged with mud, because the slow thick laughter sounds like bubbles in that substance. Apparently he has no words left, but that needn't rob Agnes of hers. He sounds like a sadistic adult trying to frighten a child in the dark, and she knows at once that he has to be in the shop. So does the woman who answered her call, which means that at least two of her supposed colleagues dislike Agnes enough to be mindlessly vindictive. If she let herself she could imagine it was everyone. "You know something," she says as the receiver falls eagerly silent, "I don't know who you are or your friend either. If you look like you sound I'm glad it's dark."

She has allowed herself to be provoked into saying too much. Half of it would have made twice the point. She swings the receiver away from her, and it meets the wall of the lift with a clang she hopes is agony for anyone who's listening. She's happy to make a noise with it in the process of locating its niche inside the compartment and fitting it in. As she slams the panel she vows that once she's out of the lift she'll learn who played the trick. She leans towards the doors and cups her hands around her mouth. "Can anyone hear me?" she shouts. "Angus? Nigel? Ray? I'm in the lift."

Too much of her voice is trapped by the doors. She feels it or her breath fluttering insect-like between her hands. She tilts her head back to shout "Anyone?" and then presses her ear against the door, which seems to shift restlessly with her anticipation. She's just able to hear Ray calling "Agnes, was that you?"

The way he can't be bothered to pronounce her name aggravates her sense of being singled out for general dislike. If she didn't answer she would feel worse than stupid, but she has to make an effort. "I'm in the lift. It's stuck."

He's silent for so long that she's beginning to wonder if he didn't hear or doesn't care when he shouts "Someone's coming in a minute, Agnes."

She mustn't start imagining he feels the need to put more distance between them as they talk. He has moved away to deal with another task; that's why he sounds increasingly remote. Now there's silence, but however long it lasts she won't give anyone the notion that she's panicking by calling out again. Once she has succeeded in reminding herself that she's surrounded by a lift's worth of air, however cramped a space she's wedged in, she's able to take deep slow breaths while she tries to make the blackness that's glued to her eyes part of the calm she's striving to achieve. After all, she's in the midst of stillness, or is it stealth? Is the lift creeping downwards so gradually that she may well be imagining the surreptitious movement? She's holding herself immobile, even her breath, in an attempt to determine whether the cage is lowering itself like a massive spider when Woody's huge but muffled voice declares "No need to call it quits down there. No need to call it a day. You can see better than us."

Is he so mistaken that he's saying this to Agnes? Of course it must mean the lights have failed elsewhere in the building, which is why nobody has reached her yet, not because they don't think she's worth reaching. Such reassurance as that offers is undermined by the way she's almost certain Woody's voice retreated fractionally above her while he spoke. She scrabbles at the gap between the doors and succeeds in parting them about an inch, which admits only blackness and a dank chill, unless there's a faint stagnant stench. She tries to slip her fingers through the gap but is unable to hold it open with one hand long enough to touch the wall of the shaft and judge if there's movement. She's afraid of trapping her hand, and snatches it back. The doors thud shut as a voice leaps down at her. "Agnes, it's Nigel. Are you all right?"

If he's also in the dark he has more important things on which to concentrate than the pronunciation of her name. She takes a breath so that her shout won't falter. "I don't know where I am."

"You're below me somewhere. I'm at the top doors. I'll come down. Down the stairs, that is."

The image of his clambering down the cable revives her uncertainty whether the weight of the lift and its burden is carrying it downwards. It's partly in the hope of learning there's light somewhere close that she pleads "Can you see where I am?"

"I can't see a thing, to be honest. Ray's gone to operate on the fuses."

They ought to be able to see before too long, then, and the lift should behave itself as well. She's giving Nigel the option of staying where he is as she calls "Will you be able to find your way?"

"No question of it. I'm coming immediately." He becomes entangled in the last words before he recovers. "I'm coming now."

She has shaken his confidence. That makes him seem more human but hardly lets her feel safe. A muffled clunk of metal somewhere above her is followed by black silence that exacerbates her fancy that the lift is crawling down the shaft no faster than a slug. She's alternately trying to breathe in calm and holding her breath while she attempts to catch the lift moving when Nigel calls "I'm on the stairs now, Agnes. I won't be long."

"Don't be," she responds, because he sounds more distant instead of closer. Of course there's now a wall between them. She closes her eyes in case that lets her detect his progress, but it simply intensifies her impression that the lift isn't as arrested as it wants her to think. Lifts can't want, and what else would? She's reminding herself she's alone in the dark except for Nigel when an ill-defined thump above her makes her doubt it. "It's me. It's Nigel," he tries to reassure her. "I'm here."

It dismays her to have to ask the question, which seems to strengthen the dark. "Where?"

295 · Ramsey Campbell

"Very close."

He sounds by no means close enough. How can he be above her if he's at the door? There's surely nowhere lower for the lift to go. Or perhaps there is; she's no expert on lifts and how they work. If the shaft extends below the level of the ground floor, it would surely not make sense for it to reach far. Vague noises of activity overhead must indicate that Nigel is doing his best to open the doors to the shaft. She can't be certain whether the noises are sneaking away from her, but it's clear he isn't achieving much. Can she aid him? She finds the slit between the lift doors and claws at it but seems to be growing as feeble as some of her colleagues would like to think she is; this time it won't open wide enough to let her fingers through, only to admit a faint moist stagnant smell. A good deal of her effort is spent in craning sideways over the trolley to the gap. She's still wrenching at it as the edge of the trolley digs into her hip when Nigel calls "Hold on."

She's thoughtless enough to straighten up gratefully before she realises he can have no idea what she's doing. "I've seen something I can do," he explains, "and then I'll be back."

This has to be hopeful. She wants to believe it means he can see. She holds her breath in case that helps her gather what he's doing. In a few seconds she hears a clank that tells her he's opening the delivery doors. The light outside won't depend on the fuses in the shop. That being so, why has Nigel fallen silent? Why can't she hear him at the doors to the shaft? Obviously because he'll be ensuring the delivery doors won't close, she tells herself just as they shut with a resounding clank.

She restrains herself from calling out at once, but she's on the point of doing so when a muffled thump puts an end to the silence. A pause is followed by another thump, and she understands that Nigel is trying to shoulder the delivery doors open, which means he has somehow managed to evict himself from the building. Either he's weakening or, even worse, his sounds are perceptibly receding to leave her deeper in the blackness.

The one reason she has to be grateful is that her parents are un-aware of her situation. They'll have gone to bed by now, and she hopes they're asleep. If she had used Woody's refusal to let her contact them as an excuse to leave she wouldn't be trapped now, but is she going to allow the realisation to trap her as well? She isn't paralysed, and she can still make herself heard. If it takes more than one person to open the doors onto the shaft, there are plenty on the sales floor.

She struggles past the corner of the trolley and inches along the front of it. The edge of a shelf digs into the small of her back while the corners of book after book catch on her spine. With her hands flattened against a door on either side of her she feels as if she's pinned to the metal. She's keeping her breaths shallow to render herself as thin as she'll go; otherwise the metal chafes her breasts. She has to remind herself more than once that she isn't suffocating before the toe of her right shoe snags the crack between the doors. She thrusts all her fingers in and hauls the doors wide enough to stuff her foot into the gap.

She's taking a few seconds' rest in preparation for heaving the aperture wider to call for help when the stagnant smell drifts in. It's rising from somewhere under the lift, and has grown so over-whelming that she can't doubt its source is approaching or being approached. She makes herself advance one hand through the un-seen cleft in the blackness. She's hoping that despite all her im-pressions she's at the doors to the lobby, but her fingertips nudge slippery brick.

She's afraid to reach up, yet she does. As far as her arm will stretch she feels only brick. Straining up on tiptoe, she works her fingers between the top of the lift and the wall of the shaft. Just enough of the bottom of the lobby doors is within range for her fin-gertips to blunt themselves against it. Then it withdraws farther than her fingers can extend, and they're dragged over brick.

She mustn't panic. Doesn't every lift have an escape hatch in the roof? Even if she can't remember seeing one overhead, there has to be—has to. She'll be able to climb up to it on the trolley, but she would prefer not to while she's so alone. She takes a deep breath and almost spits it out again for tasting stale. Instead she uses it for the loudest shout she can summon up, having cupped her hands around her mouth and tilted her head back. "Can someone come? I'm in the lift. It's stuck."

She's about to use up the rest of the breath when she's interrupted. She doesn't want to think it's any kind of a response; at first she isn't even sure that she's hearing the lift. "Lift opening," it says, or perhaps "Lift closing", though she could imagine that the thick slow deep voice has intoned "Still lower."

The tape must be worn to a remnant, or the mechanism is running out of the last of its power, but she can't rid herself of the notion that the voice has reverted to its true nature—that its female version was a pretence. It also reminds her far too much of the voice or voices that answered the emergency phone, a thought that seems considerably worse than pointless in the dark. She plants her hands over her mouth and nose to exclude some of the smell while she takes another long breath. She raises her face to shout again, but all that emerges is a gasp. Something has swarmed over her shoe and closed around her ankle. It's too cold and slimy to be alive.

For a moment she's able to gain some reassurance from understanding that it's water or mud. Then it finds her left foot as well and makes for that ankle, and she snatches her other foot out of the gap that's admitting the spillage. The doors meet with a thud that sounds not nearly snug enough as she labours back to the corner where at least she has room to manoeuvre. The edge of the top shelf of the trolley feels like an elongated bruise some inches lower than the incessant plucking of books at her spine, and her feet keep losing traction on the wet metal floor. As soon as her outstretched left hand locates the controls on the wall and identifies the Up button she begins to jab at it. Surely that can't be why she feels the doors betray a movement as if an intruder has wormed between them.

She wrenches herself free of the trolley and straightens up as though her stance may bring her courage. For a few seconds she carries on bruising her finger against the button. It isn't halting the descent of the lift, which feels as if it's no longer just sinking but being dragged down. Though she's afraid to retreat from the controls and the doors, she has no alternative. She gropes her way behind the trolley and stands between the metal prongs of the pallet truck. She's grasping both ends of the trolley in preparation for clambering towards the invisible hatch when a rush of a substance too solid for water and too liquid for earth drowns her feet and climbs her shins.

She doesn't cry out. She needs her breath, not least to convince her that she isn't about to suffocate. She props one foot on the bottom shelf to lever herself out of the rising flood. Her foot slips off the inch of shelf that isn't occupied by books. The splash spatters her legs all the way up to the knees and almost makes her scream. She grabs handfuls of books off the shelf and hurls them aside into the blackness, where they clang dully against the walls. By the time she has cleared the other two shelves of most of their contents the viscous icy flood is halfway up her shins, and she hears books rebounding from the walls into it with splash after thick splash. She tramps on the bottom shelf and hauls herself up to the middle one. She has barely stepped on it when the trolley topples over.

She staggers blindly into the depths of the lift until her back slams against the upturned handle of the pallet truck. A knee-high wave follows her, carrying books—pulpy lumps of sodden meaninglessness that nuzzle her legs as if for companionship until she kicks them away. She twists around, wringing pain from her spine, and grabs the handle. It's too short and certainly too unstable for her to use it to climb. Then she hears the trolley collide with the wall of the lift, where it scrapes up and down.

If the trolley floats, can't she ride it up towards the hatch? She has no other course, since she can't swim, even if it were possible to do so in the sludge that has risen above her knees. She flounders through it and the blackness while her splayed fingers ward off a mass of waterlogged books. Her knuckles bump into a more solid obstruction: the bottom of the trolley, which is floating on its side. She launches herself at it in something pitifully like triumph, and her right hand closes over an object perched on top.

It has a face, but not for long. Before her hand can recoil from the lumpy features or distinguish more than that one indolently blinking eye is at least twice the size of the other, the face sinks into the cold gelatinous bulge of a head. She doesn't know what sound she's making as she struggles backwards; she only knows that she's desperate to shrink as far from the trolley and its horrid contents as the cage of the lift will allow.

Swollen books crowd around her and behind her, hindering her progress as they encircle her upper thighs. The trolley blunders against her waist, and she heaves it away with all her strength. It crashes into the doors with an impact that makes the lift shudder. Perhaps that isn't all it achieves, because in a very few seconds the eager flood is counting her ribs. She's holding her arms clear of being engulfed, if only because she has no idea what else to do with them, when the trolley nudges her chest. She scarcely has time to start to pray that it's no longer inhabited before the remnant of a face moulds itself to hers.

It's as featureless as the underside of a slug except for a grin so wide and loose it's worse than idiotic. She claws at the quivering neckless head and peels it away from her, only for limbs to slither around the back of her neck and clasp themselves together. How can they be impossible to dislodge when they have so little in the way of bones and muscle that her fingers poke into them—when the limbs don't even seem to be certain of their own shape? They draw the head and whatever it may now have for a face closer and closer to her, so that she's almost glad the blackness filling first her mouth and nose and then her eyes and brain is more solid than any dark.

# ANGUS

**"Okay, why don't you bring a smile to my face. Tell me something's** fixed."

"I expect the fuses will be soon. Ray's gone down."

"Seems like he's been long enough, or can't I tell time any more?"

"It does feel like a while. Maybe that's because it's so late."

"He could have fallen asleep on the job, are you saying?"

"No, but he has to find his way down and do everything in the dark. Do you think we should keep a torch up here in future?"

"Kind of primitive. Oh, that's what you call a flashlight. I thought Nigel got you some light."

"It's only in here. It doesn't go downstairs."

"Anyway, what's with the silence? No need to let Angus do all the talking."

"The thing is, Nigel isn't here."

"The hell you say. We've been deserted, huh? How come he crept off?"

"Anyes is stuck in the lift and he's gone to see, well, he won't be doing that, but he's seeing if he can let her out. I don't think he has yet."

"Who?"

"Nigel. You just asked about him."

"I know what I asked. I've still got the brains I brought over here. Now I'm asking what you called the girl you say is in the elevator."

"Anyes. You must have heard her called that. That's what she likes."

"And you try to do what everybody likes, right, Angus? You don't think it could screw up our work here."

"I don't see how getting on with people could."

"There's being so anxious to please people you're scared to risk doing anything better than any of them, maybe, right? You need to know that won't help the team. Anyway, that's not what I was saying."

"Shouldn't have said it, then."

"Say again? I didn't catch that. I meant her name could be the problem."

"I don't see how."

"So think about it. You Brits go for pronouncing stuff different from it's spelled, don't you? Maybe that's why we've had shelving out of order. Another word like that ain't going to help."

"At least we don't say ain't like some of you, what do you call them, you wetbacks."

"I keep not being able to hear you, Angus. Remember there's a door. Okay, I'm glad we took time out for a chat, but I guess that's enough of a break. Here's your chance."

"How do you mean? For what?"

"Hey, what were we talking about?"

"I'm not sure. I'd say not much."

"The door. Try the door."

Angus rattles the handle and leans on it and shoves at the door but might as well be attempting to budge a section of the wall. "It's still stuck."

"We don't have time to kid around. That's not the kind of smile I need. See if you can't figure a way to let me out that involves your head. I guess Ray and Nigel won't mind if they come back and find you've saved them any more clowning around." Just loud enough to be heard, Woody adds "Sometimes I want to give up on these Limeys."

Angus lifts his foot for a kick. He doesn't mean to move the door, but Woody won't know. The noise might revive his commentary, however, of which Angus has already had more than enough. If he manages to free Woody, at least then Angus should be able to get away from him. The trouble is that even now there's silence, he's unable to think.

He assumes Nigel is busy trying to release Agnes. While he and Woody were shouting at each other he could hear them doing much the same, after which the delivery doors clanked twice, presumably having swung shut in between. Now Nigel will have propped them open to let in the light from the staff car park. Perhaps Agnes can see it, because she called out not so loudly as she had been calling, which made her sound more remote, and then went quiet. Surely Angus can put her out of his mind while he considers his task. He steps back in case seeing Woody's door at a distance shows him how to proceed.

He can't unscrew the hinges. Nigel couldn't find a screwdriver, and besides, the hinges are shut between the frame and the edge of the door. Suppose the trouble is with the lock? In a film nothing would be easier than to spring it with a credit card, but Angus suspects that if he tried, the card would bend or become trapped in the mechanism or simply snap in half. Is there anything else up here that he can use to probe the lock? He peers around the room that looks steeped in glowing fog, the dim illumination from the greyish screens that are blackened with blurred icons, until Woody's magnified voice aggravates his inability to think.

"Someone will be with you any minute, Agnes, if they aren't already. You'll forgive me saying your name that way, but I guess I could claim this is American territory, and we don't pronounce it like that. I should let you guys down there know Nigel is having to let Agnes out of the elevator, and Ray's getting ready to switch the power back on for us, are you, Ray?"

There's no response. No doubt Ray knows his voice won't reach Woody. The resumption of silence allows Angus to notice the drawers under the L-shaped shelf that holds the computers. If anyone objects to his search he can tell them Woody wanted him to try whatever might help. He's tired of feeling dull and useless, and worse than tired of being alone with Woody's voice through the door. He crosses the overcast room and pulls out Connie's drawer.

It contains half a pack of tissues in carefully parted cellophane, a ballpoint with its end pushed up the neck of a plastic cat's head stained grey by the light, a birthday card swarming with a basketful of kittens and lying on an unused envelope, an assortment of scattered paper clips. He's wondering if any of the latter could be turned into a picklock when Woody's voice returns to the door. "Still thinking out there, Angus?"

"Thought," Angus mutters as he grasps that the dark strip at the back of the drawer is not a shadow but a twelve-inch metal ruler. "Thought," he calls on his way to inserting the ruler in the slit beside the lock.

The angle of the light, such as it is, has prevented him from recognising that the frame overlaps the outside of the door by a fraction of an inch. He jams the ruler between them and uses both hands to dig it in until it grinds against the bolt of the lock. As he struggles to work the ruler around the end of the bolt, Woody remarks "You're quiet again, Angus. Stuck?"

The word Angus mumbles rhymes with that, because now the ruler won't move in any direction, even when he leans on it so hard it feels close to cutting his hot moist prickly hands. Can he break the doorframe away from the lock? He hauls the ruler sideways, which produces a faint reluctant creak. The thin line of shadow between door and frame is undergoing some change, but none that appears to make sense. How can it be shrinking or growing more vague? "Wait a minute," Angus blurts.

"I've been hanging around a whole lot longer."

If it weren't for the door they might be close enough to shake hands, that's if they weren't shoving or punching or otherwise attacking each other, but Woody's unseen presence makes Angus feel more alone with the dimness, especially since it's growing darker. When he twists around he sees that Nigel's computer is emitting significantly less light than its mates. He dashes across the office and shakes the monitor rather than switch it off and on. Do the blackened icons really quiver like dead leaves on the surface of a pool that has been disturbed? Surely all that matters is that the screen brightens, though not much, as Woody shouts "Want to give me an update?"

"We were losing power somehow."

"Yeah? It's fine in here."

If it's as fine as that Angus is tempted to leave him to it, but he knows Woody's voice would follow him anywhere he ended up. He hurries back to the door and throws all his weight against the ruler. The doorframe responds with a feebler creak than before, and Woody protests "You're quiet again. I still don't know what you're doing."

"I'm trying to get the lock open," Angus says through his teeth.

"Hey, you didn't tell us you were a cracksman. Guess I'll have to keep more of an eye on you."

Angus assumes Woody is joking, undoubtedly smiling. Nevertheless he grows clammy with anger. He hurls himself against the ruler with all his might. Something yields, and he nearly runs into the wall. The doorframe has proved more than equal to the ruler, which has bent almost in half.

At first he thinks his vision is blackening with rage or from his effort, and then he understands that the room is darkening. All three computer screens have dimmed until their displays of icons are barely visible. He runs to Nigel's monitor and tries to shake some sense into it, but if anything it turns murkier. He lets it be and taps Ray's with a knuckle. Immediately all the icons vanish as if the screen has gulped them down.

He's holding up one uncertain hand as though that may persuade the computer to spare him anything worse when the screen brightens. That has to be reassuring, though it conveys the impression that a light has swum closer behind a swollen wall of fog. He moves to Connie's monitor and knocks on the screen.

At once the icons sink out of view, and he's afraid the light will. It flickers and then steadies, but can he trust it? With a pair of knuckles he knocks twice as hard on the glass. He's reminded of tapping on an aquarium to rouse whatever creatures live within, which must explain why the greyish pallor that swells towards him looks more solid than a glow—almost solid enough for a head that's rising to the surface of the medium that has rotted it shapeless. It sends him back to the door with renewed eagerness to liberate Woody. As he leans on the far side of the ruler to bend it back into shape, it gives with hardly any resistance, flinging him past the door with a handful of metal that scrapes over the wood.

The ruler hasn't even snapped in half. Less than a third is left protruding from the gap. As prickles flood over Angus's skin, Woody calls "Sounds like you did something at last."

Once Angus has regained enough control to shout rather than scream he confesses "I've broken the ruler."

"You've broken what?"

"The ruler I was trying to pry your door with."

"You're not the cracksman you wanted me to think you were, then. I guess it's back to brute force. Want me to get you some company?"

He can't be referring to the noise behind Angus, so distant or muffled it's practically inaudible. Angus glances back and tells himself he's dreaming on his feet from being up so late; no blotchy lumps can be nuzzling the insides of the computer screens. "Who?" he blurts.

"Let's try for a couple of the jocks down there." So immediately that Angus starts, dropping the fragment of ruler, Woody amplifies his voice to call "Ray, Nigel, one of you or both, why don't you stop what you're doing long enough to open a door so Greg and Ross can help Angus. Can't imagine why you didn't think of doing that already."

Nor can Angus as he wills them to respond. It's impossible that they could have failed to hear Woody, yet they aren't answering. Could the faint sound at Angus's back have some connection with them? Perhaps it's Agnes or Nigel thumping on the lift doors. He has distinguished nothing further when Woody's voice blots out the sound. "You two outside don't have to wait, you know. Maybe if you try to get in that'll do the trick."

Before long Angus hears a series of irregular thumps downstairs. They're louder than the other sounds, which nonetheless feel closer. He's becoming less able to look behind him as Woody says in his biggest voice "How about you, Angus? You hearing anything I'm not?"

Angus feels as if replying may draw attention to him, especially since all he finds to say is "What would I be?"

"Ray or Nigel or both, I'd hope."

Angus strains his ears but only grows uncertain how many sounds he's hearing and from where. "They haven't said anything yet."

"Greg and Ross, take a breather. Angus, give Ray and Nigel a shout."

Shouting fails to appeal to Angus. He sees his pallid shadow flattening itself against the dim wall and wishes he could be as anonymous and unobtrusive. It's only because he realises Woody will harass him until he does that he yells "Ray? Nigel? Woody wants to know what's happening."

At first he seems to have invited silence, but it's followed by an outburst of surreptitious thumps as though objects too soft for hands or heads are blundering against glass. Soon Woody renders them inaudible by demanding "Any message for me?"

"I didn't hear any, sorry."

"I won't tell you I'm surprised. Sounded like you were shouting at me, not them. Why don't you go find them and report back. You sure aren't achieving much here."

Angus would be grateful to escape him and the noises in the room if that didn't take him closer to the dark. He's unable to decide which is least welcome as he sidles out of the office. He very much prefers to avoid seeing the computers, but the alternative is to watch his shadow drag itself like a stricken faceless puppet along the wall. It makes him feel like a frightened child lying awake in the worst of the night, not even certain it's his own shadow or what it will do if the light goes out. Why couldn't he have learned to drive? It would have let him turn back from the fog tonight instead of being delivered to Texts by his father. As the shadow glides ahead of him it turns elongated and distorted as an amoeba trying to resemble a man before it loses its hold on the doorway to the staffroom and sprawls expansively into the dimness. Angus remains in the doorway and plants his hands around his mouth, though his fingertips block some of the view of the indistinct shapes in the staffroom. "Ray? Nigel?" he shouts. "Can you answer?"

He doesn't want to listen any harder than he absolutely has to, not when it makes him more aware of the soft insistent blundering behind him in the office. Surely it's Woody shifting impatiently against the door as a preamble to demanding "So who's said what?"

A sly blurred voice imitates his much larger one, and Angus has to tell himself it's on the speakers downstairs; that's why it's coming from the dark. "Nobody has yet," he admits.

"Can't hear you."

"Nothing yet," Angus yells through the dimness into the dark, which appears to acknowledge him with a restless twitch.

"Still can't. Why don't you try just talking to me instead of the rest of the store."

Angus could retort that back at him, but turns barely far enough and long enough to call "They aren't answering."

"Well, that makes no sense. They can't have gone anywhere. They certainly aren't on the sales floor, am I right, Greg? I'm right. Listen, Angus, you aren't doing what I said yet. I told you to find them, not shout at us. Better not get the idea you don't have to do what I say just because I'm locked in for a while."

The choice of whether to stay in the unsteady dimness or venture beyond it feels like a nightmare from which Angus has no chance of awakening. Like a nightmare, it seems to cancel time, so that he can't tell how soon Woody demands "Did you go yet, Angus?"

"I'm going," Angus nearly shrieks and twists around to ensure Woody hears. What he thinks he glimpses sends him out of the room, even though he's leaving most of the light behind. He's already less certain, or trying to be, that grey lumps were flattening token faces against the insides of the computer screens, smearing the glass with wide loosely grinning mouths that looked both voracious and imbecilic. He's the imbecile, he makes himself think, if he lets his imagination paralyse him. All that's wrong is lack of sleep. He can still prove to Woody that the British don't let the side down.

Is Woody so concerned about being trapped in his room that he has forgotten Agnes is suffering worse? Angus dodges across the staffroom, which appears to be composed none too specifically of dim fog, and leans through the entrance to the stockroom. An unnecessary amount of darkness encloses both sides of his head. "Agnes?" he shouts. "Nigel? What's the latest down there?"

He wants to believe he hears Agnes pounding on the lift doors, having exhausted most of her strength, but the sounds aren't ahead of him. There's only silence in that dark. Is she unable to hear him or too frightened to answer? If the latter is the case he's dismayed by how much he sympathises. Nigel must have locked himself out of the building; that would explain the second clank of the doors and his subsequent lack of response. Angus is about to try to reassure Agnes that she's no longer alone and himself that she can hear when Woody's giant voice intervenes. "Angus, if you're doing what I'm hearing, try and think."

That seems not to require an answer, which at least means Angus doesn't need to look towards the office, where the foggy glow is flickering as if things are moving in it. So long as it's in and not out of, Angus silently pleads as Woody adds "Leave Nigel and Agnes and see if Ray wants help. If the fuses are fixed the elevator will be, obviously."

If that's so obvious, why didn't he mention it earlier? Angus resents being made to sound foolish to the entire shop. "Agnes," he shouts between his hands. "I'm going to help with the fuses and then you'll be fine."

His resentment of Woody's comment drives him across the staffroom to show everyone he isn't useless. So little of the wakeful dimness follows him that he's barely able to see the door to the stairs is closed. Has it been rendering Ray's shouts inaudible? Angus hurries past the time clock, not least because its dial reminds him of a porthole against which a face might flounder, and pulls the door open. He's stepping forward to shout to Ray when he collides with an object crouching outside the door.

It's a chair. Ray must have blocked the door with it, only for the action of the metal arm to dislodge it. Angus shoulders the door wide and props the chair on two legs against it before he takes another step. There's more than dark ahead of him. Are the stairs being flooded? If that's making Ray attempt to draw the longest breath he can, isn't he ever going to stop? Even if he's breathing through his mouth the inhalation sounds too large. It takes Angus far too long to understand he's hearing the muted roar of the hand dryer in the Gents between the staff lockers and the top of the stairs. The watery sound is in there as well. "Ray," Angus calls, "is that you?"

In a moment the dryer breathes its last. He waits until he's beyond wondering if that was a response, which at least gives him time to identify water splashing in a sink. Someone has left a tap running. It will have to stay like that until there's light. "Ray, can't you say something?" he urges at the top of his voice.

He's nowhere near as loud as Woody, but then he doesn't have mouths all over the shop. "Does anyone else find it hard to believe Angus is still calling and not going where he's told? You'd think he didn't want us to have light to work with."

Angus feels burdened with everyone's dislike, an extra and even more oppressive darkness. He's becoming convinced that Ray has taken refuge in the Gents, having panicked in the dark, and is too abashed to admit it; that would explain his silence. If he's hiding in there Angus won't disturb him further. He can open the door at the foot of the stairs and let in whatever light is present on the sales floor. Any that allows him to see the fuses or even to see is enough.

He paces out of the last trace of dimness, where the name-tagged doors of the lockers remind him quite unreasonably of memorials, and at once is immersed in the dark. He could fancy he's about to step over the edge of a bottomless well until he finds the right-hand banister to clutch. His doubts recede with the noise from the Gents as he hears the dryer recommence its exhalation. Doesn't Ray understand this betrays his presence? Angus would rather not imagine what state of mind has brought him to playing with the machine in the lightless room. Maybe he's desperate to dry his nervous sweat, not an idea Angus welcomes. He'll be helping Ray and Agnes as well as showing Woody and whoever shares his contempt that Angus can succeed where quite a few others appear to have failed. He holds the clammy banister and steps off the edge.

A stair is waiting where his foot needs it to be, and another below that, all the way to the ground floor. He only has to trust them, because he can see his goal beyond the stairs, a horizontal glow as thin as the edge of a knife. Has Ray opened the tap further? The sound can't really be following Angus. Perhaps Ray is splashing cold water on his face in the dark. He must have retreated to the Gents before Woody suggested he and Nigel should let in Greg and

Ross. That's up to Angus now; the scrap of light confirms it by jerking closer with each step he descends. Then a surface with no edge strikes his right foot. He's at the bottom of the stairs.

The floor glistens with faint light. He hangs onto the banister while he lowers his other foot, and then he strides across the lobby. His gaze is fixed on the light under the door, but there's nothing like enough to let him watch his step. He doesn't even glimpse the object that catches his feet and sends him sprawling headlong into the dark.

Is the blackness deeper than it ought to be, or is something vast rising out of it to meet him? When the floor slaps his palms they immediately start to throb, which seems reassuring by comparison. Then the pain begins to dull, allowing him to wonder what tripped him. He raises himself gingerly away from it, but not before gaining an impression that the obstacle is a body. Someone is lying far too still on the floor in the dark.

Angus shrinks against the wall and then makes himself reach out. His fingers touch the soles of a pair of shoes. They feel thin and flimsy, and are splayed away from each other in a position that puts him in mind of the gait of a clown. The right sole is marred by a cavity into which he flinches from inserting a fingertip. It's hardly information Ray would want him to have. He shuffles forward on his knees and locates one of Ray's hands, which is or has been clawing at the linoleum. Angus lifts it by the wrist to search for a pulse, not that he has ever done so before; he isn't even sure he'll be able to distinguish any from the pounding of his own bruised hand. Ray's fingers flop against the back of it. Their touch distresses Angus, not least because they are damaged somehow; they've been subjected to violence. He keeps hold of the wrist, but his bruises prevent him from being certain there's no pulse. He lays the hand down gently and sidles alongside Ray until he feels his trouser legs grow wet. He's kneeling in water.

The floor on the left side of the lobby—the side where the fuses are—is waterlogged. Now he understands why he sees it glistening and why he thought the sound of water was following him downstairs. If Ray was standing in water while he tried to fix the fuses, and with a hole in his shoe—Aren't modern fuses built to be safe even under such conditions? The unspoken question seems to rouse Ray. Angus hears movement to his right, and as he strains his eyes he glimpses the faintest outline of a raised head.

Instinctively he stretches out one bruised hand to support the back of Ray's neck. His fingers sink into the swollen mass all the way to their first knuckles. He gasps and chokes, and as he snatches them away he feels the substance closing up like mud. He isn't quick enough to avoid a pair of thick cold flabby lips that mouth against his palm. Then the object that was squatting on Ray's chest flops off him with a sound like the fall of a sack loaded with jelly, and slithers heavily to take up a position between Angus and the door.

He can hear voices arguing beyond it. His colleagues aren't far away, but there's no use yelling for help; they weren't able to open the door from their side. He can't from his. The prospect of touching or being touched by the squat soft object in the dark has robbed him of the ability to move or speak, until his panic sends him lurching to his feet to stagger back where he came from. He knows he's leaving Ray behind, but Ray is in no state to care; if he were he couldn't have borne having the object on his chest. Angus seizes the banister and attempts to retreat backwards, but he's so afraid of tripping up again that he swings around and hauls himself upwards, his face to the dark. Water spills past him on the other side of the stairs, and he does his best to ignore the sound so as to reassure himself that he can't hear anything creeping after him. He's well over halfway upstairs when he discerns a noise that isn't water. It's above him.

It has to be Woody. He's been able to release himself somehow. His footfalls are soft and deliberate, dropping on a stair and pausing before the next descent. Nobody could blame him for being careful. Angus closes his fist around the banister, wondering why he can't sense that Woody is holding onto it too. "Woody?" he calls. "Go back. There's—"

His voice has begun to falter as soon as he spoke Woody's name, because it provoked a response. It can't be described as a word, but it's unquestionably a denial, a thick loose grunt that suggests the source is indifferent to forming much of a mouth. For as long as the newcomer takes to plod two steps towards him he's unable to move, which enrages him so much he heaves himself up a stair. "I'm not afraid of you," he shouts or screams or tries to. But he is, and twists around sightlessly with nowhere to go. He feels as if even the stairs have had enough of him, because they sail out of reach of his feet as the banisters avoid his desperate clutch. For longer than he could have dreamed it would take there's only breathless blindness. Then the floor of the lobby cracks his skull open to let his brains out and the darkness in, and he just has time to sense whatever is rising eagerly beneath the dark to claim him.

# CONNIE

**"No need to call it quits down there,"** Woody hems her in by saying out of all the darkest corners of the sales floor. "No need to call it a day. You can see better than us."

Connie doubts it in his case. She wouldn't want to be any of the people trapped upstairs with no windows and no light, but he can't lack that if his monitor is working. She hopes he concentrates on opening his door. She feels demoted enough by the way her badge wouldn't let her at the fuses, without having him watch her actions and direct her as if she's just another of a troupe of puppets. Though she wishes she weren't the solitary manager downstairs, she's more than capable of taking charge. She only has to accept the sight of the sales floor now that it has been overtaken by the glare from outside. As well as draining colour from the hordes of books, the greyish light appears to have brought in fog to settle over the shelves along the rear wall, where the shadows are thick as mud. She surveys the faces of the staff who have retreated towards the windows and the best, such as it is, of the light. All of them look flattened and diminished by the stark illumination. Greg has remained in his section and is doggedly lifting books off the floor to squint at them so hard it pulls his mouth into an unconscious grin each time he hunts for the right place on a shelf. "No point arguing, is there?" Connie tells everyone. "We're lucky to be where we are."

She wouldn't mind more of a response to her attempt to raise their spirits out of the greyness than a bunch of shrugs and mutters. Even Greg seems too busy to agree, unless he thinks his display of commitment elevates him above the need to answer. "Don't ever be afraid to tell me I'm wrong," Connie says. "Hands up anyone who'd rather be upstairs."

Jill straightens her lips while her eyes hint at the slim possibility of a smile, and Mad's fingers stir as if she might consider conceding the point, but nobody else goes even that far. "Well then," Connie is trying to enthuse when Ross mumbles somewhat too distinctly "Rather be in bed, though."

"I'm sure, but none of us can be there just now, can we?"

Connie doesn't immediately realise why she oughtn't to have said that while her eyes were meeting Mad's. She flashes Mad an apologetic smile, which seems not to help; she feels as if she has simply tried on the expression Woody hasn't urged on them for some time, thank God. "Let's see which shelves we can work on," she suggests to everyone, "till Ray gives us back some power."

"I didn't think we had much of that to begin with," murmurs Jake.

"That sort of comment won't improve anything," Greg objects. "No need for you to sound like Agnes while she isn't here."

"There are worse people to sound like."

"Why have you got to sound like a woman at all?"

"Some of us might think there's nothing wrong with that," says Mad.

She accompanies this with a look at Jill alone, and Connie tries to keep her resentment out of saying "We'll concentrate on the shelves by the window. I don't suppose you'll have a problem with that, Jill."

"I'm just glad if someone's going to give me a hand with my section."

"I could use a few of those occasionally," says Mad.

Connie suspects Ross may take this as a cue for a response that Mad even more than the rest of them mightn't want to hear. "Can we all make an effort to get on?" she says. "Having to cope ought to bring us together."

Jill has as many stubby aisles as there are staff downstairs, which means Greg has no excuse to stay in his. "Actually, Greg, I meant everyone should gather over here," Connie lets him know.

As he holds up a book, the rudiments of a glistening face appear to rise to the surface of the cover before the light loses its hold and they sink back. "I'm trying to see where this goes," he says. "Never leave a job half done."

She isn't about to feel rebuked. When she finds she has wasted time in searching for a comment that will demonstrate she's in charge she retreats into one of Jill's aisles. While she picks up discoloured books to shelve she watches Greg sidelong until he deigns to join his colleagues. She's so aware of him that she misses the beginning of an exchange between Jill and Mad. "I don't like it either," says Jill.

Connie tries and fails to ignore them. "What don't you two like?"

"The way it looks out there," says Mad.

"It looks like it has been to me, and anyway we're in here."

"Mad was saying it looks as if the shop's drawing the fog."

It's Connie's fault that everyone hears this. Only Greg ostentatiously refrains from looking out of the window and makes certain he's heard shelving. As Connie wishes that the fog—its pallor, its hesitant stealthy progress that leaves a glistening track—didn't remind her of an enormous snail's belly that is lapping up from beneath the darker body of the unseen sky, a huge voice surges out of the greyness. "Someone will be with you any minute."

Woody pauses just long enough for Connie to assume he means the staff downstairs before he names Agnes, though not the way she prefers to be named. He discusses the pronunciation at some length, not least how it falls short of being American, then reveals that she's trapped in the lift. His voice settles back into its nests in the corners without having earned an update on Ray's progress at the fuses, and Connie makes for the phone at Information. She's only lifting the receiver when it says "Yes, Connie. I'm right here."

"Are we sure Nigel will be able to let her out?"

"I guess we'll see."

At least Connie understands why she heard the delivery doors open twice a few minutes ago: Nigel must have been letting in some light again, having neglected to prop them open to begin with. "How long has she been in there?"

"Must be since the outage."

That's far too long for Agnes to have been imprisoned with no light. However annoying she can be, under the circumstances Woody's remarks about her name were pretty well unpardonable. It takes some effort for Connie to say only "Do you think we should call the emergency services? I expect they're used to letting people out of lifts."

"I hadn't thought of them. I'll do what ought to be done."

"You'll have their number, will you? I don't need to tell you it isn't the same as in America."

"Right, you don't."

"So I'll leave it to you, shall I? Calling them, I mean."

"You bet. Why don't you concentrate on pushing your team down there a bit harder. There's already going to be plenty of time to make up when we get the light back."

Connie has scarcely put the receiver to bed when Ross says "Is he calling them?"

"I understand so."

"That's what he said."

"He's calling them."

"So long as he said that," Mad apparently feels obliged to comment. "Only he was just telling Anyes, wasn't he, how they don't always speak like us. She could have done without all that while she's stuck in the lift."

"Woody's shut in too," says Greg. "Perhaps he thinks they'll just have to bear it for a while."

"It's not the same at all," Jill says. "I'd a lot rather be where he is, in his position, I mean."

"You'd like to be in which position with him with the lights out?" Instead of asking that, because she has no idea what put it into her head, Connie says "Can we at least make sure we're shelving if we feel we have to chat? We need to pep it up a bit."

"That's everyone, is it?" enquires Jake.

"Every single, absolutely."

He lifts his chin and pokes his face over the shelves at Greg, who scowls and parts his lips, revealing clenched teeth. "I shouldn't leave your mouth open too long, Gregory," Jake is delighted to advise him. "You never know what someone might be tempted to slip in there."

Connie feels as though the murky light is robbing everyone of more than colour—as though it and the interminable night are reducing them to some stark essence of themselves. "I think we've had enough conversation for a while," she says. "It isn't helping us work."

Greg ducks furiously to grab a book. Jake smiles to himself before he stoops for one. Connie fears she may exacerbate matters if she says any more, and tries to focus on shelving instead. She has to hold each unshelved book towards the window to catch the grudging light; she could imagine that each repetition of the gesture brings the fog edging closer. Greg is either determined to set an example or challenging anyone to match his speed; he's making so much noise with books that it virtually blots out a short-lived commotion from the lobby where the fuses are. It can't mean Ray has fixed them, since the lights stay dead. Connie is wondering if she ought to find out how he's coping when Woody proclaims that he and Nigel should let in Greg and Ross.

"They could have done that by now," Greg complains, but that appears to be the sole response. Apart from the thudding of books on shelves there's no sound—no hint of activity beyond the doors. Connie is unable to judge how much of the time that feels inert as fog is used up before Woody declares "You two outside don't have to wait, you know. Maybe if you try to get in that'll do the trick."

As Greg strides towards the door that leads to Ray, he glances back to urge Ross to the other. Connie can't help resenting how Greg fits his badge to the plaque as though it might be readier to acknowledge him than her. She really oughtn't to feel secretly gleeful that it fails to recognise him either. He and Ross start to compete at ramming their shoulders against the doors, and Ross is the first to give in. "I don't—" he gasps and takes a breath. "I don't think Nigel's there."

"I thought he mightn't be," Greg says and deals his door the winning though pointless thump.

Connie succeeds in restraining her irritation enough to ask "Why's that, Greg?"

"I heard him go out before. I'm sure now that's what I heard. He'll have gone to fetch security. He must have seen they're needed at the lift."

"Why wouldn't he phone them?"

"He couldn't where he was, could he? He'd have had to go all the way back upstairs in the dark."

Connie feels stupid for needing to be told that, especially since she must have known the answer. No doubt he's all the more convinced he would make a better manager, not least because she's a woman. As she struggles to think how he might be wrong about Nigel, Jake says "Explain Ray then, Greg."

"I'm not aware of anything that wants explaining. He's a good manager."

"Except he seems to be hiding from you."

"I wouldn't be the one he'd have—" Greg's shadowy face produces its own darkness at his having let himself misunderstand. "If you're asking why he hasn't come to the door, he'll be too busy with the fuses. It'll be a hard enough job as it is without being left halfway."

"You ought to be able to hear him," Ross says. "Did you?"

"Not while we were both making so much noise."

"How about now we aren't?"

"Not at the moment."

"Try shouting to him," Connie suggests, "or would you rather I did?"

"I'm perfectly capable." Greg turns his back on everyone and leans towards the door, where his shadow shrinks into itself. "Ray?" he shouts as his shadow hands merge with the faceless silhouette of his head. "Ray," he yells between his hands. "Ray."

"Sounds like three cheers for nobody," says Jake.

Connie is about to hurry to the door Ray must surely be beyond when Woody's voice reappears overhead. "Angus, if you're doing what I'm hearing, try and think."

"Can't imagine what Woody doesn't want him doing with himself in the dark, can you, Greg?" Jake calls.

"Jake, do give it a rest for a while," says Jill.

"Well, I'm sure I don't want to bother anyone."

Connie's in no doubt that Greg feels a duty to respond. She's about to head off his retort when Woody interrupts. "Leave Nigel and Agnes and see if Ray wants help. If the fuses are fixed the elevator will be, obviously."

Mad thuds a book onto a top shelf before protesting "It's not that obvious, is it? The lift mightn't be on the same fuses. The phones aren't."

"Woody's bound to know what's what," says Greg.

Woody doesn't know that Ray isn't answering or that Nigel has gone for help. Nigel seems to be taking his time, and meanwhile what is Agnes expected to do? Connie marches to the door outside which Greg is loitering and raps on it with her knuckles. "Ray, can you at least let us know you're there?"

She doesn't shout. Being shouted at may have distracted him and made him too annoyed to answer. She presses her ear against the door in time to catch a restless shuffling that sounds impatient, and then a curt grunt. He must be too busy or concentrating too hard for words. "Success, Greg," she says. "Maybe some things need the female touch."

"I didn't hear him."

"I did." She's very close to losing her temper with his willingness to interfere. "And he doesn't want us disturbing him when he's fiddling about with no light."

She gazes at Greg with a patience that makes her eyes feel like hot weights until he retreats to his shelving. She's amused to observe that he can't let himself appear reluctant to move, which might imply a lack of commitment to the task and to the shop. Then Woody's voice demands "Does anyone else find it hard to believe Angus is still calling and not going where he's told? You'd think he didn't want us to have light to work with."

Is Angus another of the distractions that made Ray unresponsive? Connie returns to the aisle where she's shelving and picks up a book in each hand for extra speed, only to find that trying to read two covers by the stifled glow makes her feel retarded to half her pace. She reverts to her old method, hoping furiously that Greg didn't notice. She has shelved a few books with thunks that are meant to sound triumphant but that strike her as just dull when Mad says "Am I the only one that thinks we're assuming a lot?"

Apparently she is, because Greg clunks two books home before Ross gives in to asking "What about?"

"Obviously you heard Ray, Connie, and I understand why he's not saying much, but why are you so sure Nigel's gone for help, Greg?"

"Perhaps you'll tell me where else he could have gone."

"Suppose he just couldn't bear the dark any more? Maybe there's no light at all in there."

"Please." In case she doesn't have the wit to grasp why he's out-raged Greg adds "Management doesn't act like that."

"I might."

At once Connie wishes she hadn't admitted that, even to suggest Mad may have a point, because Greg emits a low brief hum she thinks is the most insulting noise she has ever heard. She's about to train her icy rage on him when Jill asks her "Even if you'd be leaving Agnes, Anyes in the lift?"

"You're right, I can't see Nigel doing that, or me."

"If he went for help," Mad persists, "why isn't he back? He's had time to stroll all round Fenny Meadows since we heard the door go."

"Obviously," Greg says, only to leave his audience in suspense while he stoops for a book and lifts his smug grey face above the shelves, "they weren't in their hut and he's had to track them down."

He glances through the window and then peers at the book. For an instant Connie thinks she glimpses activity in the fog, but the unstable shapes that she must have imagined were nowhere near as tall as Nigel or a guard. She expels the impression from her mind as Jake says "Am I allowed to speak yet?"

"It sounds as if you've started," says Greg. "Try and make sure it's worth hearing."

If anyone needed to give Jake permission it surely ought to have been Connie. She's on the brink of saying so when Jake turns ostentatiously away from Greg to ask "Was that Angus I heard?"

"When?" says Mad.

"When you were arguing about Nigel."

"Nobody was arguing," Greg informs him. "We were establishing the situation. Some of us try not to make everything into a squabble like schoolgirls."

Jake looks to see who's offended, which leaves Connie feeling as unsympathetic to him as she already was to Greg. "Whatever you call it," Jake insists, "you were making a row."

His victory seems to terminate all conversation. With visible reluctance Jill asks "What did you think you heard?"

"Angus calling out or trying to. He sounded a bit shrill."

Greg's expression suggests that the shrillness is all Jake's. "Did anyone else hear anything like that?"

While nobody appears to want to take Greg's side, everybody's silence does. "Well," Jake says, "if it wasn't Angus it must have been Ray."

Greg utters a short laugh of pitying disbelief, but Connie wonders if Jake's persistence is making Greg as nervous as she's growing, or if he hasn't the intelligence. Before she can tell Jake to keep his fancies to himself, Jill says "Why aren't we hearing them?"

"I'm surprised at you, Jill," Greg says, leaning on her pronoun. "Obviously because there wasn't anything of the sort to hear."

"I don't mean that, Connie. Angus must be down by now, so shouldn't we be hearing them talk?"

Connie tries not to resent having needed to be told as she stalks along an increasingly dark aisle towards the exit to the staffroom. The illumination at the exit isn't much better than no light at all. The door has begun to remind her how her bedroom looked once when she was little—when she wakened in the middle of the night to catch all the doors in the room skulking in the dimness and holding themselves motionless on behalf of whatever had taken up residence behind them. She almost pounds on the door to render it harmless and elicit a response. Instead she calls "Sorry to disturb you, but is Angus with you, Ray?"

"Oh yes."

It has to be Ray's muffled voice, unless it belongs to Angus. Whoever spoke must be preoccupied, since he barely forms the words. Though she won't pretend she's eager to hear it again, Connie asks "Are you both all right?"

"Oh yes."

At least they both answer, though the words are even less clear;

she could fancy that their mouths are growing somehow looser. She has the grotesquely unnecessary notion that she's deluding herself she recognises them; she can't tell which is which. More to the point, she sees no reason why her questions should amuse them. Her impression that they're close to bursting into laughter goads her to demand "How are you getting on?"

She would like not to believe that they repeat their answer, if in voices so thick they sound muddy with mirth. The sluggish syllables are barely comprehensible, not least because they're almost blotted out by Woody's overbearing intervention. "What's happening with you, Connie? Doesn't look like much."

She grabs the nearest receiver, which looks like a glimmering bone. She has to duck close to the stand to distinguish which button will enlarge her voice. "I'm trying to find out what Ray and Angus are doing. I thought you'd want to know."

In a moment he transfers himself to the receiver. "So what are they?"

"I'm not sure. Listen for yourself." Holding the phone towards the door fails to relieve her of much of her nervousness, because her shadow elongates itself grub-like across the spines of books. "Ray, Angus," she nevertheless shouts. "Woody's hearing you on the phone if you want to let him know where you're up to."

She braces herself for another repetition of their phrase, but has to conclude they meant it as a laddish joke at her expense as she's met by a silence that feels more mocking still. "Come on, you had enough to say before. Woody wants to hear it now."

She pokes the receiver at the silence so angrily the earpiece almost knocks against the door. Once her arm begins to ache with stretching the cord she snatches the phone back to her face. "They aren't answering."

"Could be they don't like your tone."

This strikes her as wholly unfair. "Perhaps you'd better show me how to do it, then."

"Give me a smile and you've got it." When she bares her teeth fleetingly at the ceiling Woody says "I hope you can set the team down there a better example than that" and sends his voice into the air. "Ray, Angus, Connie's holding the phone outside the door. One of you talk to me."

Fishing at the dimness appeals to Connie less than ever. The door isn't shifting, about to spring open; she's simply unable to hold the shadow of the phone still. After quite a few seconds Woody booms "Are you sure they can hear me?"

"If you can hear me," she shouts, "you'll be able to hear them."

"Ray or Angus, speak to me."

Connie has to watch the door appear to tremble restlessly for altogether too long before Woody's voice shrinks into the receiver. "Tell me you heard them and I couldn't."

"Not this time."

"What did they say before?"

"Nothing that made any sense."

"To you, maybe, could that be?"

"To anyone." She makes herself turn her back on the door to call across the shop "What did you think they were on about?"

The five grey faces grow dimmer and less defined as they swing towards her. Once they've all finished pivoting they seem to delegate Jill to murmur "Who?"

"Them," Connie says, confining some of her anger to jerking a thumb over her shoulder. "The comedy team. Ray and Angus."

"I don't know how funny you'll think this is, but I didn't hear them."

Connie's about to indicate how little she's amused when she realises the others are pleading deafness too. "Well, I did," she says and finds her cheek with the receiver again. "I heard them, except they weren't saying much at all."

"Guess they're too busy doing what I told them to."

He has brought her back to a conclusion she reached some interminable time ago. She's gaining the impression that their ability to think and communicate is close to falling dormant and already dragging time down with it. "Do you want me to leave them to it, then?"

"Hey, that's some plan. Why don't we try that."

She's lowering the phone so as not to be tempted to blurt a retort when Jill hurries several paces down her aisle, brandishing one palm. "Connie . . ."

"Have you decided I wasn't hearing things after all?"

"No, I was wondering if you should ask when they're coming for Agnes."

Connie wants to be out of the worst of the dimness but lifts the receiver once more. "I wonder—"

"I heard what someone wondered. No need to do their talking for them."

"Then what's the answer?"

"No."

She has to take time to be certain it isn't the fault of her brain that the reply seems wholly unrelated to the question. "You're saying . . ."

"Why do we need to call anyone when Nigel's there?"

Connie sucks in a protracted breath to begin an explanation that she's afraid will outdistance any patience she has left, and then an idea struggles from beneath whatever's weighing down her mind. "Because they could let you out as well."

"You got me there. Why don't you try calling."

"I will, then. I'll just . . ." She waves a hand in a generalised fashion at her colleagues and fumbles to plant the receiver on its stand before he can say any more. She wants to be closer to the others and the window, not least because of an unpleasant though surely irrational notion that someone has shuffled to the opposite side of the door and is quivering with mute amusement. As she hurries through the muddy darkness of the Psychology aisle her shoulders grow tense in case Woody's voice falls like a spider on her. She reaches the counter without being questioned, however. "Don't let me slow you down," she says, since even Greg has stopped to watch her. She picks up the nearest receiver and dials

999, then stares at the fog as if her parched gaze may help bring a response.

It only confuses her. She imagines she can hear the surges of the fog, pretending to give ground but actually stealing nearer. Of course the noise is static, even if it sounds increasingly thick and solid. She ends the connection and leans towards the keys to be sure she's obtaining an outside line, and dials again. The same sound oozes out of the earpiece, and a third attempt seems to entice it closer. Rather than yield to the fancy that it's gathering in her brain, she cuts it off and thumbs the intercom button to dial Woody's extension. "I can't get out to anyone."

"I could have told you so."

"Why didn't you?" she says through her unsmiling teeth.

"Figured you might as well find out for yourself in case any of you thought I was trying to stop you phoning."

Connie supposes he's right, but it distresses her to realise they've become so distrustful. It seems to intensify the threat of the lurid unnatural light and of the shadows that have engulfed much of the shop. "I'm sure nobody can now," she tries to reassure him or herself.

"I guess that's worth a smile."

"I expect so."

By the time she understands he isn't asking one of her she has sent it guiltily towards the ceiling. His only rejoinder, if it's even that, is "I'm through talking if you are."

She turns from laying the receiver down to find Jill watching her. "What were you so pleased we can't do?" Jill says at once.

"Nothing, Jill, honestly. I'd be happy if we could all do the same thing."

Jill's immediately expressionless face tells Connie she shouldn't have used those words. It must cost Jill an effort to say only "What are we going to do about Agnes?"

"What would you suggest?"

"Did we just hear you say Woody wasn't able to phone either?

Nigel's had more than enough time. Someone else should go for help."

"Are you volunteering?"

Jill blinks out at the fog, which appears to greet her by proposing a slithery dance. "If nobody else does."

Every other face turns inert as the grey light until Ross clears his throat unevenly. "I will."

"To do what?" Greg objects.

"Had you better try security first just in case, Ross?" Jill suggests with her back to Greg. "If nobody's there you'll have to phone from Stack o' Steak. They're open all night, aren't they?"

"Nigel will have thought of that," says Greg.

"What do you want us to do then, Greg?" Jill demands, whirling to face him. "How long would you like Anyes to stay in the lift in the dark?"

That silences him, though perhaps he's mutely answering the question. "It won't do any harm for someone else to get help," Connie intervenes. "If you have to call emergency, Ross, you can always ask if anyone already has."

The thud of a book on a shelf conveys Greg's opinion of this. "Are you going to be warm enough, Ross?" says Jill.

His hand gropes at the unbuttoned collar of his shirt, which looks doused in the grubby light. "I'll run."

"Will you be all right on your own?" Jake says.

Greg mutters something Connie would ignore if Mad didn't ask "What were you inspired with just then, Greg?"

"My mistake. It's not a ship."

His comment had to do with rats and sinking. "Thanks anyway, Jake," Ross says. "I expect I'll be faster on my own."

"Depends who's coming after you, would you say, Greg?"

Greg's face grows so furiously blank it's clear that he was thinking along those lines. "If you're ready then, Ross," Connie says and hurries to the exit. As she reaches for the keypad on the door, her fingers falter inches short of it. She can't recall a single digit of the code.

Exhaustion must have driven it out of or too deep into her brain, but the harder she strives to dredge it up, the more her head feels as if it's filling up with some of the fog that's prancing shapelessly beyond the glass. She has been reduced to fingering the air in front of the keypad in case her hand remembers, the same way it knows the layout of the computer keyboard, when Woody's voice darts out of all the darkest corners at her. "Gee, am I watching more not work?"

She tries to make light of it as she uses the nearest phone on the counter. "Just my brain."

"Uh huh."

She wouldn't mind a reply that sounds less like agreement, even though he isn't announcing it to the entire shop. "I can't remember the exit code," she tells him.

"Right."

Surely he doesn't mean the situation is. "Could you remind me?"

"Why are you going to want it now? Doesn't look anything like daylight down there to me, and there's a whole lot of work to finish."

"We'll get it done faster if we have Anyes to help, and besides, we really need to let her out. We don't know how much air is left in there."

"In an elevator with just one person in it? Plenty, I'd think."

She's dismayed to suspect that she could have persuaded him by concentrating on the notion of releasing Agnes to work. "She's in the dark as well," Connie nearly pleads. "How can we leave her like that?"

"Nigel isn't, is he?"

The prospect of explaining in any detail about Nigel makes her head feel stuffed with worse than dullness. "It doesn't sound as if he's had much success."

"Seems like he isn't on his own there." Before she can decide if that's aimed at her, Woody says "So it's Ross you figure is expendable, right?"

"He put himself forward."

"You'd maybe wonder why he's anxious to desert."

"I don't think he's that at all."

"He'd tell me the same if I asked him, you think?"

"I'm sure he would."

"Then I won't bother. The one that wants to go has to be the one we need least. Go ahead if that's your decision."

Static rushes into the silence Woody leaves behind, and she's afraid he has forgotten or no longer cares what she asked. "You were going to remind me of the code."

"Which one was that? Numbers or behaviour?" The static sounds like breathing over his shoulder. "Okay, see what this does for you," he says and gabbles digits.

How mocking does he mean his voice to be? He surely wouldn't give her an incorrect code, but is he thinking the right one won't work? She returns to the exit and uses a single finger to ensure she's pushing just the numbers he helped her recall. She closes her fist around the handle, which feels like the chill of the fog solidified, and tugs.

The door snags on nothing she can see and then swings inwards with a glassy creak. It seems to invite the dankness and the stale smell of the fog. Although Ross didn't hear Woody's comments she feels bound to encourage him, but can't think of much that would. "Don't catch cold and don't get lost," she tries saying, and has to add "Only teasing. Anyes will be grateful. We all will. Hurry back."

He's out of the shop before she has finished speaking. She trails after him to watch. As he passes the window, almost running, he throws Mad an uneasy sidelong glance. He hasn't reached the end of the building when the fog starts to fray his outline and fade him. It engulfs him and muffles his footsteps until they sound as though the pavement is growing soft. She's hearing them dwindle and wondering if she should call out a last reassurance when Woody demands "Have we lost Connie as well?"

She could imagine the entire shop is doing duty as his mouth. She steps back through the doorway to shake her head at whichever camera is on her. The interior of Texts resembles the night outside more than she likes: the grudging flat discoloured illumination, the clinging insidious chill, even the way the opposite side of the room appears to recede into a greyish dimness more substantial than air. She shuts the door hastily and jabs a finger at the keypad, but has second thoughts. Why is she locking Ross out? Suppose she's unable to let him back in? She can't face an argument with Woody over this. She fingers each digit of the code without any pressure, and then looks up at the cameras as she heads for the drumming of books on shelves. "Now you got it, Connie," Woody declares. "Everyone else check it out. That's what I call a smile."

# ROSS

**"Don't catch cold and don't get lost,"** Connie says and follows it with a giggle so stifled by embarrassment she sounds as if she's producing it in her sleep. "Only teasing. Anyes will be grateful. We all will. Hurry back."

Just now Ross would rather not even glance back, because everything about the shop looks like a nightmare he's having. He's out of it—the shop, at least—before Connie has finished talking about Agnes. As he flees past the window he risks a blink at Mad. Her appearance and everyone else's still dismays him: her greyish face and dim eyes balanced on flesh bruised by shadow make her resemble a corpse put to work, and her mechanical actions—stooping to lift yet another book, rising stiffly to find a place for it—don't help. She sends him a quick smile meant to be heartening, and a response tugs like a tic at his lips. Then he's past the window, and has the notion that the fog has hidden him from Connie. She mightn't notice if he makes for his car.

His entire body wavers towards the staff car park, but he won't give in. He doesn't care whether Agnes is grateful or how much of a pain she continues to be; he can't leave her trapped in the dark. At least now he's able to see what he's doing, more or less. The emergency services can surely restore power to the shop, which will give Mad and the rest of them their looks back. He has told everyone he'll help. He can't let them down, especially Mad. He hurries past the alley, averting his gaze.

All the same, he wouldn't have minded some company. If Greg had kept his mouth shut for once, Ross might have had Jake. Still, no doubt Jake would be anticipating aloud what may lie ahead. Ross concentrates on walking fast, not giving himself an instant to think of a reason to falter. His footsteps sound isolated and shrunken to childishness by the silence, which is as oppressively pervasive as the fog. Even when he remembers that the motorway is closed, that doesn't make the silence seem any less unnatural, though since the retail park is artificial, isn't black silence closer to its natural state? He feels as if each of his breaths is gathering fog to lie stagnant in his lungs and seep into his brain. Under the floodlights that are fattened like cocoons restless with eagerness to hatch, the glaring murk drags itself over the deserted pavement and the tarmac bare of vehicles and peels itself reluctantly away from the shopfronts. Posters in the window of Happy Holidays remind him of a dozen or more places he would rather be, although he thinks several of the handwritten destinations are misspelled, or is he too tired to recognise how they should be spelled, or both? In TVid someone has left the televisions on, presumably tuned to a sports channel, since they all show people fighting, figures so blurred and unstable they appear to be sinking or melting into the darkness behind or below them. In Teenstuff the air-conditioning must be on; flimsy clothes shift in the dimness as though at least one intruder is crawling behind them, unless the intruders are too small to need to go on all fours. He even fancies he sees a head, or rather less than one, writhe into view from the neck of a bellying dress on a hanger. He hastens past that and the sight of far too many identical cloth faces staring glassy-eyed out of Baby Bunting, but his speed does him no good. He's left with the impression that among the dolls he glimpsed a face pressed as flush as the underside of a snail against the pane; he also imagines he saw its flattened grey blobs of eyes move, smearing the glass, to watch him. When he twists around, of course he can locate nothing of the kind, and surely the glistening vertical trail down the pane must be condensation. Now he's alongside Stay in Touch, where any number of mobile phones on stands blink nervously in the dark. He has no idea what has set them off, but he's assailed by the notion that they all have the same message for him: perhaps that if he owned a mobile he could have made the call without venturing so far, or might it be information he would welcome even less? Walking faster only brings him to the unoccupied section, where the words scrawled on the boards over the shopfronts have abandoned all resemblance to language; trails of moisture have distorted them and the crude figures that accompany them so much that they suggest first attempts at writing and drawing by a mind too elementary to be called childish. All this is beginning to make him feel as though Fenny Meadows has reverted to a state worse than primitive, an era before there was anything worth describing as intelligence in the world. He finds he's grateful beyond words to hear a voice.

It's down the alley by the nameless properties. It's in the guards' hut, a long white almost featureless box with small smeary windows as grey as the backdrop of fog. Ross is unable to distinguish a word, but that doesn't matter. There must be at least two people in the building; indeed, two sets of muddy footprints lead to the door.

Suppose Nigel's in the hut? What will Ross have to say to him? He's starting to feel awkward and embarrassed, but slowing down even slightly allows the chill to fasten on him. He rubs his arms so hard the chafing muffles the voice, which he's beginning to suspect may not belong to anybody in the cabin. If it's on the radio, someone has to be listening. Perhaps there's only one listener, since one trail leads out of the building, the other in.

His shadow smears itself across the whitish door like another example of vandalism as he reaches for the metal handle. Whoever's in the cabin must be asleep to have allowed the radio to drift so far off the station. The misshapen voice sounds as though it's trying to force its words, if there is more than one, through mud. "Hello?" Ross shouts and knocks on the flimsy door.

That seems to rouse a guard to switch off the radio, but not to answer. "Hello," Ross calls, resting his fingers on the icy handle. At the end of a pause that lets him watch several of his breaths join the fog he realises what is causing him to hesitate. To be so muddy, wouldn't all the smudged footprints need to have started from outside the hut? That simply means they don't belong to whoever is inside. "I'll come in, shall I?" Ross shouts and pushes the handle down.

The door swings inwards, disclosing that the cabin is lit only from outside. It doesn't contain much to illuminate. A shelf extends along the left side to a metal sink. The shelf is strewn with pages of a basic newspaper and also holds a microwave oven, an electric kettle, an empty mug and one half full of a liquid that must be tea or equally stale coffee, however much it imitates mud. Beside it an ashtray is stuffed with butts, and at first Ross thinks at least one of them is smouldering, but he must have stirred the ash by opening the door; the hint of drifting greyness surely can't be fog. To the right of the sink an open door reveals a toilet with an upright lid, which the dimness turns into an oval mask so primitive it's featureless. Two swivel chairs, one behind the other, face the entrance, but of course they didn't swing to greet his knock, nor did their occupants jump out of them to hide. If that's absurd, is the situation any less so? The cabin is deserted, and he can't see a radio.

There has to be one, which must have wandered off the station as he knocked, though in that case shouldn't he be hearing static? He shoves the door against the wall as he's compelled to step into the cabin to discover what he hasn't understood. The bare floorboards yield underfoot more than he likes, but where in the cramped dimness could anyone be hiding? If he let himself he could think they're behind the door. It isn't as close to the wall as he assumed; there's an obstruction between them. As he leans hard on the door without wanting to define why, he senses that the soft obstacle is exerting an equal pressure; perhaps it's about to push harder. It isn't an experience he's anxious to prolong. He slams the door after him as he dashes towards the shopfronts.

Even Texts seems like a refuge, but he still has to summon help for Agnes. Once he reaches the spillage of discoloured light along the alley he twists around, but the door of the hut hasn't opened. He's less sure that the thick voice hasn't recommended mumbling; perhaps the hindrance behind the door was the radio, which he managed to set off again. He hurries out of the alley towards Stack o' Steak.

He's passing the supermarket when he falters. Is someone working late? Will they let him phone if he shows them his Texts badge? He advances to the nearest door and squints past the unstaffed checkout desks into the aisle where he thought he glimpsed a figure crouching or kneeling at a shelf. "Anyone in there?" he shouts and knocks on the glass door, which tolls like a drowned bell. "I'm from Texts. We've got a problem."

Perhaps Frugo has as well. Belatedly he notices that the only illumination in the supermarket comes from the spotlights. Would anyone be working late in that? He has to lift his wrist almost to his face to discern through the condensation inside the plastic on his watch that it's past two in the morning. They must have locked a stray cat or a dog in Frugo by mistake; at the far end of the aisle the indistinct hunched shape is flinging packets off the next to lowest shelf. Ross doesn't linger to watch. He's supposed to be phoning from Stack o' Steak.

The fog mocks his pace by grudging every inch it releases of the supermarket before it yields up any of the diner. The k and a and e of the sign, bright yellow letters embedded in fat orange outlines, look not just dulled but doused by fog. He thinks it has stolen their glow until he sees it has kept none for itself. The sign doesn't matter, but the fog appears to have overcome the light inside the diner too. He plants his hands against the window with a concerted thump he's desperate enough to hope will bring the staff to find out what he wants, and leans his forehead against the cold glass.

The chill fails to enliven his brain, which feels tired past stupidity, unable to stop insisting like a child denied a treat that the diner is meant to be open twenty-four hours. His breaths swell up and fade from the pane while his hot eyes do their best to persuade him that the interior is lit as it should be. At last he grasps that the light beyond the window is more of the sludgy glow he's standing in, because the kindergarten colours of the furniture and ketchup containers and oversized cruets have all been simplified to shades of grey or black, as though a child too unintelligent to make any use of the items has muddied them instead. He can only assume the diner is closed because the motorway is, but that needn't mean the staff have gone home. He tramps to the glass doors and drums his fists on them. "Anyone still here?" he shouts. "I'm from Texts."

He's about to explain that it's the bookshop in case it has always been as invisible to them as it is now to him when he notices marks on the floor in front of the counter. Footprints oughtn't to be so nearly circular, and what kind of dance has someone been performing? As he grows aware of the photograph of a giant hamburger among the unlit images above the grill behind the counter, he recognises the objects strewn across the linoleum. They're hamburger patties glistening with rawness. There are at least a dozen, and every one has a piece missing. If those are bites, they're all the more disconcerting in their lack of shape.

He doesn't want to interpret the sight. It can't touch him except by letting the chill of the fog overwhelm him. His legs have begun to shake as they once did when he was a child with a fever that felt like a nightmare from which he couldn't waken. All he can do with them is run while he rubs his arms with hands he can barely feel, but which way does he run? To his car to drive to the nearest telephone box, and the route around the stretch of pavement he hasn't already traversed is shorter. Besides, it will take him past the shop so that he can inform Connie of his plan, or perhaps someone else should take over. Ross might prefer to stay with his colleagues, however the suffocated light makes them look. He's beginning to feel as if he has been cast out in the fog for not saving Lorraine.

He can still save Agnes. Though that isn't remotely as serious, it's something he's able to achieve—something Woody can't prevent. Perhaps once Ross has called about Agnes he may allow himself to get so lost in the fog that the only route he knows will lead home. The prospect lends speed to his agitated legs, and so do his surroundings. The building next to the diner is practically completed, but instead of windows it has sheets of whitish plastic that appear to billow stealthily as Ross dashes past, unless he's seeing the antics of his own faint distorted shape. Beyond that shopfront the murk bristles with poles that sprout from a shop-sized rectangle of pallid concrete, as if the metal sketch of a building has been abandoned because nobody could think how to finish it. The fog that trickles down the poles reclaims them as he sprints past a foundation surrounded by the lowest courses of its walls, which put him in mind of a ruin or an ancient construction whose purpose has been forgotten. Would the route across the car park be quicker? He's running like a puppet along the pavement while he struggles to decide, and a wall so mud-caked and uneven he can't believe it's newly built has loomed into view ahead, when someone calls him.

At least, he thinks it's his name. It's a whisper that's mostly a hiss, and surely he doesn't recognise the voice. "Lorraine?" he gasps.

"Ross."

Growing louder has lowered its pitch, and he's dismayed that he mistook it for Lorraine's. Remember but get on with living, his father advised when he saw what a lump of depression Ross kept turning into at home, as if the man knows anything about failing to save someone rather than just being unable to keep her. "Nigel?" Ross calls with a good deal more certainty. "Where are you?"

"Here."

He's somewhere behind the unfinished buildings. Halting makes Ross begin to shiver like a twig in a storm. As he heads between the abandoned stubby walls he feels as if he's blundering into a land of dwarfs no taller than the topmost bricks. The fog uncovers the wet black road that leads past the retail park to the motorway, and the spiky six-foot hedge along the far side of the road pokes blurred holes in the rotting curtain of murk. "I can't see you," Ross complains.

"Here."

Nigel is in the field beyond the hedge, which has broken out in beads of fog like sweat. However welcome Nigel's company is, Ross is cold enough without risking wet feet. "What are you doing there?" he calls.

"See."

He must be impatient if he has so few words at his disposal. Perhaps he's as eager not to be alone as Ross, who jogs across the deserted road to search for a gap in the hedge. Its countless beads have begun to remind him of dull yet watchful eyes. He's behind the diner when he finds a stile half overgrown by the bushes on either side. He takes hold of the right-hand post and steps on the lower rung. The wood feels spongy and slippery, and his handful of it exudes moisture as chill as the fog. Resentment close to disgust makes him shout "I've lost you. Where have you got to?"

"Here."

Nigel's somewhere on or near the muddy glistening path that extends out of the blanket of shadow draped across the hedge, impaled on it. As Ross clambers over the stile his silhouette appears to lift its head above the roof of the diner before flinching out of sight like a soldier ducking into a trench. He pretends he didn't see that or feel it was in any way inappropriate as he plants one foot on the earth.

Under the lush sodden grass it's even less firm than he expected. His heel slithers over it before sinking at least an inch, and he glimpses moisture swelling up around his shoe. Surely the terrain has to be more solid farther on for Nigel to sound so unconcerned about wherever he's waiting. Ross lowers his other foot and attempts to steady himself before he relinquishes his grip on the oozing stile. As he plods cautiously forward his shadow hauls itself with a series of jerks out of the trench it's part of and begins to merge with the darkening earth. He's out of the darkness cast by the diner, but with every squelching pace he takes the fog around and behind him grows dirtier, as though it's sucking up mud. He hasn't progressed more than a few hundred yards along the flattened slimy trail when he finds he can barely distinguish it from the rest of the soaked field. "How much further?" he protests.

"Here."

Nigel sounds close. The question is whether the last of the glow from the retail park will have fallen short by the time Ross finds him. He must be able to see, otherwise how can he show Ross what's there? Perhaps that's it ahead, a low mound about six feet long over which the hem of the fog is trailing. No, it's a man stretched flat on the earth to peer into some kind of burrow. It's Nigel. "What are you doing?" Ross blurts.

Nigel doesn't answer. He's so engrossed in his discovery that he doesn't even move. What could be so fascinating it would make him lie in the mud? Ross hurries to him, but his haste is worse than useless; his vision has to catch up with the thick shifting gloom, and he can't separate the hollow Nigel is examining from the overgrown earth around it. He crouches, gripping his knees so their shivering won't topple him over, and ducks his head as near to Nigel's as he can without losing his balance.

His eyes still aren't equal to the dimness. He won't even consider what he appears to be seeing. With a grimace he rests one hand on the earth, which seems to shift to greet it, and brings his head almost level with Nigel's. The choked glow from the retail park begins to settle faintly on it—that is, his vision starts to grasp what's in front of him. He struggles to believe he's mistaken, but the sight is just too clear to be illusory. There's no hollow around Nigel's head. His face is buried so deep in the soil that it covers his ears.

How long has it been since he spoke? Surely not long enough for him to have stopped breathing. Ross stays more or less in his crouch as he shuffles frantically to grab Nigel's shoulders from in front. Has Nigel already tried to raise himself? Every joint of his thumbs and every inch of his fingers are buried in the earth at the ends of his arms flung wide. Ross heaves at Nigel's shoulders while he labours to stand up, but Nigel won't budge. In desperation Ross thrusts his fingertips into the mud, squeezing it under his nails, and locates Nigel's cheekbones. When he tugs at them Nigel's head wobbles up on its stiffening neck as the ground that was moulded to his face emits a slobbery gasp. Tears of relief or gratitude stream down his blackened cheeks, and then Ross sees the liquid is part of the mud that coats not only Nigel's face but also his eyes, which would otherwise be staring blindly. It has plugged his nostrils too, and appears to have forced his jaws to gape their widest so that it can fill his mouth.

The sound that escapes Ross as he flounders backwards leaves its words behind. Nigel's face slaps the earth, which sets about re-claiming it at once. Ross sprawls full length on his back and jack-knifes upwards, terrified that the mud will swallow him. He's unable to think or to orient himself. Although he seems to remember approaching Nigel from the far side, the glow from the retail park is behind Ross now. As he staggers upright it's strong enough to spill his faint shadow over the mound of hair, all that remains visible of Nigel's engulfed head. It looks as though one of the tufts of muddy grass has been mounted on his neck. Ross strives to clear his mind of the sight as he flees, shivering with his entire body and maddened by the icy wetness that clings to the whole of the back of him, towards the retail park.

Yet another reason why he's close to panic is that the fog is thick-ening. That has to be why the light appears to be retreating into it, matching his pace. Shouldn't he have reached the stile or at least the hedge by now? He risks looking away from the glimmering track long enough to glance over his shoulder in case he can judge how far he has progressed. Nigel has been erased by the fog into which Ross's footprints trail, an irregular series of depressions in the flattened path. He faces forward, only to wonder what he overlooked. His head throbs with the effort and then with realising. There was just one set of his footprints behind him; there are none ahead. At this moment the glow he's following ceases to hover. From sailing as high as a floodlight it sinks through the fog into the earth, abandoning Ross to the dark.

He stumbles to a halt, or at least as much of one as his shivers will permit, and glares at the suffocating blackness. His eyes are so parched of sleep that they're dreaming of light, shapeless waves of it that drain away and reappear in time with his pounding heartbeat. Though his vision is useless, he should still be able to find his way back. He only needs to turn the way he came, and surely he'll be able to discern enough not to trip over Nigel by the time he reaches him. He inches his left foot around until it's more or less at right angles to the other. His stance feels unstable even when he presses his feet together, but he simply has to repeat the manoeuvre and he should be ready to walk. He's edging his left foot away once more when behind him Nigel speaks his name.

Ross spins around without thinking. His feet skid on marshy ground, and he's terrified of losing his balance. He flails at the clinging invisible fog with both arms and manages to remain standing, but now he has absolutely no idea where he is in relation to the shops. He's turning his head as gradually as his latest fit of shakes will allow, and narrowing his eyes in the hope that may help him identify some hint of light, when Nigel calls out again. His voice is at the level of Ross's waist and sounds close enough for Ross to touch him.

Ross shrinks away. His fingers dig into his palms rather than risk brushing against Nigel's face stuffed with mud. He finds himself striving to recall anything his father has told him that can help, but his skull is cluttered with sayings of his father's like chunks of useless rubble sticking out of murk: be yourself, do what you have to, don't drive tomorrow unless you're sure you're awake . . . How can Nigel speak when his mouth is packed with earth? But he does, this time from the direction Ross recoiled in. Ross hurls himself forward with no thought except to dodge out of range. He no longer cares where he's treading, but he should. The ground slides his feet from under him, pitching him into blackness.

He thrusts his hands out just in time for them to sink into unseen mud, taking his wrists with them. As he props himself on his quivering arms, Nigel's voice addresses him. "Ross see here," it chortles sluggishly, and before it has finished speaking it echoes itself from the other side of him: "Ross see here." He hears the pair of mimics take shapeless shuffling paces towards him, but all he's able to think is how pointless the whole game has been; why bother enticing him into the dark when he was helpless once he fell beside Nigel? At once he's almost throttled by a sense of vast resentment of his ability still to think—a sense of malevolence with a solitary purpose as primitive as itself: to reduce him to its own mindless state. As though aroused by his understanding, it fills his nostrils with an exhalation that smells like water stale beyond words, like the breath of an ancient toothless mouth—the mouth that gulps his arms up to the shoulders. Before it closes over all of him it gives him time to experience how it's composed not quite of mud, not quite of gelatinous flesh, but worse than both.

# JAKE

**He's so on edge with straining his eyes for Ross or headlights every** time he thinks he glimpses movement of something more solid than fog that Woody's giant voice almost makes him drop a book. "Hey, I'm the only one around here that needs to wait. Any idea how I can help all of you work?"

Jake's first reaction is to duck guiltily to find the right location for the book or at least pretend he has, but he can't resist watching Connie frown at Greg in case he presumes to respond. The only aspect of the present situation that gives Jake any pleasure is how Greg has started to annoy people besides him. Greg is either unaware of Connie's feelings or ignoring them. He raises his face as though catching more of the slimy light may help him think, unless he's miming thought for Woody's benefit. As Connie emits a compressed breath like the reverse of a sniff, Mad says "What's that?"

She's peering down the aisle she's in and along the one that leads to the exit to the staffroom. "What are you seeing?" Jill asks across the shelves.

"Under the door."

Jill cranes her neck and then ventures down her aisle to veer into the one Mad hasn't glanced away from. "I can't see anything," she admits.

"Me neither with you in the way."

"Sorry," Jill says, to some extent as though she is, and backs against the nearest shelves, only for Mad to complain "Now I can't either. I could have sworn there was, I don't know, a big stain on the floor."

Jill is following her frustrated gaze out of politeness when Woody demands "What am I seeing now? Who called time out?"

"It's nothing," Connie tells him. "Just a mistake. I expect we're all getting tired." Before Greg can raise the objection he's opened his mouth for, she adds "Some of us, anyway."

Mad takes the criticism to be aimed at her but seems uncertain whether to focus her resentment on Connie or Jill. As Connie tramps back to her shelving Jake returns to his. He's hoping it may conceal him from the tensions he feels gathering like a storm, but it offers no refuge. Once he has found space for yet another of Jill's novels he has to retreat one shelf further from the window, and now he's unable to read the names on the packed spines except by pressing his neck against his shoulder and crouching like a hunchback within inches of the books. He straightens his head up and stoops lower to grab the next lump of cardboard and paper from the heap of them. Sweat collects behind his knees, clamminess encases him but keeps giving way to a chill, both of which make him feel so feverish he surely ought to be in bed. He wishes he were there with Sean and no fever except the kind they create between them. Since there's no possibility of that, he wants Sean to be peacefully asleep, not least so that he'll be ready to collect Jake if the sun ever rises. The dead glow through the window seems to have rendered time as inert as itself, and Jake has to squint fiercely at his watch to be certain why it appears to have lost a hand. He's about to speak when Connie says with hardly any patience "What now, Mad?"

"It mustn't be anything. You told Woody it wasn't. I expect it's just me being mad."

"Don't be like that," Jill says. "If you—"

"Don't be childish like you think everyone else is, you mean?"

"You are," says Connie, "if you don't tell us if there's something you should tell."

Mad stares towards her shelves along the rear wall and takes a long loud breath. "I thought I saw someone on the floor. Go on, say it's me imagining someone's been messing with my section."

Jake peers towards the alcoves, which are dim as the depths of the fog. For a moment he fancies he glimpses a head that inches around the end of an aisle and immediately shrinks or shrivels into hiding, but its owner would have to be on all fours or no taller than an infant. Nevertheless Jake is tempted to come to Mad's defence even before Greg remarks "Either that or Agnes has got out."

Incredible though Jake finds it, Greg apparently intends this as a joke. Jake is sure the girls would side with him if he attacked Greg for it, and has to force himself to concentrate on a more important issue. "It's quarter past three, no, seventeen past. When did Ross leave?"

"Some of us were too busy to be watching the clock."

"That isn't fair, Greg," Jill objects. "Jake wasn't. That's why he's asking."

"He's been out there too long," says Mad. "All night, it feels like. Even longer."

"I wouldn't put it past him to have sneaked off home," Greg says. "If we're expected to believe Nigel could have, Ross certainly could."

Jake is delighted Greg can't have realised he has given him the cue to say "Then someone else will have to go."

"So there'll be even more work for anyone who cares about the shop, you mean."

"No," Jill says, "because Ross mightn't have thought of going more than one way."

"That's clear as mud to me."

"Maybe he won't have gone on the motorway if he forgot the phones up there will still be working. If he'd found a phone box on the other road someone would be here by now."

"That's assuming he bothered to try."

"If he didn't," Mad retorts so furiously she sounds close to abandoning language, "that's all the more reason for someone else to, isn't it?"

Greg's face grows dull with understanding that he has trapped himself. He picks up a book and stares at it as though nothing else matters. "So what plan is anyone suggesting?" Connie asks.

"Someone tries the motorway," Jake says, "and someone tries the bottom road in case there's a problem."

"Don't tell us," Greg mutters just audibly. "You'd like to take the bottom road."

"I'd like to help, that's right. Agnes has been shut up long enough. But I haven't got a car."

"I'd rather not go out by myself if I'm going," says Mad.

"I don't see why you should." Connie waits for agreement to begin spreading over Greg's face before she says "Go out by yourself, that is."

As Greg shelves the book with a thump like a fist on a table she returns to the counter. She's only reaching for the phone when Woody's voice falls on her. "Let me guess. The cavalry's here at last."

"Not exactly. Well, not really at all. We think something may have happened to Ross or he'd be back by now and there'd be help."

"All the news is bad, huh? That's why you all look like you're stuck in mud. Okay, let's see if I can get you moving," Woody booms like an uncle talking at a child, and begins to sing. "Goshwow, gee and whee, keen-o-peachy . . ."

"We're just deciding what to do." Connie raises her voice to give it some authority or counter his. "Actually, we've decided. There's more than one place we could phone for help from, so we think it'll be best if we make a concerted effort."

"Talk English, Connie. I don't get why you Brits have to dress things up fancy."

Jake feels like shouting that they invented the language, but he would only be extending the argument that seems to be gathering around them, embedding them in the stagnant twilight. He has the notion that Connie intends to free herself of it by saying "I want to send people out to both of them."

"And how about the reason we're all here?"

"Getting the shop ready for tomorrow, well, today, you mean."

"Tell me another if you know one."

"We're never going to be able to finish in time now. I'm certain your New Yorkers will understand."

"Yeah? I don't. See if you can make me."

"The light's too bad. The further you go from the window the worse it gets. We don't want people ruining their eyes for nothing and having to go home, do we? I wouldn't be surprised if we all end up in bed with colds as well."

"You think that's too much to ask of the team when they promised to fix up the store."

"We've already been through that. There won't be time. Don't worry, you won't be on your own. I'll stay."

"You won't be the only one," Greg declares.

"Greg's saying he will too, and there's Angus and Ray even if they haven't had any luck with the fuses."

"That right? You two still there? I'm talking to Ray and Angus."

They grunt beyond the door in the darkest corner of the shop, so nearly in unison that they might be speaking in a single muffled voice. "They said yes," Connie transmits.

"So they're still working on the fuses, right?"

"Yes," the double voice responds.

"Tell me, Connie."

"They say they are."

"So let's give them a while longer. Could be they're almost there."

"Don't you think Agnes has been brave long enough? If I were her I'd be making a lot more fuss by now." With a movement that suggests an attempt to wriggle free of the retarded discussion Connie turns, covering the mouthpiece with her hand. "Anyone who's going, go. I'll take the responsibility. The door isn't locked."

Jake lingers to replace on the pile the book he's holding rather than simply dropping it. He and Mad and Jill are abreast of the counter when Woody says "I don't believe what I'm seeing. Looks like the dogs are out of their gates."

"They're all trying to leave," Greg shouts. "It doesn't need them all, does it? I don't think they'll come back."

"Try it shriller and maybe he'll hear you," Jake says before he realises Woody can through the receiver Connie is no longer soundproofing.

"I guess maybe I don't either. Okay, everyone back to the shelves."

"I said go," Connie insists, jabbing the receiver towards the exit.

"You wouldn't say that if he wasn't out of action," says Greg.

Jake's eager to watch her squashing him but is even more anxious to leave. As he hurries past the counter with Mad and Jill in his wake, Woody says in a voice like a huge false smile "Hey, am I not getting through any more? I can hear myself fine."

"You are," Greg shouts and nods hard at the ceiling. "Everyone can hear."

Jake closes his fist around the metal handle, which feels as cold and wet as a stick pulled out of mud. He has to blame his handful of sweat, which must also explain why the metal gives the impression of crawling with rust. He tugs at the handle, and the glass door vibrates against its twin with a faint low gong note, but that's all. "Connie," he says higher than he means to. "It's not unlocked."

"It shouldn't be, either," Greg remarks.

"It is, Jake. That's how I left it. Just push, pull, I should say."

Jake does both, vigorously. The glass clanks like a large loose pane in a storm while the fog beyond it stirs as though it's either mocking the movement he's desperate to produce or gathering itself to confront him. He shakes the door until it jangles, and then says as calmly as he's able "If it isn't locked I don't know what it is."

Connie plants the receiver firmly on its stand and strides to give both doors an interrogative shake. "I don't understand, but it's all right," she says and types numbers on the keypad before triumphantly flinging the doors wide. At least, that's clearly her intention, but the result is no more than a paralysed glassy clank.

"Forgotten the code again?" Woody enquires, audibly smiling. "Don't ask me."

"That was right. I know it was," Connie assures everyone but him, and keys it in a second time, then hauls at the doors until they creak. Jake almost cries out, afraid that they'll shatter, leaving her clutching the handles and riddled with fragments of glass. At last she lets go, panting "It's got to be something to do with the power."

Jake is about to break the silence, which feels like the imminence of thunder, when Jill says what he's thinking. "We'll have to break our way out, then."

"I don't know if I want to be responsible for that," says Connie.

"Just don't be responsible for stopping us," Jake blurts.

"It'll have to be broken sooner or later," Mad says. "How else are the emergency people going to get in?"

Connie fingers her lips as if she's feeling for her own expression before saying "What would you use? We can't have anybody hurt."

None of them has noticed that Greg has dodged behind the counter to the phone until Woody says overhead "Something you think I should know, Greg?"

"They're saying they'll smash the door down."

"They won't be doing anything like that. Tell them so nobody can say they didn't hear."

"Woody forbids it," Greg says and, as if to please him further, doesn't entirely resist smiling.

"Pass me the phone, please." By the time she finishes speaking Connie is opposite Greg at the counter and thrusting out a hand. "Give it to me," she practically spits.

"Woody, do you want me to—"

"Do as you're told." She grabs the phone away from his face, and the earpiece clubs him on the ear. "That was your fault," she informs him, turning away from him. "If we don't open it somehow, Woody, what's going to happen to Agnes?"

"Nothing that hasn't already. Maybe nothing I'm not putting up with myself."

How can anyone side with him after that? It seems to Jake that Woody has ensured Connie won't oppose any means of escape, and at once he knows what to do. He dashes to the trolley he has unloaded and drives it towards the exit. Mad and Jill look shocked as they catch up with his plan, but they move to either side of the trolley to help ram the door. He's backing off to take a longer run at it when Greg darts from behind the counter, rubbing his ear to make certain everybody knows it's injured, to position himself in front of the door, arms and legs stretched wide. "You've been told," he shouts.

"You're my man, Greg," Woody bellows. "They shall not pass."

"Better get out of the way," Jake warns Greg, nudging the trolley in his direction. "Stay like that and you'll get this up your arse."

"Yes, move, Greg," Mad urges.

"We're going to do this," Jill says. "You'll have to move."

Connie slams the phone down and folds her arms. "You've made your point, Greg, and now will you please step aside. I'm in charge down here, and I don't want anyone coming to harm."

"Woody can see everything, so you can't be in charge."

Jake feels as if the women's frustration with Greg has been added to his own loathing. Perhaps they're experiencing that emotion too, because it has grown so oppressive that he needs to discharge it somehow or he'll suffocate. As the trolley thunders forward he visualises how it will burst Greg's crotch unless he dodges. At almost the last moment he veers the trolley at the glass, but Greg sidles rapidly as a crab to block it. Jake exhorts himself not to falter, but the trolley shudders to a halt inches short of Greg. "Move," Jake nearly screams.

"Who's going to make me? I don't see any men to."

Jake shoves the trolley backwards and flies at him. A contemptuous smile is parting Greg's lips before he realises he has brought Mad and Jill on himself as well. They grab his arms and strive to budge him while Jake manages to refrain from seizing him by the throat and digs his nails between Greg's ribs instead. Greg attempts to laugh, but it isn't amusement that bares his teeth. In a few seconds he loses enough balance for his attackers to hurl him aside so violently he staggers behind the counter.

Jake runs to the far end of the trolley while Mad and Jill grab the sides. It has barely started to trundle forward when Greg lurches into its path. As he makes to arrest it Jake rams it into his stomach. He gasps and flounders backwards, and Jake wonders with no apprehension at all whether Greg will be the object that shatters the glass. But Greg surges red-faced at the trolley, and Jake darts around it to keep him off.

He has to rob Greg of more balance than last time. He tells himself he's being rational, but it also feels insanely satisfying to kick Greg on the shin with all the force he can draw from his hatred. As Greg recoils hopping, fighting to grin away his tears, Jake chases him and hooks a foot behind his ankle. A shove at his pudgy chest overbalances him to thump the floor behind the counter with his shoulders or, for all Jake cares, his head. "Do it now," Jake shouts at Mad and Jill.

He's advancing to stand over Greg when Connie cries "Jake."

Doesn't he only intend to keep Greg where he is? He's about to tell her as much, even though he grudges any reassurance that may offer Greg, when the thunder of the trolley culminates in a shrill peal. For a moment the right-hand door stands its ground, and then it collapses outwards, strewing the pavement with hundreds of fragments as though an immense jewel box has spilled its contents. Mad and Jill flinch back, and Jill wheels the trolley away from the hole as though she's rescuing it from a sudden swell of fog. The two women are stepping forward almost hand in hand when Woody speaks, so loud and all-encompassing that Jake could imagine the voice is in the fog as well as in the corners of the shop. "Anyone that leaves the store now, don't bother coming back."

Mad and Jill hesitate in front of the threshold composed of shattered glass. Connie stares at Greg's left hand, with which he's gripping the edge of the counter to haul himself into a crouch. Jake thinks she's about to hammer on Greg's fingers with her fists or otherwise disable him. He's disappointed when she takes Greg's robustness as an excuse to head for the exit. "That can include me, then," she says. "I've had enough."

As Jake follows her towards the gap the alarm begins to squeal. Greg wobbles to his feet and shows Jake his teeth as if he believes the shop is accusing the deserters. Jake is enraged by growing nervous that the noise may alert someone, presumably a guard, for who else could it call out of the fog? It falls silent for as little reason as it made itself heard, and he's waiting for the women to finish picking their way over the debris when Greg stumbles towards him. His face is heavy with determination not to let Jake escape. Jake treads on glass and twists around to wait for him, stooping for a handful he can grind into Greg's eyes. Then Connie says "That's as far as you go, Greg. Remember what Woody just said about leaving the shop."

The frustration that narrows his eyes and mouth is feeble compared to Jake's. This is so intense it feels vast, as if a presence the size of the fog is experiencing it too. He could almost think the huge voice belongs to such a presence. "Let them go, Greg. You're all we need."

Greg doesn't look entirely comfortable with this as he takes a reluctant pace backwards. Jake resists the temptation to kick glass at him. He's following the women past the window full of books that seem drained not just of colour but of any meaning when Woody booms "You can hear me out there, right? I guess you're hoping I'll change my mind and let you in."

Connie increases her pace, and the other women trot to stay beside her. Before Jake catches up with them they dodge around the corner of the shop, leaving him alone with Woody's giant muffled voice. "I know you're listening. Let's see your faces. How many of you are there? Let's see them all."

Jake has the disturbing notion that the words are aimed at the fog. Otherwise there's silence apart from his panicky footsteps; there's no sound from the alley into which the women disappeared. A succession of shivers, not only because of the clinging fog, overtakes him as he dashes to the corner. The women are close to the far end of the alley, which looks walled off by mud. As he hastens to join them he sees that it's a thick mixture of fog and darkness. "What's happened to the lights behind the shops?" Connie seems to think someone ought to know.

"Will it be the power?" Mad suggests.

"Whatever it is I don't like it. Can one of you start her car?"

"What's wrong with yours?" says Jill.

"It's further round than someone else's. If they start theirs we'll be able to see."

A shiver tries to propel Jake into the dark. "We can all go together, can't we?" he says in case that's reassuring.

"Mine's nearest," Mad says impatiently and tramps into the murk.

Jake has time to feel pitifully grateful that all the women are wearing trousers with pockets for their keys as he leaves behind the last of the suffocated glow along the alley. Past the side of Texts he's just able to distinguish Mad lowering herself into a block of darkness. As it shuts her in he hears a huge voice muttering, but not its words. The Mazda emits a rasping cough that adds to the fog, and then the engine roars and the headlights slap a luminous patch on the concrete wall. "Shall I drive over to yours, Connie?" Mad rolls her window down to ask.

"I hope I'm not quite that incapable just yet. There are only a few years between us, you know. I can still walk."

"I meant I could bring you more light," says Mad, but only Jake hears. Connie is already at her Rapier. Jill hurries past it to her Nova, which is less certain of its shape and colour. As Jake waits for someone to offer him a lift he feels as though the frustration he experienced on sparing Greg has accompanied them under cover of the fog. The way Mad's car keeps flaring its lights while it roars like an infuriated beast aggravates the impression, even when she explains "I'm seeing it doesn't die of cold."

Connie's engine acknowledges its key with no more than a click. A second try produces even less of a response, a third no sound from the engine at all. Connie opens her door and leans out, looking diminished. "I don't know the first thing about this. Can anyone help?"

"Not as capable as you thought, hey?" Mad lets her hear.

The oppressive imminence seems to close around them, and Jake fears they'll act it out somehow. "Sean doesn't like to get his hands dirty, so I'm the mechanic," he says with more confidence than he feels. "Can you open your bonnet, Connie?"

She stares at him as though she wonders if he's suggesting she's unable to perform the task, and then she reaches under the dashboard. A different kind of click indicates she has released the bonnet as Jill thinks better of entering the Nova, instead peering past it. "Isn't that Ross's car?"

Jake sees it is but has no idea what to say. He's hooking his fingers under the metal edge when Mad climbs out of her car and joins Jill behind the vehicles. "There aren't many ways he could have walked," Mad reassures everyone. "One of us should find him if we keep our eyes open."

The hood flies up and Jake leans over the engine, scraping his shoulder against the wall of the bookshop. The light is dim, and the metal innards are further obscured by his shadow, so that all he can immediately distinguish is that the engine appears to be clogged by a greyish mass. He stretches one hand along the rim above the radiator grille and stoops closer. Just as he begins to see what he's ducking towards, Mad's engine cuts out, and so do her headlamps.

"Sorry," she calls, and runs to the Mazda. Jake's eyes have adjusted enough to let him separate outlines from the dark, but he isn't sure if he's seeing or remembering or, his entire being pleads, imagining that although the humped mass is sufficiently fluid to have oozed over the whole of the engine, it's well on the way to having a face. At least, low down on a rounded lump that's no longer flattened by the bonnet, a gap like a slit in jelly is widening in an unmistakable if mindless grin. Such a violent shudder overwhelms him that he's terrified his arm will yield, thrusting his face against the gleeful swelling. As he flings himself backwards, skinning his elbow on the concrete wall, his hand slips. He doesn't know if anything reaches out to detain it, but he feels as if he has stroked a slug. He stays within range barely long enough to slam the bonnet as Mad revives her engine and her lights.

At first he thinks all the women are gazing at him because they know what he glimpsed, but of course it's worse than that: they want him to tell them. He can only cling to his first impression and wish it were the case. "It's frozen. Burst, I mean," he babbles. "It burst because it froze and now it's frozen again."

Connie waits until she's certain this is over and says "So are you just going to leave it?"

"Have to. Nobody can do anything."

Both Mad and Jill look inclined to disagree, and he's terrified they'll go further than arguing. Can he hear a bulk slithering about under the bonnet in anticipation that someone will insist on seeing? "Honestly, it needs a proper mechanic," he hears himself pleading rather than simply maintaining. "We'll just have to go two in a car."

The idea is received with so little apparent enthusiasm that he wonders if it could be unwise, but what alternative is there? He shivers with silently urging Connie to put some distance between her and the Rapier. At last she emerges from it, saying almost as reluctantly "I'll ride with Jill if you'll have me. You're the closest to me. Where you live is."

Mad's lights flare again, staining the murk faintly red and encouraging it to grow more solid. "So who's heading which way?" she calls.

"You take the motorway," Connie says. "Don't forget you're looking for Ross as well as a phone."

Mad plainly resents the implication that she needs reminding. Jake is suddenly afraid Jill's car won't start, which is yet another reason why he shudders uncontrollably as he asks "And then what?"

"Go home and wait to hear. I'll ring the shop later if nobody's rung me. Don't worry, I'll be defending everyone the best I can. Greg as well."

That sounds like the germ of another argument that could keep them trapped in the fog. Jake suppresses a retort as he watches Connie open the passenger door of the Nova. He must be loitering out of some sense of protectiveness, since he's alone in knowing what has invaded Connie's car. Jill's engine utters a choking sound and dies. He's about to urge them both to travel with Mad when the engine of the Nova splutters and revs up. He and his ill-defined shadow that looks half absorbed by the fog dash to the Mazda. "All right," he gasps as he slams himself in.

"I should think we must be now. No rush, is there, when it's like this?"

"Maybe not," he says with far too many syllables, "but what are we waiting for?"

358 · Ramsey Campbell

"You to put your seat belt on, I hope."

As Jake drags the belt across himself his elbow stings as if the fog has penetrated an open wound. The Mazda begins to withdraw from the patch of light, which dims as it grows more diffuse. He's only dreaming that the shop is determined not to release it; perhaps the blurred web that one splintered headlamp lens is casting on the wall has given rise to the idea. Is the fog behind the car retreating less than the wall? He tries not to fancy he's helping it trap them by saying "Shall we wait a moment?"

"That isn't your idea of being female, is it, changing your mind."

He has to tell himself she isn't like Greg. "I want to see the others get away, don't you?"

"I was going to till you distracted me."

He mustn't argue. She needs to concentrate on driving, however unreasonably she's behaving, even if fighting to stay quiet beside her feels like trying to breathe underwater. The Mazda swings backwards in an arc, illuminating how Connie's car is holding itself so still it could almost be mistaken for deserted. When a dark glistening shape inches out of hiding beyond the Rapier a cry begins to prise his lips apart, and then Jill reveals it's her car by remembering to switch her headlamps on.

He doesn't know if Mad is taking her time so as to pay him back for suggesting she ought to. She doesn't follow Jill's rear lights until they're smouldering with fog. As the Mazda cruises past Connie's car he seems to glimpse the bonnet raising itself a fraction, like a trap about to be sprung. He does his best to find it again in the mirror without alerting Mad, but the fog hides it before she steers around the corner of the bookshop.

As the cars veer away from the shopfront Jake thinks he hears an incomprehensible voice as muffled as it is enormous. He sees Greg, a greyish silhouette that ducks and shelves a book and ducks again so fast it looks determined to finish all the extra work. Is the voice manipulating it like a puppet? The silhouette rears up and either sends the cars an ironic salute or shades its eyes to watch them, only for the fog to deny it the pleasure, if that's what it's having. Then the nearest saplings drift by, dripping as though they have been dredged up, and the Mazda puts on speed. It creeps so close to Jill's angry lights that Jake wonders if Mad wants her to feel threatened for guiding them so close to where the Mazda ran Lorraine down. Until the fog swallows the broken tree-stump and Mad eases her foot off the accelerator, he has to restrain himself from treading on the brake.

He's increasingly unsure whether he's continuing to hear a wordless mutter underneath the fog. The impression refuses to fade, which aggravates his sense that the cars are being held back. The tarmac oozing from beneath the Nova resembles a stream of mud so closely that he has to keep renewing his belief that the vehicles are advancing, though far too slowly to outdistance the memory of his glimpse inside Connie's car. When Jill's brake lights brighten he's afraid to learn why until he sees that her headlamps have lit on the diner, which is shut and unilluminated from within. "So Ross couldn't have called from there," Mad says.

Just now it's more important to Jake that they're at the exit from the retail park. Shadows as low as the furniture parade through the diner while Jill's headlamps turn towards the gap. As the Mazda follows, Jill drives across the deserted road into the lane between hedges bristling their tarry spikes as though the beams have roused them. Jill sounds her horn, and she and Connie wave at the mirror above the windscreen. Mad echoes Jill, and she and Jake both wave, but he isn't sure the others see this before the fog extinguishes the rear lights of the Nova. With a sigh he prefers not to interpret, Mad steers left behind the diner.

He won't be able to breathe easily until he can be certain what he glimpsed behind Texts isn't pursuing them under cover of the fog. He peers nervously towards the buildings and the open space they're helping the fog to obscure. He has to clench his teeth until they ache so as not to urge Mad to drive faster. The diner is succeeded by an unfinished block with polythene for windows, which he tells himself are nothing like eyes so weighed down by cataracts they sag out of their sockets, and then there's even less of a building, mostly a roofless cage of metal. It lets more of the glare of the floodlights reach the car, but why is a portion of the light so close to the ground? Because it belongs to a vehicle that lurches between the incomplete buildings into the path of the Mazda. "Watch out," Jake deafens himself by screaming as he clutches at the wheel.

The car is almost in the hedge on the far side of the road before Mad regains control. "What the—" She remembers she's a lady and demands only "What are you trying to do to us, Jake?"

"Didn't you see? You must have seen. There was a car or something."

"Where?" To his dismay she tramps on the brake. "Show me where."

He wants to plead with her to drive away, but he twists in his bonds to stare through the rear window. One skeletal corner of the building under construction is visible, but there's as little sign of another vehicle as he has to admit he saw when he grabbed the wheel. "It must have been the fog," he says.

"Yes, well, whatever you think you see from now on, can you leave the driving to me? I'd expect Greg to try and take over, not you."

She eases the car back across the road and picks up almost no speed. The unfinished buildings crouch lower as if the earth is swallowing them. The murk settles over the last of them as the tunnel under the motorway yawns ahead, a cave daubed with giant drooling symbols and inhabited by wakeful fog. As Mad steers up the ramp to the motorway, which Jake was expecting to be blocked off, she says "Do you think it's because we're so tired we've all been getting at each other?"

"I wouldn't know."

In fact he believes tiredness is the least of the reasons, but can't be bothered thinking about it when she has accused him of resembling Greg. The car ventures onto the motorway, having hesitated at the top of the ramp, and she matches Jake's resentment. "Maybe you can speak up if you see a phone or Ross for that matter."

Jake is tempted to retort that Ross would hardly have wandered onto the motorway, but is that the case? He might have in search of the nearest phone. The lights of Fenny Meadows fall away below the car, and it appears they were diluting the fog, which closes down in front of the windscreen as though a skyful of unshed rain has settled on the blanked-out landscape. The rays from the headlights butt it with a feebleness not far short of exhaustion, but the car must be maintaining its progress, because a marker of some kind has loomed into view beside the road. Is the fog beyond it thinning? No, Jake is seeing another of the lights he saw in the retail park, and now he knows what they are. A fen is a marsh, and marshes sometimes emit will-o'-the-wisps. As a child he read about them and wished he could see one, and he has been granted his wish. He's about to point out the phenomenon to Mad when she frowns across him at the marker. "Is that for the next phone? How far does it say—"

The light hurtles out of the fog and splits into the beams of a pair of headlamps on the wrong side of the motorway—in the same lane as the Mazda. Above them the windscreen of a Jaguar wags its wipers in reproof. Beyond one cleared segment of the glass the driver, a man whose forehead is bagged in a leather cap pulled down low, is grimacing at a mobile phone. As though to demonstrate he's even stupider than this suggests, he takes his other hand off the wheel to gesture drunkenly. Having time to assimilate so much detail convinces Jake that Mad is able to avoid the collision; she's already spinning the wheel. Then the speed of the Jaguar does away with the distance between the cars, which turn into a single explosion of metal and glass. In that instant Mad seizes

Jake's hand, which he closes around hers. There's a moment in which he yearns for hers to be Sean's, and yet he's grateful for her closeness, because something that's delighted by the crash doesn't welcome their reconciliation at all. Indeed, it spews whatever's left of their intelligence into the dark.

# JILL

**She beeps her horn and Mad's car answers, which puts Jill in mind of** the start of a hunt. When she waves at the mirror Connie imitates her, except there's no reason to think of it like that—no reason to suppose Connie's making fun of her or indicating slyly that she regrets not being in the Mazda. The fog drags the Mazda away by its headlamp beams, a reddish tinge fades from the glaring nothingness between the hedges, and then the mirror shows Jill only the gap, which continues to shrink between the hedges as the Nova coasts forward. "Shall we get going now?" Connie suggests.

"We are."

"All right then if you aren't comfortable driving any faster. I just feel uneasy leaving Anyes shut in any longer than we absolutely need to. Woody too, of course."

Jill wonders about smiling at the dutiful afterthought but isn't sure that Connie wouldn't think she was presuming, a possibility Jill resents more than somewhat. "You can blame me if you have to," she offers instead.

"Thanks, only it's really my responsibility."

Jill isn't going to pretend to herself: she would rather have Jake as her passenger. Connie made it clear when she just about asked that she wished she needn't travel with Jill. The wet blackened spikes of the hedges close in behind the car. As they and the fog solidify into a single lightless mass, Jill says "So you'll take all the responsibility, you said."

"I'm not sure if I can quite do that, can I? Not unless you want me to drive."

"I certainly don't, thanks."

"Then you'll have to be responsible for that, won't you? Some people think I'm not too bad."

"I don't recall saying you were."

Connie turns her head as if to force Jill to acknowledge her expression. When Jill concentrates on the illuminated scrap of road the veil of fog is doling out, Connie says "At driving."

"I've got people like that too."

"I expect your little girl's one."

"She'd be on my side, don't you worry." Jill grips the wheel harder while she tries to regain control of her words. "She's one reason why I asked how much blame you're going to take. She's the best reason."

The moist hiss beneath the car fills another pause during which she refuses to look at whatever expression Connie's showing her. Eventually Connie says "None at all."

The curtailed road seems to quiver with Jill's disbelief until she recovers her grasp on the wheel. "You'll never get away with that."

"There's nothing to get away with. I didn't come along till a good while after you and Geoff split up. I hope you aren't telling your daughter I did."

Jill feels as if her brain is growing maggoty with disagreements that hem the car in even more oppressively than the fog. She doesn't understand how she could have let the misunderstanding develop, yet part of her wants to use it as an excuse to confront the other woman now that she has her trapped. It requires quite an effort for her to say only "I was asking if you're going to tell whoever needs to know you were behind us breaking out of the shop. I wouldn't mind keeping this job."

"I don't think we're too likely to do that, or Mad or Jake either."

Now Jill feels like a child cheated out of a promise and stupid enough to protest "But we broke out for Woody as much as anyone."

"Did we? He might think we were trying to get away from him."

"You won't say that, will you? Who's it going to help?"

"I'll be helping by phoning. That'll have to do till I've had some sleep."

Jill no longer understands what Connie means, if her remarks signify anything except less oxygen in the car. "Just let me drive, then."

"I don't remember starting the argument."

Nor does Jill—it's as though the memory has been swallowed by the dark—but she dislikes feeling accused. "Can't we try to get on with each other while we're stuck with this?"

"You think I'm not trying."

"I don't suppose you want to be in this situation any more than I do."

"Even less."

Jill has made all the effort she's making. They can't argue if they don't talk. She focuses on ignoring the inert lump of hostile silence into which Connie has subsided, because their progress can't distract her from Connie's presence. The black road crawls incessantly towards her under the fog the hedges appear to keep retarding, and only the bends of the lane oblige her to be even slightly vigilant. Even they emerge so gradually that she could dream they're taking time not to disturb her. She has no idea how many have sunk back into the fog or how far the Nova has advanced when Connie says "Are you doing it on purpose?"

"All I am is driving that I know of."

"That's what I mean. Are you deliberately going the slowest you possibly can?"

"No, I'm going the safest."

"There's such a thing as being too safe. No wonder—"

When she interrupts herself Jill is certain Connie intends her to know she's thinking of Jill's marriage that was. Jill sucks in a stale-tasting breath that's designed to suppress any answer, then hears herself demand "No wonder what?"

"It'll be a wonder if we aren't both asleep before we get anywhere at this rate. I feel as if we're hardly out of Fenny Meadows."

Jill resents sharing Connie's impression, but her own goes further. Her notion must be the fault of her lack of sleep—the notion that their arguments are contrived to be an extra hindrance. This strikes her as so idiotic that she snaps "You'd rather I went faster and ran us into the ditch."

"I can't see any ditch. I can't see any anything except what I've been seeing since it's beginning to look like forever."

"You want me not to be able to stop if we meet something coming."

"Who else is going to be along here at whatever time of night it is in this? They'd hardly be driving to Fenny Meadows, and there's nowhere else to drive."

Jill almost cites the motorway, except of course it's shut and in any case she has never seen anyone use this route to it. She still won't be told how to drive, especially by Connie. She's overwhelmed by an impulse to twist the wheel and ram the Nova through the hedge to speed across the field. "Fast enough for you?" she can already hear herself enquiring. Only reluctance to damage the car holds her back, and she isn't certain that it will if Connie antagonises her any more. She's daring her to add to her uninvited comments when Connie slaps herself on the forehead as if a mosquito has bitten it. She can hurt herself all she likes as far as Jill's concerned, but apparently the blow aimed to wake her brain up, because she says "We'll have to go back."

Jill lets the car carry them a good few yards before she bothers asking "Why's that?"

"Not now. When I've phoned about the shop and my car. I'll need to be with it when they come to fix the engine."

Jill refrains from treading hard on the accelerator to outdistance the proposal. "It can wait till you get home, surely."

"And how do you expect me to get back from there?"

Jill is expecting nothing to do with it, and if it were possible she would care even less, but says "Can't you get whoever you call to pick you up at home? Use your charm or be helpless. I'm sure you're good at one of those."

Connie turns her face towards her yet again, and Jill grows clammy with refusing to look at the wad of flesh Connie is poking at her. The wheel seems to prickle as she grips it so as not to lash out. She's hoping for both their sakes that she can dislodge Connie's gaze by saying "Anyway, I thought you'd want to go home first so you can catch up on your sleep."

After a pause Connie faces the suffocated glow they're following. "Maybe I won't be able to sleep for thinking. That's how I get sometimes."

"It's only a car, Connie. It won't be going anywhere."

"I suppose you think I'm acting as if it's my child."

"Well, since you ask—"

"I didn't, and I really will need to get back to it."

"Not in my car, I'm sorry. Not now we've come all this way."

"All what way? I keep feeling we've gone nowhere whatsoever."

As Jill begins to steer around the latest protracted bend, she blames Connie for giving her the senseless notion that all the curves of the lane are about to add up to a circle that will return the car to Fenny Meadows. She's convincing herself that some of them will cancel out the others when Connie murmurs "Did you say you wanted to hang onto your job?"

"I'd like to. I haven't got just myself to feed."

"Then maybe you'd better think of doing what I asked. I haven't stopped being a manager yet."

The yearning to drive off the road shivers like electricity through

Jill. She's aware of nothing but her foot poised on the accelerator and her hands preparing to swing the wheel. She doesn't immediately register how Connie's tone changes, or her words. "Who's that? Is it Ross?"

Is she trying to divert Jill from her plan? Fog surges to cover where Connie was peering, but Jill doesn't believe there was anything to see except the bony black-clawed tangles of the hedge. Even when Connie leans towards the windscreen, this looks like an attempt to make Jill forget what was threatened, too late. Then the stretch of hedge resurfaces, twig after dripping twig, and Jill sees that a dim figure is indeed crouched in a hollow of it. "That isn't Ross," says Connie.

The edge of a headlamp beam finds the lowered head, which seems wet enough to have been rescued from drowning, and inflates it twice its size with shadow. The figure squirms as if to shake off the light and then lurches to its feet, blinking violently and yawning. If Jill hadn't recognised who it is by now she would know the yawn for Gavin's. He tears his right sleeve free of the hedge and stumbles in front of the car.

Jill wrenches at the handbrake while tramping on the brake pedal just in time not to overbalance him or worse. As he limps stiffly around the Nova she lowers her window. "Gavin, you nearly—"

"What time is it?" He leans one hand on the roof and knuckles his eyes redder still. "Is it over?"

"What?"

"Have you finished working at the shop?"

That sounds like a revival of Connie's threat, but she keeps it quiet. "Don't stand there, Gavin," she says instead. "Get in."

He fumbles open the rear door and takes some care over bending himself to fit the seat. Jill shuts her window well in advance of his slamming his door. "Have you been out here ever since you phoned?" She means this to express sympathy, but it sounds inanely obvious.

"Feels like longer. Were you looking for me?"

"Mostly for a phone. I don't suppose your mobile could have come alive again."

He fishes it out and holds it towards the faint glow through the windscreen. When he thumbs a key, it fails to light up. Indeed, for a moment it appears to turn as grey as their breaths are being rendered by the fog that followed him into the car. "Didn't think so," he yawns. "Wasn't the box any use?"

"Which box?" Connie's impatient to learn.

"I found one, don't ask me when. If I'd phoned I'd have had no change for the bus, and anyway there wasn't much reason to."

Jill's instincts deny this, but before she can grasp why, Connie demands "Whereabouts was it?"

"Somewhere along here. Didn't you pass it? I thought I've been heading for the main road."

Jill thinks hostility is making Connie look so dull she would call it brainless. "Don't say you drove us past a phone," Connie says.

"I won't. You'd more chance of noticing with less to do. There's bound to be phones on the main road when we get there. I've told you I won't go back."

That's meant to challenge Connie to repeat her threat in front of Gavin. Jill's frustrated when he interrupts the confrontation by asking "Why do you need a phone?"

"Woody's got himself stuck in his office," says Connie, "and Anyes has in the lift."

"You're making it sound like their fault," Jill objects.

"Well, it isn't. I'd say it's anyone's that lets them stay stuck any longer than they have to be, wouldn't you, Gavin?"

Jill would like to think his yawn indicates he's bored with the question. "We're phoning from the main road," she says, releasing the handbrake.

He has a yawn for her too. She doesn't know how many of those she can stand. She's tempted to increase her speed to outrun some of them, but the sluggishly retreating fog entangled in the hedges looks more ominous than ever. She searches her murky brain for some way to enliven him instead, and succeeds in dredging up the memory she was trying to retrieve before. "What were you going to tell me if we hadn't lost you, Gavin?"

"It doesn't seem like much now. Woody didn't think it was."

"But you did. You thought it was so important you rang us back. You'd seen something, you said."

"Just on some videos I took home. People fighting instead of what was meant to be on them."

"I'm with Woody," Connie says.

Rather than inform Connie she wishes she were, Jill asks Gavin "Why did you want us to know?"

"It seemed like there had to be something wrong. Two people that lived, I don't know, forty miles apart brought them back."

"I'll bet they were the same sort of tape, though," Connie says. "Do I win?"

"They were both concerts. So?"

"You check and see if they weren't released by the same company. It'll have been a glitch when they were copying the tapes."

Jill doesn't know whether she remains unpersuaded because she prefers not to agree with Connie. Gavin's faceless silhouette in the mirror has fallen silent. She's willing him to take issue with Connie when he sits forward. "This looks like it could be it."

The road is doubling back on the curve she has just negotiated. As the lit patch of fog extends itself more dimly through a gap in the left-hand hedge, Gavin says "The phone was down somewhere like that."

Connie lifts a hand towards Jill. "I see it. There it is."

Jill doesn't know if Connie is imperiously gesturing her to stop or even considering a grab at the handbrake. When she halts the car just ahead of the gap she enjoys imagining that the pedal underfoot is part of Connie. She narrows her eyes at the track leading away from the road. It's either bare churned earth or tarmac encrusted with mud, and the object in the fog to which it meanders could be a wide tree-trunk chopped off about seven feet from the ground.

"I don't think so," she decides aloud. "Would you drive along any-where like that in this?"

"If it got help to some people who need it," Connie retorts, "I certainly would."

Jill doubts it, and steers the car into the gap to clarify her objection. The blurred object by the track grows no clearer; indeed, the fog ap-pears to be gathering around it, which may be why its outline seems less regular than a phone box ought to be. Jill lifts the headlamp beams to it, but this only blinds her with fog. She squeezes her eyes shut to find she's so tired that she begins to see images that Gavin's description must have put into her head, of people fighting sav-agely and sinking on if not into the earth. She gropes to dip the head-lights and opens her eyes once they feel ready for use. Now the shape ahead reminds her of a totem pole, though of course she isn't seeing the rudiments of faces starting to materialise, one piled on top of the other. "I'm sorry," she says, "I'm not happy going any further."

"Maybe Anyes isn't too happy right now either," Connie says.

"We don't know that, do we? Mad and Jake may have sent for help."

"And they may not have. All right, let's vote whether we drive to it or I've got to end up muddy. Gavin?"

"You want us to be democratic now, do you? It's not long since you were acting as if you were in charge." As Gavin's hand begins to waver in the mirror, Jill continues "No point in voting. We aren't driving, I am. It's my car. If you don't like it you can get out and walk, but don't expect me to hang around."

She's confused by the delight that her speech seems to intensify, because the glee doesn't feel like hers; it feels as if it's closing in. It confuses her so badly that she imagines she sees the tree-trunk or the object that resembles one twitching with eagerness. "It isn't even a phone box," she tells Connie. "Go and look for yourself if you can't see that."

"Will she wait while I do, Gavin? Could you make her, do you think?"

He disagrees with one or both of those, mostly with a yawn. They can give Jill all the arguments they like, but it's her car. She jerks it into reverse and swings it out of the gap, scraping the front offside wing on the hedge. As the headlamp beams veer away from the field, she seems to glimpse the object in the fog splitting like an amoeba and the topmost segment hopping or collapsing onto the earth. How tired must she be? Not too tired to drive, which she does in the midst of a frustrated silence like a lack of breath. Then Gavin yawns again, perhaps at the spectacle of yet more fog oozing backwards over the same wet black patch of road and dragging itself through the hedges. "Gavin," Connie almost shouts, "for the love of I won't say it will you stop that wretched yawning all the time."

For once Jill agrees with her, but has to grin when Connie yawns furiously. "You're doing it as well," Gavin points out.

Amusement hasn't finished tugging at Jill's lips when a yawn forces itself between them. "It's you," Connie retaliates. "We weren't till you came. Keep it to yourself, can you? We've enough problems without not being able to stop doing something."

"Tell me how I can help it, then."

Her answer is another enraged yawn, not the only reaction Jill thinks Connie is unable to control. Obviously when she complained of problems she meant Jill, but Gavin was hardly in the car before Connie turned on him. It seems not to matter whom she attacks as long as it's someone. A yawn that feels like a dismissal of the notion overcomes Jill, carrying with it the wish that she had failed to brake in time when he stumbled in front of the car. Suppose she asks him to walk ahead as people used to precede vehicles in fog? Still better, why doesn't she suggest that Connie keep him company? She wouldn't mean to run them over, but she's so exhausted that nobody could blame her if she lost control, if she forgot which pedal she had to push down hard—

It isn't just the childishness of the plan that snatches all her breath. It's the exultation that her thoughts seem to bring to the surface, a joy too vast and savage, surely, to be hers. "Can we all stop arguing till we get out of this?" she pleads. "I mean really try and stop."

"We might if you did," Connie says.

At least Jill made an effort to suppress her irrationality, but Connie sounds like a child in a schoolyard. Jill senses delight welling up again, drawn by her own contempt. They've all reverted to thinking and behaving like fractious children, her included—and then she sees more in the situation. She has observed it all too often, children fighting when another child relishes slyly turning them against each other. She opens her mouth to pass on the insight, but she already knows how Connie reacts to being included among the childish. She's about to let her thoughts subside into her dull mind when she senses they're being engulfed by more than her fatigue. The impression so resembles lurching awake from a dream that she gasps "I know why we mustn't fall out any more."

Gavin doesn't quite yawn, but barely pronounces "Why?"

"Think about it." Jill is doing so aloud, which seems to help. "We've all been arguing all night, haven't we? And before that too for I don't know how long at the shop. Something wants us at each other's throats. Why, you even saw people fighting on your tapes."

At once she's afraid that her last remark is one comment too many. At least Gavin isn't yawning. She glances away from the reflection of his silhouette she hopes is thoughtful. She's watching the road, though the dim ill-defined enclosure of fog has begun to make her feel helpless as an insect trapped under a glass, when Connie says "Well, I'll vote that's the silliest thing I've ever heard."

Words won't suffice as a response to that; not words alone, at any rate. Perhaps she'll believe they are little better than puppets if Jill gives her a demonstration. "This is even sillier," Jill says and shuts her eyes before pressing the accelerator.

At first nobody notices. She's beginning to think she can judge the road without looking when Connie says "Careful, you'll have us in the hedge."

"Better do something about it, then."

"I just did. Careful," Connie repeats with an edge.

"I need more than that. Which way do I steer?"

"Left, of course. You can see—" As Jill eases the wheel leftwards, Connie says "I'm not falling for that. You haven't got both eyes shut."

Jill shows Connie her face and releases a smile that feels dry as a crack in dead earth. "All right, you've made your point, whatever it was," Connie says, and when Jill doesn't relent "You're the driver. You drive."

Jill's seat quivers as Gavin leans between it and Connie's. "Right now. Right," he urges, no longer sounding inclined to yawn.

"I was about to tell her, Gavin. There was time," Connie says and adds "Right."

"It's going to need both of you with a driver like me."

"We weren't saying anything about your driving," Gavin protests.

"You will," she assures them and faces forward as she presses the pedal harder. In a moment she feels Connie clutching at the wheel. "All right, you steer," Jill says, letting go. "But I want Gavin to tell you which way. If he doesn't I'll drive faster."

She has to do so before they're convinced she's serious. "Left," Gavin directs in a choked voice, and she feels the car slew that way. She's glad he and Connie are too preoccupied with the situation to ask her what she's doing, because she can't explain it even to herself; it just feels right, perhaps by accident. She has the notion that she's beating some vast idiocy at its own game. She thinks she senses it pacing the car behind the hedges or under the road or both. That makes her desperate to speed out of its reach, and she doesn't know if she's yielding to the impulse when Connie cries "Jill, slow down. Think of your little girl."

"You said I was too slow before. Can't you make your mind up, or haven't you got one?" Connie is the last person she needs to remind her of Bryony; indeed, Jill resents it so much that she can't decide if she ought to chance driving faster. Suppose she will otherwise never see her daughter again? She imagines Bryony in the Christmas play with only Geoff to support her, unless he takes Connie, but of course Jill has Connie at her mercy in the car. Whichever of these thoughts is compelling her to accelerate, she's amused to hear Gavin cry "Right" and Connie respond in the same agitated tone "I know." She's close to feeling that she's dreaming the journey, that the pictures within her eyelids are more real: the crowds of greyish shapes struggling to destroy one another or tear themselves separate from one another, if not from the morass into which they're sinking, unless they're emerging from it. Her fascination with all this is one reason why she's in no hurry to respond to Connie's entreaty. "We're there."

"Where's that?" Jill hears herself ask sleepily.

"The phone. You're passing it. You've passed it. The phone box."

Jill slits her sticky eyelids and is confronted by a multitude of eyes glinting at her out of the dark. They could belong to hundreds of swollen spiders or a single immense one, but then she recognises them as beads of moisture on the tips of the hedges. She can't see a phone box, not until the brake lights paint its lower section crimson in the mirror and splash the interior dull red. She leaves the engine running to power the lights while she says "I'll phone about the shop. What do you want to do about your car that doesn't involve me driving back?"

Connie seems almost too enervated to say "Just get us home."

The call may take too long for Jill to risk leaving the lights on with the engine off. She's certainly not about to trust Connie or even Gavin with the key in the ignition. She snatches the key and gropes her way out of the car to pace alongside, one hand on the slimy roof. Two diagonal paces away from the rear bring her close enough to the phone box that she senses it looming over her. She fumbles at the door, which feels moist enough for rot, and locates the drooling metal handle. As she lets herself in, the box lights up with a glow that she could think has floated upwards rather than appeared beneath the cramped ceiling. It stays lit as the door shuts with a creak that seems to find an echo in the hedge behind the box.

There's no directory on the rusty metal shelf, but she doesn't need one. Someone has sprayed incomprehensible symbols over the mirror and the framed notices, rendering all the words unreadable and trapping her exhausted face in a thick web. The tarry paint has caught the phone as well. As she lifts the chill receiver, the light dims as though it's shrinking from a waft of fog. She taps one of the most basic three-digit numbers in the world as soon as she's greeted by the dialling tone, muffled though it is. When it's silenced by a click, she calls "Hello? Operator? Hello?"

"Operator."

It's hardly surprising if so late at night the female voice sounds somewhat mechanical. "I'm not sure which service I need," Jill admits.

"Which?"

"It's an emergency. Someone's been trapped in a lift for hours, and there's no power in the building at all. Can you connect me with whoever will deal with it?"

"Connecting." Before it reaches the last syllable the voice cuts itself off, and in a very few seconds one so similar Jill could mistake it for the first if she let herself says "Power emergency service."

"All our electricity has gone off. That's you, yes?"

"Electricity. Yes."

"It means someone's stuck in a lift. Can you fix that too?"

"Yes."

"I don't know if you'll know the area. It's quite new. Fenny Meadows."

"Yes."

Jill hasn't heard so much agreement for a while; by now the voice sounds positively enthusiastic. "It's a shop there," Jill says. "Texts, the bookshop."

"Yes."

"I ought to tell you it's very foggy there. It is here too, quite a way away."

"Yes."

The enthusiasm seems misplaced now, though Jill assumes it's intended to be reassuring. "I can leave it with you then, can I?" she suggests.

"Yes."

Perhaps she has asked one question too many; the voice has dipped half an octave, which makes her think it's impatient. "Thank you," she says, and hangs up the scrawled receiver on its similarly defaced hook. At once she feels foolish for not giving her name in case management would have learned she made the call, and shouldn't she have ascertained whether Mad or Jake has already been in touch? The apparently sourceless light flickers overhead as if it's about to fail, and she doesn't want to be shut in the box in the dark. She shoves the door so wide it catches the twigs outside; that must be why the hedge gives a creak extensive enough to suggest that something is raising itself behind quite a length of it. She runs to the Nova and lowers herself into the driver's seat just as the box and the livid patch of hedge around it are engulfed by blackness like a rush of mud. "That's dealt with," she says, and succeeds in locating the ignition to revive the engine and the lights. "Everyone ready to move?"

"I don't think I came this way," Gavin says.

"Just let her drive," Connie blurts. "We'll have to get somewhere."

"All right, forget I said it. Sorry, Jill."

Jill can't help smiling like a fool when she realises they're afraid of how she may behave if they start another argument. That's close enough to agreement for her, and when the Nova coasts forward she's sure she has done something right; they're leaving the hungry frustration behind. Although she has no idea what that means, it's enough that the view of the fog doling out the road and the hedges no longer seems nearly as oppressive. She hasn't taken many foggy breaths when Connie hopes aloud "Is that the main road?"

There's certainly light ahead. In not too many seconds it's brighter than the glow Jill's headlamps are lending to the fog. It's bright enough for floodlights; indeed, that's what Jill thinks the source may be. Then the fog thins while retreating, and she sees a tall streetlamp beyond a gap between two pairs of bulky houses. "This isn't where I came along from," says Gavin.

"It doesn't matter, does it?" Connie says. "We'll be out in a minute."

Once Jill has crossed the dual carriageway so as to head for Manchester she realises Connie was referring to the car. "Stop," Connie orders. "I'll take this cab."

Jill has scarcely braked when Connie flings herself out of the Nova and sprints ahead, waving and shouting if not screaming at the taxi. As it halts and backs up she calls "Gavin, do you want to share?"

"I might if you don't mind, Jill."

"Why should I mind? I want to get home like everyone else."

"I'll see you, then." He yawns and stretches in the process of opening the rear door, then lingers to say "I'll see you, won't I?"

"We don't know at the moment, do we? I expect we'll find out soon."

"I don't think I know what soon feels like any more." He's demonstrating this by the speed at which he leaves the car when Connie shouts "Are you with me or not, Gavin?"

"Thanks for getting us out," he murmurs to Jill, and hurries to the taxi as fast as his lingering stiffness allows.

The taxi switches off its roof light and races away. Jill follows more slowly, and in a short time she's alone with the parade of twinned houses on either side, mostly dark except for the towering streetlamps. The blocks of light are softened, but it's only fog. She can't recall when that became the case, let alone what she means by it. Perhaps she will once she has slept. A few minutes' drive shows her that she joined the main road a couple of miles past the route she took to Fenny Meadows some unimaginable period ago. At least there's another way to the bookshop, which ought to bring more custom if someone erects a sign for the retail park.

Before long she reaches the motorway to Bury and leaves behind the last of the fog. There's nobody about to object to her driving as though she's in a built-up area. Eventually she is, where the clocks among the shops inform her that it isn't much later than four in the morning, though she can hardly believe she hasn't missed Christmas. A few windows embroidered with fairy lights or occupied by trees laden with coloured bulbs only make her feel the season has passed her by. Of course she will be spending it with Bryony, but she's so tired that the thought of not doing so starts her rubbing her eyes, both to stay awake a little longer and so as not to weep.

A milk float prowls moaning down the next side street as she turns along her road. There's plenty of space outside her house for the Nova, but nevertheless she scrapes a tyre against the kerb while reversing. The dandelions she prevented Geoff from denying Bryony sprawl over the path; they're bedraggled by dew and flattened by the harsh light of a streetlamp. Jill unlocks the front door none too expertly and pushes it past whatever obstruction it always encounters. She finds the switch for the hall light, then types the alarm code, a date that feels meaningless just now. She plods into the kitchen to fill a glass with water and raise a feeble toast to her reflection in the window. Having run another glassful, she's sipping it when she's confronted by muddy footprints all along the hall.

They're hers, of course. She forgot to use the doormat. She shuffles her shoes clean on it, but the carpet will have to wait until she's awake. Instead she trudges to the phone and dials Geoff's number. Once he has finished saying he's on tape and the rest of it, she murmurs "Only me, Bryony. Just wanted you to know I'm home. I'm off to bed now. I hope it'll be you that wakes me up."

She replaces the receiver and carries the glass past the exhibition of pony drawings. Perhaps sometime she'll be able to afford riding lessons for Bryony, she thinks dreamily, though how likely is that if Jill's out of a job? All that matters is that they'll be together and manage somehow. Jill brushes her teeth in front of the foggy mirror, having performed the rest of the minimum required by the bathroom. She gives the faint muddy tracks on the stairs a reproachful blink as she heads for her room, where she wriggles gradually into bed before switching off the final light. As she closes her eyes she holds Bryony in her mind in case that brings a dream of her. Perhaps Jill won't hear her coming upstairs. Perhaps Jill won't know she has company until she wakens to see a small face close to hers.

# GREG

**"Keep it up, Greg. You'll go down in the history of the store. I only** wish I could be with you. If there's anything else I can do, just say the word."

Greg isn't going to ask for a break. If Woody doesn't think they can afford the time, how can he disagree with that? Far too many of the staff have succumbed to weakness without his succumbing too. He stoops to retrieve book after book and hold them close to his face while he deciphers each author's name and each title. Another dozen or so and he'll be able to move to the opposite shelves at the end by the window. He's crouching in the dimness to locate Khan when Woody says "So where did I go wrong, Greg? Advise me on that if you can."

Greg would have to leave his task to do that, and Woody mightn't want to hear that he could have chosen better personnel. As Greg finds the book a place among its tribe, Woody says "Okay, let me tell you. I guess you'd be too modest to admit it, but I ought to have hired more guys like you. Pity I couldn't just clone you and have a storeful of Gregs."

Greg lifts the next book—King, which is a step up from the previous author—and permits himself a humble smirk for as long as it takes him to rise halfway. "Hey, award yourself a smile or two," Woody urges so close to the phone that his huge voice grows blurred. "I wouldn't mind seeing a few."

Greg sends one in his general direction before concentrating on the mass of royalty that occupies three shelves. He hasn't identified where the thousand or more pages in his hand should go when Woody booms "Another, maybe? It's getting kind of lonely up here."

His words and the closeness of his voice have started to make Greg uncomfortable. He's unable to separate them from the waves of heat and chill that flood him each time he exerts himself. Whenever he bends or straightens up, the ache in his bruised shoulders fastens on the back of his head where it struck the floor. Perhaps Woody didn't see that Greg was knocked down by, of all people, Jake. Greg hopes not. He's certainly not about to tell Woody, let alone his own father, who he's sure would finally conclude Greg isn't worthy to be called his son. It's enough for Greg to know he remained, having played the man against the mob. He forces a smile and directs it at the ceiling before he reverts to searching for the gap he should make for the book. "Don't do it just for me," Woody says. "I'm sure you can use it as well."

Greg does his best to smile at finding more Kings at his feet. Of course he's in favour of the monarch, all the more so if it were a man, but the repetition of the word seems to drain it of meaning. Perhaps that's the fault of the dimness that is stinging his strained eyes. As he turns books to face outwards so as to clear space for additional copies, Woody says "You didn't answer my question back there. You're making me feel kind of useless."

With a book in each hand Greg glances at the dark where he can almost visualise Woody hovering, and stretches his arms wide. He means to mime incomprehension, but Woody says "Up to me to figure out how I can help, huh? Let's try this."

When he begins singing Greg can't react until he has planted both volumes on the shelf. By then Woody has repeated "Gosh-wow, gee and whee, keen-o-peachy" several times, though not always the melody. Greg smiles with all the energy he can summon and waves his hands on either side of his head to chase away Woody's behaviour. "Say, since it's just us listening I guess I can say you look like a minstrel in this light," Woody says. "Join in if you like."

Greg shakes his head as he ducks for books, and feels as if the clammy insubstantial burden of Woody's voice is pressing him down. Woody has stopped singing, but for how long? As Greg holds his breath for fear he'll recommence, Woody says "No? Don't let me distract you from that fine job. Holler if there's anything you need, that's all I'm asking."

What Greg needs is not to be alone in shelving. He jerks his hands at the shelves around him. "Say what?" Woody enquires. "Speak to me."

Greg stands up with a pair of Kings and mouths "Angus" at the ceiling. "Still not getting it," Woody complains.

Greg marches to the counter, where he drops the books beside the nearest phone and snatches the receiver. "Does Ray still need Angus? Couldn't Angus see if he can come through the other door?"

"Try the one they're at again first if you like."

This feels like being put in charge downstairs. Greg doesn't know how long it has been since either of his colleagues was heard from. Ray must have told Angus to keep quiet or sent him packing. Greg sets down the receiver and strides after his shadow, which the dimness stretches into anonymity. He's annoyed by the need to keep glancing over his shoulder, but the exit is open since the deserters smashed their way out, though he did his best to block the gap with a pair of double-parked empty trolleys. He can't help feeling that some mischief has been or is going on around him; perhaps that's because he's unable to discern the order of the books he's passing or even to remember whose responsibility they used to be. He's some yards short of the exit to the staffroom when he shouts "Ray, will you let us know what stage you've reached?"

Apart from the last of his footsteps there's silence. He understands Ray has to concentrate, but that surely needn't entail rudeness. Can Ray have fallen asleep on the job, and Angus too? Greg pounds on the door with the side of his fist in case anyone requires wakening. "Could someone answer, please?" he shouts and leans his ear against the door.

In a moment he hears a repeated sound but can't identify it. However much it resembles the dripping of water, it must have to do with the fuses. "Angus," he bellows. "We want to know if you're at a loose end."

Because of his position most if not all of his voice seems to stay outside the door. Nevertheless he hears movement, and is straining to interpret it when Woody demands "What's going on?"

Greg marches to the nearest phone and gropes for the receiver. He's distracted by an impression that the children's books are as jumbled as Madeleine kept claiming they were. It's too dark to be certain, and if they're disarrayed he more than suspects she's to blame. As he squints to distinguish which button to press, Woody connects them. "Here I am, Greg. You're not on your own."

"I'm assuming they both have to be there, but I haven't had an answer yet."

Woody's voice expands to fill the shop. "Ray or Angus, Greg's outside by himself. He needs to know you're there."

Greg wouldn't have phrased it quite like that, and isn't wholly happy with the response it brings. The movements beyond the door sound as if somebody is coming to life in mud; the shuffling seems not just aimless but unpleasantly soft. The best, if hardly acceptable, explanation Greg can find is that Angus is rousing himself from whatever he found to lie on. "Well, don't stay there," Woody exhorts. "Go to the door."

Greg is about to echo this when he realises it was addressed to him. While he resents being classed with Angus, he would be wrong to show it. As he strides to the exit, Woody says "Greg's there now, Angus. See if the two of you can shift that goddamned door."

Greg applies his badge to the plaque as he thumps the door with one shoulder, sending an ache across and up his neck, but he might as well not be a member of staff. He runs at the door and bruises the heels of his hands on it with no other result. He's labouring entirely on his own. At first he hears Angus rubbing part of himself over the far side of the door—both his hands, perhaps, since the surface sounds large enough for his face. Is he too stupefied to locate the metal bar? Now he seems to be shuffling about as though he's prancing with idle delight, so loudly it suggests Ray has joined in. Greg hurries to the phone to report "I'm making no headway, and I've no idea what anybody else is up to."

"You can hear me, right, Angus? Anything more you can do to help Greg?" After not much of a pause, Woody's voice shrinks into Greg's ear. "Anything?"

"Nothing at all."

"Okay, Angus, why don't you see if you can find your way down to the door by the elevator. You can check how Agnes is."

The shuffling recommences, though now it sounds like meat being dragged across the floor. Greg hasn't managed to sort out the noise when Woody addresses him without bothering to keep the phone between them. "Plenty of shelving to finish while you wait, Greg. Give him a yell when you're down, Angus."

Greg has to restrain himself from stamping back to retrieve the books from the counter. He isn't one of the women or Jake. As he makes his measured but speedy way across the sales floor he discovers how tired he is: sufficiently to glimpse squat shapes withdrawing into the aisles or collapsing into themselves like grey jelly.

Surely he didn't take his attention off the entrance long enough for anyone to have sneaked in, and besides, no intruder could look like that. He shelves the books and the rest of the regal heap so that he can return to the end of the aisle by the window.

The illumination lacks the strength he thought he remembered, but that's no excuse for him to slow down; there are no excuses, as his father often used to say and still does. Greg crouches and straightens his back and does his utmost to have found the right place for each book as soon as he's at attention. Here's a Lamb, but it's not for him to sacrifice: only God should do that, because it was part of God turned into flesh. Here's one by Law and three by Lawless, which just about sums up the state of the world. Here's Lone, which is what Greg is at the moment, with no reason to complain— his father has to deal with greater difficulties every day he's at the barracks. Greg would be there too or patrolling somewhere in the world if his mother didn't upset herself at such length whenever she thinks of his coming to harm. He thought his father might appreciate his helping people improve themselves by reading, but the shop contains few books Greg would be happy to recommend. He'll have to take a stand if Texts intends to promote the likes of Brodie Oates, men so ashamed of being their sex that they want to be women. His father and the other real men are forced to have them in the forces now. Greg knows what kind of force they deserve, but is his expression as grim as his thoughts? When he trains a smile on the ceiling, that earns him no response from Woody. He busies himself with more volumes—Mann, which looks like a man determined to prove he's one; Marks, not Marx, Greg is glad to see; May, which you might assume has sunk out of the language. He thinks of a joke he would like to tell ("These days May ought to be filed under Can") just to show he has a sense of humour. He gazes upwards, but Woody doesn't ask what's on his mind. Greg could share it with Angus if he ever bothers to arrive at the door by the lift; how long does Angus mean to let it take him? The dark would be no excuse for a soldier, and it shouldn't be for anyone. It isn't

Angus who makes Greg replace May on the stack at his feet, however. He's sure he glimpsed movement outside, almost concealed by the fog.

He flattens his hands against the window and peers through his breath on the icy glass. Before the fog obscures it he sees a blurred light prowling the car park. He has been so intent on shelving that he forgot to look out for the emergency services; perhaps he doubted any of the renegades would call them. He swings around to raise his face and shout "Here at last."

Woody doesn't respond. He must have fallen asleep. As the manager he deserves more rest than anybody else, and Greg feels left in charge. Ray and Angus must have heard him, and seem to be throwing themselves about with glee, leaping up and landing with soft thuds and bumping against the doors, Angus having reached the other one at last. Greg can do without their antics, not least because it has distracted him from events outside the window. When he stares through it he realises the lights are lost in the fog.

He sprints to the entrance so fast he jars pain from his shoulders into his head. He shoves the trolleys aside and is on the pavement when he falters. What sounds like huge breaths in the glaring murk—like the moist snuffling of some gigantic beast in search of prey? As it trails off into an expectant silence he understands that it can only have been the noise of a vehicle that has halted out of sight. "Over here," he shouts. "We called you here."

Apart from the frolics of Ray and Angus, which have started to annoy him even more than they bewilder him, there's silence. He can only assume that the driver of the vehicle is contacting a control room, inaudibly to Greg, but that may not help. He cups his hands around his mouth to yell "Can't you hear me? We're here. The bookshop."

The engine gives a snuffle that he takes at first for a response. When it subsides he's afraid that the driver can indeed not hear him. "Woody, I'm just going to get them," he shouts, pointing with his hands into the fog. "They don't seem to know where to find us."

Woody stays asleep. Greg considers using the phone but doesn't want to waken him abruptly. Besides, he might be allowing the driver time to move off. He can't help resenting how Angus and, yes, Ray have left him to do so much, but it shows that he's equal to any number of tasks. He blocks the entrance with the trolleys and hurries away from the shop, calling at the top of his voice "Hold on. I'm coming to you."

He hears an exhalation that must be air brakes, however large and eager it sounds. "That's the drill, wait there for me," he bellows, sprinting across the tarmac. The fog trails over it like a mass of sodden rotting cloth, from which the nearest trees unpick themselves, two saplings and the stump left by Madeleine's car. He dodges around the strip of lush grass in which the trees are rooted. The noise of brakes was beyond them—beyond the saplings that the fog momentarily unveils a couple of hundred yards behind them too, apparently, or could the vehicle have crept away unheard? "Where are you?" Greg demands so vehemently his throat feels raw with fog. "We're the ones who called you. You've found us."

This appears to have some effect, thank the Lord—Greg was beginning to wonder how much of an invitation the fellow expects. The noise like an excited breath is repeated not too far ahead. It has acquired a slobbering quality that Greg could live without, and sounds as though it's emerging from somewhere lower than makes sense, which must be a trick of the increasingly dim fog. It sinks into silence, but not before he locates it in the middle of the car park. He makes for it so fast he nearly loses his footing on the muddy tarmac. There are the lights of a vehicle about a hundred yards ahead, so blurred they seem less to penetrate the murk than to be part of it. Are they retreating? Half a dozen strides fail to clarify his view of them, and he can't distinguish the vehicle at all. He's opening his mouth to call out, though it fills instantly with fog, when the lights swerve and rush at him.

Has he come to the same end as Lorraine? He doesn't deserve it;

even Lorraine didn't. Then the lights fly apart and merge with the fog on either side of him. Too late he realises he was in no danger. He started to run from the lights instead of facing them down, and now he has no idea which direction he came from.

At least it's clear that he was right to be suspicious. None of the deserters has bothered to put in a call, or help would have arrived by now. So much for their pretence of solidarity with their colleague in the lift, never mind setting Woody free. Greg has no doubt they would be delighted to know they've caused him to lose his way in the fog. Of course that's an exaggeration; the retail park is too small for anyone to stay lost for any significant length of time. What would his father do? Remain on the spot, he thinks, and turn slowly until a landmark shows itself. He's beginning the manoeuvre when he hears a voice as blurred as the fog.

"Goshwow, gee and whee, keen-o-peachy . . ." It has left many of its consonants behind, and almost anything that could be described as a tune. He isn't even certain who it is until he realises Woody is singing, if it can be called that, in his sleep. Greg could never have dreamed how welcome this would be; it tells him that the shop is about a hundred degrees to his left. In a moment the mumbled song trails off, but he doesn't need it any more. He starts in its direction, only to jerk to a halt. What has crept up to surround him?

Until he takes a guarded pace he's able to believe he's seeing merely fog and darkness. As he shifts his weight, however, the tarmac under the hem of the marquee of fog blackens and grows visibly wetter. When he retreats he hears a muffled sucking sound behind him. He swivels in time to see moisture welling up to meet the edge of the fog, and then he has to fling his arms wide to maintain his balance as he feels the tarmac underfoot dip towards the jagged watery perimeter. He stands his ground, but that's no solution. All around him, lazily but relentlessly, the tarmac has begun to sink.

He twists around wildly, perhaps enough to disturb the fog,

which withdraws far enough to let him glimpse a tree to his right. He can see nothing else as solid. The tarmac beneath his feet is inclining itself like the deck of a ship towards a surge of black moisture as long and as uneven as the edge of the fog, which may be hiding more of it. Water oozes up outside the concrete rim that boxes in the strip of grass where the tree and its companions are planted. He flings out a hand as if he's clutching for a lifeline and makes a dash that fills his mouth with the stale taste of fog. He staggers coughing onto the grass and closes both hands around the trunk.

It's no thicker than a small child's arm. Beneath the ragged grass scattered with rotting leaves the ground is bony, obviously with roots. Are there insects or spiders in the branches? He hasn't finished spluttering out fog when his skin starts to crawl. It feels as if something akin to electricity is swarming over him. There's no discernible reason, yet he seems to hear a faint but piercing whine or buzz that reminds him of mosquitoes. As soon as he has caught his breath he stumbles to the middle tree and leans against the discouragingly slender trunk.

He won't loiter any longer than is necessary. The last few minutes have exhausted him so much that he has no idea what happened. His confusion is letting unwelcome thoughts into his head; the image of being supported by a tree between two others threatens to become unforgivably blasphemous. He makes himself stand unaided, as a man should. He's turning his head minutely in search of the bookshop, and willing Woody to help by uttering any kind of sound, when an object drops on his left wrist.

The object is black and glistening and unappealingly shapeless. It must be the remains of a leaf, Greg tells himself, glancing upwards as he shakes it off. His gaze snags on the first tree, however. A few leaves still cling to it, and the undersides of all of them are turned towards him. They're pallid as the fog; at least, the little that's visible is. Most of the foliage is covered if not encrusted with insects. The same, he sees, is true of the branches above him, on which a dripping blackened swarm of crawlers of no species he would like to name has started to demonstrate how flimsily attached portions of some of them are. For a moment he imagines that the trunk is shivering with the activity overhead, and then he realises that a mass of insects is squeezing out of cracks in the bark and flooding down the tree towards him.

He hurls himself away from the infested trunk, but his skin persists in crawling and prickling. Even if he can't see what's there, he's sure that insects are biting him—draining his strength. At first he thinks that's why his legs give way before he has taken a proper step: he's poisoned, he's weakened. But the soaked ground has yielded, not him. He's stronger than it is, and he almost shouts a challenge as it drags his ankles down. Before he can draw breath, he's up to his shins, his calves, his knees in icy glutinous mud.

He won't let the sensation cow him. While he's alive he can fight. His fingers scrabble at the earth where the tree's roots ought to be, but they must be clustered on the far side of the trunk. Mud grates under his nails as his feet plunge deeper, burying his chest and dragging his hands out of reach of the concrete rim of the stretch of grass. The fog stoops hugely to press him down. There are handholds to his left—two domed greyish rocks. By throwing all his weight in their direction he manages to grasp both.

His right hand can't sustain its hold. It slithers down the rock and uncovers its furrowed brow before his fingertips catch on the lower lids of both eyes full of mud. As he struggles to let go, his other hand claws all the way down the face of the second man he last saw reluctantly quitting his chair in the shop. Greg's fingers land on the bottom lip, tugging the slack mouth into a wide idiotic grin. He recoils, nauseated by the spectacle, and the corpses submerge into the morass as his shoulders follow them. He makes one last desperate grab for anything that may help, but the grass is as slippery as a slug. He thinks he can feel his body merging with the ground, which is worse than a marsh. The hungry gelid substance is digesting him. This is pointless, he wants to scream. It's stupid beyond words. He even opens his mouth, but mud drives his protest back inside him and fills his ears with a liquid hiss like a gigantic eager Yes.

# WOODY

**Is he watching a religious channel or a scientific one? Perhaps the** latter, since it seems to be dealing with a form of life so primitive it has little consciousness of anything except itself. It splits off portions of itself for companionship, but is so hostile to any other creatures and in particular the threat their intelligence represents that it reduces them to its own state in order to consume them. Yet the origin of life and of religion appears to be involved as well—the lives the shapeless entity creates out of itself, and the savage worship it attracts, simply to reward any sacrifice by engulfing the worshippers too. Only one, Woody keeps thinking or hearing, only one. How can the screen be conveying all this to him when he's unable to see any image on it beyond a blurred restlessness? It occurs to him that this is the merest fraction of the entity under consideration, so small a part and so close to the screen that he's incapable of focusing, or his mind is. The idea is enough to startle him awake.

He is indeed sitting in his chair below the screen, but it shows nothing like his dream. He rubs his eyes and wonders how long he has been asleep: long enough to have dreamed all manner of disasters—power failures, Agnes trapped in the elevator, mutineers abandoning the store. Every quadrant of the screen shows people diligently shelving, though for the moment he can't see who is who. A glance at his watch tells him that the sun will soon be up. He feels abandoned for having slept, but at least nobody has taken that as an excuse to slack. He reaches for the phone and thumbs the button for the speakers. "You're doing good, guys. Keep this up and—"

All the figures crouched in front of the shelves raise their blurred heads, trailing veils of grey. He has the impression that they're about to rise to their feet to celebrate his awakening, but the quiver that passes through them all sends them crowding through the aisles without having gained the least stature. He's unable to discern anything else about them, not least because the images on the screen are wavering like water that's about to yield up a secret. He can't be seeing the figures squeeze one after another under the door that leads up to the staffroom. The images stabilise, revealing that the store is far less brightly lit than he thought he just saw. Nevertheless the light through the windows is enough to show that the shelves have been ransacked, strewing books the length of every aisle.

Rage and dismay are all he feels or thinks. He stands up so fast that his chair slams into a filing cabinet with a clang like a rusty bell. He's stalking to the door when he realises that if the power failure is real, everything else must have happened too. He's still shut in, except that when he wrenches at the handle the door swings open at once.

Every computer in the outer office is switched on. Each screen displays a muddy blur rather too reminiscent of his dream. When he glances back he sees that's true of the security monitor as well. Their illumination is what matters, and he lets it urge him across the office into the staffroom, which is darker. "Are you there, Ray?" he shouts. "What's the latest with the fuses?"

He hears movement down the unlit stairs. It sounds like a herd of soft bodies shuffling about in the darkness, or a mass as large as the lobby slithering over the floor. Just now he isn't anxious to discover any more about it. He hurries past the table and the stagnant brimming sink into the stockroom.

The entrance to the aisle is defined by outlines of racks the colour of dim fog, but beyond them is little besides darkness. That needn't faze him if he walks straight—surely he's sufficiently awake—but he has taken only enough steps to lose count when he cracks his elbow on the corner of a metal shelf. This simply enrages him further. He swings around and walks backwards, guiding himself by the silhouettes of shelves against the glow from the office. He has no idea why the light is shifting, nor does he care. All that matters for the moment is to set Agnes free.

He pilots himself backwards by grabbing the edges of shelves until he arrives at the doors to the top of the elevator shaft. He gropes past them and finds the banister above the stairs. Has the soft shuffling mounted the other staircase? In a fury he clings to the banister and tramps downwards, faster once he has gauged the depth of the treads. The banister ends, and he holds onto it while he plants his feet on the floor of the lobby and turns to face the elevator. "Agnes?" he shouts, and when there's no response "Anyes."

Even this brings no answer. He hopes that's because she has fallen asleep. He's about to knock on the doors as a preamble to trying to part them when he notices a thread of dimness on the far side of the lobby. It's beneath the delivery doors, which should provide all the light he needs.

He hurries through the empty blackness and shoves at the bar. It feels rusty, but after a second's resistance it gives with a clank, flooding the lobby with illumination not unlike clouded moonlight. He leans on the right-hand door until it jams too wide for its metal arm to haul it shut, and then he runs back to the elevator. He takes a deep breath that tastes of fog and braces himself to exert all his strength. Digging his fingertips between the door and the frame, he strains to increase the gap. In a moment the door slides all the way open.

Why couldn't Nigel have done that? Admittedly he still has to deal with the door of the elevator. It's just as accommodating, however. He almost wishes it were not, given what it reveals. Agnes is standing upright only because she's trapped against the elevator wall by a trolley in front of a pallet truck. Most of the books from the trolley are scattered across the floor. They resemble lumps of the mud that covers Agnes, not least her blindly gaping face, and fills her nose and mouth.

It's too much. His feelings are exhausted. All that's in his head is the knowledge that anyone who sees Agnes will know more happened here overnight than simple failure and walkouts and vandalism. He drags the trolley out of the elevator and catches her as she topples forward. Did her eyelids flicker? No, the light changed because its source moved. As he swings around, cradling Agnes by her shoulders, it recedes further and he hears a choked snuffle of brakes.

"Wait," he shouts, feeling as though his brashness has robbed Agnes of peace. He slips his other arm behind her knees to lift her. She's so light his eyes blur. Whoever's outside will take her wherever she must go. Perhaps Woody ought to accompany her once he has let Greg know, but where is Greg? If he's not on the sales floor, Woody can't leave; the store would be unguarded. Only one, he finds himself thinking again, only one. First he should take care of Agnes and then deal with the store. He eases Agnes head first out of the exit and paces into the fog, over the blackening tarmac, towards the lights and the moist snuffling. As he advances he takes a moment to prepare his face. Whatever his burden, he still represents Texts. The least he can do is smile.